THE FAIR MAID OF KENT

THE FAIR MAID
OF KENT

CAROLINE NEWARK

Matador
9 Priory Business Park,
Wistow Road, Kibworth Beauchamp,
Leicestershire. LE8 0RX
Tel: 0116 279 2299
Email: books@troubador.co.uk
Web: www.troubador.co.uk/matador
Twitter: @matadorbooks

ISBN 978 1788036 597

British Library Cataloguing in Publication Data.
A catalogue record for this book is available from the British Library.

Printed and bound in the UK by TJ International, Padstow, Cornwall
Typeset in 11pt Minion Pro by Troubador Publishing Ltd, Leicester, UK

Matador is an imprint of Troubador Publishing Ltd

For Richard

LIST OF MAIN CHARACTERS

Joan	(Jeanette), daughter of Edmund, late Earl of Kent
Joan's mother	Margaret Wake, Dowager Countess of Kent
The King	Edward III of England, Joan's half-cousin
The Queen	Philippa of Hainault, wife of Edward III
The King's Mother	Isabella of France, Dowager Queen of England
Edward	Son of the King and Queen of England
Isabella	Elder daughter of the King and Queen of England
Joanna	Younger daughter of the King and Queen of England
Lady Catherine	Catherine, Lady Montagu, Countess of Salisbury
Sir William	William, Lord Montagu, Earl of Salisbury
Uncle Montagu	Sir Edward Montagu, Sir William's younger brother
Margaret	Joan's cousin, daughter of the Earl of Norfolk
Alice	Margaret's younger sister

Elizabeth Montagu	Eldest daughter of the Earl and Countess of Salisbury
William Montagu	Elder son of the Earl and Countess of Salisbury
Lady la Mote	Governess to the girls in the royal nursery
Thomas Holand	A soldier, later steward to the Earl of Salisbury
Otho Holand	Thomas's younger brother and confidant
Countess Jeanne	Jeanne de Bar, estranged wife of the Earl of Surrey
Lady Arundel	Previously Lady Beaumont, later Countess of Arundel
Bishop Simon	Bishop of Ely, Sir William's brother
Bishop Grandison	Bishop of Exeter, Lady Catherine's brother
Bishop Bateman	William Bateman, Bishop of Norwich
Nicholas Heath	A Bachelor of Canon Law at Salisbury
John Vyse	A Bachelor of Canon Law and, Sub-Dean of Salisbury

Prologue

The lord of Albret wiped the blood from his hands and considered his visitor with a cold eye.

'Is she a virgin?'

The Englishman smiled.

'But of course. Would my master offer you anything but the best?'

'Ah yes. Your master, the King of England and his desires.'

It was no secret to the lord of Albret that the King of England coveted the French throne. As the only living grandson of the great Iron King he had a better claim than Philip of Valois who was a mere nephew. But the Estates in their wisdom had chosen the Valois. If his informant was to be believed, the English king had not given up the fight and encouraged by his unspeakable mother was planning war. Christ's blood! The Valois would be shitting his breeches at the thought.

'I'm not sure there is enough in your master's proposal to attract me,' mused the big man, scratching his ear.

The Englishman sighed in exasperation. He knew the big man's neighbours were talking to Philip of Valois's envoys and the old fox enjoyed nothing better than threatening him with a flirtation with France.

'Your son would boast a close alliance with our king,' he said persuasively. 'The girl is not some distant kin, you understand, but a cousin germane, the daughter of his favourite uncle. And very beautiful.'

The big man rubbed his fingers together, wondering if the French might offer more. The Fleur-de-lys was said to be full of fears and misgivings, and stubborn as a mule when cornered. But he was rich.

The Englishman was becoming impatient. This particular fortress on the edge of the Landes, a half day's ride from Bordeaux, was draughty, and the steaming damp from the marshes seeped into his bones as it did everywhere in this godforsaken country. If it wasn't for the river traffic, all those creaking vessels making their laborious way up the Gironde, bringing the Englishman his barrels of wine and the king a fortune in taxes, nobody would bother with Gascony. But things being as they were, it wasn't simply a matter of English pride to defend this last bulwark of the great Angevin empire, it was fast becoming a necessity. The wine trade suffered in time of war but when the whole of Aquitaine was theirs once more, the vineyards in the *haut pays* would fruit again and the English king would reap his just rewards.

'My wife is ailing,' said the big man. 'A great inconvenience to me. Her women send messages to say she has taken to her bed.'

'I'm sorry to hear that,' said the Englishman, wondering if his host's lady was sick to the point of death or merely trying to avoid his attentions. He'd heard nothing of an illness despite paying some *damoiselle* in her household to bring him information.

'I may shortly be in need of a wife myself.'

Ah, thought the Englishman, so that's the way it is. The image of the beautiful virginal English girl had stirred the old lecher's appetite and he wanted her for himself. Doubtless there'd be some other bride for the son. It made no difference as long as the matter of the betrothal was settled soon.

'I'm sure my master would not be averse to a slight change in our plans, although I would remind you the girl is very young.'

'But biddable.'

'Oh yes, extremely biddable. She has been raised in the royal nursery with the king's own daughters and knows her duty.'

1

We drifted on through clear grey water. It was July and after five terrifying days at sea the King of England's fleet of more than three hundred ships was sailing slowly down the estuary of the River Scheldt in a smooth and lazy fashion. Our canvas sail gave one last despairing sigh but the forty-foot long coloured streamer adorning the top of the mainmast didn't stir; it hung like a giant's discarded headcloth, limp and forlorn and forgotten.

By the time we edged round the final bend there was barely a breath of wind. In front of us the *Christopher*, one of the king's favourite ships, was being drawn slowly towards the walls of the little town of Antwerp where thousands of people on the foreshore could be seen cheering and waving and throwing their hats in the air. It promised to be a very grand arrival.

Once, when I was too young to know better I'd asked Lady la Mote if the king was my father.

'Certainly not,' she'd said, a flush creeping up from her wrinkly neck to the edges of her soft white veil. 'He is your royal cousin.'

The flush had deepened to cover the whole of her face while her fingers twisted her sewing into a crumpled ball.

'Has your lady mother not told you about your father?'

1

My mother never told me anything. She had left me in the royal nursery when I was three years old and almost never came to visit. Sometimes she took my little brother away to inspect what she called "his inheritance" but she never took me. Once a year she allowed me to kiss her old woman's hand and receive her blessing but I knew she didn't love me, not the way a mother should, not the way my cousin the king loved me.

It was Margaret who first told me about my father. We were sitting on the wall at Framlingham eating cherries and inspecting my uncle's deer park which stretched from Brabling all the way to the corn mill at Saxtead.

'He's dead, you lump-head!'

'He can't be,' I cried. 'He's my father.'

'Well, he is. He went to Winchester for the parliament and never came home. the king had him executed. Father said they cut off his head.'

'I didn't know that,' whispered Alice who was a small pale shadow of her older sister.

I was six years old and felt sick at the thought of my father's head being chopped off. I wasn't stupid, I knew these things happened. I'd seen plenty of blackened heads with sightless eyes rotting over the gates on London's bridge.

'What had he done?'

'Nobody said.'

'But he was my father,' I wailed. 'The king would have called him "uncle". Why would he want him dead?'

Margaret spat out her cherry pip and lowered her voice to a conspiratorial whisper. 'It wasn't the king who wanted him dead. It was the king's mother.'

2

I clutched at Alice who nearly fell off the wall in fright. I was scared of the king's mother. She swept through the nursery rooms at Woodstock in her rich brocades and fine black veils looking for all the world like the witch Margaret said she was. She smiled with her sharp little teeth at the king's children and gave them costly gifts, but she glared at me as if I had no right to be there and she would like to scratch out my eyes.

'The king must have signed a death warrant,' worried Alice. 'There has to be a death warrant, otherwise it is murder.'

'Father said the king's mother held a knife to the king's throat to make him sign,' said Margaret. 'And if someone is holding a knife to your throat you don't have a choice. You'd be a fool not to sign.'

I thought of the king with his large capable hands and his loud carefree laugh and wondered how he could have done this to me. How could he have allowed my father to be killed? I was his cousin. I was his little Jeanette. I had sat on his knee and played with his beard and he had kissed me. He had tickled my chin and told me I was his sweetheart. He had said he loved me.

Slowly my eyes began to fill with tears.

'Oh don't be such a cry-baby,' said Margaret.

'But my father is dead,' I wept.

'I know,' Margaret sighed. 'It's a pity but it couldn't be helped. Here, have another cherry and see if you can reach the path this time.'

Elizabeth jabbed me with her elbow. 'What can you see?'

The quayside at Antwerp was dominated by a huge

platform draped in black cloth and on a dais, raised higher than anyone else and surrounded by black and gold banners, was an exceptionally tall man. His upper lip curled, his black brows furrowed and I thought he looked extremely dangerous.

Elizabeth pulled herself up on the rails to get a better view. 'That must be the Duke of Brabant,' she announced. 'He's the king's cousin and a person of great importance.'

Flanking the duke on either side were several other richly dressed men, equally important judging from the quantity of jewels and costly silks on display.

'The princes of the Low Countries,' sighed Elizabeth, gazing at the glittering magnificence. 'My father says they've come to fight with us against the armies of the French king but of course you wouldn't know that, Joan, would you? People don't tell valuable secrets to girls like you.'

I had endured a whole year of Elizabeth's particular brand of friendship: the pinching, the hair-pulling, the stealing of my ribbons and the hissing of "traitor's daughter" into my ear. I hadn't wanted to leave Woodstock to live in her mother's household but I had been given no choice.

The order had come from a frosty-eyed Lady la Mote who had charge of the girls in the royal nursery, and she had been unforgiving,

'But why?' I said. 'What have I done? Why am I being sent away?'

'You are trying to tell me you don't know?'

She drew up her shoulders and began speaking rapidly as if she couldn't wait to rid herself of what needed to be said.

I didn't understand the words she used or the halting descriptions of my behaviour: impropriety; intimacy of a sort that no young girl should ever be a party to; a gross betrayal of Her Grace's loving trust. Never before had she, Lady la Mote, had a girl in her care who had so blatantly disregarded everything she had been taught and behaved in such a disgraceful way. Impure thoughts, immodesty, the need for contrition, repentance, and lastly, when the whole of her face had flushed to an alarming shade of crimson, a suggestion of the attentions of older men and a hushed mention of His Grace, the King's knee.

'How could you have behaved in such a way? And in front of the queen and the royal daughters?'

It had been the day of the visit of the royal children to their parents, an afternoon of great excitement with singing and laughter and special games. I remembered Isabella loudly demanding her father's attention, Joanna rolling her little woollen ball across the floor and Edward, as usual, leaning on the arm of his mother's chair. The king had circled his arm around my waist and drawn me close.

'Too old to sit on my lap, little cousin?' he had murmured.

'No, Your Grace.'

But sliding myself awkwardly onto his knee I'd found I was now tall enough for my white satin slippers to touch the floor. Beneath the thin silk cloth of my gown I could feel the firm pressure of his legs on mine and the tightening of his fingers on my waist. I'd leaned back into the solid comfort of his shoulder where the blue velvet smelled of spiced perfume and his cheek was warm against my hair. But something had changed and as the queen's eyes met mine I knew she was thinking I was no longer a child and had no business sitting on the knee of her husband receiving his caresses. I had displeased her but at the time I didn't realise how much.

Lady la Mote's lips were set in a thin disapproving line. 'As soon as arrangements can be made you will join the household of Lady Catherine Montagu at Bisham and you will remain there for as long as the queen wishes it.'

Our arrival in Antwerp was just as I had expected. As soon as we set foot on dry land there was the usual embracing and lengthy speeches of welcome which accompanied my cousin wherever he went and afterwards we walked in slow and solemn procession to the Church of Our Lady to give thanks for the safe arrival of the King and Queen of England and their friends. Then there were yet more speeches and kissing and exchanging of gifts before we were escorted to our hired lodgings where we would spend the first night.

I barely noticed my tiredness or the way the ground shifted unsteadily beneath my feet because of the strangeness of everything. I kept reminding myself this was Brabant, not England, this was another country where things were done differently. What was most surprising was the lack of solid ground as most of Antwerp appeared to be half-afloat. The crooked houses with their odd-looking roofs were separated, not by paved or cobbled streets, but by wide smelly ditches full of water, with bridges and steps and ridiculously narrow pathways. All around was a watery light which made the early evening sky shimmer and beads of damp crawl up my arms.

I should have known that my first night in such a strange place would not be peaceful but whatever other surprises I might have imagined, the last thing I expected was a summons. The girl and her escort arrived at dusk, just as the candles were lit, when the milky sky of morning had turned to an evening haze of soft purple and grey.

'Lady la Mote requests that the Lady Joan should come at once,' the girl said, keeping her eyes on the floor. 'The Lady Joanna won't stop crying. The nursemaids can do nothing. She weeps and calls for the Lady Joan and won't go to sleep.'

Lady Catherine sniffed as if the girl had brought the stench of the ditches into the house. I could see she didn't want me to go. She was the wife of the king's closest friend, Sir William Montagu, the Earl of Salisbury, and she had never liked me. That first day at Bisham when I'd stood in front of her, trembling in my water-stained clothing, waiting for her approval, her lips had twitched in annoyance and she had looked as if she'd wanted to slap me.

Now, she was struggling with what she interpreted as a royal command. She didn't want to say yes, to make me seem a person of importance which in her eyes I was not, but she couldn't, in all conscience, say no.

'It is very late but as the child is the king's daughter you must go,' she said, her mouth twisting with disapproval.

I bobbed a curtsey, murmuring my gratitude for Lady Catherine's kindness and almost ran from the room before she could change her mind.

It was still warm from the heat of the day as I followed the girl outside. Our escort carried torches and were armed. This was not our country and even though we were honoured guests in the territory of the Duke of Brabant, I think none of us felt completely safe.

'It is very strange, the place where we're lodged,' whispered the girl. 'The lord who lives there is called Sir Two-Faces. The man in the kitchen, who speaks some English, says his master wishes people to know how rich he is so he has offered his house to the English king.'

The wealthy townsman's house where the king and queen were lodged for the night was a large painted building with carved gables, very ornate and rather grand and set well away from the ditches. It was made of wood like all the other houses. The two-faced townsman couldn't be as rich as people said he was or he'd have built his house with stone which is what rich men did in England. Perhaps all the duke's people were poor because the rambling fortress by the edge of the river and the Church of Our Lady in the middle of the town appeared to be the only stone buildings in the whole of Antwerp.

The girl led me past the guards and up the stairs to a room crowded with women. Lady la Mote was there, wringing her hands in despair, while five nursemaids fluttered uselessly around the bed twittering and fussing. I could hear Joanna, a thin mewing cry like a trapped kitten.

I pushed past the people loitering at the door and walked over to the bed.

At the sound of my voice she stopped wailing. Her little round face was red and streaked with tears.

'Nettie,' she hiccupped.

'Yes Jo, it's me.'

'Bella,' she wailed and started crying again.

'She's missing her sister,' said Lady la Mote. 'She wants the Lady Isabella.'

'Don't cry, sweetheart,' I said, stroking my finger over Joanna's smooth cheek, feeling the damp softness and wondering why she, of all the royal children, had been chosen to accompany her parents to Antwerp. 'Your lady mother doesn't want you to cry.'

'She was sick on the sea voyage, poor little mite,' said Lady la Mote. 'And now we're here she's frightened of the people and the peculiar way they speak.'

I thought of the odd-looking men in the streets of Antwerp and the dreary flat countryside outside the town walls which was not in any way like home, and knew exactly how Joanna felt.

'Would you like me to sing to you?'

Joanna nodded her head.

I clambered up onto the bed and made myself comfortable. Joanna snuggled herself up against me with my arm curled round her shoulders. I began to sing. It was only a little made-up lullaby, nothing special, but it had the desired effect. Soon her eyelashes drooped, her breathing became slower and after a few moments she was asleep.

'May Our Lady bless you for that,' said Lady la Mote.

'I'll stay with her,' I offered. 'But Lady Catherine must be informed and I'll need my nightgown.'

'Lonata has a spare one.'

I smiled at Joanna's maid.

'She doesn't know yet,' said Lady la Mote quietly, gazing at Joanna. 'She's so young. It seems cruel to send her away.'

'Send her away?'

'To Vienna, to the Austrian court. She is to be brought up alongside her betrothed.'

'Oh no!,' I gasped. 'Surely not. She is the queen's baby girl.'

But of course this is what happened to the daughters of kings. They were married off to men they had never seen, whose customs they didn't know and sent far away from their families. Their happiness counted for little compared to the sealing of an alliance or the making of a peace. Margaret said that many years ago the king's mother had sold her little daughter to the Scots for the price of a worthless treaty.

'Perhaps the queen's next child will be a girl,' said Lonata, handing me her nightgown.

'Hush!' said Lady la Mote sharply. 'Don't gossip.'

Lonata coloured and lowered her head.

The nightgown wasn't as fine as mine but it was clean and smelled of lavender. When I slipped it on I was surprised by the roughness of the linen against my bare skin. I wriggled my shoulders to make it more comfortable and less scratchy and then after saying my prayers, climbed in beside Joanna.

While the others prepared for bed I lay thinking of Joanna being sent away to live with her betrothed and wondered if my cousin had a marriage in mind for me. Had the king's mother whispered in his ear and might I too be sold to an enemy as her little daughter had been? And what would a husband like that do to me?

Eventually the snuffling and shifting and sighing stopped and all I could hear were the rumbling snores of Lady la Mote and the whimpering of the youngest nursemaid who was missing her mother. Then, nothing but breathing.

The blue-grey half-light had gone and the room was full of inky blackness. No glimmers of torchlight filtered through the shutters and apart from a single candle which barely shed its light onto the floor let alone through the bed curtains, we lay in the dark.

I must have drifted off to sleep. I was dreaming of water: water on the quayside lapping greedily at the toes of my boots; smelly green water in the little ditches of Antwerp; and the dark slow-flowing river water which I saw each morning from the door of the beautiful Montagu manor at Bisham.

I awoke. At first there was no sound. I sniffed and wrinkled my nose. The kitchen boys must be up early. I moved my head to make sure Joanna was asleep. Her lashes fluttered against her cheeks but she didn't wake.

I sniffed again. Smoke! A boy had put wet logs on the fire which was no surprise. In this watery world it must be hard to keep anything dry.

I closed my eyes and then opened them again. Someone was shouting. Then a scream. I sat up. The smell of smoke was worse. I turned back the cover, climbed out of bed and tiptoed my way across the floor trying not to step on any of my sleeping companions. When I reached the door I opened it a crack then quickly slammed it shut.

'Wake up!' I shouted, shaking the shoulder of the nearest girl as I made my way back to Joanna.

'What is it?' said the annoyed and sleepy voice of Lady la Mote.

11

'Fire! The house is full of smoke.'

At that moment the door burst open and one of the king's men appeared in the doorway. The smoke came after him, swirling like mist across the floor.

'The Lady Joanna?' he asked urgently, looking around him for the precious bundle of the queen's daughter.

'She's here,' I said, climbing back onto the bed and waking Joanna.

'Come, sweetheart. Let me wrap you in your cover.'

But the man didn't wait. He snatched a startled Joanna from her bed and raced to the door, 'Remove yourselves! As quick as you can. It's fire.'

The next moment he was gone.

Two of the nursemaids began screaming as if Satan himself was at the door. A girl fell to her knees and another clutched Lonata shrieking for Our Lady to help her. 'Oh Holy Mother of God, save me,' someone murmured.

'Shall I pack the chests?' a girl's voice wavered as the question died on her lips.

'*Sainte Vierge*! We're going to die!'

In the panic someone knocked over the candle and we dropped into darkness. From outside came screaming and shouting and the sound of people's feet. I could hear Lady la Mote muttering, '*Sainte Vierge, aidez-nous, aidez-nous*,' over and over again. I kicked the girl crouched on the floor. 'Get up! Get down the stairs!' She scrambled up and I felt her run.

I stumbled my way to the door using my hands to tell me where I was. I could see nothing. The smoke was getting thicker and there was a strange roaring noise from somewhere under my feet. The outer chamber was crowded with people shoving and pushing and crying. Men's voices shouted for their servants and women screamed for their children.

I couldn't remember which way led to the stairs but it didn't matter because the press of people was so great I was pushed along in the crowd. I had no idea where the others were. I twisted round to see if there was light behind me but could see nothing, just shapes in the darkness. I started coughing. Smoke was burning my throat.

Now the roaring sound was getting louder and I could feel the heat and hear the sparks. At that moment someone behind me shoved against my back and I fell sprawling to the floor. No-one stopped to help me. No-one took any notice. Feet pushed past my face and trod on my fingers and toes. I tried to get up. I raised myself to my knees but a man's boots knocked me down again. This time my head hit the wall and I lost my nightcap.

I hauled myself upright but had no idea where I was or which way was safety. Tears ran down my face as I struggled for breath.

A woman grabbed me by the shoulders and thrust her face into mine. 'Babette?' she shrieked. But I wasn't who she was looking for. She pushed me aside, sending me crashing down onto my knees again. I could see a man with a lantern, just a little wavering light. There were two men carrying an iron-bound chest between them which prevented people behind from getting past. There were shouts and blows and the lantern fell to the ground. I was plunged back into darkness.

By now I could hear the crackling of flames. I began to pray. I was going to die. I knew I was going to die. I curled myself up into a little ball on the floor and tried not to think what it would be like to burn. I coughed and spluttered as smoke billowed about my head.

I tried to pray to St Polycarp, whose blood put out the flames when the Romans tried to roast him at the stake. He knew what it was like to burn. But all I could think of was my cousin's face and the way he used to smile at me. I would never see him again.

'Holy Mother of God, Blessed Virgin,' I prayed. 'Forgive me my sins.'

All of a sudden I felt two hands slip round my shoulders and under my knees, and someone I couldn't see lifted me bodily up. I was too exhausted to struggle and wondered for a moment if this could be St Polycarp. I hid my head in the rough cloth of a man's jacket and tried not to breathe in the smoke which was swirling around us. His large hand pressed firmly against my hair so that I could neither see nor hear anything other than the roar of the flames and the pounding of my heart.

My rescuer held me tightly as we pushed through the crowd. I felt myself jolted up and down. That must be the stairs. People bumped against us but my rescuer had me held so tightly I knew if I fell, so would he. The journey down the stairway to the door took an eternity, a burning, choking, smoke-filled lifetime but just as I thought I could bear it no longer, I felt cold air on the back of my neck and the roar of the flames receded.

We were outside. His grip relaxed and I lifted my head.

The house was ablaze and I could see a woman in her nightgown surrounded by mounds of baggage. She was weeping pitifully over the loss of a favourite piece of finery. Next to her stood a man with hollow eyes holding the charred remains of a fur-lined cloak. A half-naked groom was leading a terrified horse to safety from the stables where the thatch was already alight and a boy was wailing for his mother.

My rescuer carried me to a place far from the burning building and set me down on a bench. I was filthy with smoke in my hair and dirty smuts of black on Lonata's borrowed nightgown. My feet hurt, my eyes stung horribly and my throat was raw. But I was alive.

'All well?' He was coughing too.

I nodded. 'Where are the others?' All I could think of was Joanna and her little household.

'Who have you lost?'

'The Lady Joanna, the king's daughter. One of the king's men took her.'

He smiled; a surprising flash of white teeth in a face that was probably as black as mine. 'She's safe. I saw them carry her out. And our king and queen, they're safe too. I saw them leave.'

In my panic I had forgotten about my cousin and the queen.

'Everyone's safe,' said my rescuer. 'We were the last. I'd have been out sooner myself but I saw you curled up asleep and it was quite a struggle to get to you. I had to fight my way across the room so next time would you please choose a place closer to the door as your bed for the night.'

He wasn't old. A few years younger than my cousin, I thought, and his voice told me he was English. He had dark hair, or at least it looked dark, and his face and clothes were filthy. They were smudged with black marks and covered in ash. He certainly wasn't anyone I knew.

'I wasn't sleeping,' I said indignantly. 'I was praying.'

'I should use the chapel for your prayers in future.'

'I was praying to St Polycarp and to Our Lady to save me.'

'How sensible. And your prayers were heard because here you are safe and sound.'

'Thank you for rescuing me,' I said politely. In my relief at being rescued from the fire I had forgotten to thank him and, despite his rough appearance, it had been a kindly act. I touched my waist but of course I didn't have my purse with me. It was awkward because I should have given him a coin.

'The pleasure was mine.'

He was looking at my nightgown. I shivered and wrapped by arms around myself.

'Are you cold?'

'A little.'

I couldn't understand why I was cold because I could still feel the heat from the burning building on my face.

'Wrap this round you.' he said, removing his cloak.

It was thick rough cloth without any fur either as a lining or as a trimming. It smelled disgustingly of horses and leather and smoke.

'Thank you.'

He nodded his head, watching me carefully as despite the cloak I continued to shiver. 'It's the same after a battle. Men feel cold and frightened just when there's no further need and everything is over.'

'Are you a fighting man?' I asked.

'Yes. I'm one of the king's men. I give my sword to his service.'

I smiled at him.

'And you my young friend? What do you do for the Lady Joanna? Sing her lullabies?'

How funny. He thought I was a nursemaid. I looked down at the plain linen nightgown and thought about my hair and my face and my bare feet. I must have looked like all those other weeping women, covered in smoke and grime and smudges of ash.

'Yes,' I said truthfully. 'That's what I do. I sing her to sleep and make sure she sleeps soundly.'

'Just what I'd expect from a pretty little maid like you. And I can think of nothing sweeter than to be lulled to sleep by a soft voice like yours and wake in the morning with you by my side.'

I felt myself blush. He was flirting with me which was wholly improper for a man like him. Of course he didn't know who I was and perhaps that was an excuse.

'I think I should look for Lady la Mote,' I said primly trying to cover my confusion. I'd never had a man flirt with me before. Elizabeth and the older girls were always getting smiles and sideways glances from various young men but nobody had ever bothered with me.

'Is she your mistress?'

'She is the Lady Joanna's governess.'

'Ah,' he said. 'The senior lady of the household who wields the big stick. Would you like me to ask? That's if anyone knows where anyone is in a melee like this.'

'Yes please,' I said in a small voice, aware that the churning in my belly was getting worse.

'What's the matter?'

'I think I am going to… I don't feel very well.'

'It's the smoke. Here, let me hold you.'

He sat down beside me and placed his arms round my shoulders and held me while I retched. I lost my supper onto the cobbles and sat there shivering and crying in his arms.

'There, there, little girl,' he murmured, his face in my hair. 'Don't cry. It's all over now. I've got you.'

He sat me upright and smoothed the tangles away from my eyes. He smiled. 'You do look a sorry mess.' He took the edge of his cloak and spat on it and proceeded to wipe my face. He was surprisingly gentle for a rough soldier but he really shouldn't have been touching me.

'It's no good, he said. 'We need water. Wait here.'

Before I could protest he was off into the crowd. I sat wrapped in the borrowed cloak, waiting for his return. I sniffed a bit, feeling very sorry for myself and looked to see if there was anyone I knew. Probably half the town was out on the streets. There was no sign of anyone from the royal household and nobody I recognised but with all the black-streaked faces that was not surprising. Probably none of my friends would recognize me. My legs felt too weak to stand and by now I was frightened to move in case I got lost. This was a strange place with strange people and somebody had tried to burn us to death in our beds.

My rescuer returned carrying a small bowl and a large cloth.

'I got it from a woman in the house over there.' He gestured with his free hand towards a row of houses where women and children were crowding out of their open doors. 'From what she said I gather we've given the townsfolk of Antwerp a good night's entertainment.' His smile widened. 'And I discovered the king and queen and their little daughter have been taken in by the sisters at St Bernard's, so now we know where you belong.'

He thrust the bowl at me. It was full of greenish-looking water. I splashed my face. The water was cold but welcome. I began to wipe with the cloth but had no idea if I looked any cleaner.

'Let me,' he said, taking the cloth from my hands. I closed my eyes while he scrubbed my face and round my neck. 'There! Now you look less like an urchin from the city ditches and more like a nursemaid who rocks the royal cradle. I've cleaned the worst of it off but your hair needs combing. And I suggest you change your nightgown as soon as you can as it's not fit for a beggar.'

'Thank you.'

'Now, let's see about getting you back on your feet.'

He put his arm round my waist to help me up. My legs trembled but I just about managed to stand. He didn't remove his arm. I stood there rather awkwardly, aware of the pressure of his hand and the unaccustomed nearness of this man whom I didn't know. There was a moment of fear. Where was he going to take me? What would he do with me? Every girl knew how dangerous men could be.

'I think I shall be alright by myself,' I said in a small voice, moving away from him and looking to left and right in panic, wondering where I should go.

He laughed and came closer. 'I don't think you will. Night streets are dangerous places for young girls out on their own, particularly ones as pretty as you.'

He put his hand on my shoulder.

'No, really,' I said, trying to move sideways.

'Listen, my young friend,' he said, tightening his grip. 'Stop struggling. It is a rule of war; soldiers who capture prizes are allowed to keep them. There is always a price to pay and captives don't go wandering off just when they feel like it. The ransom must be agreed first.'

'I'm not a prize.'

'That's where I beg to differ,' he said, smiling and turning me round to face him.

'Please,' I said, my eyes filling with tears. 'Take me back to the royal household. I promise I won't run off, but please take me back.'

He shook his head and smiled again. 'If I'd known what I was getting myself into I would have left you behind curled up on the floor. It seems that rescuing young maidens is a thankless task.'

'Oh no,' I said. 'I am truly grateful. It's just that...' I stopped.

'Yes?'

'It's just that I've never...'

He looked at me enquiringly. 'What? No stolen kisses down in the laundry? Don't tell me a girl as pretty as you has never felt a man's lips?'

I stared at him in an agony of embarrassment. My heart was thumping and I could think of nothing to say.

After a moment he patted my hand. 'Don't worry, sweetheart. I won't harm you. I'm not a brute.'

But before I could stop him he had lowered his head and touched my mouth with his. He was gentle. I should have jerked my head away or slapped his face but I did neither. I stood completely still. My lips trembled and then

20

yielded to the pressure. He stayed like that for a moment, then drew away and laughed.

'There, that wasn't so bad, was it? I think next time you'll enjoy it more. But for now, the ransom has been paid and the hostage is free to go. Shall we see if we can find the Abbey of St Bernard and the rest of the royal household?'

I nodded, unable to speak, the feel of his lips still stinging my own and the strangest of feelings curled tight in my belly.

'It was the kitchens.' Lady la Mote was quite adamant. 'The boys were careless with the fires. The cook left them unsupervised.'

'They say there's nothing left,' said Lonata in an awed voice. 'Just some lumps of roasted flesh and a few charred bones. Nothing else.'

'Well, that's a mercy,' Lady la Mote replied briskly. 'It will save the duke from having to hang them.'

But I was not convinced. I thought someone had deliberately tried to burn us in our beds and that such a man would find it hard to disguise his hatred of the English king. I was certain it would show in his face if not on the singed tips of his fingers.

At the welcoming feast, which was prepared in some other great man's kitchens, I peered at each of the princes in their costly robes to see who had evil in their eyes as well as in their heart.

The Duke of Brabant in his customary black and gold looked sour but I couldn't believe he had tried to burn his cousin alive on his first night in Antwerp. It would be against the Church's rules on hospitality and the duke was supposedly very devout.

The man next to him had plump cheeks like the queen and seemed friendly.

'Who's that?' I asked the dark-haired man standing by my shoulder. He was one of a group of exotic foreign knights who said they had come with the Margrave of Juliers.

'The Count of Hainault. He is the brother of your queen and his wife is the duke's daughter. Her mother was cousin to the French king.'

This daughter kept her chin up and her mouth turned down. Either she didn't like her sturdy husband or she didn't like the company he was keeping.

I was shown the queen's sister and her husband, the Margrave of Juliers, and an older grizzled man who was glaring at the woman next to him.

'The Count of Guelders,' said my helpful companion. 'And his countess, your king's sister.' He lowered his voice. 'Husband and wife, they do not like each other.'

Further along the table was a nervous narrow-shouldered youth.

'The Count of Namur.' My informant spoke into my ear. 'What a fortunate young man. A fifth son. Never expected the honour to be his. Unmarried. He'll be rich when the old mother dies. A good prospect for some lady's family.'

Elizabeth looked with undisguised interest at the Count of Namur but I could have told her that a prince of the Low Countries would never consider marriage with a mere earl's daughter from across the sea. She would be of no use to him. He would take a girl from another ruling house and I hoped I didn't have to marry him. He was all hairless chin and bulging pale blue eyes.

'There is an empty seat at the table,' said my new friend. 'Do you not see who is missing?'

I shook my head.

'Why, the Emperor, the Bavarian. He has stayed away and it is not a good sign. Perhaps he is not as keen on this adventure as your king believes.'

'Perhaps he holds out for more gold,' said his companion on my other side whose arm was pushing uncomfortably against my own. 'Your English king is rich. The Bavarian knows he can afford more.'

'If the Emperor doesn't want to join with our king perhaps it's better he stays away,' I ventured.

The two men laughed and moved a bit closer.

'If the Emperor doesn't come then the princes of the Rhinelands will go home. They won't fight without him.'

'But the others will fight, won't they?'

'If they are paid,' said the second man.

'We can pay them in wool, like we will pay the Flemings?'

I knew the people of Flanders had overthrown their count in order to embrace the English king and his promise of limitless wool for their cloth makers. The count had run away to Paris and left his towns unguarded. Perhaps he had heard of our coming and was nervous of my cousin's armies.

'There is no more wool,' laughed the first man. 'Everybody knows that. The store houses are empty. And the princes want gold not promises.'

'I thought men fought for honour.'

The men laughed again and the first one put his hand on my arm.

'Honour doesn't put food on the table or armour on your back, and promises can prove to be as empty as a drunkard's purse. For the princes up there it's money first and then they'll fight for the honour of it. It's not as if this is a Holy War.'

'Now,' said the second one. 'Shall we have a little merriment?'

After the feast it was a summer of entertainments and picnics and journeys across the river. We girls in the Montagu household visited churches and wandered through the grasses and played games with the younger children. We listened to the duke's minstrels at the evening displays and wondered at the acrobats while we watched the young men who had come in the princely entourages. We giggled when water slopped over the rim of our boat as we were rowed across the Scheldt, and on the other side we arranged ourselves prettily on little travelling stools waiting to see who noticed us.

The princes paid friendly visits to the queen bringing their wives and their children but the queen's brother didn't come, not even once. Somebody said he was wavering in his support for the king's war and it was very difficult for the queen.

But as the end of summer drew nearer, the princes spent more and more time closeted with my cousin, devising their strategies and planning what should be done. And there was still no sign of the Emperor.

I was frightened Philip of Valois and his army would arrive before my cousin and his friends were ready. He would attack and we would be trapped. There would be no escape. He might burn our ships and we would have no way of getting back to England.

'Where is the French king?'

'Hiding in his grand palace near Paris,' said one of the girls. 'He's been told by his astrologer not to meet our army in battle because he will lose.'

But she was wrong because the very next day my cousin received word from his spies: Philip of Valois was marching towards Amiens with the war flag of France. The French king was preparing to fight.

It was time for the King of England to settle matters with the Bavarian.

At the end of the month we travelled to a place called Herenthals where Joanna's household joined with my cousin's for the long journey into the unknown lands of the all-powerful Emperor.

'We will rest with the queen's sister, the Empress, at Koblenz before we travel on to Vienna,' said Lady la Mote with understandable pride.

'When will you return?' I asked politely.

Lady la Mote looked regretful. 'We won't. The Hapsburg court will be the Lady Joanna's home for the rest of her life.'

The queen wept. She didn't want Joanna to go but Joanna was her father's child and everyone knew she must carry out the duties of a royal daughter. Her little household left, weighed down with cartloads of jewels and furs and glittering gifts, and as we waved them farewell, I looked at the queen's drawn face and thought of the king's mother and wondered if Joanna had done something to anger her grandmother. Why else was she being sent so far away?

Gloom descended over the whole household and as soon as we returned to Antwerp the queen retreated into her new lodgings at St Michael's Abbey and held no more entertainments. I thought she probably wanted to weep in private. I understood how she must feel because I too felt like weeping.

Throughout the autumn everyone said we were edging closer to war. After my cousin's visit to Koblenz, the Emperor was now our friend and had given my cousin a golden crown. But this must have annoyed the French king because he captured some of our ships and burned the town of Southampton. When Elizabeth's father returned from Arras he said he couldn't see the point of all this talking as nobody wanted peace except for His Holiness; the French king was determined to keep the duchy of Aquitaine for himself and the King of England would never agree to that. War was inevitable.

As the weather grew colder, occasional flurries of snow blew from the east and the water in my bowl became rimed with ice each morning. To my joy, Alice arrived for the Christmas festivities, but this was not the Alice I knew. Like Margaret she was now a married woman. My uncle after a long deliberation had agreed a marriage for her with the Earl of Salisbury's brother, Sir Edward

Montagu. I thought him rather old to be a husband for Alice but nobody had asked my opinion. When she came into the room, two steps behind Lady Catherine, she barely acknowledged my presence and when I smiled she lowered her head and refused to look at me.

In the days which followed, Lady Catherine and Alice paid numerous visits to the queen, who was recovering from the birth of yet another baby, but I was not invited to go with them.

'Are *you* having a baby?' I asked Alice.

'No.' She blushed and lowered her head.

'Does your husband mind?' It was almost a year since the wedding and the earl's brother looked an impatient man.

She flushed a deeper red. 'Yes,' she whispered. 'He wants a son.'

It was almost the feast of the Epiphany and the Christmas celebrations would soon be over. When I'd heard Edward and Isabella were arriving for a Christmas visit to see baby Lionel, I'd expected an invitation to join them but there had been nothing. I'd been forgotten by my cousin and the queen. However much I regretted what I'd done and no matter how hard I prayed for forgiveness, I knew I would never again be part of their family. They had remade the tapestry of their lives without me and I was nothing but an unwanted ravelling, cut off and discarded onto the floor.

But next morning a royal summons arrived at the Montagu lodgings.

'Today,' said Lady Catherine, running her eye over the note which had come with the king's messenger. 'You are to attend the king at the abbey.' She pursed her lips and frowned. She didn't like me being favoured in this way.

'Is it an entertainment, Lady Catherine?' I enquired politely.

She tapped her fingers on the table and looked at the note again.

'I have no idea why the king wishes to see you and it is not important you know. Now, the matter of your clothes.'

I spent hours in the wardrobe selecting something suitable to wear as I was determined to look my best. Outside there was sleet on the ground so with the help of one of the maids I put on my heavy silk under-gown, the blue one with the lambswool lining. I smoothed the folds and thought how well it fitted me now my figure had grown a little rounder in certain places.

I slipped on my red surcote and let the girl comb out my hair, fixing it in place with a narrow gilded chaplet. I peered into Alice's little silver mirror. I did look pretty. I hoped my cousin would notice.

One of Lady Catherine's women came to see where I was and ask why I wasn't in the hall as the king's man was waiting. I shrugged myself into my hooded winter cloak, bit my lips to make them redder, and ran down the stairs. I could feel the flush on my cheeks. I was being brought back. the king had remembered me and I had been forgiven. I was still his favoured cousin, his little Jeanette.

Lady Catherine stood by the foot of the stairs. She had a faded sort of beauty like a rose whose petals are about to drop but there were lines about her mouth and below her chin the flesh was slightly pouched. She ran her gaze over my clothes, peering closely at every seam, looking for something to criticise. I saw the serpent of jealousy in her eyes and knew she wished it was her being summoned to the royal presence.

'The king has sent an escort for you,' she said, snapping out the words.

She nodded in the direction of a man standing in the shadows at the back of the hall. At that moment I should have known who he was but I didn't. He stepped forward and my heart lurched. It was him!

He was clean. No streaks of dirt, no ash smudges, no black marks on his clothes, no filthy smoke-filled hair. Dark clothing, the leopards of England on his tunic. He stood looking straight at me but betrayed no sign he knew who I was. Did he know? Did he remember? Did I look so very different all dressed up in my fine clothes? I felt my hands begin to shake and tucked them quickly into the folds of my cloak so that he couldn't see.

I was unable to stop looking at him. I should have dropped my gaze, I knew I should. Girls did not stare at men, particularly men they didn't know. Girls kept their eyelashes lowered and their faces averted.

'My lady,' he said, bowing correctly. Just the right degree for a girl who was the king's cousin but somewhat in disgrace. Not too low but not insultingly shallow.

He looked me straight in the eye but still betrayed no sign he knew who I was. Surely seeing me close to, he must know? He stepped back to let me walk through the door and down to the courtyard. At every step I felt his presence behind me, walking and watching. I gripped the rail tightly, afraid I might stumble. I heard the creak of his boots and the rasp of his breath and wondered if he could hear the thumping of my heart.

I walked unsteadily to the water steps.

'Shall I help you down, my lady?'

He knew! I was certain he knew. I could tell from the way he asked the question, from the way he spoke the last word and the way he stood just that little bit too close.

I kept my head turned away from his. I didn't dare look at him. I bit my lip and swallowed hard. I didn't know what to say and I didn't know what to do.

'My lady?'

His voice was flat and impersonal. He didn't know. I was imagining it.

'Thank you,' I said as graciously as I could.

He stood on the lower step holding out his hand. I felt the pressure of his fingers on my embroidered glove. He was strong, but I knew that already. My cloak brushed his face as he helped me into the barge and escorted me to the raised seat beneath the canopy.

The space on either side of me was empty and I would gladly have offered to share it with him but I didn't dare. I sat amidst the cushions all alone.

'Are you ready, my lady?'

'Yes,' I whispered.

We travelled upriver on the running tide in complete silence. Each time I summoned up the courage to speak, the words died on my lips when I saw his closed expression. I began to think I had made a huge mistake and he was nobody I knew at all. But the next moment I was certain I wasn't wrong. He looked the same, he sounded the same. It must surely be him.

The journey to the abbey was only a little way but seemed endless. I kept my head lowered and was surprised when a bump indicated we had arrived at the water steps. I peeped out of my hood and saw him standing talking to some other men. A moment later he remembered his duty and came over to hand me out, taking great care the hem of my cloak didn't fall into any puddles. As our eyes met for a brief moment I thought I saw a flicker of recognition, but when I turned to thank him, he had gone and one of the king's attendants was at my shoulder waiting to lead me into the light and warmth of the abbey.

I was taken through a maze of richly painted rooms, each one more gloriously decorated than the one before, until at last we reached an echoing space with two vast carved doors at the far end. People were gathered in small knots talking and nodding, some in a great state of agitation. This had to be the king's outer chamber where men and women waited, hoping for an audience with my cousin.

The two men-at-arms in royal livery who guarded the doors with crossed halberds looked curiously at my reddened cheeks, my unbound hair and the sleet melting on the folds of my cloak, but after a hurried conversation with my escort, they signalled for us to go ahead. A soft knock at the door and it was opened silently from the inside.

I stepped through. The room was dark and shadowed apart from the glowing circle of light where my cousin sat. He looked as he had always done: hair gleaming tawny gold above the furred collar of his robe, eyes a piercing blue. When he turned his head and smiled, the memories came flooding back of the last time at Woodstock when I had sat on his knee. The queen, who had been seated at his side, had failed to smile at me embracing her husband and in her displeasure had sent me away.

Today, the person in the chair beside my cousin was not the queen, it was a grey-haired old man. He was being very familiar, laying his hand on my cousin's sleeve and leaning towards him so that their shoulders touched. He spoke easily like a friend would and laughed at a joke my cousin was telling. They were totally absorbed in their conversation and didn't notice me until the man looked up, tapped my cousin's arm and nodded in my direction.

My cousin crooked his finger, summoning me forward. I walked unsteadily into the pool of light, held the heavy folds of my skirts between my fingers and lowered myself to the ground. I heard the blue silk rustle and was glad I'd worn it. I wanted him to know how sorry I was, how I regretted my banishment, how much I wanted to return to being his little Jeanette.

For a moment there was no noise at all and then I heard a sound so slight it was almost silent.

It came from the old man.

I raised my eyes. He was staring at me with the expression some men have when the priest raises the Host.

'As you say, *mon cher*, a veritable prize.'

He was the second man to describe me in that insulting way. I waited where I was to see what my cousin wanted from me.

He leaned forward and touched the top of my head. 'Up, little one.'

32

I rose with great care making sure I kept my chin raised and my back straight but to my dismay this time the silk didn't rustle.

He looked at me carefully, taking in the blue of my gown, the rich red surcote with its silver embroidery and the pretty golden chaplet. Then he leaned back in his chair and ran his eyes over me once more. I hoped my hair hadn't blown too much in the cold breeze on the river. He waited a moment and then smiled.

'You've grown, little one.' He paused. 'Come closer and let me see you properly.'

His voice was kind. It was soft and caressing not hard and stony as I feared it might be. He cared. The queen might still be angry and exclude me from her presence, but he had forgiven me. He was my cousin, the man who had loved me when I was a child. He had protected and cared for me and yet had allowed my father to be killed. But when I was with him I would have forgiven him anything, even that, because I loved him and wanted him to love me.

I stepped right up to his knee, remembering the times he would circle me with his arm and pull me onto his lap. I was so close I could smell the creamy smoothness of the sandalwood oil on his skin and the scent of something spicy deep within the folds of his robes. When his gaze caught mine I saw candlelight shining in his eyes.

'I have someone here who wants to see you, little cousin.'

I moved my gaze to the other man.

Holy Virgin, but he was really horrible! Long grey hair and flowing beard and no colour at all in his ancient washed-out face. He had sunken rheumy eyes hidden amidst a web of wrinkles, and gouges like plough strips furrowing his cheeks. When he spoke, his inner lips were moist with snail slime and his teeth were yellowed. There was a whiff of foul breath about him and a pungent smell of garlic.

He leaned forward, screwing up his pale blue eyes as if to see me better. He looked tall but his gown hung loosely on his bent shoulders. I thought him probably a scrawny man beneath the dark red velvet but wrapped in those robes it was hard to tell. It wasn't an English fashion. The sleeves were too wide and too short and the cut was wrong, but the cloth was of good quality. I wondered where he came from.

'What do you think?' My cousin's voice was soft.

The man shook his head, peering closely at every part of me. I felt like a mare under the appraising eye of a horse dealer.

'Perfection,' he breathed. 'Oh perfection. Look at the hair, the way it catches the light. What a depth of colour. And so heavy. Can you see how it falls against the cheeks? It shines like the most precious of silks. And the skin. Quite luminous. His Holiness has such a one in Avignon, a painting of the Virgin with the Christ Child in her arms.'

He stretched out a hand as if to touch me. I wanted to shrink away. The back of his hand was covered in hideous blotches and his fingers were like claws, curled up and bent, with shiny yellow knuckles. He was ugly, like all old men.

'Come here, child.'

I glanced at my cousin who nodded his head. I took two steps until I was almost standing between the man's knees. Now I could smell a strange exotic perfume beneath the garlic and the rotting teeth. He put out his right hand and smoothed my hair, following the cascade of gold down almost to my waist. I shivered at the feel of his fingers. What did he want? Why was he touching me?

'Does she please you?' My cousin spoke quietly but intensely as if the answer the man would give was of great importance.

The man moved his hand to my face. He traced the curve of my cheek beneath my eye and let his fingers run down the soft skin in front of my ear. He stroked the tiny wisps of hair which had escaped from the chaplet and then touched my lips. Little soft movements almost like kisses.

His gaze followed the fall of my hair, across the swell of my budding breasts to the dip of my waist to where my gown slid over my narrow hips, all the way down to the tips of my feet.

'Oh yes,' he said, his breath warming my skin. 'I could not have wanted for anything more beautiful or more desirable.'

With a rush of understanding, I knew what this was. I was to be given to this old goat. He wanted me for his wife. I was to be sent away to some distant land, like Joanna, somewhere where I would be quite alone. He would imprison me in a castle high on a rock and make me dance for him every night before he would take me into his bed and slither his loathsome tongue between my teeth.

'She is her father's daughter,' said my cousin. 'In every way.'

'So I see,' laughed the man. 'Look at the length of the under-lip, you can always tell. I have an astrologer who tells me these things are written at the moment of birth, and by the bones of the blessed St Thomas, this one is a feast for the senses.'

I knew what would be expected of me in marriage. "They do it whenever they like," Margaret had said. "There's no escape. You have to submit."

'I thought you would want to see her,' said my cousin. 'The sight of her comforts me in some of my blacker moments, when I am chased by the demons of the past.'

'We are all chased by those demons, *mon cher*,' said the man quietly. 'I more than most.'

They continued to talk, ignoring me. The conversation was about Philip of Valois and his many failings.

'Your lady mother said he was a man afraid of his own shadow.'

My cousin nodded his head in agreement at this considered assessment of the French king.

I felt ice slide inside my veins and chill my belly. This man was known to the king's mother. It must have been she who had persuaded my cousin to give me to him in marriage. Everyone knew how much power she wielded and on the question of a foreign marriage he would be bound to defer to her wishes. She wanted me sent away and had chosen the vilest and most hideous old man of her acquaintance to be my husband.

At last my cousin remembered me.

'Come here, little one.'

Obediently I went to his side, too frightened to do anything else. He put his arm round my waist like he used to and pulled me close.

'Too old to sit on my knee now, I think, Jeanette, but not too old to give your cousin a kiss.'

With his free hand he turned my face to his and gently placed his mouth on mine. He tasted of salt. I enjoyed the touch of his lips and happily kissed him back. Too soon he drew away and smiled into my eyes.

'Oh yes!' he said. 'A lucky man who has you in his bed, my little cousin, a very lucky man indeed.'

'Your Grace?' I whispered.

He raised his eyebrows. 'Yes?'

'Are you sending me away?'

He laughed. 'I can hardly keep you by my side, little one. What would the queen say?'

'But I do not wish to go.'

'Everyone must do their duty,' he said, his tone serious. He removed his hand from round my waist and leaned back in his chair. 'A girl's duty is to marry where she is bid and you are nearly old enough for marriage.'

'Yes, Your Grace,' I said miserably, wondering how long it would be before I would have to go. Lady la Mote had said Joanna's marriage was so many months in the arranging she had despaired of the contracts ever being signed.

My cousin patted my arm. 'Off you go, sweet cousin. You can return to the care of the lovely Lady Catherine. I shall tell her it is settled. After the summer campaign when we are flushed with victory will be the perfect time for a wedding.'

I lowered myself to the ground again and whispered a farewell.

He nodded his head towards his guest. I turned to the man and said in a low voice. 'Fare you well, *monsieur*.'

Before I could move away, his hand shot out and he drew me towards him. I trembled at being so close. He held his grey wrinkled face up to mine.

'You may kiss me,' he murmured, little drops of spittle spilling out of his mouth.

What horror! I closed my eyes and quickly placed my dry lips on his furrowed cheek.

He laughed. 'I'm not as desirable as your king, it seems.'

I felt the heat rise in my face and stepped back quickly before he demanded I place my mouth on his.

'*Monsieur*?'

'How the wheel of fortune turns. In my youth I had women dance naked on tables and throw themselves at my feet, but now all I get is a dry peck from an unwilling young maid. *C'est dommage!*'

He chuckled into his beard as he waved me away.

I picked up my skirts and practically ran from the room.

Outside the king's servant was waiting, ready to escort me back to the courtyard. I wasn't to see the queen or Edward or Isabella and I wasn't to join in the last night of the Nativity celebrations. I had been brought here to be paraded like a slave girl in front of the horrible old man so that he could decide if he wanted to purchase me. He needed to see if the bargain he had struck with my cousin was worth the price he was paying.

I favoured the royal servant with an encouraging smile and, after a little gentle flattery, he told me everything I wanted to know about the old man, except for his name.

'A stranger of the utmost importance, little lady. His presence is a closely guarded secret.' He lowered his voice. 'Some call him "the Welshman" but he's not one of those scurvy weasels, not talking like he does. Speaks French perfectly and can read a Latin text. He dines alone with the king and queen and is given the choicest of dishes and the best cuts of meat.'

'Does he have servants?'

'There's a boy,' said the man, standing rather too close and nudging me into an alcove. 'Says his master's a friend of His Holiness. Prattles away about papal palaces, but he's witless so pay no attention.'

My heart sank. His Holiness, the Almighty's representative here on earth. If the Holy Father had sanctioned my marriage there was nothing to be done.

'Where does he come from?' I asked.

'I reckon he's a Gascon, come from the duchy. Doesn't look like one, they're mostly short-arsed, but they're saying in the kitchens the lord of Albret is here to see the king. A matter of a marriage contract.'

Like all men he wanted payment for his information so I allowed him to squeeze my waist. It wasn't very pleasant and I was glad when we were disturbed by a group of rowdy grooms dressed in their Twelfth Night finery.

Outside in the cold, it was dusk and the sleet from earlier had turned to snow. My escort was waiting for me, leaning against the arched entrance to one of the buildings, his hat pulled low over his face. What with the dreadful happenings inside the abbey I had almost forgotten him.

He moved to the foot of the water steps and without so much as a single word offered me his outstretched hand. I climbed in but refused his further help, stumbling past the oarsmen to my seat at the back of the boat. I watched from under my lashes as he talked to one of the men, sharing a joke and doubtless giving orders. He had an easy manner which didn't surprise me in the least. He'd had an easy manner with me last summer. He was the sort of man who would always have an easy manner with anyone, particularly with a girl.

As we slid away from the steps, he began walking up the boat towards where I sat perched beneath the canopy. For a moment I thought he might speak but he merely settled himself down on the servant's bench whistling softly under his breath. I felt disconcerted to have him so close but contented myself with gazing upwards at the yawning entrance to the watergate and the shimmering vaulted roof slipping slowly past.

As soon as we left the shelter of the abbey walls, a sharp wind, which blew in each night with the tide, began to bite and I pulled my cloak more securely around me.

'It's bad out on the river tonight, my lady.' He was looking at me through the gloom. 'You'll get frozen in that elegant finery of yours.'

He stood up and pulled off his heavy cloak. Hesitating for a brief moment, he laid it over my knees, pulling the thick cloth round my skirts and making sure my feet were well hidden. He didn't smile.

'I thank you,' I said politely.

'It's nothing.'

It was as if what he had done was of no importance. I watched the snow settle on the sleeves of his jacket and thought he was being very rude. I had thanked him and the least he could do was be grateful for my thanks. I could have ignored him. I decided I *would* ignore him.

In the gathering dark, the water had deepened to a rich damson colour, almost black, but streaked with occasional shafts of gold and silver from the riverside torches. I stared out across the Scheldt but could see very little amidst the flurries of snow other than the bobbing lanterns of other boats.

I stole a glance at him.

'Are you angry with me?' Even to me my voice sounded small.

He made a dismissive movement with his head and for a moment I thought he wasn't going to answer. When he did his voice was tight with resentment.

'They tell me you are the king's cousin. Is it true?'

'Yes.'

He looked away at the snow, great grey flakes lost in the night sky and the swirling waters of the river. After a few moments he gave a deep sigh and turned back to face me.

"The girl I rescued that night last summer was just a nursemaid, a pretty girl like dozens of other pretty girls who cross my path. She was nobody in particular, just an ordinary person, like me. She was far below the notice of princes and kings; they would not even have known of her existence. She was not some grand young lady dressed up in velvets and furs with a fortune in jewels stitched onto her clothing. All she had was a torn nightgown and a corner in which to lay down her head. She didn't even have any slippers.'

'I didn't intend to deceive you.'

His eyes were unfriendly, as if he didn't believe me.

'I went to find her but when I returned to the abbey and asked in the laundry and the kitchens, nobody knew anything and I had no name. When I returned a second time, a few weeks later they said the Lady Joanna's household was leaving for Herenthals and wouldn't be coming back. I was told the king's daughter was travelling to the Emperor's court to meet with the Hapsburg family of her betrothed and was taking her maids with her.' He shrugged. 'So I stopped looking.'

'I didn't know.'

'No, you didn't.'

'If I'd known…'

I stopped. What could I possibly have done if I'd known? This man was not someone I could have brought into Lady Catherine's hall to enjoy the entertainments or dine in private with the family. I might as well have invited the boy who carried the meat into the kitchens to share our table.

'I'm sorry,' I said but my voice was so low he probably didn't hear.

In the distance, Antwerp's Twelfth Night celebrations were in full swing. I could just make out the flickering torches as the townspeople made their way through the streets towards the great bonfire in the market square. Above the singing and banging and rattling of rommelpots came the deep boom of the midwinterhorn reminding us that the year had turned.

I raised my face from the folds of my cloak and said as meekly as I could, 'Might we go closer? Would that be possible?'

I didn't want to sound too grand as if I was ordering him about.

'Of course, if that is what you wish, my lady.' His voice was flat again. It was obviously of no interest to him if he walked me through the streets of Antwerp or if we carried on down the river to the Montagu lodgings.

He gave orders to the men and we turned in towards the bank. As we came alongside the town steps he leapt out and in that moment I saw him clearly, outlined against the torchlight. He was not quite as tall as I remembered but he had wonderfully well-shaped legs.

He offered me his arm as I clambered up the slippery steps.

'In the streets, my lady, you will have to stay close because I wouldn't want to lose you.' He paused. 'Not for a second time.'

Now that we were ashore he seemed in no hurry and we ambled slowly along the busy streets with flakes of snow settling and then melting on our cloaks and gloves. After a few minutes of silence I ventured the words I had been wanting to say for some time. 'I don't know your name.'

He gave me a long cool look. 'My name is Thomas Holand, my lady.'

Thomas Holand. The king's man. Not a count, not a lord, not even a knight, just an ordinary man as he had said, an ordinary man who had given his sword to his king. He probably had a wife and a string of children back home in England but of course that was of no interest to me.

'Are you married, Master Holand?'

His face showed he found the question amusing.

'No, my lady.'

'Why not? I thought all men of your age were married.'

'I haven't had the time to look for a wife. I've been too busy fighting.'

'Did your father not arrange a marriage for you?

43

'No.' He sounded as if he didn't wish to discuss the matter further which was very annoying. Perhaps he had no money and couldn't attract a wife. I didn't know how rich fighting men were. He didn't look wealthy, he simply looked very ordinary. His clothing was not of good quality, but sturdy and rather drab. He had a warm woollen cloak, the one he had lent me, but his boots were badly worn.

'I am to be married soon,' I said. I wanted him to know I wasn't ordinary in the slightest.

'Of course you are.' He sounded as if he couldn't care less if I was to marry or not.

'It will be a very grand marriage.'

'Of course it will. What else would the family of a girl like you expect but a grand marriage?'

I felt irritated. I wanted him to acknowledge my importance.

'I shall doubtless have a title.'

'Doubtless.'

'And a vast wardrobe.'

'Most certainly a very vast wardrobe.'

'And my betrothed will shower me with gifts and jewels.'

He nodded his head sagely. 'A prince's ransom in jewels.'

I felt he was making fun of me and I didn't know why.

By now we had arrived in the square where the crowds had gathered round the fire. After the events of last summer it was rather frightening to be so close to a wild, uncontrolled blaze which might come roaring towards us. I stepped nearer to Master Holand so that my skirts touched the top of his boots and my sleeve brushed against the dark brown cloth of his jacket.

'Don't be frightened,' he said. 'We're perfectly safe.'

'I'm not frightened. Why would I be frightened?'

A roar erupted from the crowd as a bough of winter greenery was flung onto the blaze and flames leapt up into the night sky in a shower of bright red sparks. The woman next to me pushed sideways and I clutched at Master Holand's arm to prevent myself from falling.

'If you climb up here, my lady,' he said. 'You'll be safer and get a better view.'

He guided me to a set of steps leading up the side of what looked like the sort of warehouse where my cousin might store his wool. There were no windows, just huge doors. I climbed up part way. The steps were rather steep and, I thought, not very safe.

'Will you catch me if I should fall?'

He looked up into my face where I stood perched two steps above him. 'Yes, my lady. If you fall, I'll catch you. But if I were you I'd keep a tight hold of the rail.'

Just at that moment, the sound of his voice, the roar of the flames and the acrid smell of the smoke, brought everything back. It had been summer then and I'd been young and foolish and thought my mighty cousin might care for me, now it was winter and I was older and wiser and knew better. My cousin loved me, but not enough. What he wanted and what the king's mother wanted, would always come first. His alliances and his treaties and her desires mattered more. He would send me away to marry the old man, to be shut away in one of his castles and never see my family again. Edward and Isabella would quickly forget and Alice and Margaret would be lost to me forever.

I wondered if that was what had happened to my father. The king had loved him too, but just not enough.

On the other side of the bonfire some men started singing and soon everyone was swaying from side to side. I didn't understand the words but thought they were probably rude judging by the gales of laughter. Small children darted in and out of the crowd, dodging as close to the flames as they dared and one old woman bent over, lifted her skirts and wiggled her buttocks, much to the crowd's delight.

'I think it is time we went, my lady.' The voice came from by my feet. 'It's getting late.'

I held onto the rickety rail and climbed down the steps one at a time, being careful where I placed my boots. When I reached the last one I stood with my face level with his. I had forgotten what a pleasing countenance he had. He wasn't handsome like my cousin but it was an open, honest face. I had thought his eyes were brown but now I could see there was a hint of green and gold in the depths. He had long dark lashes of a sort which would have pleased any girl. His mouth was well-formed and when he smiled, which he was doing at that moment, I could just see the white of his teeth. Most common men smelled of sweat and horses and the midden, but he didn't.

'Master Holand?'

'Yes?' He held out his hand.

'Do you think… if it would please you… would you kiss me?'

'Christ's blood, my lady! He snatched away his hand

and stepped back in alarm as if he had been struck. 'Are you trying to get me hanged?'

He had no manners at all. What had I done to deserve such rudeness?

'Listen, my lady,' he said, coming close and practically whispering in my ear so we couldn't be heard. 'I know this is the last night of the celebrations and the world is upside down and I know the king's servants in the abbey are running riot over their masters and poking fun at their betters. But this is the end of it. Tomorrow the world will be set back in its proper order and you must know I cannot do what you ask.'

'I haven't asked you for anything, Master Holand,' I said sulkily. 'There isn't anything a man like you could possibly offer a girl like me.'

'My lady, I may not be the cleverest of men but I know about young women and I know exactly what you were saying and I cannot listen to you if you speak like that.'

He took my gloved fingers and helped me to the ground but immediately afterwards removed his hand as if afraid of what I might do.

'So we cannot be friends,' I said.

'Not if I value my neck, my lady, which I do.' He must have seen the flicker of disappointment in my eyes. 'Listen, my lady. There is a gulf between my world and yours and it's as wide as the River Scheldt; you must know that. It's a gulf of birthright and privilege. I am in the king's service and you are his cousin. I can have no place in your life, not as a friend or anything else.'

'My betrothed is very old,' I said, hearing the quiver in my voice.

'If you will permit me to say it, my lady, you are very young and doubtless many men look old to you.'

'But he has a great regard for me.'

'I'm sure he does.'

'I don't like him.'

'But he is rich and powerful, I'll wager?'

I thought of the sumptuous velvet of the crimson robe, the jewelled rings and the casual intimacy he'd shared with my cousin. 'Yes. He is rich and he is over-friendly with the king.'

'Then you have nothing to worry about. It is a good marriage.'

We walked back across the bridge and through the streets, side by side, neither of us speaking, with that gulf he had talked of widening with every step we took. At the river's edge he took pity on me. His face was half-hidden in shadows but this time his voice was soft. 'I don't wish to be unkind,' he said. 'I wish you well and I hope it is a good man they have found for you to marry. You are a very...' he paused as if seeking the appropriate word. 'You are a very pleasant young woman and you deserve to be happy.'

'Will you go with the king to fight next summer, Master Holand?' I thought I would converse with him like any person might, how any girl who was quite uninterested in being his friend or anything else, might converse.

'Yes,' he said. 'And if the king and the blessed St Thomas permit, when it is over I shall go home to England and find myself a wife.'

Alice was waiting for me in the warmest place, beside the dying embers of the fire. One of her husband's many torn garments lay neatly on her knee and she was carefully applying tiny stitches along the seam.

She raised her head as I entered the room.

I stripped off my cloak and collapsed onto the stool at her side.

'I am to be married,' I said miserably. 'That's why I was summoned. To be shown off to my betrothed, not to share in the entertainments. Oh Alice, he's old enough to be my grandfather and I don't know if I can bear it. He was horrible. He wasn't what I imagined a husband would be and he treated me like a horse from the stable yard to be prodded and poked.'

I shivered at the memory of his fingers on my face.

'Who is he?'

'I don't know.'

'But you must have some idea,' said Alice gently.

'One of the king's friends.'

'Rich?'

'Oh yes,' I said grudgingly. I knew this was the only thing of any importance in marriage: how wealthy a man was and what were his connections to the king.

'One of the nobility?'

'The servants say he's a Gascon lord.'

Alice put down her needle and clapped her hands together.

'But that's wonderful. A lord, maybe a count.'

'No!' I cried. 'It's far from being wonderful. I won't marry him.'

'Don't be childish,' snapped Alice. 'Margaret was quite right. You really are the most stupid of girls. Of course you will marry him. It's not up to you what you do. If the king has chosen this man, then you will marry him. From what you say it's a splendid marriage. Just imagine what your life will be like. You'll have a horse of your own and a groom to care for it. And there'll be gifts. A rich husband will give you jewels and furs and you'll be admired by everyone. You are very lucky.'

'I'm not lucky and I'm not stupid,' I cried.

'You have no idea what the world is for a woman,' said Alice firmly. 'Look at me! I am a king's granddaughter but my father took no more care with my marriage than he did with Margaret's. Do you imagine we enjoy our positions as our husband's wives? Do you think I like Lady Catherine looking down her long nose and treating me as no better than a servant simply because my husband is inferior to hers? When she is a mere baron's daughter, do you think I like it that she is a countess and I am not? And how do you think Margaret feels, married to that nobody, John Segrave? You are extremely fortunate so stop complaining. I wish I had had your luck.'

We continued arguing until Alice made herself ready for bed. She murmured her prayers and crawled beneath the covers. I lay beside her in tears. The pillow was warm and damp beneath my cheek but Alice's words were hard as granite and just as pitiless.

'Stop snivelling, Jeanette. You don't have any choice in the matter so you'd better get used to it. Think of your family. Imagine how pleased your mother will be.'

'I don't wish to marry him,' I mumbled tearfully into my pillow, the softness swallowing up the words. But there was no reply. Alice was already asleep.

That summer my cousin took his men to war. Together with his allies he invaded the territory of the French king, burned his villages and laid waste his land. But there was no great battle. When the two armies met, the Valois turned tail and scuttled back to Paris like the coward he was.

'There'll be another campaign,' whispered Elizabeth. 'The French king has to be defeated in battle.'

My heart leapt. Perhaps my betrothed might not live to see the French king vanquished. Perhaps he would die before I had to marry him. Or perhaps I would grow old and die a spinster in Antwerp, still waiting for my cousin to win his war.

The cold weather returned and with it the tedium of discussions within Lady Catherine's rooms of compulsory staples, forfeitures and papal interdicts. To my surprise there was a treaty of friendship with the Flemings giving them limitless supplies of English wool and allowing my cousin and his army safe passage through Flanders to the borders of the kingdom of France. Lady Catherine said that before long Philip of Valois would hear us knocking on the gates of Paris.

2

GHENT 1340

'Where is my girdle?' shrieked Elizabeth, her nose deep in a chest. 'Who's taken it?'

'Nobody,' I replied. 'You lent it to Lady Alice.'

'But I need it. Someone must go and get it.'

She looked in vain for a willing slave but every other girl had her arms full of clothes and the maids were nowhere to be seen. The room was awash with silks and shoes and serviceable woollen gowns, the beds strewn with satin ribbons and bits of embroidered cloth, and the little table by the hearth was hidden beneath a pile of fine linen sheets.

Only yesterday we had been told we were leaving for Ghent. Everything must be got ready and packed into chests because this wasn't like the week we had spent in the little town of Brussels enjoying my cousin's tournaments, this time we were not coming back.

Clutching a tangle of coloured stockings to her breast, Elizabeth favoured me with a special smile. 'Please, Joan,' she pleaded. 'I'll let you borrow my green ribbon.'

'Oh, very well,' I said. 'But don't steal anything out of my box.'

I thought Alice might be in the courtyard so I hurried through the outer chamber and ran down the steps as fast as I could. As I rounded the final turn I found myself confronted by a dark figure with a foot on the bottom stair. I put out both hands and clutched the rails to stop myself from falling.

'By the Saints! Here's a surprise!'

It was Thomas Holand looking at me with an ever-widening smile.

'Are you planning to hold the stairway against all-comers, my lady? Because if you are, I would suggest you find a weapon.'

I couldn't speak. It was a whole year since I'd seen him last and I hadn't expected to see him again.

He put his hand to his belt. 'I have a dagger if you'd care to borrow it.'

I could feel the flush rising into my cheeks.

'No, thank you, Master Holand,' I muttered. 'I have no need of a weapon.'

'Ah, my lady, wrong on two counts. First, I am Master Holand no longer; I am Sir Thomas Holand. And secondly, a young woman should always pay attention to her defences. Who knows when she might find herself in need of protection?'

'You are a knight?'

'Yes. His Grace did me the honour. But as you know, my lady, I'm really just an ordinary man and ordinary men seldom expect such rewards.'

Sir Thomas! I thought. How wonderful for him.

'Will you be returning to England?' I asked, feeling a need to fill the growing silence.

'Why would I do that?'

My cheeks burned. I would have given anything to escape this embarrassment but he was blocking my way.

'You said you wanted a wife.'

He put his head on one side and considered me for what seemed like an age. Then his eyes narrowed and his smile widened still further.

'I had planned to return for the winter, but I've been offered a position here which, on second thoughts, I think I shall accept.'

I looked up and met his eyes. 'Who is your companion?' I said quickly.

He cast a sideways glance at the man standing at his shoulder.

'Forgive me, my lady, I forget you like to know the name of every man who crosses your path however lowly he may be. May I present my younger brother, Otho Holand.'

The young man bowed. I could see the likeness: the prominent cheekbones, the wide-set eyes, the straight nose. He was about the same height but of slighter build and the hair beneath his cap was fair. He didn't have the firm mouth and well-drawn lips of his elder brother and his chest was not as broad. He looked ill at ease. Perhaps it was something I'd said.

I smiled one of my smallest smiles and acknowledged the greeting.

'And what of you, my lady?' Thomas Holand's voice was perfectly even. 'What of the vast wardrobe?'

He was laughing at me and I found myself unable to speak.

'Not yet?' he said more gently.

I shook my head. 'No, not yet,' I muttered. 'But soon.'

'Of course,' he said. 'Soon.'

His brother gave him a nudge and whispered something I couldn't hear. Sir Thomas gave a short laugh and spread his hands in a gesture of apology.

'I have been remiss, my lady, and my brother reminds me of my duty. You see, it is always wise to have a man like my brother at one's side when doing battle no matter how well-disguised the enemy might be. He's saved me from many an ill-conceived action. You were clearly on your way to some engagement when we stopped your progress, so may we have the honour of escorting you?'

'No thank you, Sir Thomas.'

'There are many people out there, my lady, people you might not care to meet: undesirables, cutpurses, young girls bent on deceit.' His eyes creased with amusement. 'And I really wouldn't want you to get lost.'

He was being very rude. Perhaps that was what happened when you were raised up by the king. Perhaps he now considered himself my equal. But he could never be that. I was a king's granddaughter whilst he would never be more than he was, just an ordinary man honoured by his king.

'My lady?' He looked at me enquiringly. 'May I be of service?'

I looked up in an agony of indecision. Perhaps I should accept his offer. Perhaps I ought to say something. Perhaps I should ask if he'd be coming with us to Ghent. I gulped and felt that unaccustomed sensation of disquiet deep in my belly.

'No, thank you, Sir Thomas,' I said quickly. 'I have no need of you.'

In January we travelled into Flanders with the English archers singing as they marched. It was horribly cold and the rivers and marshes glittered with ice but nothing dampened the high spirits of my cousin's men. In the bright winter sunshine, sword hilts sparkled, spurs gleamed and everyone believed we were marching towards a great victory. My cousin's new banners, quartered with the leopards of England and the fleur-de-lys of France were, so Elizabeth said, a statement of the rightness of his claim to the French Crown. When he stood in the market place in Ghent and declared himself King of England and King of France, a champion of Christendom, the crowd roared their approval and I knew that nothing could stop him.

But I was to be disappointed. For two months we idled our time in St Bavo's Abbey while my cousin spent his days with his close advisors and the queen made preparations for her confinement. There were no entertainments and nothing to think of but what lay ahead.

Then one day, with the king absent on secret business and the season of Lent fast approaching, the queen disappeared into her rooms with her favourite ladies leaving us girls to enjoy our new-found freedom.

'We hear there is no money.'

It was the first day of Shrove feasting and I had failed to notice our old friends, the two knights of the Margrave of Juliers' train, sidling up to my shoulder.

I turned slowly, not wishing to appear too eager for conversation. 'Who has no money, Sir?'

'Why, your king, *damoiselle*,' said the older one, pressing himself close. 'As I told you before, the wool sheds are empty. Now we hear the English commons will not support him and his credit is no longer good.'

'That is nonsense.'

'Alas, no, *damoiselle*,' he said. stroking my sleeve with one of his fingers. 'You must understand, the princes want the gold they were promised and your king is unable to pay. He has returned to England. He has abandoned you. Left you to your fate.'

His friend, who was edging close to Elizabeth, spoke quietly. 'We have heard that your queen, the great lady from Hainault, is in low spirits. She is angry your king has fled to England. They say she weeps.'

Elizabeth looked at me as if to say, what would these foreign knights know about the goings on in the queen's rooms.

'It is believed his affections are much engaged elsewhere,' the man whispered in my ear. 'They say the damsels of the queen's chamber are no more than whores for your king, and that his closest friend is forced to wear cuckold's horns.'

His companion placed a proprietorial hand on my waist, 'And they say, and I am certain it is true, that when your queen is recovered from her present *accouchement*, she will take a lover.'

'That's a lie!' I protested, amazed they would talk of such matters to us.

Both men held up their hands. 'We only repeat what we hear, *damoiselles*, and what we hear is that the marriage of the King and Queen of England lies in disarray.'

It was untrue, of course it was. The marriage of the king and queen was strong; you couldn't put a single hair between their closeness. But there were uncomfortable memories: Lady Catherine's scented garden where Elizabeth said she often entertained the king; my cousin's hand resting on her arm and a meeting of their eyes; a pretty maid dropping a basin at the king's approach and, at the tournament in Brussels, a wisp of silk which was not the queen's, tucked into his padded jacket.

Next day, Lady Catherine emerged from the queen's rooms and Elizabeth spent most of the afternoon with her mother.

'We are not to worry,' said Elizabeth on her return. 'The king has gone to consult with the parliament. And she says I am to be married soon. It is certain to be a man of good family. My father wouldn't waste me on someone unworthy. What of your mother? Who does she want for you?'

I remembered that Easter at Bisham with my mother visiting: endless dark spring days, fog-filled and damp, with lengthy recitations of my sins, deeply disapproving silences, numerous penances for my many misdeeds and woven through it all, the unmistakable thread of maternal dislike. The queen, it was made clear, had been more than merciful because my behaviour at Woodstock had been unforgivable.

'I don't know,' I whsipered.

'I'm sure they'll find someone,' laughed Elizabeth. 'Some toothless old greybeard with a sagging belly and scrawny legs who won't mind you being a traitor's daughter. If they pay enough, they're bound to find someone.'

I hadn't told her about the old man in Antwerp. I hadn't told anyone except Alice. And Thomas Holand.

That evening I too received a summons from Lady Catherine. She regarded me from the far end of her polished table with a smile which started and ended with her teeth.

'I have a letter from your mother. She enquires after your spiritual education and says she wishes you to be married. She asks if you are ready. Are you ready?'

'Yes, Lady Catherine,' I muttered, blushing.

She eyed me as if I were a juicy little sweetmeat, tempting but possibly laced with poison and hence unwise to eat.

'The king is generous,' she said. 'He has brokered this marriage and you are extremely fortunate to have been chosen.'

She was almost crooning at the thought of the king's generosity. I wondered what he had given her.

'Marriage means one thing above all else, Joan, and that is obedience to the will of your husband and his family. You do understand?'

'Yes, Lady Catherine.'

She didn't believe me. She considered me stupid.

'You must learn to curb your own desires because they have no place in a woman's life.'

This was a repeat of the lectures I received at regular intervals: don't question, be obedient, be prudent, be virtuous, be merciful, be good.

'There is nothing finer for a young girl than to serve God through her husband. That is where true joy lies. And when you have given him a son you will have accomplished God's purpose.'

I gulped. A son! With that monstrous old man! And if there was no son he would probably beat me. He might even kill me!

I raised my eyes. Lady Catherine was idly running her fingers over my mother's letter. There had been no mention of wedding clothes, no talk of measurements or fittings, no holding up of lengths of silk or discussions about my hair which was certain to be heavily veiled.

'Will my marriage be soon, Lady Catherine?'

She sniffed. 'His Grace has requested we wait until he returns. He wishes to see you wed.'

'When will he return?'

'That is not your business.'

She looked at me severely as if I needed to be reminded of my place, which in her eyes was very low indeed.

'We must none of us forget what we owe the king; you most of all.'

She shouldn't have said that. I knew exactly what I owed the king. I owed my fatherless state to the king. It was he who had signed the death warrant which had taken my father to the executioner's block and however much I loved my cousin I could never forgive him for what he had done. My father hadn't been worth fighting for and he hadn't been worth saving.

I left Lady Catherine's room, dragging my feet down the stairs and out into the cloisters. Beyond the arches on the far side of the paved area a man was lighting torches and in the distance the abbey dogs were barking.

I heard a faint chink of metal. Someone was in the shadows.

'Who's there?' I said nervously.

'My lady?'

Thomas Holand. Of course. Who else?

'What are you doing here, Sir Thomas?'

'Seeking solitude, my lady. And you?'

'I too wanted to be alone.'

'Then we are both destined to be disappointed.'

I'd been very careful to keep well out of his way these past weeks and was annoyed at finding him here but I could hardly turn round and leave, that would not be polite. He didn't say anything else and the silence lengthened and grew, filling the cloisters like a fog, until I could barely breathe.

'When I am married I shall not speak with you,' I said in a rush. 'My husband would not allow it.'

'Naturally not.'

'As a married woman I must do as my husband bids me.'

His teeth gleamed in the darkness

'If I were your husband I would keep you under lock and key, my lady.'

He took a step out of the shadows and now I could see him clearly. He wore a new cloak of some quite expensive cloth. Of course he was a knight and my cousin would have given him some manors.

'Are you rich Sir Thomas?'

'Are you after a loan?'

I dipped my head. 'No, of course not.'

He looked at me thoughtfully. 'I wondered if you might be in need of ready coin. I know how these things work for young ladies.'

'So, you *are* rich?'

'No, my lady, I am not. What little money the king has given me has been spent. Suits of armour are expensive and good horses even more so. It's a costly business being a knight and a man can't appear impoverished, not if he wishes to make his way in the world.'

'But have you no other income?'

Surely he must have something, how else could he manage?

'I am a second son.'

'Has your father not made provision for you?'

He hesitated. 'My father is dead. He died in difficult circumstances.'

'What sort of circumstances?'

He sighed. 'You are a very inquisitive young woman. If you must know, he was killed, a matter of revenge for something he'd done, something his enemies regarded as a betrayal. So they cut off his head and sent it to the man who had ordered his killing.'

I clutched the pillar to stop my legs from giving way. My father had lost his head for something he'd done, something the king's mother regarded as a betrayal.

'They cut off my father's head,' I said in a small voice.

He looked at me carefully.

'Who was your father?'

'He was the king's uncle.'

I blinked. I couldn't cry, not here in front of Thomas Holand.

'I know nothing,' I said. 'I don't know what he did or why he was killed and no-one talks of it.'

'What happened to you and your mother?'

'My cousin Margaret says we lost everything.'

He nodded as if he understood. 'It's hard being the wife of a man branded a traitor. My mother had daughters at home and nothing to live on, and I was no longer welcome in the lord's house where I'd been sent because no man wants a turncoat's son whispering his secrets and seducing his wives and daughters when the candles are out.' He gave a wry smile. 'I was barely twelve years old.'

Twelve was nothing. I thought Thomas Holand with his sleepy eyes and twisting words would have been capable of corrupting his nursemaid in the cradle.

'What did you do?'

He smiled. 'What any sensible younger son would do. I offered myself to the king. I said I would fight for him. I said I was brave and strong and would be loyal and true to his banner. Then I demonstrated my skills by knocking down the first half dozen boys who tried to take me on. I was an aggressive little brat with hard knuckles and I was determined to succeed. So I became one of the king's men and fought in his battles.'

'And that's why you are poor?'

He laughed. 'Oh, I'm not poor, my lady, it's just that I'm not rich; not yet.'

'But one day you hope to be rich?'

'If a man is prepared to take risks there are many ways to become rich.'

I should have known he was a risk-taker and like any sensible young woman, should have had a care to my defences because where Thomas Holand was concerned I had begun to realise that my fortifications were badly in need of repair. But I told myself he was just an ordinary man and so it didn't really matter.

Two weeks later, with rain drumming heavily on the abbey roof, the queen gave birth to a son – John. A message was dispatched to England, the Duke of Brabant indicated his pleasure at being asked to stand sponsor and Lady Catherine bestowed a smile on the assembled company. I gave a sigh of relief. Nothing had really changed. Everything was how it should be.

But nothing was how it should be because no amount of kind words from the duke or smiles from Lady Catherine could delay the awful day of my marriage.

The Béguinage of St Elisabeth lay in a quiet corner of the town some little distance from the abbey. I had never visited but had heard others talk of what a pleasant place it was.

'The béguines will not expect a formal presentation,' said Lady Catherine briskly. 'It is simply a little gift, nothing of value, merely to let them know they have not been forgotten during Her Grace's confinement.'

She looked at me, impatience and annoyance shadowing her eyes.

'It will not be long until you are a married woman, Joan, and charitable giving will then be part of your duties. Your husband will expect it. You have stitched many cloths for the sisters of St Frideswide and seen how broken meats are given to the poor at the gate so you are not unpractised in these matters.'

Not long! This marriage was perilously close and I didn't know what to do. Perhaps I could run away like St Frideswide; hire a boat and escape into the oak woods. But I had no money and had foolishly refused the offer of a loan and I had no idea where there was an oak wood of sufficient size to shelter me.

'I would go myself,' continued Lady Catherine, 'but naturally it is impossible with the queen still confined and His Grace due back any day. I have arranged for Sir William's steward to accompany you and one of the maids will carry the basket.'

At the bottom of the courtyard steps I found a plump dark-haired woman waiting patiently with a cloth-covered basket placed firmly at her feet. I looked round anxiously for Sir William's steward.

'My lady?'

It was Thomas Holand, smiling the way he always did.

'May God keep you well, my lady.'

'I'm going out,' I said, not wanting to be drawn into conversation.

'I know,' he replied. 'I am to be your escort.'

'You?' I was panic stricken. 'Why you?'

'Oh, I fancied a ride in the sunshine as a man does and the earl has no need of my services this morning.'

'You are Sir William's steward?'

'I am. I told you I had been offered a position. Do you not approve?'

I looked at my feet. 'It is nothing to do with me,' I muttered. 'You may do as you please.'

'He laughed at my confusion. 'I shall.'

He called a groom to bring the horses and I eyed the cushioned seat behind Thomas Holand's saddle with dismay. Lady Catherine disapproved of a girl riding astride, spreading her legs across a horse's back. She said it gave rise to wicked thoughts.

He swung himself easily into the saddle and waited while the groom lifted me up. I sat there, turned sideways, barely touching him, not daring to lean against his back, but when he pulled the horse round I had to grab at him to prevent myself from falling off.

On any other day I would have noticed how glorious the streets of Ghent were, how pretty the houses, how grand the churches and how delightful the little sparkling canals; but with my cheek hard up against Thomas Holand's broad back and my fingers clutching his belt, I was aware of nothing but his nearness, the rise and fall of his breathing and the dusty male scent of his clothing.

At last the swaying movement slowed. Ahead lay a cluster of brightly painted houses laid out neatly behind a low lime-washed wall. To one side was a vast drying meadow shimmering with hundreds of gently billowing cloths, and beyond the meadow, an orchard.

'The béguinage,' said Thomas Holand, making to dismount.

I snatched my hands away as in one fluid movement he was off the horse and standing at my feet.

'Alone, or would you care for my assistance?'

I peered at the beaten earth far below me.

'I would be grateful for your help,' I said reluctantly.

With what seemed maddening slowness, he placed his hands on my waist and lifted me down. His fingers pressed firmly against the stuff of my gown and my breath caught in my throat. The closeness of a siege was not what I'd expected. I'd thought it would be a single well-aimed arrow, easy to see coming and easy to avoid but the next moment I was on the ground and he was giving instructions to the groom.

I smoothed out my skirts. 'Please remain here, Sir Thomas.'

With my face aflame and behind me, the maid clutching the basket, I approached the door of the béguinage and pulled on the bell. Almost immediately a woman poked out her head.

'Greetings, lady, greetings,' she said, her whole face one wide smile. 'It is my honour and privilege to welcome you to the Béguinage of St Elisabeth.'

She opened the door wider and ushered me inside. She was youngish, quite pretty and dressed in a plain brown gown with a wimple over her head. I gave a little nod and explained who I was and why I was here.

'Ah, the kindness of your queen. Such munificence. How would we manage without the boundless generosity of the ladies of Ghent? If you would care to put your basket here.'

The queen's gift, covered with its fine white cloth, was placed on the table beside what I presumed were other people's offerings: two pairs of shoes, a pile of warm woollen blankets and a box of rather wizened quince.

'Such kindness,' murmured the béguine. 'Would you care to see the infirmary? Everyone who visits wants to see our infirmary.'

She led me out from under the shelter of the gatehouse into a sun-filled courtyard.

'Not what you imagined, eh?'

She smiled at my open mouth. It was like a pretty little village all on its own, set apart from the town by its smooth white walls and shallow moat.

'It's not like other convents, is it?'

She laughed. 'Look around! Do you see any high stone walls or locked doors?'

I shook my head.

'We are not like our Cistercian sisters. We béguines are free to come and go whenever we wish. Everyone is like you on their first visit. "How strange it is!" they exclaim. "How beautiful!" And all the time they are wondering what I am doing in a place like this.'

'Were you placed here by your family?' I asked politely thinking it was a shame she hadn't been allowed a husband.

My remark caused her to break into peals of laughter again.

'No, no, no! On the contrary, I had to battle against my family. They'd picked a fine young man for me to marry. My mother wanted grandchildren and my father coveted the young man's wealth. But I knew what God wanted of me and I was determined to live the way He intended that I should.'

'So you chose the béguinage?'

'Yes. Here I serve God with my prayers and my hands. I am like Martha. And I serve my fellow béguines. Not all are young and strong like you and me and some have no money at all.'

She led me past the gardens where a couple of old women on their knees poked diligently at the soil.

'The seeds are up already,' called one. 'God has blessed us this springtime.'

'The vegetables,' explained my companion. 'Some of the beguines would spend all day planting and hoeing if they could. Now, what do you think of this?'

It was an imposing building, beautifully decorated and painted.

'The infirmary,' she said with undisguised pride in her voice. 'For the old and the poor and the sick. It is our pleasure to care for them. It is why we are so grateful for your offerings.'

'I thought you would spend your days praying.'

'Oh no. We do God's work in whatever way we can. Those béguines who have no money but some learning go into the town and teach the children of wealthy merchants because there are many men who wish their daughters to rise in the world. They know a wife unable to manage her husband's accounts is of no use to any man be he a weaver or a banker.'

'What of those who have no money and no learning?'

'If they are young and strong they take in laundry from the rich houses. Behind these buildings you will see our drying meadow. It grows larger each year. I think we wash linen for every household in the whole of Ghent.'

She showed me the church and the cabins where the béguines lived, and a large building where I admired the plain wooden benches.

'We come here to discuss what needs to be discussed and make our decisions. We are not ruled over by a man.'

'But surely you have a bishop?'

'No. We elect one of our own to guide us. This is a place where women are at peace and do God's work without the interference of men.'

I was silent. The idea of a woman choosing her own life was so odd that I had to examine it over and over again in my mind. My new friend's family had arranged a marriage for her and yet she had defied them. She had chosen this life. It was not what her father or her brothers wanted and it was not what her cousin had ordered her to do. If he had presented her with an elderly lord from a faraway duchy, she would have refused the marriage. She would have chosen to live here.

As we walked back along the path the mid-March sunshine warmed my face, but somewhere in a dark corner of my mind the seed of an idea was beginning to grow. If it was possible for a béguine to choose her life, why then should it not be possible for me?

She kissed me on both cheeks and bade me farewell, then slyly suggested a stroll amongst the early blossom in the orchard. With a final murmured blessing and a wave of her hand, she disappeared through her little wooden door.

I stepped out of the shade of the archway and into the light. Thomas Holand was waiting for me, sitting comfortably on the wayfarer's bench with his legs stretched out in front of him. When he saw me he got quickly to his feet.

'My lady?'

I hesitated. I wasn't comfortable giving him orders and yet it wasn't right to ask his permission.

'I wish to walk in the orchard and I need you to accompany me in case…' I stopped. I felt the colour rise in my cheeks. I could think of no good reason why I should need Thomas Holand. 'In case I…'

'In case you become lost?' He obligingly finished my words.

I nodded. 'Yes, there are a great many trees and it might be…' I was going to say "dangerous" but he might think me foolish if I did, so I said nothing and left the missing word floating idly in the air.

We walked along the path which bordered the wickerwork fence until we reached the gate. He undid the latch and stood back to allow me through. A small breeze rose up from nowhere but it wasn't enough to stir the grass, and under the trees it was warm.

I didn't know about orchards. I thought the grove of gnarled old trees whose lichen-covered branches almost touched the ground might be quince but I wasn't sure. The stately trunks with canopies high above my head looked more familiar. There were trees like this, with branches covered in early blossom, in the queen's secret garden in Woodstock where we used to play as children. They were pears.

As I walked further in amongst the trees I could see huddles of leafless bushes growing untidily in small secretive clusters and beyond them dozens of delicate spindly trees laid out neatly in rows. Perhaps they were cherries or possibly damsons. I didn't know and had no-one to ask. A wisp of sheep's wool was snagged on the bark of what I believed might be an ancient plum but there was no sign of its owner.

When I could no longer see the beautiful buildings of the béguinage or the shiny pointed rooftops of Ghent, I stopped. I could be anywhere. I could indeed be lost. A faint drift of sweetness filled the air, and a softness. It smelled like home, like the fields beyond the park at Woodstock: the grasses, the fresh green leaves and the welcoming scent of springtime. I thought I had come to puzzle out what to do but now I was here I felt nothing but a steady calmness and an inner peace.

I knew he was behind me.

'I am to be married,' I said at last. 'At Easter when the king returns.'

There was a pause and then he said, 'I know.'

It never occurred to me to ask him how he knew.

'I must marry the man my cousin has chosen for me.'

He said nothing.

My flesh crawled at the thought of marriage and what it meant: the old man's hand creeping under my nightgown, his wrinkled face pressed up against mine and his tongue sliding into my mouth. He would devour me at his leisure and I would have to submit.

I turned to face him. 'What can I do?'

He looked at me curiously. 'Are you asking me for advice, my lady?'

I nodded. 'Please help me. I cannot marry him.'

'But it is a good marriage.'

Of course it was. My cousin would never give me to an unworthy man.

'I don't want it,' I said with rising panic.

I had no idea how I could defy my cousin. No girl could think of refusing marriage. It was impossible. Lady Catherine would lock me up and have me beaten if I showed the slightest disobedience in this matter and I had no-one to protect me.

For a few moments neither of us said anything. My mouth was dry with fear and he was only Sir William's steward and could have no opinions of his own, or none that could be voiced aloud.

'I have a sister,' remarked Thomas Holand. 'A little older than you, I think, but she finds herself in much the same situation. She doesn't wish to marry the man my brother has chosen for her. It's a good marriage, a very good marriage, but she's adamant she won't have him. She's set her heart on someone else.'

'So what is to happen?' I asked politely, knowing his sister couldn't possibly be in my situation.

He smiled. 'This other man admires my sister. He wants her. He showers her with gifts and has made my brother an offer.'

'Is he rich?'

'Immensely.'

'So there's no problem.'

'As far as my brother is concerned there is a very great problem. The man is married. He wishes my sister to become his concubine.'

I blushed. How dreadful! How could his sister even consider such a thing?

'Do you think she should refuse him and marry the man she has already rejected, the man she doesn't wish to marry?'

I tried to imagine myself as Thomas Holand's sister, pursued by a rich admirer, but all I could think of was the horror of those clawed fingers and rheumy eyes.

'I have no wealthy admirers.'

'But you could marry someone else, someone of your own choosing. If you did they couldn't make you marry this man.'

Someone else? Marry someone else? My mind skittered over the men I knew, the sons and brothers of my cousin's friends. Their names and faces were a blur and I could think of no-one. Only Edward; and they would never let me marry him.

'There is no-one,' I said in a small voice, aware of the impossibility of following any other course than the one chosen for me by my cousin. 'I thought it might be possible to choose a different life, one that I could accept, but it's not.'

The air was very still, the slight breeze lost in the trees. All I could hear were the voices of two béguines in the drying meadow calling to one another as they laid out the sheets.

'You could marry me.'

Above my head a bird began to sing. The noise was pure and sweet like those first clear green days of springtime before the heat of mid-summer burns everything to dust. A small yellow butterfly wavered in mid-air, danced briefly and then flitted away out of sight.

At his first shot my fragile defences had been breached.

'That would not be possible,' I whispered.

I thought I might have imagined my words but he answered me.

'Why not?'

'You are too poor. You couldn't provide for me.'

He gave a short laugh. 'I shan't always be poor, my lady. As I told you, one day I shall be rich and then, if you were my wife and if it gave you pleasure, I'd scatter jewels across our marriage bed.'

It was an appalling image: Thomas Holand casting jewels across my marriage bed. My knees trembled. I closed my eyes to hold the picture sharp in my mind.

'And I would look after you very well,' he said softly. 'Very well indeed.'

'They would never let me marry you.'

'We shan't ask them.'

The thought was so shocking, I gasped.

'But they would…' I wasn't sure what my cousin or Sir William would do but I knew their revenge would be terrible.

'Are you afraid of them?' He seemed amused.

'Yes.'

'What's the worst that could happen?'

I sensed the hardness of the king's eyes, the scrawled *Edwardus Rex*, the dripping wax, the impressed seal, and my father's bloody head rolling onto the waiting straw.

'They could kill you,' I whispered.

'For marrying you? An honourable marriage?'

'A very dishonourable marriage, done without the king's permission. You may be able to marry any woman you like, Sir Thomas, but I can only marry with my cousin's consent and he would never agree to this foolishness.'

He touched the tips of my fingers with his.

'Is it so very foolish?'

I couldn't look at him. I could never be his. Never. It was impossible. He was not someone I could even consider. I was the king's cousin and he was nobody.

When I spoke it was almost in a whisper. 'It *is* foolish. You know it is. And it's dangerous.'

My heart skipped a beat and then stopped as his fingers closed over mine.

'Perhaps as a fighting man I'm used to danger.'

His hand was firm, a soldier's grasp. If he held me he wouldn't let me fall. I'd be safe.

'You must be acquainted with many girls, Sir Thomas. Why would you want to marry me?'

He smiled gently. 'Do you need to ask?'

I felt a shiver run through me as I remembered how he'd held me in his arms and kissed me when he'd thought I was nothing more than a nursemaid. He hadn't known my value in the marketplace and yet he'd prized me; he'd wanted me and had sought me out. I lowered my lashes. I couldn't look at him because I knew what was written on my face.

'You are very sweet, my lady,' he said quietly, 'and very beautiful. I think any man would want you as a wife.'

At the softness of his voice I looked up and that was my undoing. His eyes spoke of something I'd never seen before. I thought it might be love. I was very young and knew nothing at all about men but I thought I saw the flicker of desire in Thomas Holand's eyes.

He released my hand and stepped back. Now an empty coldness lay between us and I felt more alone than before.

'Think about it, my lady. Think carefully but don't delay. The king will return in a few weeks and the vast wardrobe won't wait long.'

He was gentling me with words and the steady persuasiveness of his voice, but it wasn't necessary because, although he couldn't know it, his battle was already won.

He glanced up and down the rows as if expecting someone to step out from amongst the trees. Then he looked back at me. He didn't press me further. He'd shown me my escape route if I was brave enough to take it.

He turned towards the gate.

'We should go.'

The River Scheldt had narrowed to a tricking stream, so slight I could bridge it with a tiny step.

'Please,' I said, placing one foot hesitantly across the abyss which had once divided us. 'Please. Don't go. Don't leave me. I... I don't need to wait.'

'So?'

He sounded less than interested. I stared uncertainly at the toes of my boots. What if I'd been mistaken and he hadn't meant what he'd said? What if I was about to make a fool of myself? What if he laughed?

I opened my mouth to speak but the words died on my lips. I tried again.

'I... I think I would like to marry you.' My voice tailed away into a whisper.

For a moment there was no sound at all, not even a bird or an insect or a breath of wind. I wished I was somewhere else. I waited for his laughter and embarrassed explanations of how I had misunderstood his words, but nothing came. When I thought I could bear it no longer I felt his hand touch mine.

'I'm glad, my lady, because I very much want to marry you.'

'You do?' I looked up.

He smiled at me with my whole world reflected in his eyes and at that moment I had no need of anything else.

'How would we do it?' I whispered, distracted by the unaccustomed sensations in the pit of my belly and a sudden wish to have him place his mouth on mine. 'The bishop would never agree to marry us.'

He laughed. 'No, he wouldn't. But we don't need the bishop. You can leave that to me; I'll arrange it.'

'What about Lady Catherine and Sir William?'

He began to stroke my hand with his fingers.

'We must keep this a secret.'

'But everyone will know. How can they not know?'

'Listen' he laid his hands on my shoulders. He looked very serious. 'For now this must remain a secret between the two of us. After we are married you will continue to live in the Montagu household and...'

'I thought we would live together,' I said, not liking the idea of returning to Lady Catherine one little bit. 'I thought we would have our own lodgings. I know how to run a household if that's what's worrying you. It's what I've been taught to do.'

He reverted to stroking my palm again. 'No. I won't have you live like I do now, you deserve better. Later, when I've made my fortune, I shall come and take you away.'

'And we'll be together?'

'Yes, but until then if they try to marry you to anyone else you'll be able to say that you're already married: to me.'

My toes tingled at the thought of being married to Thomas Holand. Now that I could see clearly, I thought him very good-looking.

'How will you make your fortune?'

'War makes men's fortunes, my lady. It's easy. Rich towns to plunder, merchants to be stripped of their wealth, wagon-loads of jewels and furs to be taken, and the greatest prize of all – a ransom. Look at my friend Walter Manny; one moment nothing but an esquire carver in the queen's train and ten years later, admiral of the northern fleet, the king's man in Merioneth and a fortune in ransom money stashed in his saddle-bags.'

'And you could be like that?'

'I could.'

I liked his vision of the future and never considered for one minute that he might fail.

'When can we marry? Can it be soon?' A girl shouldn't ask such a question but our conversation was already so peculiar, like something imagined not something real, that he didn't seem to find it odd in the slightest.

'The princes are coming to the abbey tomorrow to speak with the queen and her advisors. The place will be overrun with strangers. Half the queen's ladies are being moved out of their chambers to make room for the great men. There'll be so much coming and going you'll be able to slip away and no-one will notice in amongst the chaos.'

He put out his hand as if to touch my face but changed his mind.

'You do understand what will happen, my lady? You do know about marriage?'

I blushed and couldn't look at him. 'Yes,' I whispered. 'I know.'

'When we have exchanged vows it will be necessary to lie together. You understand what that means?'

'Yes.' My face was the colour of the setting sun it was so hot.

There was a long silence.

'Good. It's settled then. Tomorrow, when the Vespers bell sounds I'll send my brother to the postern gate. You remember my brother, Otho? And you must bring one of your women, someone to be a witness, someone you can trust to keep silent.'

Alice, I thought. With her husband returned to Ypres, I would ask Alice. I couldn't possibly bring the maid I shared with Elizabeth as she was a Montagu servant and probably spied for Lady Catherine. It would have to be Alice.

We walked slowly back to the gate, saying nothing for there was nothing left to say. We had made our promises and I would think of him as my betrothed. How thrilling that sounded! He unlatched the gate and swung it open.

'My lady?' For the first time since we'd entered the orchard, he sounded uncertain of himself. 'You're quite sure this is what you want?'

'Oh yes,' I breathed, 'I'm quite sure. I won't change my mind.'

'A word of advice. Say nothing of our conversation, especially not to your friend.'

'Which friend, Sir Thomas?'

'The earl's daughter, the Lady Elizabeth.'

'We've been put together by Lady Catherine but we're not friends. I tell her nothing of any importance.'

'Good.'

He helped me onto his horse and we rode back together in what I took to be companionable silence. I rested my cheek against his back and wondered at his strength and the way his muscles moved beneath his clothes.

In the courtyard, just as we were about to enter the abbey, I remembered something. I touched his sleeve. 'Will there be minstrels?' I was embarrassed to ask as he hadn't made any mention of entertainment, but I didn't want a wedding day which was dull and dreary.

He looked surprised.

'Minstrels?'

'For the marriage feast. There will be a feast, won't there? There's got to be a feast. And minstrels.'

His lips twitched. 'Whatever you wish, my lady. I'll make a note of it: minstrels and a feast.'

'And silver coins,' I said, remembering the pennies showered over Margaret and John Segrave: a glittering waterfall of shining silver.

'Silver coins.' His voice was steady. 'Anything else?'

I shook my head and smiled up at him, trying to hold a picture of the silver coins in my head until tomorrow.

Alice was in the little room at the top of the stairs, far from anyone's attention. I was hardly through the doorway when I blurted out my story. I thought she'd be pleased but she gave me a look of utter horror and dropped the book she'd been reading onto the floor.

'My brother-in-law's steward? Are you out of your mind?'

'No,' I said sulkily. 'Why would you think that?'

'This is a joke, I presume. A jest or some such.'

'It's not a joke, Alice. I'm going to marry him.'

She rolled her eyes upwards and sighed deeply. 'Jeanette. You cannot marry the Earl of Salisbury's steward. It's ridiculous. What are you thinking of? The king and Sir William decide who you marry. It's nothing to do with you.'

I shrugged off my cloak and dropped it onto the chest.

'I don't want it to be like that.'

'It doesn't matter what you want, it's what the king and Sir William want. I've told you this before. Men decide these things. You can't please yourself. Don't be foolish.'

'Please, Alice.'

But Alice, it was becoming clear to me, was not going to be swayed by my pleading.

'Jeanette, you tell me the king has already decided on your future husband; the other women say Lady Catherine is preparing for a spring wedding so there's nothing you can do; you will be married as the king wishes.'

'Yes, I will be married but it won't be to that monstrous old man. I'm going to marry the man I choose to marry.'

'And where did you meet this man you think you wish to marry? In the stables?'

I wasn't going to tell her about Sir Two Face's house and the night Thomas Holand had kissed me because I knew she'd be shocked. I needed Alice to think well of Thomas Holand and I didn't want her thinking him a common adventurer who molested any girl who crossed his path.

'And what do you know about him?'

'He is a knight.'

'And his family?'

I tried to remember what he'd told me that evening in the cloisters.

'They are a worthy family. His father is dead but he has a mother and several brothers and sisters living.'

I wouldn't tell Alice one of his sisters desired to be a rich man's concubine.

'I presume he has a house and is not expecting you to grub by the roadside with him.'

'He's a second son,' I said defiantly, knowing what this would mean in Alice's eyes. 'But he's not a nobody; the king thinks very highly of him.'

'The king thinks very highly of his cook but he's not going to let you marry him, and a second son will have nothing to offer.'

'Alice, it doesn't matter what you say, I intend to do this.'

'You can't. They won't let you.

It was very hard to keep my mind on the orchard and the sweetness and not be bruised by Alice's objections

'Nobody will know,' I said stoutly. You are the only person I shall tell.'

'You can't marry without permission.'

'Sir Thomas says we can.'

'How do you propose to marry a man without the king's permission? You're his cousin; you can't just marry whomsoever you please. Girls have been put away for less. Is that what you want? To live out your days in a nunnery?'

'We shall marry in secret.'

'Now I know you're mad.'

She was getting angry; I could hear the irritation in her voice and Alice was the sweetest-natured of people.

'I am going to marry him no matter what you say.'

We argued like this until the sky darkened and a groom came in to light the candles. When eventually we lay down to sleep she turned her back. I lay there in the shadow and warmth of her body and thought about tomorrow. It was much closer now than I thought it would be. If I screwed my eyes up tightly I could believe what lay ahead was a garden of delights, full of delicate sweet-smelling lavender and scented roses, but a peep at Alice's hunched shoulders and rigid back made me afraid I was wrong and what lurked beyond the walls of

St Bavo's Abbey was nothing but a ditch full of nettles and a thicket pricked with thorns.

A muffled voice said, 'I shall tell Lady Catherine.'

I grabbed at her night cap. 'Alice, please, you mustn't.'

Thomas Holand's life would be in danger if she told anyone else. My cousin would not take kindly to having his plans for me thwarted and I already knew how terrible the vengeance of a king could be. Good men died when my cousin wished it so.

The onset of evening brought with it an unexpected chill in the air and, as we hurried down the narrow pebbled path at the back of the abbey, I was glad of my warm winter cloak. Alice had agreed most reluctantly to escort me as far as the postern gate. She had spent much of the day praying and I knew she regretted not telling Lady Catherine.

The postern gate of St Bavo's was sunk deep into a wall, hidden from sight by a line of stunted trees and guarded by an elderly porter. I worried that we were too early, that we would have to loiter when we had no reason and could be discovered at any moment. Then I was convinced we were too late and Sir Thomas's brother would have given me up for lost and left. But when we arrived, Otho Holand was there, waiting for us.

He looked up from the lonely contemplation of his boots. He bowed politely but when he saw Alice he hesitated and regarded me with worried eyes. From the quality of her cloak and the expensive leather of her gloves he must have known she was no maidservant.

'This is Lady Alice Montagu, my cousin,' I explained.

Alice regarded Otho Holand, taking in his appearance and his obvious lack of wealth or position.

'Master Holand,' she said. 'I am here solely because my cousin has asked me to come. I don't agree with what she is intending to do and I cannot think your brother knows what he is about and the danger he is putting her in.'

But Otho Holand was well-prepared to defend his brother.

'I understand your difficulty, Lady Montagu. I am sure you care deeply for your cousin, but you must believe me when I say my brother has her best interests at heart.'

'Hers?' said Alice sharply. 'Or his?'

'Oh hers; he will be a very good husband.'

'I know nothing about your brother,' retorted Alice. 'For all I know he has a wife already.'

'No, Lady Montagu, my brother has never married and believe me, he will look after your cousin very well.'

I felt Alice stiffen and I reached for her hand.

'Please, Alice. Come with me?'

'No,' she said. 'If you wish to ruin yourself you may do so on your own. I have done all I can. I shall pray for you, Jeanette.'

But at the last, she seized Otho Holand's hand. 'Master Holand, I beg you, take care of her. She's very young. Please don't let your brother hurt her.'

The old man was undoing the bar to open the gate.

Otho Holand took my hand. 'If you would put up your hood, my lady, and hide your face. There are rough people out there and I wouldn't want you recognised. I've brought my brother's boy. He's good with his fists and handy with his feet but I'd rather we avoided trouble altogether.'

'Is it far?' I whispered as we slipped through and out into the street.

'Past the bridge, towards the square.'

It was an unfamiliar route, past buildings I didn't know, with an urchin of uncertain age and smelling greatly of the stables scampering in front of us, leading the way. Hidden in the deep folds of my hood, I could barely see anything but I could hear plenty. Every army commanded by the princes must be roaming the streets of Ghent for there to be this much noise and I wondered how safe I really was with my meagre escort. I kept very close to Otho Holand and held on tight to his arm.

We crossed the bridge and after several twists and turns our guide disappeared like a little shadow into a narrow alleyway on our left. The houses on either side towered over us shutting out what daylight was left, making the lane dark and sinister. About half way along the boy stopped at a door next to a house where the sign of an apothecary hung on the wall. Otho Holand knocked and the door opened.

Inside was a dull-faced woman wearing a grubby linen cap who was surreptitiously drying her hands on her skirts. Behind her I could see a couple of tow-headed children peeping round a doorway and a set of worn stairs. I followed Master Holand up the stairway into the gloom. As we approached the top I could make out a glimmer of light, a single flame, and Thomas Holand with a candle in his hand.

I saw his eyes widen in alarm when he realised I was alone.

The room was something of a shock. Even in the half-light I could see it was very small, built into the roof, barely big enough for two people, with nothing but a trestle table a bench and a bed. There was no decoration: no hangings or carpets or painted walls, and nothing on the floor but plain unswept boards. Sir Thomas's sword in its scabbard lay propped in the corner together with his belt. The pallet bed tucked hard against the wall was narrow but the pillow and covers looked reasonably clean.

On the table was a wooden platter with some bread and a covered dish. There was a jug and some cups. I looked for the priest but there was no sign of him. We must be going elsewhere for the wedding, I thought, because we couldn't possibly marry here in this tiny room amongst the dust and the cobwebs.

Sir Thomas came in with the candle. He bowed to me.

'God keep you well, my lady. My apologies. I know this is not what you're used to in any way but it was all I could manage at such short notice. The princes' men have snapped up the best lodgings; some are even reduced to sleeping in the stables.'

He was being very charming. He set the candle down and wiped the bench seat with his sleeve.

'Please, sit. I've sent my brother to fetch the woman of the house. I cannot allow you to marry me with no woman present. It wouldn't be right.'

We waited in silence until we heard the sound of footsteps on the stairs. The woman of the house sidled in, staring at me with undisguised curiosity. She didn't look at the two men.

'I have explained,' said Otho. 'She understands.'

Sir Thomas held out his hand and pulled me up.

'Come, my lady, we'd best to business.'

'Here?'

Now the moment had arrived I wasn't sure and was filled with a sudden desire to run back to everything familiar. If there had been ritual and formality I would have been more certain but everything seemed too simple, too easily won and I was nervous.

He nodded his head. 'Are you ready? You don't want to change your mind? You're perfectly free to do so if you'd rather return to the abbey. I won't have anyone saying I bullied you into this.'

'What about the priest?' I whispered.

'We don't need a priest. It's not necessary. We're not marrying the priest, we're marrying each other. All we need are our two witnesses.'

'But surely…' I bit my lip, too frightened to continue.

'My lady, people will say you must have a priest's blessing at a marriage but truly it is not necessary. A marriage like this is perfectly sound. Hundreds of people marry in this way and are none the worse for it. And although the Church would rather take your money for a blessing, to marry without is recognised as a true marriage and prevents a couple from marrying anyone else.'

He was reassuringly certain of everything and of course that was the reason for this marriage; having once married Thomas Holand, I would be unable to marry anyone else. I gazed admiringly at the openness of his face and the set of his shoulders. He was strong and he was brave and I knew he would protect me. And he was something else as well but I hadn't allowed myself to think too much about that.

'What about the ring?'

There was a moment of silence in which Thomas Holand for once appeared less than sure of himself.

'I have a ring,' he said. 'It is nothing but a tawdry little thing I bought for a pittance. I hesitate to offer it to you.'

In the orchard he had promised to scatter jewels across our marriage bed to give me pleasure and I knew that one day in the future, when he was rich, he would do just that, so a trumpery little ring on our wedding day was of no consequence.

'It doesn't matter,' I said in a low voice. 'Whatever you have will do.'

I stood facing him and he took my right hand in his. The first touch of his fingers on mine made me tremble and, in that brief moment when there was still time to change my mind, I knew exactly why I was marrying this man I barely knew.

I didn't know what to say as I'd never married someone before but he led me through the words with care. He promised to take me as his wife and I said I would take him as my husband. He slid the little ring onto my finger and gave me a brief kiss on my cheek. And that was all. It was very quick, barely more than a few moments and it was done. We were married.

I examined myself but I didn't feel any different.

Before the woman disappeared downstairs, Sir Thomas slipped her a coin and thanked her for her help in the matter of our marriage.

'My lady?' My husband offered me a cup. 'The best I could find.'

There was wine at our wedding feast and there was bread, not white and soft but rather coarse and earthy, and difficult to chew. And there was some sort of dried fish which tasted disgusting. Even the men rolled up their eyes.

'I'm sorry,' laughed Sir Thomas. 'Being Lent there was no meat to be had and the woman said this was a speciality of Ghent.'

It wasn't much of a feast and I wondered if things would get better or if we would always dine on brown bread and dried fish. I told myself it was unimportant.

I glanced up at Sir Thomas. Surely he hadn't forgotten the other things?

He smiled at my face as if he knew what I was thinking and turned to his brother.

'Otho, my wife wishes for some minstrelsy.'

'Oh! I thought...'

'... that I'd forgotten? I'd be a poor husband if I had. Otho is the songbird in our family and he'll sing for you.'

'For me?' I was enchanted. Nobody had ever sung just for me. People sang songs for my cousin and for the queen, but not for me.

He had a beautiful voice. It was clear and sweet and filled the room. The first song was a ballad about a girl and her boy. It was very tender and very sad.

I clapped my hands in appreciation. Sir Thomas leant back against the wall and said, 'Something less mournful, Otho. This is a wedding feast not a funeral.'

The next song was bawdy and I giggled. It was about a man doing business with a woman but there were too many words I didn't understand.

'Otho! Enough!'

I tuned to Sir Thomas. 'Isn't he wonderful?'

He smiled and thumped Otho on the shoulder.

'Off with you, brother, before my wife decides she prefers you to me.'

Otho Holand flushed with pleasure and embarrassment, wished me a safe night and went quickly out of the door.

I lifted a cup from the table because I didn't know what else to do and thought a sip of wine might give me courage, but the cup was empty.

My husband checked the door was closed and barred and we couldn't be disturbed, then, with slow deliberation, took the cup from my hand. He put it on the table. His expression gave nothing away.

The moment had come, as I knew it must, and now it was here I didn't know what was expected of me.

I stood there in front of him in my best wool gown with ribbons in my hair and a plaited girdle at my waist. I was still only a girl and in spite of what I'd thought, I wasn't sure I was ready to be a wife. I swallowed twice and twisted my fingers together.

'Sir Thomas?'

He undid my fingers and held them to his lips.

'Yes, my lady?'

'Should I call you "my lord" now we're married?'

His mouth twitched as if he was trying not to smile. 'No. You should call me Thomas.'

He pulled me close, so close I could smell the warmth of him and see the tendrils of hair which curled over his ears and the small dark flecks deep within his eyes. He put his mouth gently on mine and I felt the pressure of his lips and tasted the wine on his breath.

He kissed me in a way he hadn't before.

'Thomas?' I whispered.

He kissed me again and this time I opened my lips slightly and kissed him back. I liked what we were doing but kept thinking about what else he might want me to do.

The candle guttered and spluttered and nearly went out. There was almost no light from the little window in the gable wall and, with no fire, the room was becoming cold.

He let go and put his fingers on the plaited girdle I wore round my waist. He gave a little tug as if he was going to lead me like a dog on a leash.

'We'd best remove your fine clothes, my lady,' he said quietly. 'I wouldn't want them spoiled.' His voice sounded different as if he'd drunk too much.

I gulped and wished I'd brought a maid with me. I'd never been undressed by a man. Perhaps I could suggest he returned to the abbey to fetch someone? But it was too late; his fingers were insinuating themselves into my clothing and touching my undergarments.

He removed my surcote and then lifted up my right hand and kissed the soft skin of my inner wrist until I shivered and bit my lip and wanted him to go on for ever.

Without saying a word he turned me round and began undoing the laces of my gown. The touch of his fingers as they travelled down the length of my back was almost more than I could bear and I wanted him to slide his hands around my waist and pull me tight against him. He gave one swift tug and the soft blue cloth fell to my feet. I stood there, half-naked in my linen shift.

I shivered.

'Cold?'

'No,' I whispered.

'Frightened?'

I shook my head, although I was.

'Good.'

He led me to the bench and sat me down. Then he knelt at my feet and held my ankles while he took off my shoes. By now my cheeks were burning with shame. No man had ever seen me without my gown and I felt most uncomfortable, yet I didn't want him to stop.

He lifted the hem of my shift and slid his hands slowly up my legs and fiddled with the ribbons whilst all the time watching my face. Without taking his gaze away, he carefully rolled down my pretty red stockings and drew them off. I'd worn them especially for him because they were my best but he didn't notice. Now my feet and legs were bare.

He stood up, looked at me and smiled. Before I could say anything he bent down and scooped me up. He carried me in his arms to the bed and laid me beneath the covers.

I watched as he undid the ties and laces on his clothes but when he was clad in just his shirt he turned to the table and swiftly blew out the candle leaving us in the dark.

'Thomas?'

'Shh!'

There was some rustling and a muttered curse and the weight of the cover lifted, letting in a cold draught of air. The mattress dipped as he climbed in beside me. He was completely naked.

He gathered me tightly in his arms. The feel of his thighs against mine through my shift made me shiver and

I didn't think it was because I was cold or because I was frightened.

'Thomas?'

He kissed me and began trying to remove my shift, sliding the fine linen carefully over my arms.

'Thomas?' I whispered, struggling out of the unwanted garment and being shocked at the intimate feel of his bare skin on mine. 'Thomas. I don't know what to do.'

He held me so tightly I could feel the solid curves of his body pressing against mine. 'Yes you do,' he said quietly.

He kissed me again, slowly this time with his mouth open, and gradually to my surprise I found I did; I knew exactly what to do.

At some hour in the depths of the night when there was nothing to hear but the call of a night owl and the rustle of small creatures in the roof above our heads, he kissed me awake, brushing my eyes and mouth with his lips. In a drowsy half-sleep, barely aware of what I was doing, I wrapped my arms around his neck and pulled him close.

'Please,' I murmured. 'Do it again.'

It was indescribable; it was wonderful; it was joy. Why didn't people say marriage was like this?

Afterwards, I slept, and when I awoke, a weak grey light was already lapping at the window and he was watching me. He wasn't smiling. I remembered Alice's repeated warnings of how men were born and bred to violence and thought perhaps I had offended him in some way. He would have known many women in his years of soldiering, women who excelled in the art of pleasing a man, but I had not even known what to do. Perhaps I'd been a disappointment.

I felt hot tears begin to sting the back of my eyes.

'Did I please you, my lord?' I whispered, nearly too afraid to ask. 'Was I to your liking?'

For a moment his face didn't change and then his eyes softened. 'Thomas,' he corrected me. 'And yes, you pleased me very much. Yes, very much indeed.'

He leaned over and placed gentle kisses on my eyes and then on my mouth.

'What about you, my lady? Did you enjoy what we did?'

I blushed, too embarrassed to look at him now we were no longer lying in the dark. 'Yes,' I whispered. 'I liked it very well.'

'I thought you might,' he said.

'Is it possible... could we...?'

He laughed and gathered me close, crushing me against his chest and placing his mouth on my forehead.

'There's no time. Look! Morning is here.'

'But I may come again tonight?'

'No.' He kissed my mouth gently. 'Not because I don't enjoy having you in my bed, my lady, because I do. But we can't risk a child. You're too young and it would spoil our plans.'

I hadn't thought about a child. It had never occurred to me but of course it should have; I did know about such things. I knew God sometimes blessed you with a child if you shared a bed with your husband but I hadn't thought it could happen to me. Not with Thomas. Not now.

Thomas rolled himself out of bed and started pulling on his clothes. I lay watching him, marvelling at how differently made he was to me and loving the dark hair on his chest which ran in a ruffled line all the way down his body. When he saw I hadn't moved, he grabbed the cover and pulled it off the bed. The sight of me curled naked on the sheet made him pause. I looked up at him from under my lashes, hoping he might change his mind.

'No!' he said. 'I told you; there isn't time. Up! Come on! Otho will be here any moment and I don't suppose you wish to greet him like this.'

I was embarrassed at the blood stains on the sheet and bundled it into a heap, hoping he hadn't noticed but I'd heard too many giggled stories of young women no longer *virgo intacta* to be in any doubt as to what this was. I struggled into my various garments and with Thomas's help managed to get myself into a state of some order.

'How do I look?' I said doubtfully.

He put his head on one side and considered the matter carefully.

'You look delightful but please, my lady, turn round and put on your stockings. My brother is very partial to bare feet.'

He made me laugh and I was certain this must be love.

As soon as I had pulled on my stockings and tied the ribbons he came and sat beside me. He was different, dressed in his clothes; separate from me, older, no longer the Thomas of last night and I didn't know what to say. It felt wrong to be sitting with a man on the edge of a bed.

'I have a little gift for you.' He reached into his purse and pulled something out. 'I don't have the funds for what you desired but I want you to know I haven't forgotten. Give me your hand.'

I did as he asked and into my outstretched hand he put something small and hard and round – a little silver coin.

'It's a gross, made here in Ghent. See! A cross.' He turned it over. 'And a lion.'

It lay where he'd placed it, gleaming dully in the palm of my hand.

I lifted it with my fingers and examined it closely. 'Oh but it's beautiful.'

He shrugged. 'It's not worth much but each time you look at it you'll remember me.'

'Oh, Thomas!'

He seemed embarrassed at what he'd said and got quickly to his feet.

'I'll get us some water.'

Moments later he returned carrying a bowl and a plain earthenware jug with no enamelling.

'I like my women clean,' he said, kissing the top of my head as if I was a child. 'Now you'd best give the ring to me for safekeeping. We can't risk it being discovered on your person'

By the time Otho arrived I was putting on my shoes. He and Thomas stood by the door talking in low murmurs. I couldn't hear what they were saying. There was a smothered laugh and I heard Thomas say, 'Twice!' Otho looked over to where I sat on the bed and then back at his brother. He frowned and said something. Whatever Thomas replied, amused Otho. 'You lucky sod!' he said.

They talked some more while I sat patiently waiting.

Eventually Thomas came over and offered me his hand.

'Come, my lady. We must get you back before you're discovered.'

When I was wrapped in my cloak I turned to him and whispered, 'When will I see you again?'

He hesitated. 'We are moving out today, my lady. I'm truly sorry.'

'Moving out?'

'Yes. Sir William and the Earl of Suffolk are taking us west across the Scheldt. The princes have decided to attack Tournai.'

I didn't know where Tournai was or why it was to be attacked.

'But what will I do?'

He gave a short laugh. 'Pray. It's all a wife can do for her husband when he's away.'

'The men of Cambrai are raiding the Count of Hainault's castles and if we do nothing they'll soon control the whole of the valley of the Scheldt from Cambrai to Valenciennes,' Otho explained.

'Is that bad?' I had no idea what the men of Cambrai were trying to do and why it was of such importance. I didn't even know where Cambrai was, or Valenciennes.

Thomas gave his brother a grin. 'My wife is no military planner, as you see. My lady, if the men of Cambrai control the valley of the Scheldt there is nothing to stop the French armies from marching into Brabant and the duke will not be happy facing them on his own. He'll wonder why he joined with us if we're not there to fight with him.'

'So what will you do?'

'I do whatever Sir William commands.'

'But you will come back?'

He took my hand in his. 'I will come back. This is only

a small matter. We're not marching into France. One day soon we will and then anything could happen.'

'It's what the men want,' explained Otho. 'An opportunity for glory and honour.'

'And getting rich,' laughed Thomas.

'That too.'

'And now you'd best take my wife back. I'll go and find Sir William and try to explain my absence of yesterday evening. Gut-ache will do, I think.'

'You won't tell him about me, will you?' I said, suddenly frightened at what we'd done and what the earl might do.

'Do I want a dagger in my ribs?'

'No, of course not.'

He kissed my hands and looked me straight in the eye. 'Tell no-one. Remember this is our secret. Now go.'

I pushed the sleeping boy to one side with my foot. He opened an eye but I put a finger to my lips and quietly opened the door. In the pale light coming through the cracks in the shutter I could see two grey lumps curled on a pallet and the heavy dark folds surrounding Alice's bed. The gentle sound of breathing filled the room.

I tiptoed to the bed and pulled the curtain aside. Alice turned her head. She was awake.

'I presume it's done?'

'Yes. Oh Alice, it...'

'You have ruined yourself and your family, Jeanette, you realise that, don't you? I have lain awake all night praying for you but I can see no happy ending to this. When the king finds out I dread to think what he'll do and before you utter another word I don't want to hear any more. I regret my part in last night's affair. I should have gone straight to Lady Catherine.'

Alice was so disapproving I could have wept.

I pulled off my cloak, removed my shoes and climbed onto the bed.

'He's leaving.'

'Of course he is.'

'Sir William's taking men to attack Tournai. He's going to fight.'

'Oh you stupid girl! What did you expect?'

'But what if he's killed?'

'Then you will have ruined yourself for nothing.'

Sometimes when the cobwebs of sleep were still sticky in my eyes I wondered if I had imagined my marriage and if those hours in the little attic room were nothing but a dream. It was hard to be a wife and yet no wife, to have a husband who was not a husband and could never be mentioned. When I listened to Lady Catherine's women talk of their houses and their children and their numerous burdensome duties, I felt sad to have no house, no child and no duties other than to keep my lips tightly sealed. This was all Thomas had asked of me: to keep silent.

That year was a troubling one to be an Englishwoman with a husband on campaign and I suffered no less than anyone else; perhaps even more because I suffered in private, my fears unseen and unshared. In the final days of Lent Sir William and his fellow commander, the Earl of Suffolk, were captured by the French during a skirmish. Thirty of their men were killed and only one escaped.

With no-one to stop them the French crossed the Scheldt and marched into Hainault.

I prayed more than I had ever prayed in my life before. My knees were rubbed raw and my shoulders ached but by mid-summer my prayers were answered. My cousin returned from England to fight a great sea battle where he defeated the French fleet and hanged their admiral from his own mast. He then turned his attention to Tournai.

I listened carefully as the queen read out my cousin's daily letters telling her of his attempts to bring the French king to battle: how the Valois had refused his challenge to fight body to body, how my cousin and his friends had encircled the town of Tournai and how the siege was dragging on and on. One night the queen's mother, the dowager lady of Hainault, had crossed the marshes and gone down on her knees to the Valois, who was her brother, and the English king, who was her son-in-law, and had begged them to make peace.

And then it was over. There was to be a treaty. There would be no fighting until next summer and we would keep the towns we had taken. All prisoners were to be returned and Sir William would come home to Bisham. Naturally there were to be celebrations: a week of extravagant gift-giving, tournaments, feasting and entertainments, and I knew Thomas would come for me.

We met by arrangement late one evening at dusk by the postern gate, hidden from prying eyes by the low-hanging branches. The greetings I had planned, the little speech of welcome and all the words I wanted to say, died on my lips the moment I saw him. I had imagined this moment in the drowsy hours of half-sleep but now he was here I felt strangely embarrassed. He didn't look like the Thomas of my dreams; in truth he didn't look like Thomas at all. He was leaner and darker and older and his clothing was different.

He greeted me as a husband should, removing his cap and giving a small nod of the head.

'My lady' His voice was low and very familiar. 'God keep you well.'

I tried to give a small smile to show how pleased I was to see him but somehow my mouth wouldn't do what I wanted and my lips started to tremble.

'Have you missed me, my lady?'

'Yes,' I whispered.

He seemed pleased with my answer.

'And our secret?'

'I have told no-one.'

'Good.'

'Lady Catherine says we are returning to Bisham when the games are finished,' I said. 'She believes Sir William will come home.'

He nodded his head. 'And you will accompany her.'

'But…'

He held up his hand. 'You are my wife and must do as you're bid. I need you to stay in Lady Catherine's household a little while longer because I am going away. The king's war is over and I must find another war with richer pickings.'

'Was there no prize money at Tournai?'

He laughed. 'No, there was no prize money at Tournai.'

'Where will you go?' I whispered.

'I shall go east. Pope Clement has proclaimed a Crusade. Otho and I will join with the German knights and fight against the Tartar hordes.'

'Why a Crusade?'

'For honour, for glory, for the forgiveness of my sins.'

'Have you sinned much?' I asked. I thought he probably had, he was that kind of man.

'More than most but the Church tells me I will be rewarded in Heaven if I follow a Holy War.'

'Will the Church not reward you on earth?'

He laughed softly. 'Oh, my lady, you are my earthly reward.'

That was the most beautiful thing he had ever said to me and I hugged it close.

'But you will come back?'

He smiled gently. 'I will always come back and I will find you wherever you are.'

He took my hand in his and slowly pulled me close. He held me tight against his chest. I could hear his breathing and feel the warmth of his body. I put up my face and he kissed me until my mouth opened under his and I was dizzy with wanting him. Abruptly he set me aside.

'Grant me a blessing,' he said quietly, dropping to his knee at my feet. 'A wife's duty and her privilege.'

I did as he asked, laying my hand on his head, feeling the warm hair thick beneath my fingers.

He reminded me once more to tell our secret to no-one and with a final farewell, disappeared swiftly through the door leaving me alone.

I didn't set eyes on him again before he departed and two months later in the bitter cold of a dark and miserable winter's day I too left Flanders. On the journey home to England the queen had the comfort of Joanna who had been returned, no longer wanted by her betrothed's family; Lady Catherine had the comfort of anticipating Sir William's imminent return to Bisham but I had no comfort at all.

3

BISHAM 1341

Snow began falling on the Eve of the Nativity and by dusk the world beyond Bisham lay hidden behind a veil of silent swirling white. Unfortunately my mother had already arrived. At mid-day her smart new travelling carriage had creaked under the gatehouse and, however much I wished it, there was now no possibility of her being delayed by something as convenient as a waist-high drift.

I knocked at the door of the guest chamber. An elderly woman opened a crack and looked me up and down in the insolent way only an old retainer would. Somewhat reluctantly she gave me admittance.

'Greetings, lady mother,' I murmured, lowering myself sufficiently far to please her.

The wide sleeves of her old-fashioned gown rippled slightly as she bent forward, offering me her cheek. I felt the accustomed churning in my belly which accompanied my every meeting with my mother. Her voice was the same as always: low, throaty and unrelentingly icy.

'You may kiss me.'

She smelled of dead mice and after a quick peck on her loose pitted skin I backed away as quickly as I could.

She looked me up and down, carefully examining what she had in front of her. I stood like an animal caught in the flare of a torch, frozen to the spot, too frightened to move. All of a sudden she smiled and I blinked in surprise because my mother never smiled.

'Lady Catherine tells me she is pleased with you. It seems you have learned well and have been a credit to your family.'

'Yes, lady mother,' I replied, wondering was this a different Lady Catherine from the one I knew.

The smile still lingered and her eyes softened. Springtime must indeed have entered my mother's breast because the ice was melting.

'Good news!' she purred. 'You are to be married. Of course this is not the marriage I might have hoped for if things had been different but under the circumstances it is the best we can achieve. Sir William is newly come to his riches but the title is an old one with an illustrious history and you will be well provided for. The son, so I am assured by those who know him, is not an imbecile.'

Marriage! The old man! A tremor of absolute panic ran through me from head to toe. I'd thought I was safe and Thomas would protect me. But Thomas wasn't here.

She looked down at the ring she always wore, the brilliant ruby set on a golden band.

'I was young when I first married,' she said softly. 'My husband was a fine young man. It is a kindness to marry a girl to a boy of her own age and when the king told me of his plans I could not help but be pleased for you. Of course my own wedding was not as yours will be. Lady Catherine tells me the Bishop of Ely, the earl's brother, will celebrate the nuptial mass and she expects the king and queen to honour us with their presence.

But, as my mother continued to talk of my wedding, the awful truth became apparent. It wasn't what I thought it would be. It was worse. They were planning to marry me to Lady Catherine's son; they were giving me to William Montagu!

What of Antwerp and the king's friend, the man who had stroked my face and smoothed my hair? What of him? What of Thomas? And, sweet Holy Mother of Christ, what was I going to do?

I stood there gaping like a netted fish.

'The king was delighted to offer you to Sir William for his son,' said my mother. 'He assures me this is an advantageous match. The Montagu name commands great respect both in England and abroad. The connection will serve our family well. Yes, all things considered, I am pleased with you.'

There was silence.

'Joan?'

I stared at her, too scared and horrified to speak.

'Have you nothing to say?' She expected gratitude from a daughter who could not have expected this honour from the king.

'Oh yes, lady mother. It is indeed a very fine marriage.'

'With Sir William returned from Paris there is no need for further delay. We shall have the marriage celebrations as soon as the arrangements have been concluded. Naturally it will be a magnificent occasion because you, my dearest Joan, are a king's granddaughter and the earl is man of great importance.'

William Montagu! Lady Catherine's son! I couldn't believe what I was hearing. My cousin was proposing to marry me to the son of his closest friend and I hadn't known.

Throughout the Nativity celebrations I remained in a daze, believing this could not be happening. I couldn't marry William Montagu. It was impossible. I was married to Thomas Holand. Thomas was my husband. But Thomas was somewhere on the borders of Christendom fighting in his Holy War. It might be months before he would return and in the meantime they were going to marry me to William Montagu.

After the feast of the Epiphany, the days passed in a blur of activity: my wedding gown was fitted and I was measured for new robes in the Montagu colours. I tried to pretend it was nothing to do with me, it was for some other girl, some other bride. But the arrival one morning of William, the Montagu son and heir, bought me to my senses. If I did nothing, in a week's time I would wake up to find myself Mistress Montagu!

Alice had told me what to do if the worst happened and they tried to marry me to someone else. In her considered opinion my mother was the only person who would be able to help me. But Holy Virgin! Alice didn't know my mother.

I looked in the tiny mirror Elizabeth kept in her chest and the face which stared back from the polished surface was white and drawn and haunted. I pinched my cheeks and in fear and trembling walked slowly through the old building to the new guest chambers.

'Well?' said my mother, looking up from her book. 'What now?'

The fire in the hearth was burning brightly but my mother's gaze chilled the warmest of rooms. Beneath my gown I felt the cold dead hand of fear curl stealthily round my belly like a night-time frost creeping in under the shutters.

I raised my head and before I could change my mind, I told her.

'I cannot marry William Montagu.'

There was silence while she laid the book aside.

'Cannot? What do you mean, cannot?'

'I cannot marry him.'

She narrowed her eyes to glittering slits. 'Is this some maidenly foolishness because if so it will do you no good? You are quite old enough to marry.'

'No,' I said. 'It's nothing like that; it's...' I couldn't go on. I was too frightened.

'It's what? Tell me this instant. Or shall I shake it out of you?'

So in my terror, I told her everything. I stumbled over how, when I was in Ghent, I had married a man I barely knew, a man unknown to my family, a man who had nothing to recommend him other than a strong right arm. A dark, threatening silence followed my confession and in that moment I knew what I'd done was unwise. I was a fool. I was fourteen years old and should have known better. I should never have told my mother the truth.

She hit me. She screamed and shouted and shook and slapped me until she had me crying on the floor. I tried to cover my head but she kicked me. She had used violence before and had ordered others to beat me but there had been nothing like this. This time I knew she intended to kill me.

She dragged me up and thrust me up against the wall. Then she mentioned my father's name and I knew my fate was sealed.

'I'm sorry,' I sobbed. 'I'm sorry. I'm a wicked daughter and I'm sorry.'

I threw myself down and tried to kiss her feet. I clawed at the hem of her gown and reached for the embroidered band of her shoe but she stamped on my fingers until I feared they would break.

At last her anger drained away and all I could hear was her ragged breathing and a muffled crack as a log settled in the hearth and sparks flew up into the chimney.

'Get up.'

I hauled myself painfully to my feet and wiped my hand across my face. Her eyes were unfriendly but I didn't think she was going to hit me again.

'Now,' she said, spitting out each word as if she had eaten something unpalatable. 'You will tell me the truth. And remember, if you are tempted to lie, you are not some village slut, you are a king's granddaughter.'

'Yes, lady mother,' I whispered through my swollen lips.

'This man. Who is he? What do you know of him?'

His name is Thomas Holand. He is a knight. It is a worthy family.'

She snorted in disbelief. 'What would you know of a man's worth? Is he heir to his father's lands?'

'He is a second son,' I whispered.

'*Sainte Vierge!*' spat my mother. 'And where in Ghent did this marriage take place?'

'In a house near the abbey.'

'Whose house?'

'Sir Thomas's. His lodgings.'

My mother raised her eyebrows. 'And who was the priest who risked his neck to marry you without the king's permission? Not a bishop, I'll wager.'

'There was no priest.'

I was beginning to feel uncomfortable about the lack of a priest and I could see written on my mother's face the stupidity of my actions. To marry secretly with no priest present to give a blessing was a foolish thing to have done. Thomas had allayed my fears at the time but Thomas wasn't here.

'No priest?'

'No,' I whispered.

'A marriage with no priest?' She sounded incredulous.

'We held hands and made our vows to each other. He said it was a true and proper marriage. He said we didn't need a priest.'

'And you believed him?'

'Yes,' I whispered.

'You fool,' said my mother. 'You stupid little fool. That was no marriage. That was a man using the oldest trick in the world to get a girl to raise her skirts.'

'It was a marriage,' I sobbed. 'It was. He said it was. He said we didn't need a priest to be married.'

My mother seized my wrists and removed my hands from my face, forcing me to look at her. 'Listen to me and mark this well. You have been duped. I suppose he lay with you and you happily spread your legs.'

'Yes,' I whispered, flushing at my mother's coarseness.

'He took you?'

'Yes.'

'It was not just kissing and caressing?'

'No.' My voice was so quiet I could hardly hear my own words.

'How many times?'

The heat reached my ears and I wished I was dead. 'Twice.'

'And you bled?'

'Yes,' I whispered, remembering the blood on the sheets.

'Did you lie with him again?'

"No. He said it was too dangerous.'

By now I was weeping with shame.

'Very well,' said my mother. 'You have committed the gravest of sins but all is not lost. We must plan carefully if we are going to limit the damage your foolishness has caused. Who else knows about this so-called marriage? Who was there? I presume there were witnesses. I'm sure he made certain of that.'

'His brother.'

'And?'

'The woman of the house. Sir Thomas had her brought upstairs.'

'No-one else? Not your maid? Not Lady Catherine's daughter?'

'No.'

I wasn't going to tell my mother about Alice. It would be worse than unkind to allow Alice to take any blame.

'And this scoundrel who tricked you? Where is he?'

'He has gone to fight in a Holy War.'

'Good. With a bit of luck he'll be killed,' said my mother. 'What of the brother?'

'He is with Sir Thomas.'

My mother looked satisfied at this bit of information.

'And you are quite certain there is no-one else who knows?'

'No-one else,' I lied.

'Now, listen to me. You will say nothing to anyone and one week from now you will walk through those doors in your wedding gown and marry William Montagu. Do you understand?'

'But…'

'Do you understand?'

I nodded my head. 'Yes,' I whispered. 'I understand. But I can't marry him. I'm married to Thomas Holand.'

My mother seized me by the shoulders and thrust her face close to mine.

'You are not married to him. It was not a marriage. Don't you understand? He used you. He took advantage of a young girl who should never have allowed herself to get close to a man like that. He stole from you the one priceless gift you should bring to your husband on your wedding night. He has abused you and shamed our family and for that I will see him hang.'

I thought of my father's bloody head rolling onto the straw and knew that the king, like my mother, would have no mercy. If my cousin discovered the truth, Thomas would hang and I would be sent behind the walls of a convent for the rest of my life. Unless he killed me too.

'Tell me what to do,' I sobbed. 'I'll do whatever you say. I didn't mean to be wicked. I didn't mean to be sinful.'

My mother looked at me severely. 'The Montagu marriage is a good one. Sir William is wealthy and close to the king and Lady Catherine is greatly admired. The boy is young and one day you will be a countess. So you will keep your mouth shut and do exactly as I say.'

I nodded miserably.

The elderly maidservant treated my face with salves to lessen the bruising and applied a herbal balm to heal the cut on my lip while my mother detailed a lengthy list of things I must do.

'What about Sir Thomas?' I said as meekly as I could.

'You can leave Thomas Holand to me,' said my mother, with knives in her voice. 'You will never see or hear from him again.'

That night she made me sleep in her bed, telling Lady Catherine it was a mother's privilege to have some time alone with her daughter.

I was not a married woman. I had never been a married woman and what I had done with Thomas was a sin, a sin which my mother said I must keep to myself and confess to no-one. My heart felt sliced into small pieces as I lay with silent tears rolling down my face.

How could he have done this to me? He had told me I was beautiful and that any man would want to marry me. He had held me tight and murmured loving words whilst all the time he had known what he was doing was wrong. It was not a true marriage. He knew we needed a priest and yet he had lied and told me we did not.

That night with my mother in the guest chamber at Bisham I was the most miserable girl in the whole of England.

'We have seven days to lay our plans,' said my mother the following morning as she sat warming herself in front of a meagre fire whilst her maid applied more salve to my face.

'It has been agreed there will be no bedding. You are both too young, but this is to our advantage. It gives you more time to prepare for the deception which lies ahead. Your husband must never know you have been with another man before him. If he finds out, make no mistake, he will not be merciful and for an angry husband there are many stairways on which an unfortunate wife might lose her footing. If you escape that fate, he will most likely have you put away. The disgrace to the Montagu name, if this should become known, would be so immense I cannot see how he could permit you to remain.'

'I shan't tell him.' I said, terrified at the thought of Lady Catherine discovering what I'd done.

'You little fool! He will likely know without you telling him.'

'But what shall I do? How shall I deceive him?'

My mother looked at me with ice in her eyes. 'That is your business. I have done all I can and the rest is in your hands.' She leaned forward. 'Make certain that when the time comes whatever you do is done well. Leave him in no doubt you are a virgin. Forget everything that has gone before because if you fail our family in this, I swear I, myself, will have you put away.'

A week later, outside the door of the Bisham chapel, I married William Montagu. Snow flakes swirled from a pewter-coloured sky as I walked to my wedding on the arm of my mother's brother, my Uncle Wake. He was the only other person who knew the truth and I felt the weight of his disapproval in the stiffness of his neck and the thinness of his smile.

It was everything I had once expected of a wedding and I was exactly what a bride should be. I was young, I was pretty, I brought royal kinship to the marriage and came with an enormous dowry provided by my family. I wore a blue silk gown embroidered with silver thread, especially commissioned by Lady Catherine, and a crimson surcote studded with pearls. My cloak was of azure velvet, lined with lambswool, trimmed with the softest, whitest miniver and secured at the neck by a heavy jewelled clasp. My hair lay like a golden veil across my shoulders and on my head I wore a chaplet of twisted gold and winter flowers.

I was favoured. the king and queen arrived to see me married and Lady Catherine's brother, Bishop Grandison, Bishop of Exeter, joined the earl's brother, Bishop Simon, at the chapel door. I was doubly honoured with two bishops giving God's blessing to my marriage. But I wasn't joyful.

My throat was stripped raw from nights of crying and I was barely able to form the necessary responses. William's hand, damp and hesitant, clutched mine. He was thirteen years old and had the appearance of a boy: solidly built with lank brown hair and a pale square face but he meant nothing to me.

He shot swift glances in my direction and kept pressing my fingers but he didn't speak. I too was silent. I kept my head bowed, my eyes lowered and said not a single word. A hundred beeswax candles lit the chapel and the canons from the nearby priory sang as we walked hand in hand past the men of the Montagu affinity who had come to see us wed. Showers of silver coins rained over us as we stood on the chapel steps but instead of laughing at the sight of the village children leaping to catch the shining pennies as they fell, I wept.

At the marriage feast, William and I sat side by side on two matching gilded chairs, so ornate and magnificent they might have been royal thrones. Above our heads shimmered a silk canopy embroidered with the leopards of England and the Montagu arms and at our feet, a clutch of liveried pages knelt with dishes of delicacies as if we were the king and queen themselves. Lady Catherine and my mother, dressed in almost identical finery, both carried the same self-satisfied smile stitched onto their faces and even Elizabeth looked pleased.

William leaned over and carefully took my hand in his. I let it lie there, unsure what he wanted from me.

'You are very beautiful, Joan,' he said in a voice so low no-one else could hear. 'I worried they'd get me a fat old dowager. When my father told me it was to be you, I couldn't believe my luck.' He giggled in a childish way and his pale eyes, the colour of ditchwater, glinted with pleasure. 'Edward boasted you'd be *his* wife, but instead you're mine.'

I gave him a smile. He was my husband. Over a hundred people had seen us make our vows and there could be no pretending it had never happened. My marriage to Thomas might have been swept away by a tide of my mother's making, erased as if it had never been, but this marriage would endure. It had been witnessed and blessed and committed to the records. The bare facts had been entered into the priory's great book of Bisham in which every momentous event in the Montagu family, whether baptism, marriage or death, was written down. I was now a canon's entry in elegant lettering, illuminated and decorated and set there for all time. I was trapped and the cage door was firmly shut.

Everybody kissed me.

The queen took me lightly in her velvet-clad arms and placed her soft pursed lips on each of my cheeks and told me how pleased she was to see me wed. I breathed in the familiar scent and touch of her ample breasts and the warmth of her loving eyes and wondered how it was I had been so careless as to lose her favour.

When my cousin kissed me, his mouth lingered on mine and he whispered in my ear, 'I wish I was in young William's shoes.' His eyes were bright with too much wine and the excitements of the day and I wished he hadn't spoken.

William and I were put to bed together, dressed in our finest nightclothes, scented and oiled as tradition demanded and covered by the most sumptuous of embroidered coverlets. But it was only a ceremony and despite the prayers and the blessings and the lengthy speeches, we were not permitted to touch each other except for one chaste kiss on the lips. William opened his eyes wide as he placed his mouth on mine but the brush of his lips was a mere butterfly's touch and I was scarcely aware of what he had done.

William's uncle, Bishop Simon, placed his fleshy hands on our shoulders, squeezing mine in an uncomfortably intimate way and told us to bid each other farewell. After that we were taken to our separate chambers to spend our wedding night apart.

Later, after the feasting, the gift-giving, the speeches and the entertainments, everyone departed leaving me alone with Lady Catherine and her daughters. A week later, amidst very little fuss, Elizabeth left for her own wedding. She was to marry Hugh Despenser, an older man, son of the traitor executed fifteen years ago on the orders of the king's mother. It was to be a very modest affair.

'If my father hadn't wanted you for William he would never have agreed to this,' spat Elizabeth, during the one blazing row we had on the subject of her marriage. 'The king needed the breach healed with the Despenser family and asked for my father's help. The arrangement suited both of them. My father considered you a valuable prize but nobody thought of me,' she wept. 'I'm the one who has to sacrifice my life to heal this breach, not him and not you. It's your fault.'

There had been no point in telling Elizabeth Hugh Despenser might be a good husband because, to her, the disgrace of having to marry a man from such a family far outweighed any other marks in his favour. I felt sorry for her but not nearly as sorry as I felt for myself. I was utterly and completely miserable.

It was late September, eight months since my marriage to William. The long table in Lady Catherine's room was covered by a roll of parchment full of tiny writing, detailing every penny spent at Bisham since our return the previous winter. The list was endless: ells of cloth, candles, swans, herring, olive oil, axles, traces and saddles, nails, canvas, loaves of bread, gallons of ale and numerous purchases of wheat and straw from the Montagu manors. From what I could see the clerk of the wardrobe, who hovered at Lady Catherine's side, had done a remarkably fine job. There was an entry for the sesters of wine delivered from London last month and one for two pounds of ginger comfits for the little Montagu girls and yet another for the expenses of Lady Catherine's page travelling to Windsor with her letters for the Earl of Derby who had been with the king.

I had been thinking of Thomas and wondering if I hated him sufficiently to pull out his entrails. He had lied and cheated and tricked me. He had fastened on my ignorance and persuaded me into his bed. He had used me in the worst possible way and my mother said I would never be pure again. He had taken everything of any value from me and I wished I had never listened to him. I wished I had never met him. I wished he had left me in Sir Two-faces' house to be burned alive and then I wouldn't be suffering as I was suffering now, forced into servitude as Lady Catherine's daughter-in-law.

'Joan! Pay attention!'

I jumped.

'If you can't sit still and concentrate you'd better go and occupy yourself usefully elsewhere,' said Lady Catherine irritably. 'Go and see if that little man has finished in the chapel.'

The chapel at Bisham was beautiful with a ceiling of silver stars, tall glazed windows and carvings of leaves around the doorway. Sir William was determined to make it the most glorious of all his possessions and to that end had sent for a man from Florence to decorate the walls.

I sniffed. The air smelled of fresh-picked flowers, beeswax and rich cloth, with just the slightest hint of something rather unpleasantly earthy. In the corner sat the little oak chest fastened with huge iron clasps in which the valuables were kept. I ran my hand across its surface but the wood felt rough and I wondered why no-one had seen fit to have it smoothed.

There was no sign of either of the two canons who came daily from the priory to say the Mass, or of the Italian with his brushes and messy pots of paint. But I was pleased to see he had completed both his magnificent paintings.

One was a depiction of the final day of judgement with lines of men in Montagu livery herded by winged angels up to the gates of Heaven. At the bottom was a multitude of ragged sinners being pitchforked by grinning devils down into the flaming pits of Hell. It looked horribly real.

The other was God's expulsion of man from His garden.

I contemplated Eve emerging from a small wickerwork gate like the one in the orchard of the béguinage. She had a luscious rounded beauty and in her hand she carried an apple. She displayed a great deal of naked flesh and I wondered if the earl would be disturbed by her ample curves as he tried to concentrate on the raising of the Host. There was a fluid sheen to her skin which glowed in the candlelight making her seem almost alive.

I thought I was alone but a prickling feeling down my spine told me I was being watched. I turned and there he was, half-hidden in the shadows. He was standing perfectly still and it occurred to me he must have been watching me for some time.

I was shocked at how frightened I was. In the emptiness of the chapel he seemed much larger than I remembered and much more threatening. The lines at the side of his mouth were taut and he wasn't smiling.

'My lord,' I whispered, feeling my legs start to tremble and my hands shake.

'God keep you well, my lady.' His voice was flat and told me nothing of what he was thinking.

Whatever words I might have wanted to say remained stuck in my throat as I realised this was not the Thomas of my night-time dreams, the Thomas who had held me in his arms and promised to cast jewels across my marriage bed. This was a colder more brutal Thomas, the one who had lied, the one who had forced me into sin. This was a man who might well have it in mind to do me further harm.

He stepped forward into the light and walked slowly down the nave.

'I gather our plans are undone, my lady. I hear they have married you to young Montagu.'

'Yes,' I whispered.

'Why did you not do as I told you? Why did you not tell them you were already wed?'

He was furiously angry. I could tell from the cold look in his eyes.

'I did. I told my mother, of course I did.'

'So why do I find you married to another man when you are my wife?'

I wanted to move away from him but didn't dare. He looked as if he might hit me.

'My mother said our marriage was no marriage at all,'

I whispered. 'Without a priest, she said it was not a true marriage.'

'And you believed her?'

'Of course I believed her. She is my mother. Why would she lie?'

He gave a short laugh. 'Why does any woman lie?'

'My mother always does what is right; she is a good woman.'

'Your mother would rather see you married to the devil himself than married to me.'

I gasped in horror and hurriedly crossed my fingers. 'Don't say that. What's wrong with you? What have you done?'

He sighed. 'I explained to you how my father was murdered by his enemies.'

'Yes,' I whispered. 'I remember.'

'Your mother's family regard any Holand as an instrument of evil. Can you not see why she lied? Why would she want the son of a traitor for you when she could have the Earl of Salisbury's heir?'

'But you said...'

'And then there is the matter of the money. Sir William is wealthy. She is marrying you into one of the richest families in England.'

I hesitated. I couldn't believe my mother had lied, she had sounded so certain. She had sworn a blessing by a priest was a necessary part of marriage and without it a couple were not properly wed.

'Two people exchanging promises isn't a marriage,' I said, doubtfully.

'What is it?'

'It's a deceit. You tricked me.'

'And why would I have done that?'

'You wanted me in your bed.'

He threw back his head and laughed. 'A skinny little thirteen-year-old? If I'd simply wanted a woman in my bed, I would not have chosen you. I took you to bed because you were my wife. It was my duty as a husband.' He smiled at me. 'And to my surprise, it was my pleasure.'

'You are not my husband,' I said in a low voice, not wanting to think too much about the pleasure.

'I think you are mistaken.' He seized my wrist and pulled me close to him. 'I am very much your husband.'

'You lied,' I said.

'Not to you.'

'You did. It was no marriage and you knew it.'

'It was a marriage in every particular which matters or have you forgotten?'

It was the closeness of him, the scent of his clothes, the touch of his fingers on my bare skin and the sudden memory of his leg sliding across mine beneath the covers. No, I had forgotten nothing.

'You deceived me,' I said with as much conviction as I could muster.

'I do not think I am the one who is practising deceit here. I promised to come back and I have. But what do I find? My little wife has taken a second husband. Have you told him about me?'

I lowered my eyes. 'No, of course not.'

'Poor young man. I almost feel sorry for him.'

I hadn't bothered to consider William but of course I should have done. He was my true husband.

'Is Lady Catherine a party to this stealing of my wife?'

'No,' I muttered. 'My mother said no-one must know. Only Uncle Wake. He is head of our family.'

'Wonderful! A deception of which nobody is aware. Just you and me and your double-tongued family.'

'It is not what I wanted,' I said, not sure by now what I wanted.

'Well, my lady, whether you want it or not you have two husbands. So what are you going to do?'

'I don't know,' I whispered.

'Has he had you?'

I blushed wildly, the heat rising quickly into my cheeks.

'No.'

'No?' He pushed me back hard against the wall, still holding tight to my wrist.

'They say we must wait.'

I raised my eyes to his and saw the calculation in his eyes.

'I am married to William Montagu,' I said somewhat uncertainly, very afraid of what he intended to do with me.

'I think not. You are married to me.'

I was aware of the heat of his closeness, the hardness of his soldier's fingers and the firm pressure of his leg pushing against the folds of my skirt. He moved even closer. Now I could feel every inch of him measured against me, with his breath warm on my face and his eyes glinting in the candlelight. I remembered the taste of his lips, the smell of his hair, the roughness of his cheek and the long hours of darkness we had once spent together in that attic room in Ghent.

I raised my face to his and then slowly, very slowly, he placed his mouth on mine. The kiss was sweet; soft and sweet. I should have pushed him away. Instead I parted my lips as he had taught me and found myself drowning.

Too soon he set me aside with a laugh. 'I see you haven't forgotten how to please your husband.'

I opened my eyes, drugged by the warmth and the sweetness, and saw him laughing at me. I swallowed twice and tried to remember who I was. I was not to be treated like a street wench. I was a king's granddaughter. I was married to the Earl of Salisbury's heir and this man in front of me was nothing. He was nobody. Nobody at all. He had no right to touch me.

'I think you should leave, Sir Thomas,' I said, in the tone of voice I had once heard Lady Catherine use when admonishing one of her ladies. 'I no longer wish to speak with you.'

He wiped his hand across his mouth very deliberately as if he would remove all trace of me. 'Oh I'm leaving, my lady. Why would I stay? You have made it perfectly plain there is nothing for me here. They have placed you in a gilded cage and it will take money and influence to spring this particular trap. As I currently possess neither, I shall return to the service of those who value me and hope for better days. But first I must see Sir William.'

'You're not going to tell him?'

He smiled at my discomfort. 'I wouldn't be such a fool. He'd think I was wandering in my wits and have me strung up for impugning your virtue. And if for one moment he did believe me, I'd be face down in the river before the day was out and you, my lady, would find yourself in a nunnery. Make no mistake, a single whisper of this and it will be the end for us both.'

I shivered at the thought of the danger I'd be in if he so much as opened his mouth. My mother was right; it would have been better for all of us if he'd died in battle.

But I didn't want him dead.

He seized my face in both his hands, squeezing my cheeks almost painfully, forcing me to look into his eyes.

'I shall go now. But remember this when young Montagu is climbing into your bed: you are my wife. Whatever anyone else tells you it was a true marriage. One day I will come back for you and when I do no-one will stop me; not your family, not Sir William, not even the king, because you belong to me.'

He pressed his mouth hard on mine, leaving the imprint of his kiss and bruising my lips. He let go, stepped back, gave a little bow and walked away. A moment later the chapel door banged and he was gone.

I sank to the floor and rested my forehead on the smooth cold tiles. I said frantic prayers to the Blessed Virgin to help me but in the echoing silence there was no reply. I sobbed until my throat was raw and my eyes hurt. He had gone and I thought I might die from the loss. I told myself he had lied and cheated, he had deliberately used me for his own ends and yet once, long ago, in that magical springtime in Ghent, I knew I had loved him.

After a long time, I got to my feet and looked about me at the familiar carvings on the stone: the intricately woven leaves, the fabulous beasts and, above my head, the soaring winged angels with their trumpets. But the leaves were still, the beasts silent and the trumpets mute.

There were no answers to be found here in the chapel and none by clinging to my memories of what had once been. I knew there was only one way forward and that was on the path chosen for me by God and my mother. I had no choice. My destiny was to be a Montagu wife.

4

WARK 1341

The guest chamber at the top of the keep in Wark Castle was a room no man should offer to his horse master let alone to his nephew's wife. But as I had already discovered, Uncle Montagu was not a man wedded to the courtesies imposed on him by his position. I'd always believed him an unpleasant man, now I knew him to be both brutal and uncaring.

The room was small, its unplastered walls lacking decoration, ice-cold to the touch and without the benefit of any hangings or carpets softening the unyielding hardness of the rough grey stone. There was no hearth or other means of heating and the only light came from a pricket candle and a single narrow window sunk deep into the wall with an opening no wider than my littlest finger. I didn't fancy sleeping on either of the mattresses which appeared to have been stuffed with twigs and bracken but apart from my travelling chest, which looked wildly out of place in this dingy room, being far too gaudy with its bright iron clasp and pretty incised pattern on the lid, there was nothing else. No chairs, no table, no curtained bed.

After seven days in this dismal chamber I was greatly regretting my decision to leave Cousin Margaret's house and travel north. It was gross disobedience on my part as Lady Catherine had decreed I should spend time at Croxton with my cousins while she travelled to London to visit her friends. But it quickly became apparent that Alice and I were not welcome. Margaret did nothing but snarl and snap like the meanest of stable cats and no amount of tuneful minstrelsy could disguise the simmering rows and unpleasantness which pervaded the Segrave household. When Alice received an order from her husband to join him at Wark for the Nativity celebrations, I begged to be allowed to accompany her.

'Nothing to fear, ladies,' laughed the captain of our escort as we journeyed north towards York. 'I hear the Earl of Derby has secured the border. You'll be perfectly safe.'

'Not a sniff of a Scotsman,' said the garrison commander when we reached Berwick. 'Those varmints will not be back this winter.'

My experience with Thomas had taught me that men lie, but who would have expected such bare-faced deceit from men like this. It had taken me less than a day to realise what a dangerous place the castle at Wark really was but of course by then it was much too late. The feeling of menace was palpable from the moment I set foot across the threshold. It vibrated through the air like a badly plucked lute string, crawling up stairways, sliding across floors and creeping in through the unshuttered windows.

In the downstairs hall stood Uncle Montagu distributing his own particular brand of nastiness. I knew Alice was frightened of her husband – I'd seen the bruises on her body – and the birth of a son in the summer did not appear to have altered his behaviour towards her which was alternately derisively mocking and casually cruel.

But if the presence of Uncle Montagu was unpleasant, the sight that first evening of a pink-cheeked, mud-spattered William shocked me into silence. I'd thought he was with Edward.

William's shoulders had broadened and he was so tall I barely recognised him as the boy I had married. But I was careful of this new William who looked at me with hungry eyes and who was clearly bent on following his uncle's example in everything he did. This past year I had grown in all the places which men seemed to find most desirable and William eyed me the way men often did, his gaze lingering on my breasts, seemingly unable to drag his eyes away.

I wasn't particularly scared of him but if my deceit was to be discovered, I didn't want it to be here, far from anyone I knew, where the word of Alice's husband was law and the stairways down which an errant wife might fall were exceptionally steep. That first night I barred my door, convinced my greatest danger lay with the presence of my impatient young husband, keen to sample what his father had purchased for him. But I couldn't have been more wrong. I was woken next morning by a hammering on the door and Alice's voice on the stairs. The Scots had arrived and were intent on besieging the castle. William's uncle had stolen their gold and their horses and they had come to take them back.

Alice and I spent the next seven days huddled together in my upstairs chamber, forbidden to set foot in the hall, unable to see anything of what was happening yet hearing endless blood-curdling howls as an army of rebel Scotsmen attempted to storm the castle. I knew if they gained entry they would kill the men but I prayed they would be merciful to women.

'Our grandfather condemned two of the Scottish king's women to hang in cages from the walls of his castles,' whispered Alice.

'What happened to them?'

'He left them there to rot.'

I wasn't sure that was something I wanted to know.

Our only source of news was the old man who brought us food and water and emptied the slop pail. Each morning he told us how many prisoners the garrison had taken and each evening he gloomily listed the tally of the dead.

'Help's a-coming,' he said, one morning, with slightly more enthusiasm than usual.

'From where?' said Alice, trying unsuccessfully to look out of the window slit.

'The wee lord's gone to Cornhill.'

'Which wee lord?'

'The lord's nephew.'

'William?'

'Och, I dinna know his name, lady. The wee boy who fancies hisself a man.'

I smiled, thinking William would not appreciate that description.

'You mean he's gone outside the castle walls?' said Alice.

'Aye. Rode out last night.'

'Through the Scottish lines? But he's only a boy. Why didn't my lord go? Or send one of his men.'

'Och lady, 'twas a grand game with the dice and the wee boy won. Beat the gang of them so he got to ride out.'

'Why has he gone to Cornhill?' I asked.

'They're saying yon king's there with his army.'

We waited all day while the hours crawled slowly by. Shortly before dusk we heard the noise of our royal rescuers and discovered to our surprise that the besieging Scots had packed up their baggage and melted away like phantoms into the mist. After surveying the terrain, my cousin brought a few favoured companions into the castle keep but wisely left a dozen knights and their men outside behind the walls in case the Scots returned.

I stood on the lower step in a corner of the stairway watching Alice as lady of the castle make her formal greeting to the king. He was dressed in the usual wool and leather of campaigning, his armour bright, his helm carried for him by a squire, and looked most unlike my royal cousin. His face was smeared with dirt and sweat and he seemed younger and more carefree than usual, smiling broadly and laughing with his men as his eyes scoured the hall. It wasn't long before he found what he'd been looking for and as his gaze met mine, his eyes darkened and deep inside myself I felt a bird's wing flutter.

I sat on the stool in my heavy silk nightgown with a fur-lined robe over my shoulders watching my maid fetch my slippers and the little bag containing my ribbons and combs. While she combed out the long golden tresses I closed my eyes and thought of Alice waiting in her husband's bed, of William far away at Cornhill and of my cousin, sitting downstairs, sated with food and wine. I refused to think of Thomas Holand. I had sworn I would never think of Thomas Holand again.

When at last the girl was finished, she plaited a thick braid, tied a narrow ribbon round the end and skilfully pushed the few strands of hair which had escaped, beneath my cap. While she pattered around gathering up my clothes, I knelt to say my prayers. I had just removed my robe and was preparing to get into bed when we both heard a noise on the stairs. I nodded and she opened the door a crack to see who was outside. My cousin stood in the doorway. He had discarded his campaigning clothes and was wearing a furred chamber robe of crimson velvet. None of his men were with him, he was entirely alone. I watched in silence as the girl dropped a curtsey and at a sign from my cousin, scuttled away leaving the two of us together. He stepped across the threshold and very carefully and very deliberately closed the door and dropped the bar.

'Your Grace.' I sank to the ground, as low as I could, wondering why he was here and what he wanted. I hadn't seen him for nearly a year, not since my wedding day, and it was a very long climb up the winding stairway to my room.

He signalled for me to rise and for a minute didn't speak. He simply stared at me.

'Take off your cap.' His voice was thick with too much wine.

'My cap?'

'Yes. And your hair. Unbind it. Quickly.'

I had no idea why he wanted me to remove my cap and let down my hair but naturally I would do as he asked. Memories of my last disobedience were too fresh in my mind for me to risk displeasing him. On that occasion it had only been my mother's quick thinking and determination which had saved me from utter ruin.

Removing the cap was easy but my fingers fumbled with the narrow ribbon and the awkwardness of untwisting the braid. Once it was done I bent down and placed the cap and ribbons neatly on the pallet bed and turned to face him with my hair spread loosely over my shoulders.

He didn't smile but I heard his little sigh and knew I must have pleased him. I waited, unsure what I should do next. The air was chill and I was missing my robe but didn't like to ask if I might put it on in case I spoiled this sudden closeness which had sprung up from nowhere. It was a long time since I had been his little Jeanette and I yearned to rekindle what there had once been between us.

He beckoned me forwards with his fingers, a remembered gesture from my nursery days. 'Cousin, I think you should thank me properly for rescuing you. You must understand, I could have simply sent my men, I didn't need to come myself. But when I heard you were here…'

He left the rest unsaid but I understood what he meant: the King of England, my royal cousin, had ridden all the way from Cornhill to rescue me. He hadn't come to rescue Alice or Uncle Montagu or to save the castle garrison and he hadn't come to engage in battle with the besieging Scots. He had come for me.

I went swiftly to his side. 'I am truly grateful to you, Your Grace.'

He laughed and caught me in his arms.

'Cold words, little cousin,' he said, trying not to smile. 'Not much gratitude there. Don't you think a grateful subject should kiss her king?'

And when he did smile I knew what he wanted. What foolishness! In my years apart from him I had forgotten how we behaved together. In the circle of his arms I stood on tiptoe and placed my lips on his cheek. His skin was bronzed from his weeks of campaigning and, close to, I could smell this evening's wine on his breath and I wondered if perhaps he was a little drunk.

He tightened his grip. There was nothing between us but the warmth of his velvet robe and the heavy folds of silk clinging softly to my skin.

'Not good enough,' he said quietly. 'I'd not go half a mile for a kiss like that. Shall we try again?'

I looked up into his eyes and in that instant saw what I should have seen before. It was a year since I'd been this close to him but tonight he had the selfsame look he'd had when he'd kissed me at my wedding to William. I'd seen that look in other men's eyes and at fifteen I was old enough to know exactly what it meant.

'Kiss me properly.'

Now, with the realisation of what this was, came fear. I wasn't sure I wanted to kiss him again but he was the king and I must do as I was bid. I tipped back my head and placed my mouth against his. I'd kissed him many times over the years but this time I knew what he wanted from me and it wasn't a cousinly kiss, not the sort a friend or close kin might bestow, but something else entirely.

My kiss was hesitant and trembling, like that of a nervous child, but his was a lover's kiss: insistent, devouring and overwhelming. As my lips were forced open I felt his tongue probe the edges of my mouth and his fingers thrust hard into the depths of my hair. I pushed away unbidden thoughts of Thomas and our night in the attic room in Ghent and what this kiss might mean.

'Ah Jeanette,' my cousin whispered as he paused for breath. 'Jeanette. My sweetest Jeanette. I'd thought you too young. But when I saw you on the stairs tonight… Oh Christ! Tell me I wasn't wrong. Tell me you want to please me.'

'Naturally I wish to please Your Grace,' I said, pulling my mouth away, wondering how I could escape. 'But. Your Grace, I have a husband.'

'Young William?' He laughed. 'He'll never know.'

'But what if he should find out?'

He undid the ties on my nightgown and kissed my bare shoulder.

'Hush sweetheart. Montagu will explain matters to the boy. He knows there is no dishonour in any of this. It is a privilege for a man to have his wife honoured by his king and for the woman it can bring nothing but pleasure.'

I didn't want what he was doing. It felt wrong. He was my cousin, the father I had never had. Only Thomas had touched me like this.

'Your Grace?'

His lips kissed the soft skin at the base of my throat and I began to shiver under the brush of his fingers.

'Your Grace?'

'What?' he said impatiently.

'William and I…' I whispered. 'We've never been… We've never been… together.'

His fingers stopped.

'What?'

'Lady Catherine has forbidden it.'

'You're a maid?'

'William and I have not bedded.' I said primly.

'Not even once?'

'No.'

'Sweet Jesu!'

He took his hands away and practically pushed me onto the floor.

'Christ's bones!' he shouted. 'Why didn't you tell me sooner? I can't take you if you're a maid.'

'I'm sorry,' I whispered, frightened by his sudden anger. I wouldn't tell him his assumption was wrong. Nobody must know the truth. Since my wedding to William I had spent every night telling myself I was still a maid, I was untouched, no man had ever had me.

He pulled his hand through his hair as if to rid himself of whatever demons were racing through his head. 'No, no. It is I who should apologise to you. I would not have treated you so if I'd known. I am not a barbarian.'

'Did I do wrong, Your Grace? Have I displeased you?'

He regarded me soberly. 'No sweetheart, you have not displeased me. But you must learn not to look at men the way you do. You smile with invitation in your eyes. I truly thought you were as eager as I was but, however much I want you, and you can be assured it is a very great deal, I cannot be the first. That privilege belongs to young Montagu.'

He took two deep breaths while I re-tied the ribbons on my nightgown, watching him warily in case he should change his mind.

He traced the curve of my cheek with his finger. 'I married you carefully, little cousin. There were many offers but I chose to give you to Montagu for his son. It kept you close. I didn't want to lose you.'

I lowered my head, trying to show my gratitude for his care, although I was almost shivering with fright.

'You know I would have you in my bed if I could, sweetheart. There is nothing I want more. But for now that cannot be.' He paused with his hand on the door. 'I pray you sleep well,' he said softly.

Next day Alice and I left Wark Castle with a royal escort of armed men and by nightfall were sheltering in a windswept priory somewhere south of Berwick. Alice looked weary, as if she might blow away with the flurries of snow driving in off the sea but the privacy of our tiny whitewashed cell encouraged confidences.

'The king rebuked my lord in front of his men for putting our lives at risk,' she whispered. 'It was utterly shaming and he was furious. He has lost the king's favour and blames me. He said if we had not been there he wouldn't have had to send for help.'

I tried to comfort her but there was nothing I could say to make her situation better. A man could not prosper without the king's favour.

'The king spoke well of William,' said Alice turning the pillow and testing the mattress for bedbugs.

I said nothing, not wishing to think too much about my cousin.

'Jeanette?'

'Yes.'

'Do you ever think of Thomas Holand?'

I climbed in beside her and snuggled into the warmth of her body, noticing with sadness, the fresh bruising on her shoulder.

'Sometimes. But it's past and my mother says I must forget.'

'Of course.' She paused for a moment. 'It wasn't right, I know that, but you did say he was kind.'

'No he wasn't Alice. He wasn't kind at all.'

I turned over, closed my eyes and, with a great effort of will, banished Thomas Holand to the darkness and the rising winds beyond the priory walls.

5

MARRIAGE 1341

It was almost summer. In Quarry Wood the air was full of the scent of bluebells and the little Montagu girls came home each afternoon with posies of stitchwort and windflowers and drooping rose-red campion.

There was a flurry of activity as the seamstresses were ordered to start stitching my new nightgown, and two sisters from one of Lady Catherine's favourite orders arrived with a gift of magnificent embroidered linen. When unpacked this was to grace the bed where William and I would spend our first night together and I was required to be suitably grateful. Three days later a woman was brought from Great Marlow to instruct me on my duties in the marriage bed. We met privately. If nothing else, she told me, I was to remember that a wife should be obedient.

Every time I thought about the great deception which I must practice on my husband, I shivered in fear. It must be successful because discovery would mean the end of my time as William's wife. If I avoided a push on the stairway I would be taken from Bisham to some faraway convent where I would remain, cold and hungry, paying till the end of my days for Thomas Holand's sins.

My hands trembled as I approached Lady Catherine's best guest chamber. The current occupant was William's grandmother, the elderly Dowager Lady Montagu. She had refused to attend our wedding, claiming winter travel too dangerous for someone of her age and frailty so all I knew about her was her preference for her younger son, Alice's husband, and her fanatical devotion to St Frideswide.

The door was opened by an aged crone dressed in drab grey. Beyond her were several others, creeping around with bowls and cloths, warming ale on the fire and servicing the requirements of their ancient mistress.

She sat like an eagle on a rock, arrayed in tawny velvet, waiting for a prey large enough and appetising enough to make the effort of stretching her wings and taking flight worth the while. Her eyes were hooded and very bright, her skin pouched and wrinkled. She looked extremely old.

One bony finger extended itself from the depths of her embroidered sleeve and curled round, beckoning me forward. Her mouth pursed into a web of fine lines and crinkles.

I sank down. 'Greetings, my lady,' I said softly.

'Speak up girl! Don't mumble!' she barked. 'So you're the prize they've bought for my grandson.' She looked me up and down. 'Turn around. Let me see all of you.'

I obediently moved in a small circle and came round to face her again.

'Pretty enough! I hear my grandson has been rutting like a young stag this past year. But your mother says you're a virgin. Is she right?'

The colour washed up into my face.

'Humph! Didn't think he'd dare disobey his mother. What was she thinking of, dangling you in front of him like a tasty little morsel?'

I couldn't think of anything to say. It was the bedding ceremony tomorrow and I kept telling myself I was a maid untouched. If I said it often enough and with enough conviction I could believe it. Thomas had never existed, I had never been married and we had never lain together. But I couldn't deny the images which stole into my dreams, the longing to be held, and the hunger for something I had once possessed but had irretrievably lost.

'How are old are you, girl?'

'Fifteen, my lady.'

'Old enough! Ripe enough! And ready enough if I'm not mistaken. Come here!'

As soon as I was within reach she put out a finger and poked my waist.

'Traitor's daughter, they tell me.'

I bit my lip but said nothing.

'You have his eyes. A foolish boy. He should have left well alone but as young people will, he refused to listen. Had a fancy for your mother and her all that time in love with her cousin. Now there was an evil man for you. Knew what he wanted and who could give it to him and it wasn't your mother. He had his eyes on someone else.'

She rambled on but I found it impossible to follow what she was saying. She was talking about my parents. But who was this cousin?

Next evening at the bedding ceremony, William drank steadily and with great bravado, cheered on by his rowdy friends who regarded the celebration as an opportunity to encourage the would-be husband in his excesses. I took only a cup or two of wine, hoping to remain sober, but by

143

the time we went up the stairs with a train of laughing, singing followers, my legs were most unsteady. My cheeks were flushed and if I hadn't been so scared I think I might have felt comfortably sleepy.

We knelt at the foot of the great Montagu marriage bed, an immense creation of carved wood, draped in luxurious red and silver hangings. The sheets were woven of the finest linen, and the coverlet was of yellow satin, embroidered with a design of exotically coloured birds never once seen flying in the greenwoods near Bisham.

William's uncle, Bishop Simon, loomed over us, intoning prayers for the fruitfulness and success of our marriage. Two grooms of the chamber drew back the covers. The bishop dipped his fingers into a tiny silver bowl held by the white-robed boy at his side and sprinkled a few drops of holy water over the sheets, blessing the bed in which our union was to be consummated.

There were constant mentions of Montagu generations past and the hope of Montagu generations to come and exhortations that William and I would be rewarded with numerous children, all to further the glory of God and his servants, the Montagu family.

I felt William shift as if he was uncomfortable. I had my head bent but shot a sideways glance under my lashes. His eyes were closed and his face was white. He looked sick.

After the men left, Lady Catherine loitered at the bedside showing no desire to go and every wish to remain. Margaret had once told me of a girl whose mother-in-law watched while her son deflowered his bride as she wished to reassure herself the deed was done so there could be no dispute over the massive fortune the girl brought with her to the marriage. I was consumed with terror this was Lady Catherine's intention.

What would I do? To deceive William was one thing but to deceive a watching and waiting Lady Catherine was quite another. She would whip the sheets from under us the minute the deed was done and I would have no opportunity to practice my deception.

I thought of the tiny knife my maid had hidden beneath the pillow and wondered if I could reach it without Lady Catherine seeing.

She leaned forward and kissed her son gently on his forehead, murmuring a mother's blessing and as she turned and walked out of the room I felt my whole body soften and melt.

For a moment or two neither of us said anything. I told myself I had never been to bed with a man before and any memories of the little attic room in Ghent were false. It had never happened. Never!

'Are you frightened, Joan?' William's face, despite his pallor, was full of eagerness.

Should I be frightened? Was that how a girl who had never known a man was supposed to feel? I tried to recall how it had been with Thomas, but all I could remember of that night was the joy of what we did together and my worry that I was a disappointment. I didn't think I would prove a disappointment to William Montagu. He looked as if he couldn't wait.

'I am a little frightened,' I said, thinking he might prefer it if I was. His eyes were greedy as if I was a choice piece of meat, something he longed to tear apart with his teeth and devour on the pillow.

'You don't need to be,' he said with a boy's conviction. 'I know what to do. I've done it dozens of times and I'll try not to hurt you.'

Of course. His uncle would have given him a woman at Wark. I wondered if she had been the only one or if his grandmother's words were true. I wasn't sure if I cared. He was almost a man and this is what men did.

He grasped my shoulder and pulled me towards him. He wasn't particularly rough but his hands were sticky and his breath was hot with the smell of wine. He kissed me hard on the mouth, prising my lips open with his tongue while his hands enthusiastically explored the top half of my nightgown. I thought if I were truly innocent I might recoil from this intimacy and pretended to shrink back a little.

'Oh Christ!' he gulped. 'Get that thing off.'

I tried to undo the satin ribbons but his hands were in the way and after a short wrestling match he pulled up the silk folds and sank his face into my breasts while he grunted and pushed his knee between my legs.

What surprised me at the time was how quick he was. One thrust, a gasp, a shudder and he was done.

I was immediately consumed with fear. Could he tell? I didn't think so but I was not a man and didn't know. If he suspected, would he ask? Would he accuse me to my face or would he look for some proof?

I remained perfectly still while William's head lay heavy on my shoulder. I didn't dare put my arms around him. After a few moments when nothing was said, he climbed off me and collapsed on the bed. He felt for my hand, picked it up and kissed it.

'That was good. Did I hurt you?'

I gave him a little smile to hide the fact that he had. 'Not really, William. A small matter perhaps but I wanted to be yours.'

He looked startled. 'Did you?'

'Yes,' I whispered, thinking I didn't much care for William Montagu, who was nothing more than a rough, uncouth young man. But he was my husband and I had better make the best of it.

The skin on his shoulders was beautifully smooth. He was quite good-looking, far more so than on our wedding day. There were no clawed fingers or sagging belly where William was concerned and his body was firm and well-muscled. In time I hoped he would learn better manners in our bed. He wasn't the husband I would have chosen but then no girl has a choice and he could have been worse. He could have been like his uncle.

I parted my lips slightly, lowered my eyelashes and tried to look suitably meek.

'I'd do it again if I wasn't so drunk,' he muttered, his voice thick with wine and tiredness. 'I can, you know. You'll see. Go to sleep now. I'm too exhausted to think.'

I didn't know what to do. I half-expected him to turn and carelessly pull me into his arms again but he didn't and I was glad because he had not been particularly kind or gentle and I felt bruised. The girls in Ghent had said young men were tireless between the sheets and certainly in our little attic room under the rafters Thomas had kept me awake long into the night, yet here was William, flat on his back in the Montagu marriage bed, his mouth open, snoring like a farmer's pig.

The night candle burned low and I waited for hours, not daring to move. I was listening for the Matins bell. I heard the lonely hoot from a distant owl and the clang of a man's boots on the stone outside and then a grunt and a snort from my half-drunk husband. A few moments later William's head rolled to one side, his breathing slowed and I was certain he was fast asleep.

I reached under the pillow and retrieved the knife. With great difficulty I lifted up my foot, ensuring I didn't disturb William. I said a hasty prayer, held my breath and made a slash on the soft skin of the instep. There was a sharp pain as the blade cut into the flesh. I was surprised how little blood there was but it was enough for my purposes, I only needed a few drops.

With the business done, I wiped the blade and replaced it under the pillow. I settled down and closed my eyes, confident the deception was complete. To anybody who cared to look, William had done his duty and I was no longer a virgin. As I drifted off to sleep, my last waking thought was how pleased Lady Catherine would be in the morning when the maid delivered an armful of stained and crumpled sheets.

I woke to find William standing, fully-dressed, gazing at me with a puzzled expression on his face. I smiled shyly wondering why he was wearing his clothes. This was our first night together and surely any husband should want to take me again.

'I shall see you at Mass,' he said abruptly. 'Then we'll break our fast here in our chamber. My mother says we may have a week with no duties and in that way get to know each other. She and my uncle, the bishop, have given me instructions as to what we should do during this time.'

I blinked in surprise. This was not what I had expected. It seemed our life together was to be governed by a list of instructions from William's family. I wondered would there be a strict order for when we might be permitted to pray together, to walk together and to lie together, and would there be guidance for what was to happen beneath the sheets?

My maid helped me wash and put on my clothes, lacing up my gorgeous new green silk gown and winding my hair into the golden nets over my ears. She chattered happily about the richness of the damasks and taffetas worn by the other women but carefully avoided any mention of last night.

I had given her the knife as soon as she had greeted me that morning and she had replaced it in my chest, hidden beneath a pile of my cloaks. She knew better than to enquire as to its purpose. Perhaps she thought it common for girls like me to take a knife into their marriage bed and for all I knew perhaps it was.

I walked to the chapel to hear Mass with my husband feeling important but very nervous and refusing to catch anybody's eye. I worried Lady Catherine might leap out of the shadows at any moment screaming, "Not enough blood!" Every footstep coming towards our solemn procession had me trembling with fear and the accompanying ladies must have wondered what was wrong. I saw them exchange knowing glances and smile indulgently but they said nothing.

William and I prayed together and distributed alms to the villagers who had come to gawp at us in our fine clothes, before returning once more to give thanks at the altar rail. William appeared properly devout judging from the serious look on his face and the way he bowed his head but, whatever his prayers were, I was certain they would be different to mine.

At our first meal he ate with relish like most men, tearing the bread with his teeth and chewing enthusiastically. On the table was a special rich cheese ordered from the West Country for our bedding morning. Margaret said such delicacies were supposed to give strength to a newly-married couple and aid the conception of an heir but I didn't dare mention such a matter to William.

He made no comment on my gown, although it was one I thought a husband would like with its fashionable low-cut neck and nipped-in waist. In truth he barely looked at me, giving his full attention to his food. I saw him lick his upper lip to remove any crumbs and wondered if he would kiss me again. I wasn't sure I enjoyed his kisses. He had handled me roughly last night and bruised my mouth but he was my husband and could kiss how he liked.

Afterwards we walked by the river watching the shafts of green and silver light shimmer in the water but found nothing to say to each other. I tried once or twice but had no idea what would interest a new husband. I pointed out the moorhens scattering into the reeds at our approach and the ducks dabbling at the water's edge, but he ignored me. He knew nothing of eglantine or meadowsweet or the romances which he said were fit only for foolish women who had nothing better to do with their time.

When we reached the newly built lych gate we sat on the tiny seats and stared at the flat stones where the villagers laid their dead. He didn't try to touch me and I certainly wasn't going to touch him.

'Do you play an instrument?' I asked, thinking how badly I was doing as a new wife.

'No,' he replied.

'Do you like to sing?'

'Sometimes.'

'I do too.' I smiled encouragingly but he didn't ask me to sing with him which is what I'd expected.

Hearing the birds twittering in amongst the trees edging the churchyard wall, I recalled the melancholy little ballad Otho Holand had sung for me in Ghent. All of a sudden a lump formed in my throat as if I'd swallowed a stone and tears welled up into my eyes.

William didn't touch me. Thomas would have taken me in his arms and kissed my tears away, but William did nothing. I wasn't sure he even noticed my distress. If he did he wasn't concerned. He simply sat and waited until I had stopped crying and then said we should walk back.

Things got no better. We ate together in silence. The valets who served us, moved quietly as they replaced the dishes and the groom of the ewery contrived to fill our cups without a single splash. Once or twice I smiled at William but he looked away quickly as if offended by my presence at his table.

That afternoon we sat in Lady Catherine's private garden. It was a special privilege granted by his lady mother, William said, sounding as if escorting me to a flower-filled bower was the last thing he wanted to do. He clearly thought I was nothing other than a nuisance. But it was there, amongst the roses and the gillyflowers with the sun on my face and the butterflies flitting idly from bush to bush, that I finally discovered what my husband really liked.

'The groin is particularly vulnerable,' he said, showing me the place on his leg where he'd make his planned attack. 'If you pierce that with your dagger a man is more than likely to bleed to death. I've heard it makes a fountain of blood. Think of that.'

I swallowed hard and tried not to think about blood in all its crimson horror.

'But you can easily break a man's skull with a cudgel or an axe and if he has the misfortune to lose his helmet, you can split his head apart and his brains will spill out into the mud.'

'But William,' I said, hoping he would soon talk about something else. 'I thought you'd fight with a sword in your hand.'

'Oh I will, and just think what you can do with a sword, particularly a well-made one. I could take out a man's eye with a sword or if I aim right, cut off an arm or a leg.'

I was beginning to feel decidedly sick as William continued to number the thirty different ways he knew to kill an opponent.

'Up into the gullet is one of my favourite thrusts. Men gurgle and spit out their life blood if you hit the target right. Did you know blood can be black as pitch? It's hot and sticky and smells sweet.'

He turned his glittering eyes back to me but immediately dropped them to my waist. He didn't like to look me in the face.

'Surely your enemies will protect themselves, William?'

'The breast is well-protected but it's often possible to hack off a man's head. The neck is very fragile. Here, I'll show you.'

I sat perfectly still on the bench in his mother's garden while my husband of just over a year circled my neck with his man's hands. It was the feel of those muscular fingers on my throat which made me realise just how far the boy William had been left behind. I looked up into his eyes which were close to mine. I saw a muscle in his cheek twitch slightly as he held my gaze for a brief instant but then he dropped his hands and moved along the bench so we no longer sat close together. He was giving a rose bush his full attention, a slight flush on his face.

'William,' I began, not quite sure how to raise the matter. 'Will we live under your mother's roof now we're properly married?'

He glanced over at my breasts from his contemplation of the profusion of white roses.

'No; the king has allowed my father to make over some manors to us. In a few days we'll be leaving Bisham.'

'Where are we going?' I asked, hoping it was Suffolk or somewhere equally far away.

'A half-day's ride along the river. My mother thought it good to have us nearby in the early days of our marriage.'

That night William resumed his war. Like any good captain he spent time surveying the proposed field of battle and eyeing the prize his opponent presented. There was some initial parleying to set the enemy at ease followed by preliminary skirmishes, testing the defences and removing certain obstacles which might hinder his progress. Then, just when it was least expected, he launched a determined attack with overwhelming force and the battle was over almost as soon as it was begun. No prisoners were taken and the enemy was suitably crushed.

I lay there, surprised at the speed and clumsiness of his assault, but I said nothing for what could an innocent girl who had known no-one but her husband, have to say. This was my only experience of a man. I had nothing else with which it could be compared.

William of course was not in the least concerned about me. He was only concerned with his own satisfaction and as I had predicted he didn't find me a disappointment.

'I like you, Joan,' he said, squeezing my breasts. 'My father said you'd make a good wife and he was right.'

Our new home may have been too close to Bisham for my liking but it was very pleasant, a neat little manor house boasting a tower at one end, set back from the river amongst green meadows, with a small wooded park, a cluster of nearby cottages and a tiny church.

When I pushed open the door and explored inside I discovered the house was larger than it looked. We had a hall of a reasonable size, plenty big enough for our household and any guests we might welcome; a chamber which would be William's where he could conduct his private business; an upstairs solar for me and a cramped little guest chamber up in the tower. Hidden at the back were the usual buttery, pantry, kitchen and store rooms, and on either side of the gatehouse several long low buildings which William said would be stables and barns for hay and straw and grain. In front was a walled courtyard and to the side, behind a wickerwork fence, a tiny herb garden and an orchard dotted with trees.

Our household would be run by an ancient steward who had served William's father for many years and was now nearing the end of his working days.

'My mother says he will be a safe pair of hands,' said William, delivering a lengthy list of instructions to me. 'You will need an experienced man when I'm away. Of course if I'm ordered overseas or to Scotland you will return to Bisham or wherever my mother is. I don't wish you to be alone.'

'But I won't be alone. There will be the men, and I've got a maid and soon I'll have a couple of young women to keep me company.'

William put his lips together and frowned. 'If I wish you to be with my mother that is where you will be.'

'Yes, William,' I said dutifully wondering if I would ever escape from Lady Catherine's clutches and thinking this husband of mine was turning into a gaoler.

Now he had assured himself of an obedient wife, William smiled happily. Tonight would be the first night in our new house and I was sure we would do better together away from his mother. But married life with William was not what I imagined and after a few weeks I began to wonder what else I had misjudged.

I rarely saw my husband. He spent his time with a growing circle of friends, young men from the neighbourhood who wanted to attach themselves to a man who would one day be Earl of Salisbury. They came bearing their weapons and hunted in our park. At dinner William ignored me, talking to whoever was on his other side and roaring with laughter at jokes I didn't understand. He drank a lot, like all young men, and by nightfall was often too drunk to do more than briefly take his pleasure and collapse on top of me. He never spoke except for impatient demands to lift my shift or spread my legs and he never kissed me on the lips.

He was seldom at Mass, using the time to deal with the business of our manor and dictate any necessary correspondence. Even on rainy days he preferred seeing to his hounds or gambling with his friends to being with me. I was never invited to ride with him and we never went visiting together. I began to wonder what he thought a wife was for.

Naturally I knew the answer to that: a wife's duty was to give her husband comfort in bed and provide him with sons. But I had hoped for more. I had wanted a husband who prized me and wanted me at his side. I had wanted a husband I could love and I didn't think I could ever love William Montagu.

I had my duties but running a household was easy. My clerk of the wardrobe and pantry was a clever young man. He had a clear grasp of what was needed and managed to organise the elderly steward to both his and my satisfaction. Our steward didn't like me. Although obviously the words were never spoken, I could tell he thought me too young, too frivolous and too extravagant. He demurred at my suggestions for improvements to the hall, muttering about consulting the master, and if I ordered some particular delicacy it was amazing how often it was unaccountably unobtainable.

Within a month I had acquired two women companions of my own. They were married to the sons of local knights of my father-in-law's affinity and they took it in turns to serve me. Although they were not perhaps the young women I would necessarily have chosen as friends, I enjoyed their company.

I was a dutiful daughter and wrote to my mother. I told her of our new manor and all its attendant pleasures. I told her how I was obedient to my husband's wishes and how satisfied he appeared to be with me. I told her how kind Lady Catherine and Sir William had been in providing a home for us and the men for our first household, and I told her about my lady companions and the news that I now had two maids.

But I didn't tell her about the knife hidden in my chest of clothes and I purposely forgot to mention the little guest chamber in the tower.

That summer William gave me an exquisite enamelled pendant in the shape of a bird. It was wrought exceedingly fine and I thanked him prettily. But this was not a love token from my husband, it was a reward for bringing him an invitation from the king. He was to attend the marriage celebrations in London for the king's son, four-year-old Lionel, and his bride, the young daughter of the Earl of Ulster. At the beginning of August there was to be a week of feasting and jousting and entertainments within the precincts of the Conqueror's Tower.

William's invitation was couched in the usual formal language of royal communications but made it abundantly clear that I was to accompany my husband and should be extravagantly gowned and jewelled as befitted my position. This was not just a summons for William, it was also a summons for me.

6

A ROYAL COUSIN 1342

I heard murmurs of appreciation as I walked down the length of the crowded room with my arm resting lightly on William's satin sleeve. This was my first formal appearance as William's wife and we had sparked a great deal of interest. As we approached the two royal thrones I felt my heart flutter. I hadn't seen my cousin for more than seven months and our last meeting was not something I wanted to think about. I had put it behind me and wished it had never happened.

I made a low curtsey, sweeping the ground with my blue silk skirts, but when I raised my head I saw the glint in my cousin's eye. He had not forgotten. Of course he hadn't. He was the king and a king never forgets anything.

The jousting and other entertainments were great fun but when the last of the feast was over, the young bride and groom were yawning with tiredness. With much bowing and curtseying and cheering they were returned to the royal nursery while everyone else prepared for a long evening of music and dancing. Alice was in no fit condition to dance so we stole away to Margaret's cramped chamber, hidden half-way up one of the stairways. I was certain we would be undisturbed and that nobody, however grand and important he might be, would be able to find me.

Margaret lay back against the pillows, stretched out her feet and sighed with pleasure.

'Cover my toes, Alice. I'm cold.'

Alice, heavy and ungainly with her second child, obediently pulled the coverlet over her sister's blue stockings.

'Isn't this wonderful?' she said. 'A whole evening with just the three of us. It's like the old days at Framlingham when we were girls. Do you remember, Jeanette?'

'Of course I do.'

'And the night before Margaret's wedding when we gorged ourselves on sugared plums and she threatened to drown herself in the moat.'

Margaret pulled a face. 'Sometimes I wish I had.'

Alice looked shocked. 'No you don't. It would be a sin.'

'Where have the men gone?' I asked, idly twisting a lock of hair which had come loose from its net. 'I couldn't see William anywhere.'

'Alice's husband has arranged a night's gambling and drinking,' said Margaret. 'You won't see William until he crawls back some time after dawn.'

At that moment there was a quiet knock at the door and in sidled Margaret's maid.

'The king's valet, m'lady. He's looking for Mistress Montagu. He heard she were here.'

I should have known nowhere was safe; my cousin's grasp extended into every crevice in his kingdom.

I followed the valet through the warren that was the Conqueror's Tower, down steps, along narrow winding passageways and across empty courtyards echoing with the sound of our footsteps. At the door to the king's private chamber there was a quick word and the guards stood aside to let me enter.

My cousin was seated with a quill in his hand. His private secretary stood at his shoulder, busying himself with papers, waiting for *Edwardus Rex*, the dripping of the coloured wax and the imprint of the king's private seal. They neither of them looked at me.

I waited near the door, biting my lip and wishing I was back with Margaret and Alice.

At last it was done.

'Thank you, Master Kilsby.'

The man gathered everything together, bowed, gave an incurious small glance and a nod to me and left with the door closing quietly behind him. The two grooms of the chamber padded around, folding and tidying and when everything was done they melted away. Now there was just my cousin and me.

I lowered myself, murmuring, 'Your Grace.'

The light outside was fading fast and even with the candles lit, the room was growing dark. The corners were lost in shadows and I was glad the fire in the hearth was burning. A sleek white dog slept with his nose on his paws and a falcon on a perch dozed quietly while my cousin's fingers tapped silently on the table.

'I'm going away.' His voice was low and I wasn't sure why he was telling me this.

'To Scotland?'

'No, Brittany. I'm taking my army to give help to the duchess.'

I wasn't sure where Brittany was. Somewhere across the Narrow Sea? Rocky coasts and pirates was all I remembered of people's conversations.

'Is the duchess pretty?'

He laughed. 'I've no idea but she's sent a chest of gold and asked for my assistance.'

'Is someone attacking her?'

'A nephew of the King of France. He fancies himself ruler of the duchy. He thinks it's his by right of marriage.'

'But it isn't?'

'No. The duchess's husband has the stronger claim but he's been captured by his enemies and thrown into prison.'

I clapped my hands together. 'So you'll rescue him.'

'We'll defeat the army of the Valois nephew and reclaim the duchy. And we'll make sure the new Pope's cardinals agree with us.'

If the duchess's husband was the rightful ruler I couldn't see why the cardinals would disagree.

'Will you take the princes from the Low Countries to help you fight?'

'No, they're proving less than trustworthy and have bled me dry. I'll take my English friends. They'll be happy enough for glory and the spoils of war.'

I remembered Thomas's words from long ago: rich towns to be plundered, merchants stripped of their wealth, wagon-loads of jewels and furs, and the greatest prize of all – a ransom.

'Can war make a man's fortune?' I asked, wondering if it was true.

'Why are you worrying about such matters, little cousin? War is men's business. I didn't bring you here to talk about the dirt and horrors of battle. You are far too beautiful for that.'

He waved his fingers ordering me forward. 'Come here.'

I walked slowly round the table and stood beside his chair. He had moved it sideways so that he sat facing me. Rather than look at him I stared at the intricate carving on the chair back, wondering how it had been done and if the master carver had ever allowed his knife to slip.

'Lady Catherine informed me today that you and young Montagu are living together.' His voice was curt.

'Yes, Your Grace.'

'He's been in your bed?'

I lowered my eyes. 'Yes.' My voice was getting smaller and smaller and I wished myself a hundred miles away.

There was a long pause and when he spoke his voice had changed. His words were silky on his tongue. 'So, come close.'

I moved a half-step forward.

'Closer.'

I took another small step.

'Now, let down your hair for me.'

I hesitated and then raised my arms. It was difficult without a maid but soon I had the nets and pins in my hand and my golden hair spread like a veil across my shoulders.

He sat like a man transfixed. He stared and stared and said not a word until I wondered what I was supposed to do.

'Your Grace?'

He slid his eyes back to mine.

162

'You are very beautiful. I sometimes think I am bewitched by you.'

A girl in Ghent had once consulted a wise woman but how could he think that of me? Such things were forbidden and very dangerous. The girl had needed a love charm but all I had ever wanted was for my cousin to love me the way he once had.

'I know, I know,' he said gently.

He touched the nape of my neck softly with his fingers. 'Do you remember how I stroked your hair that night at Wark, when we first spoke of this?' He paused. 'It's been more than half a year. You're a wife now and there can be no more excuses?' I heard the uneven breaths catching in his throat.

I said nothing. I was much too scared to say anything.

He put his hand under my chin and tipped it up. 'Ah, Jeanette. Look at me. You're not a child any longer. You know what this is.'

Of course I knew. I think I'd always known.

He placed his other hand on my waist and slowly pulled me onto his knee. At Woodstock it would have been my place of safety, nestled against his chest, my cheek smoothed by the velvet warmth of his tunic. But here in the royal chamber with nobody but the two of us it was shockingly intimate. This was the kind of thing a husband did.

He kissed me. He wasn't rough, not like William who bruised my mouth. His lips were gentle but determined and it was not by any means a cousinly kiss. As my mouth opened under his, he pressed harder and wound his hand into my hair.

'I could command you to my bed,' he whispered, 'but I would so much rather you came of your own free will. Oh, my dear heart, I can't continue like this. How can I plan a campaign when you haunt me day and night? I can't think, I can't eat, I can't sleep. I want you so much.'

Since the last time at Wark I had begun to have disturbing dreams about my cousin, dreams which I had admitted to no-one not even my confessor, dreams of a closeness which I knew could never be.

'I... I am afraid.'

'Ah, sweeting, you don't need to be frightened of me. I'd never harm you. I'd be very gentle. And if you came to me it would please me greatly. Don't you want to be my little Jeanette again? Don't you want to please me?'

'Oh yes,' I breathed. 'Of course I do.'

'Then come to me now and let me love you.'

I hesitated and he must have seen the doubt in my eyes because he kissed them shut and whispered. 'What can I give you in return? What gift would you like? A jewel? A new gown?'

I nearly said I would give myself freely when I realised there was something he possessed that I wanted, something I had wanted for as long as I could remember, something which was easily within his power to give me.

'There is a gift I would like,' I whispered. 'Something I would treasure.'

'Tell me,' he said eagerly, pulling me even closer.

'It costs nothing.'

He laughed at my naivety, after all what experienced woman would choose a mare's nest when she could have the mare. 'Very well, it is yours, dear heart.'

'Tell me about my father.'

He took his hands away and regarded me in amazement. 'Your father? You want to know about your father?'

'Yes. If you promise to tell me about him and why he died I will promise myself to you in return.'

He smiled and raised an eyebrow. 'A bargain?'

He was clearly amused by my choice.

'Yes, I suppose it is.'

'How do I know you would keep your side of the bargain?' he teased. 'Young women are known to be duplicitous in such matters and it would not be good for the King of England to appear a fool.'

'I would swear on the Host.'

He gave a small nod.

'Would you indeed?'

After a moment he lifted me off his knee and set me on the floor. He stood up and took my hand in his.

'Come!' He indicated the heavy curtain in the corner of the room. 'My private chapel. If we are to make a promise, we will do it before God so there can be no going back. Is it agreed?'

I nodded nervously, feeling my decision running away with me.

The room was small but beautifully painted with a crucifix on the wall, and a tiny altar. It was for my cousin's private devotions, the sort of room that only a king or a queen would have.

With great care, he removed a gilded box from a chest in the corner and showed it to me. It was heavily jewelled and inside was a tiny sliver of dark wood.

'A piece of the True Cross, the most holy relic I possess.'

I could almost smell the holiness and the suffering and felt tears prick the back of my eyes.

He knelt and pulled me down beside him, then took my hand and laid it on the closed lid and placed his own on top. I listened to him promise to tell me the story of my father's last years and his part in his death.

'What shall I say?' I whispered.

'Promise you will come to my bed. One night. That's all. Just one night.'

I raised my eyes to his and did as he asked. I trusted him implicitly.

When he had laid aside the relic, I gathered my skirts and made to rise but he placed a hand on my shoulder.

'Stay there. This is as good a place as any for the confession of past sins and I will feel more comfortable kneeling here with you at my side.'

I felt anything but comfortable but couldn't say so.

'How much do you know of your father?' His voice was quiet.

It was not how much but how little. I was fifteen years old and knew almost nothing about the man who had fathered me.

'I know it was a royal warrant which sanctioned his death and I know the signature was yours. Some girls call me "traitor's daughter" but they don't know what it means and neither do I.'

He stared straight ahead at the crucifix but said nothing. I thought perhaps he wasn't going to tell me or perhaps he was composing a lie. At last, he spoke.

'It began in Paris as so many stories do. It was snowing. Your father's wedding day and he was the happiest man alive. I remember how he laughed and how annoyed my mother was. She didn't want him to marry.'

'Why not?'

'Your mother wasn't suitable. He was a king's son and she was just a baron's daughter, a widow and much older than him. But your father loved her. I'd never seen someone marry for love. Of course it would have been better if they'd never met.'

'Why? What was wrong?'

'Your mother was Mortimer's cousin. Their mothers were sisters and she'd known him all her life.'

I hadn't known. I'd heard of the evil tyrant Mortimer but nobody had said he was my mother's cousin.

'Lord Mortimer was a clever man. He had my mother ensnared in his web. I can see now how attractive he was to my mother, a strong man, a warrior to the heels of his boots and very different from my father. She became infatuated with him. Between them they hatched a plan and soon we were sailing back across the Narrow Sea. I thought they intended to rid the country of my father's friends, the Despensers, but they had other plans about which I knew nothing. They forced my father to give up his throne to me and then locked him away. He was dead within the year.'

'Was he an old man?'

He smiled at me, a twisted smile: half sorrow, half something else.

'No, he wasn't old. I thought it was murder but said nothing. I was fourteen, almost the same age as you are

167

now. I may have been king in name but Mortimer held the reins of power. My mother was in thrall to him and did everything he said. They buried my father in Gloucester and afterwards took me north to York where I was married to Philippa.'

He looked straight into my eyes. 'I often think that without Philippa I would have given up but she gave me strength.'

I waited and for a long while he said nothing. He put out his hand and stroked my cheek.

'You are so much like your father.'

'What happened to him?'

'He discovered Mortimer's secret. It was probably your mother who uncovered the deceit because she was a clever woman, much cleverer than your father, but it was your father's plan which was their undoing.'

'What was the secret?'

He smiled again. 'I cannot tell you that. It isn't my secret to tell. Suffice to say your father's plan would have meant the end for all of us. Unwisely, he had your mother write a letter which fell into Mortimer's hands. Mortimer had him arrested and your mother imprisoned at Arundel. I doubt you remember, you were very young.'

I looked back to the past before Woodstock but there was nothing, just darkness and somebody screaming. Nothing else. It could have been anywhere or any time.'

'And my father?'

'Mortimer had him tried for treason and condemned to death: execution, save for the king's mercy.'

'But you weren't merciful,' I cried. 'You could have saved him but you didn't.'

'No. It wasn't possible. They stood one on either side of me, my mother on my right and Mortimer on my left. Mortimer put the warrant on the table and told me to sign. He explained the consequences of not signing: my death, my mother's death and the death of my wife and unborn child. My mother wept, saying how she would be torn apart and how I would be destroyed. She said if I loved her I would sign. She said if I loved Philippa I would sign. I didn't want to. But they beat me down. It went on hour after hour after hour until I wanted to scream.'

'And you signed?'

His face was bleak with the memory of his decision.

'My mother said a good king should always be a strong king and that to be a good king, difficult choices often had to be made. Yes, I signed and she affixed my seal. When it was done I returned to Philippa's arms and wept.'

'And they had my father killed?'

'Next day outside the castle walls at Winchester.'

I felt cold and numb with the pain. He could have saved my father but he hadn't. He had let him die. My father had been weighed in the balance of his kingship and found wanting.

'What happened to Lord Mortimer?'

'Later that year, Montagu led a band of his friends into Nottingham Castle and captured Lord Mortimer at the point of a sword. I would have killed him then and there but Montagu stopped me. He said there must be a trial. So we took him to London. He was tried and condemned to death. It was all done according to the law as was proper. I had him hanged.'

'And my mother?'

'She was released. I saw to it that her property was returned and Philippa took you children into the nursery at Woodstock.'

So that was why I had been brought up with Edward and Isabella and Joanna. It wasn't because my cousin loved me; it was to assuage his feelings of guilt.

I looked at his handsome profile, relaxed and smiling now the tale was told. He put out his hand and gently stroked my face. I felt the touch of his fingers on my eyelids and on the soft skin of my cheek and had to resist the urge to push them away.

'Not now,' he said quietly. 'But one day soon. I won't take you tonight. I can see you're upset and I don't want tears when you come to my bed, I want laughter.'

I didn't think I would ever laugh again. I wanted to claw out his eyes for what he had done. I wanted to throw myself against the velvet of his royal robes and beat his chest with my fists to make him understand my pain. I wanted to scream and call him a murderer. Above all, I wanted to hate him.

I couldn't love a man who had hurt me like this and yet he was the king, my cousin and I remembered I had loved him once. But tonight love wasn't the currency of our transaction. Despite the soft words and his gentle wooing, I knew he wasn't offering love. He was simply offering the consummation of desire. But I had promised myself to him before God and no matter what my feelings were I would have to keep my promise.

The lush green leaves of summer had faded to a dusty grey and the wayside flowers, which once had given me so

170

much pleasure, were gone. The track beneath our horses' hooves was rutted, the woodland edge nothing but a mess of bleached grasses and tangled bracken, and all around, the sense of something precious lost, an innocence destroyed which could never be regained.

'I shall be leaving soon,' announced William as we rode into our park.

He nodded to the old man who stood grasping the bar of one of the sturdy wooden gates.

'I shall be sorry to be without you,' I said dutifully, thinking how easy it was to lie to a husband. 'Where are you going?'

'My father and the king sail for Brittany within the month and I am to accompany them.'

This must be the expedition to rescue the duchess. It would be like the campaign in Flanders two years ago with battles and sieges and skirmishes with the enemy. No wonder William was excited.

'It will be dangerous,' said my husband, looking behind him to see if our cavalcade was safely through the gates. 'You will pray for me. I shall like to think of you on your knees. And you will gather your household together each morning to say prayers for our safety. You know how it's done. Follow my mother's example.'

'Yes, William.'

As soon as we arrived in our courtyard, William leapt from the saddle, throwing his reins to the waiting groom. He paused to fondle the ears of his favourite hound then came up to my stirrup and gripped my boot.

'When I am gone you will go to Bisham and keep my mother company. It is my wish.'

He didn't blink but kept his gaze fixed on my face. After a moment, satisfied of my obedience, he let go of my foot and stepped back. He stood watching as the groom helped me down. My clothes were disarranged from the journeying and some hair beneath my veil had come loose. William's eyes narrowed as I raised my arms to tuck the fly-away strands back in place and gather my riding cloak round me. Despite the warmth of the day a slight breeze had sent a sudden chill into the courtyard.

'I will come early tonight, Joan,' he whispered into my ear. 'We must make a son before I leave.'

The morning he left, William knelt at my feet for a blessing. His eyes were closed and with the breeze ruffling his hair and the sun falling full on his face I could almost believe I had feelings for him. He was the very model of a gallant young husband setting off for war. In this pretty tableau I was the sorrowful young wife left behind not knowing if her man would return. I couldn't be faulted and it was a shame Lady Catherine wasn't here to see.

I had deliberately dressed in my most demure gown, soft pale blue wool, high-necked with tight sleeves and a wide-flowing skirt. My white gauze veil over my coif was suitably opaque and there was little to see of that snare and delusion, my long golden hair.

I laid my hand gently on top of William's head and murmured the words of blessing. I smiled serenely and wondered if I resembled the picture of Our Lady painted on the chapel wall at Bisham.

'You will write if you have news,' he ordered, his eyes fixed on the front of my gown where he hoped a Montagu heir was already growing safely in my belly.

'Of course.'

'On second thoughts, tell my mother. She will write.'

'Fare you well, husband.'

I stepped back and rubbed an imaginary tear away from my eyes. I kept a sad little smile on my face until the last of the men had filed out of the courtyard and disappeared under the gatehouse and down the track followed by half-a-dozen pack-horses and wagons. Then I dropped my shoulders and let out a sigh of contentment. Lady Catherine wouldn't return to Bisham before tomorrow so there was no reason to order our removal until the morning.

I instructed the men as to the loading of the carts and dismissed my lady companion, telling her she could go home to her husband. I ordered my maids to start packing my chests and meanwhile I set out to spend the day wandering along the river bank.

I pulled off my shoes, removed my stockings and dipped my feet in pools of water still warm from yesterday's sun. There was no-one to see such wanton and unsuitable behaviour and as the soft mud oozed between my bare toes, I sighed with undisguised pleasure.

I lay on the grassy bank, gazing at the white puffy clouds floating over my head and wondered whether Alice's baby had been born and if it was a boy. Then I turned on my front to examine the dozens of tiny insects hopping around in the grasses and thought about Thomas Holand.

It was only in these occasional moments when I was entirely alone that I allowed myself to think about Thomas. I had sworn I would forget him and I knew I should hate him for what he'd done. But somehow I couldn't summon up the feeling any more. It was odd but all I remembered of that time before William was not the deceits and the lies but the gentle touch of his fingers and the sweetness of his smile.

In the late afternoon I returned to the house and talked with our steward about tomorrow's arrangements. He was not pleased to have me in charge and made a great fuss, slyly suggesting my husband would not approve my decisions.

It was sunset when we heard the sound of horses.

'Praise be! The young master has returned,' said the old man, shuffling off towards the door behind the screen.

But the familiar bray of a royal trumpet told me otherwise.

A wide-eyed boy ran into the hall.

'It's the king!'

The moment I saw him I knew he had come to collect his winnings.

'Is this your chamber?' My cousin cast his eyes round what to him must appear a very poor room. William and I had only the second-best hangings from Bisham and there was none of the opulent splendour of the royal chambers in the Tower.

'Yes, Your Grace.' I was determined to remain calm and distant even though my heart was racing like a cantering horse and I was horribly aware of the hovering presence of the steward.

He eyed the bed. 'I'm sorry to put you to so much inconvenience.'

I wondered did he apologise to every wife who offered to vacate her chamber and remove herself to some pokey little tower room or was this honour reserved for the women he was about to take to his bed.

'It is no trouble,' I said, my eyes lowered like a dutiful subject. 'I'll take the guest chamber.'

'Nonsense,' he said curtly. 'I'll take the guest chamber. You will stay here.'

'My husband would expect me to attend to your comfort.'

He gave a glimmer of a smile. 'I'm sorry I missed him.'

'Only by the inside of a day, Your Grace. He left this morning.'

'Then I expect we'll meet on the road.'

I doubted my cousin would ride fast. A cuckolded husband would not be any man's favourite travelling companion.

'May I offer Your Grace some refreshment?'

'Thank you. A cup of wine and whatever you have. I don't expect a feast when I gather you leave for Bisham in the morning.'

I snapped my fingers and our steward melted away, murmuring with pleasure at serving his king. I heard him call for food and wine for His Grace as if the grooms were not already running around like headless chickens gathering up the necessaries.

In no time at all the groom from the ewery arrived with wine, quickly followed by two awe-struck boys with plates of cold meat and best white bread.

'Mistress Montagu, will you keep me company?'

I bowed my head in submission. How could I say no?

We made tentative conversation. Mostly he was eager to discuss our lack of proper fortifications and made several suggestions as to how matters could be improved, all of which I promised to relay to William. After a short while he said I looked weary and he had no desire to keep me from my bed as I must be tired. I gave a deep curtsey, sweeping the floor as elegantly as I could, and bade him a safe night.

I had the girl quickly undress me and clothe me in my finest nightgown. I rejected two, casting them aside with a carelessness which would have horrified Alice and chose the one I'd worn on my bedding night, the embroidered silk. After the girl had combed out my hair I ordered her to leave it unbraided.

'You will sleep in the wardrobe closet,' I said hurriedly. 'I don't need a companion tonight.'

She ducked her head and obediently pattered away. I slid the bolt. I wanted no witness to what was going to happen and no interruptions.

I heard doors bang in the distance and a single muffled order from the steward down below. Footsteps clattered on the stairs. I had only a single candle burning but it would suffice as I knew my cousin had neither reading nor sewing on his mind tonight.

A moment later there was a soft noise and the door opened.

I glanced past him, terrified someone was on the stairs.

'Don't worry,' he smiled, 'There's no-one to tell your husband.'

He closed the door and locked it.

Although I was fully clothed, I felt naked. His gaze stripped away the soft wool of my bedrobe and the delicate layers of pale blue silk until I stood there in front of him, utterly defenceless and very scared. We had made a bargain that evening in the Tower and I had sworn on the True Cross that I would give myself to him but now the moment was here, all I wanted was to run away.

He put out his hand and said, 'Jeanette, come here.'

There was not a single inch of me he didn't explore with his lips or his fingers during that long hot night, from the soft pulse at the base of my neck to the secret warmth at the top of my thighs and the little gaps between my toes.

He took me hurriedly in the confines of the bed I shared with William, on the fine linen sheets given as a wedding gift from the sisters at the nearby convent, gasping in pleasure as he cried out my name. And he took me twice, lazily and deliberately on the Bisham furs in front of the dying embers of the fire, watching my face as he pleasured me. And when at last he was too tired for more, he cradled me in his arms and told me how he loved me.

He was magnificent and I worshipped him. His eyes held the colours of every day that had ever dawned and by morning I was totally and completely enmeshed in his being. I loved him. I believed I had always loved him. The memories of our last meetings were cold, as surely as last night's ashes were cold, and once again I was his adored little Jeanette.

'I wish I hadn't given you to young Montagu,' he whispered in my ear. 'I wish I'd kept you for myself.'

'What would you do with me?' I murmured provocatively, kissing his bare shoulder. Shining beads of sweat clung to the skin and as I tasted them on my lips, I wondered how I dared to do this to an anointed king.

'I'd keep you beside me always,' he whispered. 'I'd never let you go.'

'Can you not do that now?'

I wanted him so much I had forgotten all the duties and the ties and the other loyalties. I'd given no thought to my family, to my husband, to my cousin's children or his wife. In a single night my world had shrunk to the size of this little room where I lay with my cousin, the man who had been my first love.

I felt him smile in the darkness, his lips curving against my cheek. 'How would we explain it to young William, dear heart? And what would the queen say?'

I thought of what the two knights from Juliers had said about the plump little woman, the grand lady of Hainault, who had lost her baby this last spring. Her face was freckled and lined and tired. Perhaps, despite the rumours, he still loved her but he couldn't possibly love her the way he loved me? I was the heart of his heart, the soul of his soul, the unwavering flame in the darkness. I sweetened the arid pastures of his life and filled the rivers of his eyes with joy. I knew because he had told me so, and I believed him.

'She is the mother of my children, sweetheart. She is my helpmeet, my friend and my advisor in all things. I couldn't do without her. Everything I have and everything I am, I owe to her and without her I am nothing.'

'But…'

He stopped my protests with a kiss. 'Ah Jeanette. This is a paradise for fools and one night was what we said. Just one night.'

I must have looked desolate because he picked me up and carried me back to bed and it was a long time before he pulled himself away, groaning how the sun would soon be up and he must be on his way.

He left me at dawn, kissing my mouth, my neck, my shoulder and the swell of my breasts, telling me he didn't want to go but duty called.

For the sake of appearances, we broke our fast together in my chamber, sitting across the table from each other eating bread and cheese and drinking small ale. He asked me to leave my hair unbound and because I knew it would please him, I wore my green silk gown with the low-cut neck.

The cheese was a fine one brought up from Essex by William last summer. My cousin watched as I placed a sliver in my mouth and licked the last morsel from my lips.

'You have a good appetite.' He smiled lazily and, without taking his eyes from mine, reached for his cup.

My eyes danced and I wanted to laugh. I knew that, like me, he was savouring his memories of last night.

I tore another piece of bread and was about to put it in my mouth when I heard noises on the stairs. Voices! A woman's raised in irritation, a man's. The steward? Footsteps. The door swung open.

'Joan!'

It was Lady Catherine.

She looked at me, at the table, at the several platters and the man who had turned in his chair to see who it was. Her eyes widened and her mouth dropped open. For a moment there was no sound at all.

'Your Grace.' Her voice was strangled in her throat.

I sat frozen in my seat quite unable to move. We had been discovered and by the very worst person imaginable. My hair! My gown! I knew guilt was written right across my face. Could she tell?

My cousin rose, scattering crumbs. 'Catherine, by all that's wonderful.'

He went swiftly to her side and took her hand. He lifted it to his lips, gazing into her eyes the way he had gazed into mine.

'When they said you weren't at Bisham I thought I'd find you here. When I discovered your absence...'

He leaned forward and whispered into her ear.

She coloured like a girl.

'My little cousin gave us lodgings for the night but it wasn't the same. How could it be?' He smiled at Lady Catherine as if she was the only person he had ever wanted to see. 'Perhaps we can step outside and be alone? There seems to be a pleasant little garden where I trust we will be undisturbed.'

She looked up from under her eyelashes and placed her hand on his sleeve in a small possessive gesture which told me everything.

'Of course, Your Grace. Whatever you wish.'

They turned and left the chamber together. I sat perfectly still, feeling jealousy creep into my very bones. I was unable to move, unable to think, listening to the sound of their footsteps on the stair while the servants stood round the edge of the room waiting for my orders as to what they should do.

Later, after my cousin had gone, Lady Catherine swept up the steps with her skirts billowing angrily about her legs. I followed dutifully in her wake. This might have been my house but Lady Catherine was my mother-in-law and could command my obedience without a word spoken.

I could see her mouth was bruised and her eyes over-bright and I knew he must have kissed her out in the garden. How could he have placed his lips on hers when they must have been full of me? How could he have gone so easily to her when I was the one who had spent the night in his arms?

In the upstairs chamber the men were clearing away the last remnants of the meal, balancing cups and folding napery as they worked, but one look at Lady Catherine's scowl sent them scurrying on their way.

She turned on her heel. I stopped. She slapped me hard across the face.

'You little slut!' she hissed. 'Who do you think you are? Behaving like a Flemish whore with your hair unpinned and exposing half your bosom to the king. Luckily, he was amused. He considers you no more than a child and thinks you don't know what you're doing. But I was not amused and I know exactly what you were doing. You can't fool me. If you were not my son's wife I'd have you whipped.'

She gave me a look of pure hatred.

'If my son should find out about this, I pity you, but mark well, I will not lift a single finger to help you.'

For the next five months I lived in Lady Catherine's shadow with disapproving eyes following my every step. I was never out of her sight. I slept in her bed and spent every waking hour at her side. She treated me as one of the lowliest members of her chamber fit only for the meanest of tasks. When we sat at our embroidery I was given the dullest bits to sew: the endless blue of the sky or the tedious swirling scrolls which stretched from one end of the cloth to the other. I was quite surprised she didn't have me stitching hems with William's little sisters since I was considered so unworthy.

To the others I was an object of fascination. The older women whispered behind their hands and wondered what I could possibly have done to deserve such treatment. I must have sinned, but how and in what manner? The younger girls, who had very little sense and far too much imagination, merely giggled. They speculated wildly but didn't dare ask me to my face.

Letters arrived from my husband and were promptly deemed the property of my mother-in-law. They were read aloud to the household and in case I should complain to William, my replies were dictated by Lady Catherine to her clerk. I may have looked like a grand lady in my brocades and velvets and fur-trimmed gowns but in truth I was no better than a well-dressed prisoner.

Lady Catherine kept her eyes on my person but she couldn't pry into my thoughts. At night I dreamed of my cousin, wonderful sensuous dreams where he kissed my lips and held me in his arms and whispered how much he loved me. In the morning, when the noise of the other women stirring, forced me awake, I lay, imagining him in his bed somewhere across the Narrow Sea and wondered if he was thinking of me.

Our parting had been brief: a curtsey, a nod, a kiss

on the hand and a meeting of eyes, so swift it might not even have happened. His men were in the courtyard so obviously he couldn't acknowledge our closeness or his disinclination to leave but even so I was disappointed. I had hoped for more.

Lady Catherine had received a tender farewell: regret, a rueful smile, quiet words and a whispered promise, but he couldn't possibly have meant any of it. He couldn't have left my bed and gone straight to her, not with my scent lingering in the pores of his skin and the memory of our passion filling his eyes. I was certain he no longer cared for her. It was all a ruse. He only cared for me.

At Christmas we received a letter from my father-in-law detailing his progress. He told us how an early assault by the lord of Artois to recapture the town of Vannes had failed and the king and his Breton allies were now settled down outside the walls. I had no idea where Vannes was and Lady Catherine didn't enlighten me as I was still in disgrace and didn't deserve to know anything.

Other letters followed and in February we learned that my cousin had made an honourable truce, one which was all to our advantage. We would keep most of the towns and castles in Brittany and there would be no more fighting in Gascony or in Scotland or elsewhere.

When Lady Catherine told us the king would bring the duchess and her children with him when he sailed for England and they would be lodged in comfort in the Tower, I realised the duchess must be uncommonly pretty, possibly even prettier than me. Why else would my cousin bring her home to England? Nothing was said about the duchess's husband and when he would be released or where he would be lodged and this confirmed my worst fears. My cousin didn't want me any more; he had found someone else.

When William returned at the end of a week of storms and tempests, I was unsure how to greet him as my mind and my heart were full of my cousin. Should I be meek and docile or should I smile and be merry? Would William expect me to throw my arms around his neck or would he want me to stand three paces behind his mother and sink low in a dutiful curtsey?

I needn't have worried for as soon as he arrived, William slid from the saddle and knelt at his mother's feet.

'Lady mother.'

'My dearest son. God's greetings and welcome home.'

Lady Catherine, with tears of happiness filling her eyes, raised my husband up, kissed him on his mouth and bore him away to her chamber leaving the rest of us behind in the courtyard. She barely gave me time to make a wife's formal greeting so anxious was she to have William to herself.

It was the season of denial but even so we held a feast for William's return. Every fish pond in the locality was emptied and our men were sent to the market at Great Marlow and the wharf at Maidenhythe to see what extra forbidden luxuries could be purchased for the Montagu household. We wore our best gowns and there was a feeling of wickedness about feasting when we should have been fasting.

William sat in the place of honour where his father

usually sat. I knew if she could, Lady Catherine would have banished me to the lower benches at the far end of the hall where the grooms and the maids were sitting, but that would have been unthinkable. Instead she monopolised William's attention asking him penetrating questions about the campaign and the doings of his noble companions.

Listening to her I realised how ignorant I was. I had never thought to question my cousin's decision to take his armies to Brittany. I had assumed he was trying to rescue a beautiful damsel in distress and right a terrible wrong. It was nothing like that. He wanted Brittany for himself and he wanted it for the same reason he had wanted the treaty with the Flemings: it would give him a stepping stone, a landing place for his armies and a gateway into France to launch an attack on the Valois king. And of equal importance, it would give protection to our ships sailing to Gascony. If my cousin controlled Brittany, he could stop the constant attacks on our fleets. He had cannily brought down two birds with one stone and I was full of admiration for his cleverness.

Eventually William remembered to turn his attention to me.

'I missed you, Joan.'

'I missed you too, William,' I lied smoothly, wondering if he could tell.

'My mother says His Grace paid you a visit while I was away.'

'Yes,' I said feeling myself blush and trying not to think of what had happened between my cousin and me. 'He was sorry to have missed you.'

'I trust you gave him hospitality?'

'Naturally. I did everything as you would have wanted, William. I remembered how your mother welcomed honoured guests and tried to do what she did.'

But I had done more, so very much more and he would never know. I would never tell him of the pleasure and satisfaction I had given our guest and how much he had enjoyed his visit.

'He was concerned about our lack of fortifications,' I said, speaking too fast and tripping over the words.

'What's wrong with our fortifications? They're perfectly adequate. It's not as if we're near the coast.' William was not pleased for his house to be criticised.

'Oh, I don't think His Grace believed there was anything wrong, simply that things could be better.'

Holy Mother of God. I hoped I could remember what my cousin had said. Something about the outer walls and the weakness of the gatehouse. I should have had the clerk write it down at the time. Now I had forgotten everything except for the delicious hours I had spent behind that locked door neglecting all my duties except for my duty to my king.

'Tell me about your campaign,' I said hoping to divert him from my cousin's visit.

He smiled. I had asked the right question.

'Do you remember when we sat in my mother's garden last summer and I told you how easy it was to kill a man,' said William, slipping his hand over mine. 'In Brittany, when I killed the first one, it was like plunging a knife into a sack of corn, there was barely any resistance. I remembered how you looked that day, the little smile on your face and the sun catching your hair, making it shine like a crown of light.'

He was staring at me with a hungry look in his eyes.

'Did you kill many men?' I asked politely.

'Not as many as I'd have liked. The villagers were poor sport. They mostly ran away. The townspeople were better. One or two of the younger men armed themselves with staves and put up a good fight.' He smiled happily at the memory. 'The first one was in the garden of a house on the outskirts of Dinan. He leapt out and tried to knock me off my horse. I ran him through with my sword and the thrill of seeing the blood and his body falling gave me an appetite for more. That was when I knew my uncle was right; there is no finer sport than killing a man.'

If we had not been at dinner and if he had been anyone other than William; if he had been Thomas or my cousin or one of the two knights from Juliers, I might have raised my eyebrows suggestively and murmured that I could think of something which gave even greater pleasure. But I didn't dare say such a thing in Lady Catherine's presence and I certainly didn't want William thinking I was trying to seduce him.

That evening we sat on fur rugs warming ourselves by the fire in our chamber. I glanced sideways at the stranger sitting beside me. William was considerably taller and stronger than he had been six months ago and I realised that somewhere in Brittany, the boy he had once been had vanished. This young man whose face was familiar, was very different to the one who had ridden away from me six months earlier. The eyes were the same, pale grey with light flecks, but the skin was browner, rougher, the hair darker, and he treated me with an interest he hadn't shown before.

'Joan,' he said in a low voice. 'You're much prettier than the girls in Brittany, you know. Much prettier. They kept throwing flowers in front of our horses' hooves and wanting to kiss our feet, and they were very willing but I didn't much care for their smell and none of them had hair like yours.'

I was panic-stricken when he placed his mouth on mine. I thought he would taste my cousin's lips, but he paid no attention to my reluctance. He was firm and determined to press home his advantage. I noticed at once the difference in his kisses. He no longer attacked my mouth as if trying to devour me and as I relaxed in the circle of his arms I almost began to enjoy what he was doing.

In between his explorations of my body, he recounted more stories of the men he had killed and how much enjoyment it had given him.

'If only you could have seen them, Joan. Crawling under carts and into ditches vainly calling on God and their mothers to save them. It was a waste of breath. We slaughtered them like rats. I cornered one man before a church door and hacked off his arms. He screamed like a stuck pig before he died and the alleyway was running red with his blood. It was wonderful.'

He pulled down my stockings and with his right hand traced the lines of his father's marches on the bare skin of my thighs until he could no longer contain his excitement and ordered me to bed.

Three days later, while we still lingered at Bisham, my father-in-law returned with news. After Easter the king was to invest his eldest son as Prince of Wales. The earl had been summoned to attend the parliament at Westminster and to participate in the great feast of celebration afterwards. All the earls and the barons and the knights of the shires would be there and it was to be a splendid event. But William received no such invitation.

'It's an insult and it's entirely your fault,' he shouted, kicking open the chamber door. 'The king honours us with a visit and this happens. What did you do? Provide stale bread? Sour wine? Damp sheets? You must have done something. Why else would I be ignored. You're not fit to be my wife. You're nothing but a useless drab. And don't imagine you'll get another trinket for this. Christ's blood! You're barely worth the pittance I got for marrying you. Any fat old dowager would have managed this more cleverly than you. A slut from the alleyways of Great Marlow could have done it better. But not you with your royal kinship and your golden hair. A prize! Christ's bones! I might as well have married my father's laundress.'

'William, you're being unfair.'

I was stung into retaliating which was a great mistake with a young man like William. I would have done better to have kept quiet.

'Unfair indeed!' He threw me aside with a careless shove, sending me crashing against the chair. 'If I don't have royal favour how shall I advance? Even Edward ignores me since I married you. All the preferments will go to men like Chandos who's hardly ever out of Edward's sight and I'll be left with nothing. My father is leaving on a mission to Avignon with Lord Henry but won't take me. Says I must remain here. Says it's time to attend to my manors and to my wife.'

John Chandos was Edward's closest companion; an older man, not nobly born but the son of a gentleman. I understood William's hurt but there was nothing I could do. Friendship cannot be had simply because a man wants it. With nurturing it can flourish; little tender leaves and tiny buds which one day burst into blossom. Perhaps it could be like this for William and Edward and perhaps, just perhaps, although it did seem increasingly unlikely, it might be like this for William and me. If I kept my head bowed and behaved as a wife should, just possibly we might one day become friends.

I wondered if Thomas Holand would travel with my father-in-law and Lord Henry to Avignon but told myself I wasn't interested whether he would see the wonders of the Papal Court or whether he wouldn't. I had put him out of my mind and he was nothing to me any more. Nothing at all. Absolutely nothing. I was married to William and that was the end of it.

William and I spent the late summer travelling. We journeyed down the green lanes of England into the depths of the West Country to visit the manors given to us as part of our marriage jointure. The days were long and lazy and away from Edward's perfidy and Lady Catherine's interference we began to do better together. We found more to talk about and wherever we halted for the night, William found some pleasure in introducing me as his wife. He said he was proud of me and sometimes showed little marks of affection. He would pick up my hand and stroke my fingers and once or twice he brushed my cheek with his mouth.

By the time we reached Donyatt, where William had been born, we had taken to riding side by side sharing our thoughts and occasional smiles. We might not have been handfast lovers at night but in the daytime we were slowly becoming friends.

We rode along the narrow tracks which crossed the marshes to the abbey at Glastonbury where we admired the tombs of Arthur and Guinevere. We prayed together at the shrine of the Peacemaker and it was there, surrounded by a dozen other pilgrims with the abbey's monks hovering nearby, that I finally made my silent promise.

I knew what I had to do. I would learn to be a good wife. I would care for William's needs and be his comforter, I would manage his affairs when he was absent and be an ornament to his house. I would behave in a meek and loving manner even when provoked and bear his children without complaint. I would even learn to love his mother. I would not dwell on the sinful night I had spent in my cousin's arms and I would never, ever, ever think of Thomas Holand again.

That night as I lay in our bed in a nearby priory, William kissed me gently on my lips and told me that he loved me. I wound my arms about his neck and whispered the lie that sensible women have always told their husbands: I love you too.

In the early autumn we made leisurely progress up the march of Wales stopping at the houses of my father-in-law's friends and attending a local wedding. At Ludlow we asked for hospitality at the castle and were welcomed by Lady Mortimer herself. This was the tyrant's widow, an elderly faded little woman with a severe mouth and suspicious eyes. When I admitted to sharing the royal nursery with her grandson, young Roger, she gave a sad smile, but it was clear she didn't care for William and was icily polite in her greetings. If William had not been there I might have plucked up courage to ask the forbidding Lady Mortimer about my father, but there was no opportunity and in all probability she knew nothing, hidden away down here, far from the royal court.

We travelled slowly on up the march to our castle at Mold. It was small and in urgent need of repair and the hall was not very comfortable but we made do as best we could. There was a prolonged argument over provisions which had mysteriously failed to arrive and the only food was an undistinguished pottage and some rather tough mutton. The people spoke in a tongue I couldn't understand and the clothes in my travelling chest felt damp.

We spent a couple of evenings discussing the possibilities of what could be done with our little castle but then it started to rain. Not the usual gentle rain of an early autumn but cold lashing torrents, driven in from the west which battered the walls and seeped in under the shutters. The river flooded, the roads were awash and the roof leaked.

After a week we laughed at our predicament.

'Let's go home,' said William. 'I have a longing for our manor near Bisham where the roof is sound and the rain comes down from the sky not hurls itself sideways into your face.'

Somewhere on our long journey back along the muddy roads of Middle England I thought I might like to fall in love with my husband and by the time we saw the welcoming sight of our own gates, I believed we were part way to building a good marriage. My sins were well hidden in the past and I had done penance for them. From now on I swore I would be a good wife to William and he seemed more than willing to be a good husband to me. I had stopped dreaming of my cousin and I had promised I would never think of Thomas Holand.

We spent the Nativity celebrations that year with some friends nearby and I enjoyed myself thoroughly. William gave me a silver gilt pin as a New Year gift and told me once again how much he loved me. I gave him a pair of embroidered leather gloves which cost far more than I could afford but I wanted him to know I was his dutiful wife. And I did so enjoy buying beautiful things.

7

DEATH AND DANGER 1344

After Christmas an invitation arrived for the king's great winter tournament at Windsor. It was to be the grandest gathering of men for years and every young man with a sword would be there. For some reason William seemed to think the invitation was my doing. He grabbed me round the waist and kissed my mouth with a lingering appreciation which was something quite new. I pushed back my hood and smiled, liking my husband more and more. A few days later he gave me a ring, just a little garnet set on a narrow silver band, but it was beautiful.

'I picked it up in Brittany,' he whispered as he slid the ring over my finger. 'I thought it would give you pleasure.'

William might have been overjoyed at our invitation but I was plagued by an uncomfortable feeling in my belly which felt horribly like fear. At the royal palace on a grand occasion like this there could be no possible way of avoiding my cousin and my cousin was the one man I didn't want to meet.

It was more than a year since he had ridden away from me without a backwards look and in all that time there had been no word, no message, no token; nothing but silence. At first I made excuses for his neglect, telling myself he was far too busy with his kingship, believing he would send for me when he could, but as the months passed and still there was no word, I came to accept he no longer desired me.

One night in our paradise for fools. That was all there would ever be and there was no point in regretting any of it. It was what men did and I was the only fool for thinking it was more than a passing fancy. I had believed him when he had said he loved me and wanted to keep me at his side but I knew now I was nothing but another plaything to be picked up, enjoyed for the moment and carelessly discarded when the game was over.

When the week of the tournament arrived we travelled the short distance to Windsor with William's parents and throughout the journey Lady Catherine and Sir William spoke barely a word to each other. The earl's face was a thundercloud of fury while Lady Catherine turned away from her husband with rigid shoulders and lips clamped tightly shut. I had no idea what their quarrel was about or whether it concerned me but wisely averted my eyes and tried to think of something other than what lay ahead.

Windsor, with its great round tower and glorious rooms for entertaining, was a magnificent palace, a vast sprawling fortress built overlooking the river. I'd been there many times as a child but this visit was different. I was no longer little Jeanette from the royal nursery in her short silk gowns and white satin slippers, I was Mistress Montagu, daughter-in-law of the king's closest friend and a woman loved by her husband.

Once we had washed the grime of travel from our faces and changed into our best clothes, we joined the long procession of people in the royal presence chamber waiting to be presented. Music from the king's minstrels filled the air and at the far end of the panelled room sat my cousin and the queen on their gilded thrones.

My heart bumped and fluttered as I caught sight of him gleaming in his regal finery. He was every bit as handsome as I remembered and the red and white velvet of his robes suited his golden fairness admirably. I thought he looked magnificent. I barely noticed what the queen wore but it didn't become her. Her gown might have been cut from the richest of cloths and stitched all over with jewels but she was never going to be beautiful.

In front of us an important-looking man in the extravagant dress of a nobleman made impatient noises while a knight from Dorset stumbled over the introducing of his wife.

'Who's that?' I whispered to William.

'The Earl of Arundel, one of the king's commanders, very well-liked. His wife's a Despenser.'

I watched as the earl made his bow and conversed happily with the king and queen. William was right, the earl *was* a favoured man despite his unfortunate choice of wife. How lucky I was to have a mother whose foresight had seen me married into one of the richest and most influential families in the king's circle of friends. Despite the lingering shame of my father's death I had achieved a very prestigious marriage and one day I would be Countess of Salisbury and people would marvel at my beauty and wit and my cousin would realise too late what a prize he had let slip through his fingers.

Thomas Holand could never have brought me the honours and riches that William would bring and life with him would have been very ordinary and very dull. There would have been no royal invitations and no extravagances, no costly silks or precious gifts and I rather doubted his ability to put meat on my table. I recalled with a shudder the dried fish he had offered me in Ghent and the only jewel had been that tawdry bit of rubbish he'd doubtless picked up from some pedlar's tray. I was well rid of him and told myself I was perfectly happy with William.

We were next. As our names were called, William and I approached the dais with measured steps. My cousin looked straight at me and gave me his regal smile, a bare raising of the corners of his mouth accompanied by a haughty coolness in the eyes. He was the king and I was his subject.

I knew the smooth contours of his body, the firmness of the muscles on his arms and the softness of the golden hairs on his chest. I knew the touch of his mouth on mine, the weight of him and the smell of him, and yet here he was greeting me as if I was someone he barely knew.

I lifted my chin and smiled back, a brittle little smile. After a moment I dropped my eyes letting my lashes brush my cheeks. I had no wish for him to know how much he had hurt me and how much, despite his neglect and all my promises, my disloyal body still yearned for him.

On the first day a magnificent feast was held by Queen Philippa. Hundreds of us gathered in an upper room, giggling with pleasure at the absence of our husbands and the discovery that two handsome French knights were to wait on us. Everybody wore their finest gowns and the quantity of jewels on display would have paid the ransom for several princes and still left enough to fill a lady's chamber. I smoothed the shimmering silk of my own gown, glad William had agreed I could have a new set of robes.

'I have some news.' Alice blushed and gave me a shy little smile.

'Another child?'

She nodded. 'Yes and my husband has given me this.'

A magnificent emerald ring sparkled on her finger, not the sort of jewel which suited Alice but a wonderful gift nonetheless. Perhaps I had misjudged her husband. Of course he would want another son, men expected at least two and preferably a quiver-full like the king.

'What's afoot in the Montagu household?' asked Margaret, making herself comfortable next to Alice. 'You could hear the earl shouting all the way from the upper ward and Lady Catherine's chamber is in uproar. What's happened?'

'I don't know,' I said cautiously.

'Lady Catherine was in tears,' said Alice.

I looked at the top table where my mother-in-law sat with the other countesses. The queen was flanked by the king's mother on one side and her mother-in-law's namesake, twelve-year-old Isabella on the other. There was a plump elderly woman I didn't recognise sitting next to the king's mother being very familiar, laughing and gesticulating with her hands.

'Margaret, who's that?'

'Lady Jeanne, Countess of Suffolk. She's a tremendous gossip. It's a shame about her husband.'

'Is he dead?'

Margaret laughed. 'No! I mean her situation.' She lowered her voice to a whisper and put it close to my ear. 'He's got a woman. Keeps her in the country. She's rumoured to be very young and very comely and he's infatuated with her, just like the last one. He wants to marry her but the countess won't let him go, and why should she?'

'She's very friendly with the king's mother?'

'Yes, they're close.'

I watched how the countess tapped the king's mother on her arm in an intimate way as if they were indeed great friends. The witch knew why my father was killed and what the secret was. If she and the countess were as close as it seemed, it was possible the secret had been shared.

Afterwards, in the hall there was music and dancing and a lot of behaviour to give Bishop Simon food for thought.

'Look!' said Margaret.

It was the Earl of Arundel handclasped with the queen's friend, the widowed Lady Beaumont.

'She says he will marry her,' whispered Margaret.

'I thought he was…?'

'He is. But Eleanor Beaumont is Lord Henry's sister. A valuable alliance for the Arundels. The Despenser woman is to be set aside.'

'Is that possible? Can a man rid himself of an unwanted wife?'

Margaret laughed. 'With money, anything is possible and Richard Arundel is extremely rich.'

I joined hands with William and we danced, singing and tripping into the centre and then out again. I tipped my head back and laughed and William caught me to him and kissed me full on the mouth in front of everyone. We moved faster and the candles flickered, the torches flared and couples stole off into the shadows. On the dais my cousin whispered in the queen's ear. She blushed like a girl and smiled at him. As we moved round I came near but his gaze never drifted my way.

Countess Jeanne beamed at the sight of a new acquaintance and I smiled shyly back. I lowered myself in as deep a curtsey as I thought appropriate, holding out the sides of my rose-coloured skirts and only just able to hear the soft rustle of the very expensive cloth above the chatter of her women. William had blanched when his clerk had told him how much the silk had cost but I thought the final result was worth every penny.

'Very prettily done.'

She looked me up and down in an admiring way, noting the cut of my gown and my fashionable hair arrangement with the pearls sewn into the golden nets.

'Now,' she said. 'Tell me who you are, Mistress Montagu, and what I can do for you?'

'I am the king's cousin,' I began.

She clapped her hands together. 'Of course you are! I see it now. You are Edmund's daughter; I should have guessed. You have his eyes and his hair and the way you stand. Oh my dear; you bring it all back.' She wiped a tear from her eye.

I wriggled my toes in my slippers and wondered how much she knew.

'I believe you were acquainted with my parents, Countess?'

'We were close,' she confided. 'In Paris we were very close. I was your mother's confidante when she and Queen Isabella fell out. But it was such a long time ago and of course of no interest to somebody young like you.'

'On the contrary, I was hoping you would tell me about my father. I know so little and people don't like to talk about him.'

She smiled with a twinkle in her eye as if what she was about to divulge was something sinful but pleasurable. I guessed she was a woman who liked winkling out other people's most intimate secrets.

'What a handsome young man he was. The women ran after him. When he was young he was a heart-breaker but later he had eyes for no-one but your mother and she, wise woman that she was, accepted his courtship. Isabella was furious.'

She chuckled like a fat hen disturbed from her nest.

'Countess, do you know why he was killed?'

Her eyes widened and bulged like a startled animal. 'Killed? Oh yes, but, my dear, that was after we came back to England. A terrible, terrible time. My husband didn't know who to trust, it was truly dreadful.'

'His Grace said my father discovered Lord Mortimer's secret.'

'Ah, Lord Mortimer. Now there was an evil rogue for you. A charming man but what a rogue. I can see him now, smiling and dangerous. He had your mother and dear Isabella like that.' She held her hand gripped into a fist. 'And of course poor Isabella's son, His Grace, caught like a fly in their web.'

She stopped and smiled at me. 'You'd never think to look at us now, how much we suffered in those years.'

'Lord Mortimer's secret?' I prompted her. She was like all old ladies, prone to ramble on and forget what she was supposed to be talking about.

She narrowed her soft old eyes, until they almost disappeared into the pouches of skin, and dabbed at her lips with a cloth. 'Lord Mortimer had a dozen secrets and each one more dangerous than the next. I warned Isabella but she was beyond listening. She believed he loved her but he was like all men and loved only himself.'

'Which of his secrets would my father have known?' I asked.

'Oh secrets, secrets! Everyone had secrets in those days, girl. We learned to keep our mouths shut and our secrets close to our chests.'

She tapped her handsome bosom as if she had half a dozen stuffed down her gown but I thought with a loose tongue like hers I wouldn't trust her with anything of importance.

I felt the old frustration of being lost in a maze where everyone else knew the thread which led to the centre but no-one would tell me. If I didn't know what the secret was, I would never know why my father was killed and if my cousin could have saved him.

'I hear you're married to the Montagu boy,' she said. 'Not clever like his father from the look of him, but perhaps he warms your bed nicely.'

I murmured something about how much I had been honoured by my marriage and how good my husband was to me; the sort of words which meant nothing.

'Montagu did well for himself. None of us would have marked him down to be given an earldom but of course the king was in his debt. In and out of the royal chambers all the time, he was. Now there was a man who knew everyone's secrets.'

'Sir William?' I was astounded. It had never occurred to me that my father-in-law might know.

'Silent as a weasel and crafty as a fox. You never knew where he was hiding or what he'd heard.'

'What could he have heard?'

But Countess Jeanne had had enough. She licked her lips and sniffed,

'What do you want to know about all that old stuff? It's past and gone and of no interest to anyone now. Even Isabella has forgotten and I expect your mother has too. Nobody wants to remember those days. Leave it behind and don't ask because nobody will tell you.'

With that she patted me on the arm and made me turn so she could admire my gown some more. She touched my hair with her podgy fingers and asked to see my new slippers and proceeded to tell me a long involved story about her husband's earlier indiscretions with a woman called Maud Nerford.

'He wants a divorce but as I told him the last time we discussed the matter, marriage is indissoluble in the eyes of God. Once a man and a woman give their consent freely, the bond is forged and cannot be broken. When he married me I became his wife and I shall remain his wife until God releases one of us.'

I felt a trifle unsteady as I walked away. I had given my consent freely when I'd married Thomas Holand and I wondered what God must think of my marriage to William. Had we tried to break an indissoluble bond and if it was indissoluble, how could William be my husband?

I knew what I had to do. On our return to Bisham I would beg an audience with my father-in-law and ask him what had happened all those years ago. He was fond of me and would, I thought, tell me the truth. I needed the honesty of his words because I was certain everyone else was lying.

Perhaps I had been right that summer at Framlingham when I believed my cousin was a murderer, perhaps it was to his advantage that my father was killed; perhaps it was not Lord Mortimer's secret which was being protected but my cousin's. But I could think of no secret which could be so dangerous that it must be kept hidden at all costs, even at the expense of my father's life.

Next morning there was jousting. William looked every inch the sturdy fighter as he took the field against a burly young man who rode in Lord Henry's train. William needed to do well if he was to be noticed by Edward and yet he showed no trace of nervousness. I was immensely proud of him and had told him so early that morning as we attended Mass.

His tournament armour was new and had been commissioned at huge expense but he looked so brave and so handsome I thought I might even have forgone my rose-coloured silk if he had needed the money. Beneath his breastplate he carried a small wisp I had cut from my sleeve and I prayed it would bring him luck. I had planted a kiss lovingly on the silk before I gave it to him and would have liked to kiss his mouth but thought it would be more prudent to smile sweetly.

'Your William rides like a man determined to win,' Alice remarked after my husband had won yet again.

'No he doesn't,' said Margaret who always liked to disagree with Alice. 'William rides like a man with only one idea in mind and that's the total annihilation of his opponent. Look how his horse never veers off course and how even at the last moment his lance remains steady and true to the target. He has the courage of a true fighter.'

My father-in-law was next and a cheer from the crowd greeted one of their favourites, the man who'd been at the king's side since before I was born and who even now in middle age was a ferocious adversary. His opponent was an insignificant knight from Suffolk, all drooping shoulders and thin legs, who looked puny beside the mighty Earl of Salisbury.

I watched in admiration as William's father was strapped safely into his armour and prepared to take to the field. His glossy black horse draped in the Montagu colours stood pawing the ground and shifting its hindquarters, impatient to be off. The earl's squire passed over the helm and checked it was properly secure before helping him into the saddle.

My father-in-law looked magnificent with the burnished metal of his armour gleaming brightly and the vivid red plumes on his helmet bobbing majestically in the cold winter air. He acknowledged receipt of his weapons and his shield with a brief nod, weighed the lance in his hand and once satisfied with the balance peered through the eye slits fixing his opponent's position. His squire checked the stirrups and made last minute adjustments to the harness and at last the earl was ready.

I heard the trumpet sound and the herald call the names and saw the horses sidestep and turn and stand and at the signal gather their hooves together and begin their headlong thundering down the course. I heard the noise of lances clashing onto shields and the roar of the crowd and a moment of utter silence before the upswelling groan. He was off his horse! The Earl of Salisbury had been felled.

'Holy Mother of God!' cried Margaret, 'He's down!'

My father-in-law lay in the mud. He didn't move.

'Holy Virgin, keep him safe,' I whispered.

The earl's squire and two of the Montagu grooms ran across the grass and the lowly knight brought his horse back and dismounted, joining the small knot of people gathered round the figure on the ground. I waited to see him sit up and be helped to his feet but nothing happened.

William came, still half-buckled into his armour. A man was sent running and returned a moment later with two others carrying a board.

'They'll carry him back to his pavilion,' said Alice. 'It's only a fall, he can't be badly hurt, it's not as if it's a mortal wound or anything like that.'

But she was wrong.

He lay flat on his back, his eyes closed and his breathing shallow. His armour had been unstrapped and his arms and legs seemed straight and unbroken and there was no blood but he didn't move and he didn't open his eyes and he didn't speak. William spoke urgently to his father's unresponsive body on the litter while Lady Catherine and Elizabeth stood nearby, weeping.

'Should they move him onto the bed, make him more comfortable?' I whispered.

'How would I know?' Elizabeth said. 'What if he has broken some part of himself; they might damage him further.'

At that moment the royal physician arrived with his books and cups and proceeded to force a way through the crowd of onlookers to where the earl lay.

'He will he live, won't he?' I asked Edward's friend, John Chandos who had come to see how matters stood.

He sighed, rubbing the side of his cheek in a distracted way. 'I pray so, Mistress Montagu, I do pray so, but I've seen many men fall in that way, apparently grievously injured yet with not a mark on them and they have all died. A knight from Bordeaux once told me they bleed inside, however impossible that may sound.'

'But the bleeding might stop.'

He said nothing.

'It was only a fall,' I protested. 'There was no wound and the physician found no broken bones. Surely he'll live?'

We took him home to Bisham.

Over the next week dozens of people gathered at his bedside: his mother, his wife, both his brothers, his brother-in-law, three of his sisters and all his children, and me, his only daughter-in-law. Every one in the household wept as if tears could heal whatever afflicted the earl. His daughters were inconsolable but Lady Catherine stood stony-faced, unmoved by grief except for a single tear which trickled down her cheek. Every so often she gently wiped it away.

When we knew there was no further hope the senior men of the earl's household and his chaplain and his confessor commenced the sombre formalities of dying. At the very end it fell to Bishop Simon to impart to his brother what was required of him by the living and to receive from his lips any secrets which could in no wise be heard by anyone not sanctioned by God or by the Montagu family.

'*In manus tuas Domine*,' murmured Bishop Simon, leaning close to his brother's lips, hoping to catch a last word.

'*Commendo spiritum meum*.'

But he was too late. Dawn was breaking over Quarry Wood and the Earl of Salisbury had stopped breathing. He had commenced his final journey alone into eternity and all our prayers had been in vain. He hadn't spoken from the moment we'd left Windsor ten days earlier and had never once opened his eyes, yet I was certain he knew he had come home.

That night William and his brother kept vigil over their father's body and within two days every inch of Bisham from the great hall of the Temple knights to Lady Catherine's pretty solar was draped in black cloth. The earl's embalmed body lay in the chapel on a black velvet bier surrounded by dozens of candles and an army of weepers and I grieved at the sight.

He had been a good man and he had been kind to me. I hadn't expected him to die so soon and whatever secrets he carried, the secrets he might have imparted to me, died with him and I would never know what they were.

The funeral three weeks later was an agony of mourning. The Montagu chaplain read the eulogy and Bishop Simon spoke eloquently and at length of his brother's magnificent achievements and virtuous life. Bishop Grandison officiated at the Mass and I heard the sorrow in his voice, knowing that his brother-in-law, his great friend of over twenty years, was dead.

Every one of the earl's close companions was there: all the envoys he had served with on the king's foreign missions and the knights he had fought with in Scotland and Flanders and Castile, all the men of importance from miles around. The pages and grooms and yeoman of the household crowded by the chapel door and in the silences all I could hear was the aching sound of loss.

Only one person was missing and that was the king.

'He couldn't come,' said Lady Beaumont. 'The Montagu quarrel was public and very bitter and concerned the king. Words were said which could never be unsaid, terrible words, heard by others. There was so much talk and for him to come would only have made matters worse. It was better for him to stay away.'

'But he was his closest friend,' I protested. 'They'd always been together. They loved each other.'

Lady Beaumont sighed. 'It was a tragedy. Lady Catherine tells me she will retire into the seclusion of a life of prayer.'

'She'll take the veil?' In my darkest moments I'd thought Lady Catherine might pace the chambers of Bisham for the rest of my married life, a martyr to her suffering, and mine.

'A vow of chastity. She says there is no place for her at court now her husband is dead and she is most certainly right. What could be worse than to be publicly spurned by the king? He'd have to ignore her. You do see that don't you?'

I did. My cousin wouldn't risk his royalty for anyone. He hadn't risked his good name for me and he certainly wouldn't do it for Lady Catherine. Whatever meagre feelings he had once had for her, she had caused gossip and distress and tarnished his good name abroad and I knew he would not be pleased.

That night William returned to my bed for the first time since his father's death. He looked suspiciously at the slippery silk of my nightgown and placed his hand firmly on my defiantly slim belly.

'It is imperative you give me a son, Joan.'

This was an order which I would disobey at my peril.

'I understand, William. I too pray for a child.'

'Why haven't you conceived? We've been lying together for two years. What's wrong with you?'

'Nothing's wrong with me. I take the greatest of care of my soul as you know and I follow your mother's advice in this matter as I do in all things.'

'My sister tells me Arundel's wife was fourteen when his son was born and Northampton's wife barely fifteen. They were younger than you. And I've not neglected you.'

'No, William, you've been very attentive.'

'So why?'

William was impatient but I had no answers for him. It was a mystery why some women were blessed and others were not. Without a single word, he reached for the hem of my nightgown, prepared to force a child on me if he could. Obediently I rolled onto my back and spread my legs. This was William's own particular battleground and I had long since learned that tender kisses were not part of his armoury. A quick surrender was the best possible tactic for a wife faced with total subjugation.

It was six months since the death of William's father and this was the last day Lady Catherine would walk the halls of Bisham pretending she was the chatelaine.

For someone about to enter a life of prayer and simplicity I thought she was taking a great too many chests of fine gowns and choice linen veils, not to mention all those fur-trimmed cloaks and that magnificent silver-bound coffer overflowing with rubies and pearls. But the Montagu jewels were not leaving Bisham; those she had reluctantly passed over to William to be given to me.

To my dismay she had commanded the two best hangings from the solar, insisting they were personal gifts from her husband and needed for her new home. When I protested to William, he said the house in the outer precinct of the London convent where his mother was to live out her widowhood was large and naturally he wanted her to be comfortable.

Throughout the morning dozens of corded boxes containing enamelled ewers, bowls, napery and other items necessary for this comfort were carried down the steps to be loaded onto the wagons and I began to wonder if William and I would be left with anything.

'The dowager countess desires your presence, my lady,' grovelled one of Lady Catherine's elderly women.

I presumed the crones would disappear behind the convent walls with my mother-in-law as I certainly didn't want any of them in my chamber.

'Lady Catherine!' I swept an elegant reverential curtsey, thinking with glee that this would be the last time. By this evening she would be gone and Bisham would be mine, mine and William's.

She was seated in the best chair dressed in her widow's garb looking grey, tired and barely half the woman she had once been. The sheen on her skin was gone and the lines round her eyes and her mouth had deepened, sinking into the flesh, giving her the appearance of a wizened old woman. But those eyes had lost none of their glitter and the look she gave me was one of pure, undiluted hatred. I hastily crossed my fingers.

'I shall not see you again,' she said, honouring me with no greeting. 'After today you will be dead to me. You may be my son's wife but I shall no longer regard you as my daughter-in-law. For what you have done I can never forgive you. You may look to God for forgiveness but my prayers will not aid you in your quest.'

Her whole body quivered with such fury that I stepped back in alarm wondering which of my particular sins had given rise to this vituperative attack.

'You killed my husband as much as if you had plunged a dagger into his breast. But for you, he would still be alive.'

'I did nothing, my lady.' I protested, thinking she had run mad.

'Nothing was it?'

She beckoned me forward until I stood within her reach. Beneath the cloying perfume which permeated the heavy folds of her widow's weeds I could smell hatred on her breath. She thrust out her hand. On her finger gleamed a huge emerald the size of a pigeon's egg.

'My husband gave me this on the day he was raised to his earldom. It was the culmination of everything we had worked for all those years, the bringing of our family close to the king. You should understand that every single thing I have ever done was intended to further the honour of this family. My lord and I beggared ourselves, throwing ourselves in the way of dangers you could not even imagine, to ensure we always came first. It was what my husband wanted.

'The marriages of my other children were put at the king's disposal so we could have his favoured cousin for our son. We settled it together but when I saw you I knew we had made a terrible mistake, I knew that you, with your simpering smile and golden hair, would cause us nothing but grief and I have been proved right.'

Rather than look into her eyes as she slandered me, I stared at the glowing green jewel on her hand, but I have never liked emeralds and I didn't like Lady Catherine's ring.

'Before we left for Windsor, my lord paid a visit to my son's old steward who was said to be close to death. The man was a Montagu servant of long-standing with sins on his conscience and he wished to unburden himself. He told my husband of a night when the king came late to the house, asking for hospitality, and of the lady who made her liege lord welcome not only in her hall but in her bed. He spoke of the king's valet sent away, a maid locked in the wardrobe and cries of passion from my lady's chamber. He mumbled of a meal taken together and the lady's hair spread about her like a wanton. The old man said his duty was clear and if wrong had been done it was only right that my husband should know. He was old and befuddled and made my lord believe that the lady was me.'

Holy Virgin! I had never considered the steward. I should have done because his sly little eyes were everywhere. But in his agitation to confess, the man remembered Lady Catherine's seductive glances, her clinging to my cousin's arm, her whispering in my cousin's ear and had become muddled.

My knees trembled and I could think of nothing to say.

'My lord accused me of infidelity,' said Lady Catherine flatly.

'I am certain you were never anything other than a loving and dutiful wife,' I said opening my eyes innocently.

She had the grace to look disconcerted.

'I have never given myself to any man except at my lord's command,' she said levelly.

I stared at her in surprise. It was hard to believe the earl had instructed his wife to seduce the king but perhaps when they were young, when Sir William was eager to rise… he would not have been the first man to thrust his wife between a king's sheets to gain royal favours and Elizabeth had said her mother had been a beauty in her youth.

'We all obey our lords,' I said silkily. 'My husband bade me follow your example in every respect and you taught me that obedience is a wife's foremost duty.'

'You don't fool me,' she hissed. 'You never have. You're a little whore, nothing but a whore and a slut. I knew it the moment I set eyes on you. If you hadn't seduced the king, my husband would never have given in to his suspicions.'

Suddenly her shoulders sagged and she looked beaten

but there was nothing I could say or wanted to say which would comfort her.

'My conscience is clear,' she pronounced as if that was the end of the matter. 'He was distraught with grief at what he thought I'd done and no matter how much I protested my innocence he didn't believe me. I was angry but he was angrier by far and before we could resolve our quarrel he went straight from our chamber to the field to don his armour.' Her voice cracked. 'All those straps and buckles, all that metal, his helmet, the painted shield, the holy relics to keep him safe, and yet he died.'

She was weeping and I felt a wave of compassion. She hadn't been kind to me but in her end, I pitied her. But a woman like Lady Catherine would never admit defeat. She hadn't finished with me and with her last shaft, showed her determination to destroy me.

'My son will accompany me on my journey,' she said looking me straight in the eye. 'I shall tell him exactly what I have just told you. I shall furnish him with the knowledge of what I saw a year ago last autumn and spare him none of the details however distasteful because it is only right that a husband knows his wife is a whore. He will be left in no doubt and you will have the pleasure of awaiting his return wondering what he will do with you. You will sweat with fear, believe me, and before the week is out your bowels will have turned to water.'

She smiled with her teeth but nothing reached her eyes which were full of the cold, wet slime of black bile.

'My son is a more violent man than his father ever was, and if it was in my nature to pity you, I would do so, because you will suffer greatly at his hands.'

With that she rose from her seat, brushing past me as if I wasn't there. I heard her order her chair to be brought and her women to be summoned. She was ready to leave.

I watched from the top of the steps as Lady Catherine's retinue followed her carriage out of the courtyard, the loaded wagons creaking heavily as they passed under the shadow of the gatehouse. And I observed William mounted high on his horse, noticing the muscular strength of his hands, the mound of power in his shoulders, the sturdy grip of his thighs and I shivered at the thought of the punishments he might devise when he heard the story of my past misdeeds.

It was three weeks before he returned and from the moment he crossed the threshold, Bisham became a place of ominous silences. My mother had once told me of what might happen should the Montagu men turn against me but I hadn't heeded her. I had prepared no defences. My brother was too young and I had no father to take my part and no cousin who would shelter me from my husband's wrath.

For two days no word was brought to me and I didn't know where William was. There was no sign of him in the hall where I dined alone at the high table with the eyes of the household following my every move. The few people from Great Marlow who had come to watch us dine would have observed the richness of my clothing and the fashionable trimmings on my mourning gown; they might even have commented on what a shame it was that the lady's famous golden tresses were hidden beneath an ugly grey veil, but I doubted they would have noticed the slight tremor in my fingers or the fact that I could barely swallow.

Later, I caught one of William's grooms on the stairs. 'Where is your master?' I asked, giving him an empty smile.

'In the chapel, my lady.' The man waited, but I waved him away.

When I was a little girl still playing in the nursery, Lady la Mote had said that an unpleasant task was always best done quickly before you had time to think of a hundred reasons why you might wish to avoid it. That way you would never suffer the worry which robs you of a night's sleep. I needed to face my husband's wrath soon because I had already lost too many nights of sleep with an anxious churning in my belly.

I went swiftly back to my room and washed my face. I dabbed some rosewater on my neck and shoulders, pinched my cheeks to give them a better colour, and thus prepared, went down the stairs to find my husband.

I opened the door quietly. The chapel glowed in the light of a dozen candles but it felt as cold as the tomb and I shivered. He was kneeling on the altar steps with his head bowed, still wearing his mourning clothes. I tiptoed soundlessly until I stood behind him. His head moved slightly, indicating his awareness of my presence. I moistened my lips in my nervousness, reminding myself that this was William and he loved me.

He rose and turned his face towards me. It was streaked with dried tears but as hard as the rocks in Quarry Wood.

'My uncle beats his wife,' he said coolly as if discussing the price of a sack of wool. 'Sometimes he uses his fists but if he has a mind to, he takes a stick or uses his belt. He says a man mustn't shirk from his duty but strike until the skin is split as otherwise there is no lasting pain or hope of redemption. Once he took her to the chapel to confess her sins and had his men hold her while he whipped her.'

Alice! Oh Holy Mother of God! My legs began to tremble and I felt sick.

'He says it is the only way to assure himself of an obedient wife. Do you think I should take my whip to you? It would give me the greatest pleasure to hear you whimper as the lash cuts into your flesh and the blood runs red against the white of your skin.'

His eyes glittered.

'Or shall I put you in a nunnery? My mother tells me of a place she knows where the rule is strict. The women have barely enough to eat and spend all day and night on their knees praying for God's mercy. They are rarely permitted sleep. I need never see you again and you would remain there to the end of your days. They'd shave off your hair which would be a shame, but there'd be no-one to see and my mother says it is a snare for men's lust.'

I instinctively put up my hand to protect my hair as if William would attack me that very moment with his knife.

'A nun's habit is coarse compared to silk, but it would be so cold you'd seek warmth anywhere, even in plain homespun. And if your prayers were not sufficiently penitent I should require a shirt of goat's hair, one which would scourge your skin each time you moved. My mother says the wearing of this garment can induce such ecstasies of pain, a woman prays to whichever saint she calls her own, for a speedy release in death.'

'William, please!'

'Or I could lock you in the tower room. It's bare and there's only a narrow window. You'd never escape. But I'd be merciful, I'd let you have some straw, you wouldn't have to lie on the floor. And I'd see you fed, you could have the crusts left over from my table, sufficient to keep the flesh on your bones. I'd hold the key so there'd be no point in trying to bribe your gaoler with whatever was left of your charms. I'd visit you if I so desired, if I fancied seeing what imprisonment would do to your spirit. Women go mad in prison, you know, it's to do with the way they are: weak, feeble creatures who need a man to rule them.'

'Please, William. Don't do that to me. Please.'

I began to cry.

He ignored my tears, closing his fingers painfully on the soft flesh above my wrist.

'I can do anything I like to you, wife,' he hissed. 'Anything at all.'

He turned on his heel and strode out of the chapel, still holding my wrist, leaving me stumbling in his wake. When we reached his private room he thrust me onto a stool where I sat shivering, terrified of what would come next.

'How could you do this to me?' he hissed. 'I clothe you, I feed you, I give you gifts and honour your bed and yet you betray me. Why?'

'It's not what you think, William,' I babbled. 'I didn't want it to happen. I couldn't stop him. He was stronger than me.'

'You could have resisted. A virtuous woman would have held him off.'

'I did. You must believe me, William. I tried to resist but he told me it was an honour to be desired by the king and I should be grateful. He said a husband who stepped aside would be pleased because his wife would bring him royal favours.'

'I received no favours,' he spat. 'Not one single manor or preferment came my way so clearly you didn't please him.'

'He hurt me, William, he hurt me horribly.'

'You could have called for help.'

'He covered my mouth. I couldn't scream. I prayed for you to come and rescue me but you were a day's ride away and I was alone. I prayed to Our Lady but...'

I had spent two years carefully revisiting the events of that October and had convinced myself I'd been far from willing. My cousin had imposed his attentions on me, forced me to raise my skirts, coerced me into his arms and persuaded me into a night-long indulgence of his lust. I was totally innocent. None of it was my fault.

I wasn't sure if William gave credence to my story but with disaster staring me in the face, the deceits slipped readily off my tongue.

He wanted to believe me, I could see it in his eyes. He was only sixteen, still partly a boy, and didn't want to think I had lied to him. Somewhere in his mind he held the image of a perfect wife. I was young, I was beautiful, he desired me. I was his bedded wife so I must be true to him. It was against everything he understood as God's order for a man and a woman for this not to be so.

'Why did you break your fast with him?' he said, his eyes glinting with suspicion. 'My mother says you were half-naked with your hair down.'

'Oh William, I was not half-naked and my hair was down because he ordered it left unbound. I was frightened he'd hurt me again. I had to do as I was told.'

He placed a cold hand on my cheek.

'Did… did you let him…?'

'It was rape, William.'

There was complete silence. He chewed his lip and I sensed his anguish. But in his eyes I detected uncertainty. Please God, let him believe me because I didn't want to end my days in some dark cold place where I'd never see the light of day.

'You refused him?'

'Yes.'

'You didn't want him in your bed?'

'No. I only ever wanted you.' May God forgive me the lie but it was necessary.

'Yet you opened your legs for him.'

'It was not what I wanted.'

He knocked me sideways off the stool.

'Whore!' he hissed and strode out of the room leaving me lying on the floor.

I picked myself up, examining my face with my fingers. I was unharmed. I whispered a quick prayer, thanking the Holy Virgin. At least he hadn't tried to kill me.

He might not have tried to kill me but he wasn't prepared to live with me in amity, he made that perfectly plain. Next day, in a cold little interview where his eyes never quite met mine, he informed me that when he was at Bisham I was to keep to my rooms. I might dine in the hall when he was absent but not when he was there. Any personal duties which in the past I had carried out for him

221

would henceforth be performed by someone else and I was not to seek him out in any way.

As I watched him ride out along the road to Great Marlow I knew our marriage was irretrievably broken. In my pride and my carelessness I had damaged it beyond repair. My duty as a king's granddaughter had been clear but vanity and self-will had been my undoing. As a wife, I should have laced tighter the bonds between my new family and my royal cousin, yet I had been unthinking in my care for my husband.

During the months of our estrangement I found the barren hours filled with uncomfortable truths about myself. My mind wandered, tiptoeing through the past, my sins sliding out of the shadows, worming their way through my defences until I was forced to look them honestly in the face. I was in no way innocent. It was painful to acknowledge my complicity in the dalliance I had enjoyed with my cousin, but even more painful to admit the wrong I had done in marrying Thomas Holand. Forgetting him would be my penance.

When prayer and contemplation failed to remedy the situation I found unexpected comfort in the acerbic company of the prior. He understood my plight without my explaining anything and our lengthy discussions concerning worldly sin and God's forgiveness did much to pour balm on my bruised and battered soul. On days when I became too maudlin and was close to tears he would make me smile with stories of how the canons had hitched up their garments and taken refuge on top of the priory's wine barrels when the river had flooded. If nothing else, that long dark winter brought me to a maturity and wisdom I hadn't possessed before and a greater understanding of a woman's role in God's great plan.

Eventually, desire and loneliness drove William back to my bed and in the cold light of a rainy evening soon after the feast day of St Matthias we tentatively reconsummated our marriage. The first time brought little pleasure to either of us but gradually we learned to be kind to each other and by the summer there was reason for me to hope that all was not lost.

'I have spoken with my mother's brother, the Bishop of Exeter,' said William. 'My father regarded him as a clear-headed man whose advice was sound. He says I should forgive you.'

I gave a weak smile. 'I do not deserve your forgiveness, William, but if you should find it in your heart to forgive me I promise to be the best wife you could have. I will do anything for you.'

He looked at me with eyes which were dark and empty of any passion.

'My uncle says forgiveness is a virtue and even a lewd and sinful woman can be redeemed if she is forgiven. He says you were very young and I left you unguarded.'

The lessons I had learned from Lady Catherine in the houses of Antwerp and Ghent proved invaluable in the months which followed as I trained myself to become the perfect wife for William, and when he gave me a pretty little enamelled brooch I knew I had succeeded in transforming myself in my husband's eyes. I was dutiful and loving and never complained no matter what he asked of me.

8

THE PRINCE 1345-6

One evening at the beginning of December we sat together in William's room where the crackling fire gave out surprisingly little heat. It felt cosily domestic with just the two of us seated side by side in front of the hearth and one of William's greyhounds stretched lazily at his feet. We spoke idly of household matters and whether or not Gascony would be the destination for the king's army next year and I amused myself by wondering how I could persuade our neighbour to sell me his grey mare which I coveted. I regretfully came to the conclusion it would cost more than William could afford.

'The king is to hold Christmas at Westminster,' said William, not looking at me but staring into the flames.

I waited patiently as clearly there was more. This was William and in the past months I had studied him carefully and had begun to understand the devious workings of his mind.

'I have received an invitation to join in the festivities and have decided to let you accomany me.'

'Me?' I said, startled out of my contemplation of the curve of his rather fine legs.

'Yes, you are my wife. Why shouldn't I take you?'

I smiled sweetly and murmured that there was indeed no reason.

'Good,' he said, tapping his fingers on the arm of the chair.

Nothing was said for a few moments while he kept his face turned to the fire and I considered the exciting possibility of a new gown.

At last he spoke. 'My Uncle Grandison tells me a clever man is one who knows the value of his worldly goods and how best to work them to his advantage.'

'The bishop is truly a wise man,' I said absentmindedly, wondering why after a year and a half of keeping me immured at Bisham my husband now wished to offer me up to public scrutiny. We had been content here these past months and I was nervous of anything which might disturb the calm waters of our marriage.

He slowly turned his head until he was gazing into my face.

'You are my greatest treasure, Joan,' he said leaning over and giving me a lingering kiss on my lips causing me to blush as I remembered his passionate embraces of last night. 'At Westminster you will be by my side in the manner of a dutiful wife and I want you to use your influence on the prince.'

'On Edward?'

'Yes, I need his favour and you can get it for me. You know how to flatter a man. I've watched you weave your coils round those fat old knights who frequent our hall. It's a skill some women possess. My mother had it and you have it too.'

'You want me to flatter the prince?'

'Joan, think for a minute. Every year Edward's power advances and his influence on the king grows. If we are to further the fortunes of our family, I need to be the person who is of greatest importance to Edward. I won't be pushed aside by men like Chandos.'

'That would be very wrong indeed, William,' I said, wondering how in Our Lady's name I was to do what he wanted. 'John Chandos can never be like you, he is nothing but the son of a gentleman.'

'You understand what I'm saying? I need to be the one at Edward's side and you are to help get me there. It was a duty my mother performed for my father. She once told me that to serve one's husband in whatever way he commanded was a woman's most Christian duty.'

'She was a true inspiration,' I said, almost choking on the words.

'A wonderful wife to my father,' sighed William. 'She would have done anything to further his ambitions.'

'But William…'

He frowned at my hesitation, reminding me, in case I should ever forget, how easily his temper could be aroused. 'There won't be any discussion about this, Joan; you will do as I say. Do you understand?'

Of course I understood. I knew exactly what was expected of me but it felt underhand and I didn't like it. Edward was my friend not some fish to be lured to the net.

It was strange to return to the royal palace at Westminster after all these years, no longer a child but the wife of a man who would soon be Earl of Salisbury. It was just as I remembered. The entertainments were as extravagant and magnificent as ever, and seeing my friends from the nursery again was a delight.

But there was one person not enjoying the festivities and that was the papal ambassador, Archbishop Canali, a continuing and unsettling presence amidst the gaiety. My cousin's senior commanders went in and out of the king's private rooms almost at will but the ambassador stayed where he was, huddled with his advisors in an outer chamber, unable to secure an audience with the king and showing all the signs of a man fast losing patience. I was intrigued to know why he was here and why my cousin was refusing to meet with him.

The archbishop may have been ignored but William was making good progress. He supped in private with Edward and on two occasions rode out with the king's party in the early morning. He was often in the company of his brother-in-law, Sir Hugh Despenser, and was included in meetings with the earls of Arundel and Warwick. I rarely saw him except sometimes at dinner.

'I am shamefully neglected,' I complained to Margaret. 'William sees more of your husband than he does of me.'

She laughed. 'All women are neglected when men are planning a campaign and some of us are mightily pleased.'

She stared consideringly at the front of my gown. 'I thought you and William had been busy squirrelled away at Bisham these past months but I see your labours have been in vain. Or am I missing something?'

'No,' I said gloomily. 'And it's not just William who is becoming impatient. My mother wants a grandchild. She tells me a concoction of nettles and raspberry leaves drunk three times a day never fails but it hasn't worked for me.'

'Have you tried may blossom beneath your pillow?'

'In the middle of winter?'

She laughed. 'Holly leaves?'

'A mite prickly. I think William would object.'

She gave me another sideways look.

'You are beginning to sound like a smug married woman, Jeanette. Do I assume William is not neglecting you?'

I blushed. 'No, he's very attentive.'

'Like Alice's husband. Another girl. Did you know?'

I shook my head, remembering with a shiver William's stories of what his uncle did to Alice.

'He is complaining it was a bad bargain he made with our father, says he married Alice to get sons not useless girls.'

'I'd be happy with a girl,' I sighed.

'Your husband wouldn't. I'll wager he wants a son.'

Remembering William's instructions, I left Margaret to her own devices and set out to find Edward. I wandered through endless painted chambers looking Edward but instead found Isabella sulking in her room, refusing to see anyone.

'She's in floods of tears,' whispered Joanna at the door. 'She had a meeting with our father in his private rooms and rushed back with a face like a thundercloud. Now she's hunched in a corner refusing to tell me what's the matter.'

'I won't stand for it,' a voice screamed. 'It's an insult! I'll boil him in oil, I'll tear out his innards, I'll… I'll…'

'Someone has annoyed her,' I observed.

'I know, but she's making no sense. I'd better go, Nettie; those girls of hers are useless. They flutter about mopping up her tears and that simply makes her angrier than ever.'

Joanna gave me a brief kiss and disappeared. As the door swung closed I heard a renewed torrent of abuse followed by a sharp slap, a girl's shriek and then silence.

Eventually I found Edward gambling in a side room with his friend John Chandos and a host of other young men.

'Jeanette!' he called, spying me through the open door. 'Come here!'

I walked over and swept the king's eldest son and heir a deep curtsey.

'God give you good day, my lord,' I said politely. 'I trust all is well?'

'It is.'

He looked pleased at my deference. He was sixteen, tall and well-built for his age and if you didn't know you might have taken him for an older man. His hair was darker and less luxuriant than his father's and his eyes were brown not blue but he was cut from the same royal cloth and had the straight nose and well-shaped lips of my cousin. He had grown to be very good-looking.

'I passed Archbishop Canali,' I said. 'He wasn't looking too pleased, I trust you haven't offended him?'

'By no means, but my father is avoiding him. The archbishop wants safe conducts for his peace-making cardinals and just at the moment my father doesn't want peace.'

'He doesn't?'

'Of course he doesn't. We have recaptured our castles in Gascony from the French and Lord Henry is sweeping through the Agenais taking town after town. If you're winning a war you don't make peace, you crush your enemy and then you make peace.'

That made perfect sense and I wondered why William was never able to explain matters as clearly as this.

'I went to Isabella's chamber but she didn't want to see me. Joanna says she's discomforted.'

'Oh Christ's blood!' Edward ran his fingers through his hair. 'I forgot. I am supposed to be mourning the loss of yet another bride my father was trying to buy for me. Chandos says Pope Clement is to rule against my marriage to the daughter of the Duke of Brabant on the grounds our fathers are cousins. It's of no consequence to me but Bella is distraught. She had her heart set on the duke's son. It was to be a grand double wedding with all the usual fuss. Now she's convinced Joanna will marry before her.'

'If I may say so, Edward, you don't sound very unhappy. Surely the loss of a bride should be a matter for sadness,' I teased. 'Perhaps you could shed a tear or two.'

He looked straight into my eyes as if he would read the words inscribed on my soul and said with all seriousness, 'I only wept for the loss of one girl in my life, Jeanette. I doubt I'll weep for another.'

I knew he was talking about me but it embarrassed me to hear him speak openly like this in front of his friends so I said lightly, 'But Edward, you must surely want to marry; your royal father certainly wants it.'

'The girl I wish to marry is wed to another,' he said bluntly. 'As it seems I cannot have her, marriage will have to wait and wagering is as good a diversion as any other. Come on, Jeanette, come and play dice with me.'

'Here?'

'Why not? We can squat on the floor and you can pull up your skirts the way you used to. Chandos will keep guard.'

I looked at the tiles and considered my best damask silk gown and its new ribbon trimmings which weren't designed for crawling around on the floor. But at the back of my mind were William's instructions, so I forgot my dignity and the matter of creases and sank down beside Edward. My skirts billowed out like the petals of an exotic flower.

'Edward,' I whispered.

'What?'

'Should we be doing this?'

He made the first throw.

'I do what I like, Jeanette. Nobody tells me what to do.'

He played skilfully and he was lucky but he wagered recklessly. If I'd been as favoured I could have beggared him in a dozen throws, but as it was I soon lost the few pennies I carried in my purse. A strand of hair fell over my eyes and I cursed my maid for not securing it properly.

I started to rise but he placed his hand firmly on my arm.

'Have some more coins. I'll make you a loan.'

'Not a gift?'

'No.'

'What if I lose these as well as those I've already lost?'

He grinned. 'Then you'll be doubly indebted to me and one day when you least expect it, I'll call in my loan.'

We played some more and he let me win a little but when it looked as if I might beat him he quickly concentrated and effortlessly defeated me, throw after throw until again I had nothing left. By now the tiles were cold beneath my skirts and if I *had* been an exotic flower I would certainly have withered and died.

'Joan!' It was William's voice from far above my head. 'What in Christ's name are you doing on the floor? Oh my lord, I didn't see you there.'

Edward rose slowly and elegantly to his feet, dusting off his knees, smiling in amusement. He was taller than William and broader in the shoulders; he looked older though he was the younger by two years. He extended a hand and helped me to my feet, smoothing the folds of my gown and touching my back in the intimate way of a lover.

'It's alright, Montagu,' he said carelessly. 'You can have your wife back. I've finished with her.'

There was a hiss and an indrawing of breath from those around us. What he'd said was unbelievably insulting both to me and to William. Everybody present knew it and they were waiting to see what William would do.

My husband stood like a young bull with his legs apart and his head tipped slightly forward ready for the charge. If it had been anybody other than Edward who had said those words William would have punched him in the mouth but he couldn't strike the king's son and he knew it.

'Come away, Montagu, leave it.' John Chandos saw the danger and had his hand on William's arm. 'Let it be. Take your wife away and keep her better guarded. It's not right for her to be here.'

William did nothing. I knew he was struggling to keep his temper under control and for a brief moment I thought he would hit Edward. Then, with a swift bow, he spun on his heel, grasped my wrist and pulled me roughly through the crowds and didn't stop until we reached our chamber. There he thrust me against the wall.

'What were you doing?'

'I was doing what you told me, William. I was encouraging a friendship between you and the prince.'

'What did you promise him?'

'Nothing, William,' I said wearily.

'So what was the wager? Your virtue?'

'No. We were playing for pennies, that's all.'

'On the floor?'

'Yes, he insisted.'

'And what else did he insist on?'

'William,' I protested. 'You ask me to flatter him, to be kind to him, to gain his attention. What do you expect me to do?'

'I don't expect you to be like that.'

'Like what?' I said, truly not understanding what I had done wrong.

'The way you look at him, the way you laugh and smile and give him your hands.'

'Oh William, he is Edward. I've known him since we were children. He's like a brother to me.'

He sat down heavily on a stool and put his head in his hands. 'He doesn't look at you the way a brother would,' he mumbled into his sleeve.

It was true, Edward didn't but I mustn't think of that now.

'Do you have feelings for him?' There was a catch and a note of desolation in his voice.

I knelt on the floor in front of him and laid my head in his lap. It was warm and comfortable and increasingly familiar and I knew instinctively what was needed. He was jealous and jealous husbands were dangerous. I wound my arms part way round his waist so that I almost held him in my arms.

'I love you, William,' I murmured quietly, raising my face to his, blinking back my tears. 'Only you, nobody else. You are everything to me. You are my beloved husband and all I want is what you want.'

'Truly?'

'Truly.'

He placed his hand on my head and gently stroked my cheek with his thumb, saying nothing and we stayed like that until the boy came in with the logs and we heard the sound of a trumpet calling everyone to supper.

Next morning, I thought I was dying.

'I did warn you,' said my lady companion unhelpfully.

'I know, I know,' I groaned, my belly cramping horribly as I retched for a third time.

'Would you like me to fetch some spiced ale? It's supposed to be good for this kind of thing.' She was being sour-faced and I wanted to hit her but hadn't got the strength.

'What kind of thing?'

'A child.'

'It is not a child.'

'If you say so.'

'Just get me a cloth,' I said, pushing the bowl to one side.

She got up and her skirts wafted past my nose. I grimaced in disgust at the smell of lavender and wormwood but although my belly protested it stayed quiet and I decided that perhaps I was not going to die after all.

I sat back on my heels and took a deep breath. I knew what this was, it was the consequences of greed. Too many sugared plums.

She gave the bowl and its noxious contents to my maid but stood dithering as if she couldn't think what to do next.

'Just tell her to get rid of it,' I said irritably. 'And fetch me some water. I need to wash my face.'

'We've missed the hunt,' she whined. 'Everyone's down in the yard and they're going without us.'

I dragged myself to the window and watched the procession of horses and riders pass through the archway out into the hazy winter sunshine. Everyone was beautifully dressed, the men laughing and joking at the prospect of a day in the saddle. I swear even the hounds had smiles on their faces. William rode in pride of place next to Edward. As he had said before he left, the reward was his and his alone. He hadn't needed my help. My rash behaviour had nearly spoiled his chances and he should have known better than to have allowed me to accompany him to Westminster. Then in a piece of calculated spite, he ordered me to stay in our room. I was not to follow the hunt.

'I am going to walk by the river,' I announced to my snivelling companion. 'You can stay here as I intend to go alone and you'd better get over your disappointment by the time I get back because it's hardly my fault we're stuck here.'

It was a small act of rebellion but it made me feel better.

A low mist hung over the river and I couldn't see much, just a single boat travelling quickly downstream on the outgoing tide. A few seabirds moved along the exposed banks, pecking in a desultory way in amongst the shingle and mud. Dark clumps of reeds on the far shore appeared in and out of the shifting mist and from somewhere across the water I heard a child's voice calling for its mother. Everything looked as grey and as miserable as I felt.

I heard footsteps coming down the path but took no notice, it would likely be some palace servant on his way to the kitchens or a messenger heading for the Westminster steps. My ears registered that whoever it was had stopped immediately behind me.

I didn't turn my head. I didn't look. I didn't move so much as my little finger but I didn't need to. I had recognised the steady tread of his boots and the familiar sound of his breathing; I didn't need to see his face or look into his eyes to know exactly who this was.

Very slowly I turned around.

Thomas Holand.

There was a sensation of the ground slipping away like the waters of the river and danger lapping at my feet.

We stood looking at each other. Neither of us said a word.

It had been four years and yet he'd barely changed. His face was a bit leaner, his eyes a bit darker and there was a small scar on his left cheek that hadn't been there before. He was bare-headed and the mist had beaded his hair with a fine speckling like dewdrops which made me want to stretch out my hand and brush them away.

All the words I'd imagined saying if I should ever meet him again dissolved the moment I saw him and I found myself as tongue-tied and as awkward as a country girl in the presence of her master.

'You've grown,' he said.

I shrugged in embarrassment.

'I thought you'd gone to Gascony.' I blurted out.

'Why would you think that?'

I shook my head and stared at my feet aware of how little had really changed in those four years for all my good intentions.

'I'm only here because my husband received an invitation,' I muttered, the words spilling out in a rush. 'I wouldn't have come if I'd known.'

'Wouldn't you?'

I open my mouth and then closed it again and found myself floundering.

His mouth twitched in a small smile and he took a step closer. I immediately took a step back.

'You're every bit as beautiful as you were,' he said gently. 'Old age hasn't spoiled your looks.'

I swallowed hard, trying to remember who I was: I was the lady of Bisham, I was William's wife. One day soon I'd be Countess of Salisbury.

I raised my head and stared him straight in the face. 'Why are you here, Sir Thomas? What do you want with me?'

He lowered his gaze to where my cloak was wrapped securely over the skirts of my gown.

'I heard you were unwell.'

For a moment I couldn't believe what he'd said. It was impossible that he could know.

'Who told you?'

He smiled as if our conversation was amusing.

'This is a royal palace. No bit of information is so small as not to be of value to some great man. And where there is a willing buyer you will always find a willing seller.'

'But I was in my room.'

He gave a short laugh.

'Oh come, my lady, you know how little maids love to chatter and as I'm sure you remember, I am an extremely good listener.'

I could feel the blush rising as I recalled the hours we had spent together and the words we had spoken; the way he had patiently listened to me as we had lain entwined in each others arms.

'You shouldn't take any notice of what maids say,' I said.

'Is it true?'

I looked at him warily. 'Is what true?'

'Is it a child?'

I couldn't believe he would ask me. Men didn't talk about such things. These were matters for women.

'Don't you dare question me,' I said, trying unsuccessfully to sound fierce. 'It's none of your business. It's a matter between my husband and myself.'

'Exactly. Between your husband and yourself. I told you once that you shouldn't risk a child because it would spoil our plans.'

I half-closed my eyes. I was lying in his arms in our bed beneath the thatch. He had held me close and kissed me and told me I was too young for a child. I remembered every moment, every touch of his fingers, every beat of his heart.

'I have no plans with you, Sir Thomas,' I whispered, feeling hot tears well up at the back of my eyes.

He reached out and took my hand and I didn't have the strength or the will to resist. He must have noticed the tears because he said gently, 'I'm sorry, I didn't mean to distress you but your care is my concern, it always has been.'

He began to stroke my fingers the way he had before, the way I remembered.

'You weren't just a little trinket I picked up and cast aside once I'd had my enjoyment, you know.' He paused and bent his head forcing me to look into his eyes. 'It was enjoyable, wasn't it my lady? I wasn't mistaken, it wasn't just wifely duty, was it?'

I felt a rush of desire which caused my legs to tremble and my heart beat faster. I wanted to close my eyes.

'Go away, please,' I said in a small voice. 'Leave me alone, there's nothing you can do for me.'

He continued to gaze into my face and then he said very slowly and deliberately, 'Oh I doubt that, I doubt it very much indeed. You look half-starved.'

It took me a moment to recover some semblance of composure.

'I have eaten perfectly well,' I said. 'My cousin, keeps a good table.'

He smiled and I swear he knew how my whole body was trembling.

'I didn't mean food. A woman can find herself starved of things other than what she takes from the table.'

I felt another blush rise up into my cheeks as I realised what he meant.

'My marriage has nothing to do with you,' I whispered.

He stepped closer so that our bodies almost touched and I was unable to pull away because he had hold of my hand.

'On the contrary,' he whispered into my ear. 'I think your marriage has everything to do with me. You may have forgotten the time we spent together in Ghent but I can assure you, I haven't.'

Of course I hadn't forgotten.

I raised my eyes to his. I could feel the tears beginning to spill over.

'Please leave me alone,' I whispered. 'I don't want to get into any more trouble.'

'The prince?'

I nodded.

He made a short dismissive movement and began to stroke my cheek.

'The whole palace is talking of little else. The king's son rolling on the floor with the wife of one of his noble friends. Now that is a very choice piece of gossip.'

I had to fight the desire to rest my head against his chest and allow myself to be folded into his arms.

'I wasn't rolling on the floor,' I said wearily. 'We were dicing.'

'I shan't tell you what the kitchen boys said you were doing, but dicing didn't come into it.'

'It was nothing,' I cried. 'Nothing. I was only doing what I was told to do.'

Montagu?' he asked.

'Yes.'

He let go of my hand and placed his arm round me.

'Does he hurt you?'

I shook my head. 'No, not any more.'

'But he frightens you?'

I nodded. 'Sometimes.'

'I'm sorry.'

I pulled myself out of his arms and stood facing him.

'There's no point in being sorry, Sir Thomas. Not now. You said there was nothing you could do and there isn't. I behaved foolishly and I have to live with the consequences.'

He turned his face to the river and for a few moments we stood there side by side watching the mist thin and shift and the opposite shore come into view.

'Come on, ' he said. 'It's cold, we'll walk a bit.'

I looked around, expecting to see a crowd of people.

'Don't worry,' he smiled. 'There's no-one, we're quite alone, they've all gone.'

He tucked my hand between his arm and the warmth of his body and together we walked slowly along the bank.

'You know we're leaving,' he said after a while.

I nodded.

'The king is taking his army overseas and when we get there we intend to hunt down the French king and bring him to battle. Like all battles it will be bloody and it will be dangerous and men will die.'

My heart lurched. I couldn't bear to think of him dying.

'Perhaps the French king won't fight,' I said. 'Perhaps he'll run back to Paris like he did before. He won't want to risk meeting our army in case he should lose.'

'No, that won't happen. This time the great men of France will make him fight. It has become a matter of honour.'

I was silent. What if he didn't come back? What would I do?

We stopped beside the shelter of a little wall where we were hidden from both the river and the palace.

'Do you still have the coin I gave you?'

The silver coin was hidden amongst the pearls and jewelled brooches, locked in the tiny coffer I kept in my chest. I had only taken it out twice since I had married William and each time the feel of it, cold and hard beneath my fingers had reduced me to tears. So now I left it alone.

When I didn't reply, he said, 'I want you to do something for me. I want you to promise that if I don't come back you will throw it in the river and forget me. Let it lie forever in amongst the stones and mud with the water flowing over it. Forget Ghent and the hours we spent together and tell yourself it never happened.'

He touched my wet face with his fingers and traced the curve of my mouth.

'But you will come back?'

This was no orchard and no springtime in Ghent but he was gazing at me the way he had then and I felt the ground shift.

'Light a candle for me,' he said softly. 'If I don't come back, light a candle, nothing more.'

'When are you going?' I whispered.

'The beginning of March.'

'But that's only two months away.'

'It has to be soon. The campaign has been a long time in the planning and we can't wait any longer.'

I nodded miserably. 'Of course, I understand how important this is.'

'Will you do as I ask?'

I nodded. 'Yes. But…'

He raised his eyebrows. 'But what?'

'I shall pray you come back.'

He laughed. 'If I can, I will. Now I must go. I am meant to be joining the hunt.'

He lifted my hand to his lips and slowly kissed the tips of my fingers one by one. Then he turned my hand over and kissed the palm.

'Thomas.' It was half a breath, half a whisper, said almost to myself.

Without another word he placed my hand over my heart and hurried back up the path with his cloak flapping wetly against his boots.

He'd gone barely a few yards when I called out.

'Thomas!'

He looked round.

'What?'

I hesitated.

'It was plums,' I said. 'It was just a surfeit of plums.'

He stared at me, not understanding. Then he smiled and his smile widened into a grin and he turned away. I heard him whistling as he walked back up the path and I watched as he went through the gate and disappeared under an archway of leafless branches.

I stood where I was for a very long time listening to the distant sound of hunting horns and the pitiful cry of a lonely seabird wheeling and diving in endless circles high above the water. I gazed at the relentless ebb and flow of the river and wished with all my heart that I was back in that tiny attic room in Ghent.

One day in late January William came to find me. I was in the solar engaged in the soothing occupation of sorting my silks. I would lay them on the table one by one and gaze at the bright colours trying to decide if they were pleasing together and whether the blue was exactly the right shade for the sky. My plan was to embroider a large new cloth while William was away. It was a daunting proposition and I hadn't yet decided what design I would have but it was a suitable occupation for a wife left at home and I hoped it would please him, because little else did these days. Since we had returned from Westminster he had been surly and bad-tempered, finding fault with everything I did.

He walked over to the window and looked out across the frosted fields.

'There is a man in the stable yard asking for you,' he said abruptly.

'For me?'

For a heart-stopping moment I feared it was Thomas but that was too ridiculous for words and even if it was, I wouldn't agree to see him. I wasn't stupid.

'Who is it?' I asked, not really wanting to hear the answer.

'Just some servant. He's asking for Mistress Montagu so I can only conclude he means you.' William's voice was cold and decidedly unfriendly.

'What does he want?'

'How would I know,' William said sulkily. 'It's none of my business. He has something for you, a gift.'

My mind was a complete blank. My mother was not in the habit of sending me gifts, she was more likely to send a letter citing my failure to provide her with half a dozen grandchildren. Margaret might buy me a little fairing but she wouldn't send it, she'd bring it herself and the idea of William's mother sending me anything other than an apple laced with poison was just laughable.

'I don't know anyone who would send me a gift.'

'Apparently you do. The man is wearing the prince's livery.'

'From Edward? For me?'

He shrugged. 'You'd better go and see. As I said, it's got nothing to do with me. I'm yet to be the recipient of a royal gift. You seem to be the one who is favoured.'

I hurried down to the yard wondering with a skip of a heartbeat what Edward could have sent me and hoping for William's sake it wasn't something too intimate. There was very little that I, as a married woman, could accept without my husband's approval. A jewel, I would have to return, I couldn't possibly keep something so extravagant, but a more modest gift, a trinket or a little enamelled brooch or a decorated pin, surely not even a jealous husband could object to something so insignificant.

I ran down the last of the steps and through the archway imagining all the glorious gifts Edward might have sent and wondering how I could persuade William to allow me to keep them. It wasn't as if Edward was my brother or close kin, he was the son of my cousin who if you wanted to be accurate was only a half-blood cousin at that.

The day was bright and cold and the yard half-deserted as I looked around for a man carrying a small package. But what I saw was something else entirely and not at all what I had expected.

She stood in the middle of our yard, the most beautiful creature I had ever seen in my life: dappled grey with a silvery-white tail and a mane like spun silk, slender legs and an elegant neck which arched like the curve of a bow. At the sound of my footsteps she turned her head gracefully and regarded me with her huge liquid eyes.

The man holding her rein smiled and gave a little bow.

'Is she for me?' I could barely believe that this enchanting creature could possibly be mine.

'If you are Mistress Montagu, my lady, then yes, she is for you.'

He fished in his pouch and handed me a letter. I hurriedly broke the seal and ran my eyes over the contents. It was very short.

"My dearest and sweetest cousin,
Greetings. Because I know you are sorely in need of a
mount of your own I am sending you this gift from my
stables. Her name is Blanchefleur and I would have
you treat her as you would treat me.
I remain your devoted and most loving friend
Edward
Given this 24th day of January at Kennington"

Sweet Jesus! This was a love letter and I was a married woman!

I read the words again, running my fingers across the smooth parchment and wondering if it smelled of him. I should send it back, I knew I should send them both back because it was wholly improper to accept a gift from another man, even from Edward. And a gift of such magnitude. But I couldn't send her back. It would be an insult and she was too precious, too beautiful, too much of what I had always dreamed: Blanchefleur; enchanting, magical, beautiful Blanchefleur.

In one long hot summer of our childhood he had been Sir Perceval, the knight who sought the golden Grail and I had been his sweetheart, Blanchefleur. Hidden amongst the bushes at Woodstock, as we crawled across the barren wastelands towards the secret castle of the Fisher King, he had kissed me, a boy's kiss but on my mouth and told me he was going to marry me. The leaves and twigs beneath my knees had been sharp and thorns had scratched my face but his clumsy kiss was what I remembered best, that and the way he had grasped my hand.

The mare warmed my cheek with her breath and gently nudged my shoulder.

'She's looking for a treat,' the man said. 'The prince likes me to look after her kindly so she's used to scraps of bread or an apple.'

'She's wonderful,' I said, stroking her long velvety nose.

She twitched her ears forward at the sound of my voice and leaned her head against mine.

'She knows her mistress,' laughed the man.

'Will she let me ride her?'

'Of course, my lady. She's used to the feel of a lad on her back and your skirts won't bother her. She's as docile as they come but with a big heart.'

'I don't know if my husband has a suitable saddle,' I said sadly, thinking of all the complications of Edward's gift.

The man smiled broadly. 'The prince had one specially made for you, my lady. It's in the wagon. It's a rare piece of workmanship, I've never seen a finer lady's saddle.'

It was very wrong of Edward to send me such extravagant gifts because he must know how insulted William would be, but as he had told me he always did as he liked. He didn't care what others thought.

William sulked for three whole days before I managed to persuade him that the gift of Blanchefleur was as much a tribute to him as it was to me and that it showed how much Edward appreciated him.

'Think, dearest,' I cajoled. 'If a man wishes to please another man, what better way than to send a gift to his lady. It is an oblique compliment, a clever way of showing how much he values you. And don't forget, it was you he chose to ride beside him on the hunt, not John Chandos. It was your company he sought.'

William grunted and continued his contemplation of the dregs in his cup.

'And he could hardly have given the mare to you,' I teased. 'Your legs are much too long.'

That brought a smile to his lips. He always enjoyed me complimenting him on his rather fine figure and I knew how proud he was of his shapely legs.

'I'll wager the next surprise will be for you and it will be something of much greater value than a horse, a silver cup or maybe some preferment.'

'Yes,' he said brightening up. 'If that rogue Walter Manny can be made the king's man in Merioneth, just think what I could be.'

I didn't show William the note but kept it tucked carefully into my clothing, reading it only when I was certain I would be undisturbed. I felt warmed by the steadfastness of Edward's devotion, smiling at the memory of that childish kiss and the promises he had made. I didn't love him, of course I didn't, but there was no harm in an idle flirtation with an old friend, especially one who was not only deliciously handsome but wonderfully generous and so very, very rich.

And I reckoned it was safer to think about Edward than to think about Thomas.

William finally left Bisham in the last days of May, dressed like a prince and accompanied by his Uncle Montagu and half a dozen local men who were riding with him. This was to be the greatest expedition ever undertaken by an English king and yet two months earlier it had seemed doomed to failure. Great storms had lashed the south coast of England and ruined my cousin's plans. Twice he had to reset the date for the departure of the fleet and twice William had raged and cursed and shouted as if the delay was entirely my fault. But now at last he grudgingly admitted everything was ready.

The requisitioning officers had done their job well and hundreds of ships lay at anchor in the harbour at Portsmouth. The army was not as large as my cousin had hoped but William said thousands of men were encamped in the meadows around the town and half way up the London road, all eager to set sail. Arrangements had been made for the protection of the coast and on every cliff top from Kent across Sussex and Hampshire and down into

Dorset, beacon towers had been built to give warning in case of a French attack.

I thought they would leave as soon as they found a fair wind but it was more than a month before I received a brief note from William. He was to sail on the afternoon tide. He didn't know where they were headed as their destination was a close-guarded secret but the captain of his ship had sealed orders which he would open once they were at sea. He would write again when they reached land.

I looked at the date. The eve of the feast day of St Peter and St Paul. I counted on my fingers. Three days ago.

'We can do nothing but wait,' I said to the men of my household. 'Wait and pray they arrive safely.'

It felt as if William's ship had been cut adrift and I feared my cousin was bent on leading his men to the uttermost ends of the earth. For those of us left behind it seemed like a dangerous journey into the unknown, one which might end in disaster.

I stitched a little ship on the very bottom of my cloth, a red one with a pretty white sail. I would stitch another one tomorrow and one the next day, one for each day until we heard they were safe.

By the middle of July and with no news, the household at Bisham started laying bets, every man convinced he knew exactly where the king's fleet had gone.

'It's like as if they've fallen off the very edge of the world,' said the little page from the ewery, carefully setting down my cup of ale.

I gave a tiny gasp.

'I'll edge of the world you, my lad,' said the steward. 'Don't you go frightening our mistress like that. And if you spill one drop of that good ale I'll see you never set foot in the hall again. You'll spend the rest of your days cleaning up horseshit.'

'Thank you, that was beautifully done.' I smiled at the boy who reddened to the tips of his ears and scuttled out like a frightened fawn.

'It's Gascony,' said the steward. 'It's got to be Gascony. My sister's husband knows a man who heard the French king's been given money for his war chest by that Frenchie Pope. It's paying for an army to destroy our Lord Henry, God bless him and bring him victory. Our king will not stand for that. He'll take his army to Gascony to help Lord Henry, you mark my words.'

'They're saying in Maidenhythe, the Earl of Northampton's been securing harbours on the coast of Brittany,' said the clerk of the wardrobe. 'He'd hardly be doing that if the king wasn't going to use them, would he?'

'My husband said the earl was returned from Brittany and planned to sail with the king,' I ventured.

'That proves it, my lady,' said the clerk of the wardrobe. 'Came to give the word first-hand, wouldn't trust anyone to carry the news but himself.'

'Last week in Great Marlow a silk merchant on his way to Oxford, said it's Flanders,' said the yeoman usher, pulling up a stool. 'He'd heard it straight from a Fleming in London and you can't get much closer to a horse's mouth than that.'

The clerk of the wardrobe spluttered into his ale and had to be thumped on the back by the usher.

'I'll wager it was a dockside tavern,' laughed the steward. 'Don't trust a man in a London alehouse if he says he's a Fleming because he might just be a Frenchie. My sister says the place is teeming with them. They're like rats, they're everywhere. They listen to what you say and then scurry back over the sea to tell their master.'

'Have you not heard anything, my lady?' said the usher.

'No, not yet, but I'm sure we'll hear soon. My husband promised to write when they reached their destination, but people say it's a very long way to Gascony.'

At that moment there was a shout from the yard and the sound of a horseman and almost before anyone could move, one of the little pages was up the steps and into the hall shouting that a messenger had arrived.

It was a letter from William, a proper letter, water-stained and well-travelled and this time there was no Lady Catherine to pluck it from my grasp.

With trembling fingers, I undid the seal.

"My dearest and most beloved companion"

Oh William, I thought. How conventional an opening. Perhaps he simply left that sort of thing to his clerk, I could imagine him waving his hand and instructing the man to "start in the usual fashion".

I smoothed out the letter and began to read.

"You will be glad to receive news that we have landed safely on the Wednesday before St Margaret's day after a journey of many travails. We lay at anchor off a great

252

open beach to the south of a little port called La Hogue
in the part of Normandy called the Cotentin."

I looked up at the expectant faces. 'Normandy,' I said, smiling, 'The Cotentin.'

"No ships were lost and all the fleet has now arrived.
As soon as we disembarked the king knighted me and
the Prince and several others and then Prince Edward
knighted many more."

'The king has knighted my husband,' I said. 'He is Sir William.'

'Ay, and you are now Lady Montagu, God bless you, my lady,' said the steward.

My eyes skimmed across the page.

"... baked bread... went to Barfleur... town as big as
Sandwich... eleven ships all of which we burned... My
Lord Warwick has skirmished with the enemy... we
killed many and captured many more... men at arms
have all withdrawn into the towns and the common
people have come over to us. Tomorrow we leave and
commence our march across Normandy and thus
make our way into France."

'I shall read it to the household at supper,' I said, laying the letter aside. 'At last we know where they are and we know where they're heading.'

'Normandy,' mused the clerk to the wardrobe. 'How wonderful if our king were to reclaim the Conqueror's lands for himself. Now that would be a grand day for England, that would.'

'Wonderful indeed,' I said, still not quite sure where Normandy was but prepared to believe it was a place of tremendous significance for my cousin.

'And will it be Paris for Christmas like they're saying in the kitchen, my lady?' said the usher. 'Will you be lodging in the French king's palaces and dining off his plate?'

'I think before we plan our Christmas revels we should arrange for a Mass to be said, to give thanks for the king's safe arrival on the other side of the sea,' I said, thinking how pious I sounded and how impressed Lady Catherine would be if only she knew.

'Bravely said, my lady,' said the steward. 'I'll send a boy to the priory and gather the household. We must never forget the Almighty who guides our every step and brings us safe to shore, although I do have to say I wish He had chosen Gascony instead of Normandy, then I'd not be a purseful the poorer.'

Two weeks later another letter arrived from William and this time his excitement leapt from every page.

"We rose early, before dawn, and at midday on the Wednesday we approached the town of Caen where many knights and men at arms had taken refuge. The king offered to spare the lives of those within if the town surrendered but the Bishop of Bayeux refused and held the king's messenger in chains. the king wanted to delay the attack on the town but our common soldiers without leave rushed the bridge which had been well

strengthened with a barricade and the Prince and my Lord Warwick joined them along the line of the river and together they won the bridge. Thus we entered the town and defeated the enemy. The constable of France, who had taken refuge in the gatehouse, surrendered to my late sire's steward, Sir Thomas Holand, and the chamberlain surrendered to one of the Prince's own knights, Sir Thomas Daniel."

At this, a cheer rang round the hall from the many men who remembered Thomas in the days when he'd served my father-in-law. I waited until the noise died down and then carried on reading.

"We killed or captured more than one hundred valiant knights, and many thousand squires, citizens and commons were taken or killed in the streets or in their homes or gardens. 'We found wine and food in great quantities in the town, which is bigger I am told than any in England save for London, and we are well-provisioned. Our ships followed us along the coast and have destroyed many warships and other vessels and the sailors went ashore and burned everything they could find. The sky is blazing red for miles around and in the other towns the people will be in despair because they know the English King and his host will soon be at their gates. We have been here in Caen for three days and tomorrow is the last day of July and the king will order us to Rouen where if God is willing we will find the army of the French king."

This would be the great battle that Thomas had spoken of, the battle which would decide everything and allow my cousin to ride in triumph into Paris. He would truly be King of France and every Frenchman would bow his knee and swear fealty to the King of England. There would be another treaty, one which would give us back our lands in Gascony. The fighting would be over for ever and our men would return home.

By the early days of September we had finished the greenwood and were making good progress on the little hill with its castle perched on top. I was generous and allowed my lady companion to stitch the delicate flower garden next to the castle walls because, if I was truthful, her stitches were neater than mine. I contented myself with the wall surrounding the park which stretched right across the top of the hill and down into the trees. It looked very dramatic undulating up and down below the sky.

'It is the Grail castle,' I said, carefully threading a needle with an appealing apricot-coloured silk. 'Do you think this colour will suit?'

She paused in her work to consider the matter but she was one of those women who would never disagree with the lady of the house and I didn't know why I'd bothered to ask.

What with William's letters and the managing of his affairs, the summer had not been without its excitements but as we drifted into autumn I found myself tired of our endless days of stitching and tedious conversations about my companion's children. Outside, the same sounds that I'd heard yesterday floated up from the courtyard and I swore it was the same dun-coloured bird twittering loudly in the bush against the wall that I'd been hearing all week.

'I sometimes think that little page was right and they have fallen off the edge of the world,' I said with a sigh. 'It's been weeks and we've heard nothing.'

'Perhaps they are lost in a dark wood,' said my companion, who was very attached to the romances and had an over-fertile imagination.

'That would be impossible,' I said firmly. 'The king has thousands of men. They'd fill a wood.'

'There could be werewolves,' she suggested. 'Or it could be a wicked enchantment.'

'You listen to far too many stories,' I said sharply, probably more sharply than I should. She was a pale-faced milksop of a woman who believed if we heard howling at the time of a full moon it must be the great pookah hound foretelling a death. She couldn't help but be credulous but there were times when I wished she had more sense.

What neither of us admitted was our greatest fear, that our army had been defeated in battle by the French king and all our men were dead. At night I dreamed of men slumped over town walls and bodies lying lifeless in the shallows of a great river; blood filling the streets of Paris while the French king stood laughing on the steps of his palace, and from somewhere outside in the cold and the darkness, Thomas was calling for a candle.

There was a commotion and shouting from down in the hall and footsteps running up the stairs. I looked up from my stitching as one of the men from the pantry was admitted.

He fell to his knees in front of me.

'Oh my lady,' he gasped. 'They're saying in the town it's a great victory, a great victory for the king.'

My heart raced and I felt faint.

'Where? What have you heard?'

'In Great Marlow, my lady. A man from London. He says proclamations are being read out at every street corner. He says eleven princes of the enemy are dead. Eleven! Including the King of Bohemia and the Count of Flanders. Near two thousand of the great men of France and many thousands more French corpses on the battlefield and their holy flag of war trodden in the mud.'

'And the Valois? The French King?'

'Fled into the night.'

'And what of our men?'

'Barely any lost, twenty at most.'

'And the king?'

'Triumphant. And the prince. "Worthy to keep a realm", His Grace said. Oh my lady, it is a great, great victory.'

The man had tears streaming down his cheeks and could hardly believe his own words. I laid aside my silks and rose to my feet. A victory, and such a victory. I could barely believe it myself. In a daze I walked down to the hall where all I could see was a crowd of expectant upturned faces. I gave orders for the household to be called together and for a cup of ale to be poured for everyone. Today we would honour our men in the traditional way as my mother-in-law would have done because whatever else I was, whatever else I wished myself to be, at this moment I was the lady of Bisham.

Crécy was the name they gave to the battle and by the end of the month there was not a man, woman or child in England who didn't know exactly what miracle had happened there, how the king and the prince with their great dragon banner had triumphed. People talked of the thousands of English and Welsh archers who had rained arrows upon the enemy; they sang of the courage of warriors like the Earl of Northampton and Sir Reginald Cobham and how our men, outnumbered by a French army nearly twice their size, had come to glory. It was unbelievable and yet it had happened.

As I stood in the hall that first morning amidst the noisy celebrations with a cup of ale in my hand, I realised the men of my household were right. It would be what they had all been hoping for, what everybody said it would be – it would be Paris for Christmas.

9

CALAIS 1347

I was wrong. We were all wrong. It wasn't Paris. It wasn't even Rouen or Amiens or some other great place. It was a nasty little fortress town called Calais, perched on the edge of a swamp. And we weren't to be lodged in the town itself, we were to camp outside its walls. This was no victory celebration with my cousin dining in state in one of the defeated Valois king's magnificent palaces. This was a siege.

I didn't want to leave the warmth of Bisham and travel overseas to somewhere I had never heard of but I was given no choice. Queen Philippa commanded the wives of the king's leading men to accompany her to Calais. We were to bring comfort and relief to our husbands and there were to be no false excuses, no prevarication of any kind as our attendance was the king's most urgent desire.

'If we defeated the Valois at Crécy and killed most of his great men, why didn't the king press on towards Paris?' I asked the new Countess of Arundel as we rode in the queen's train along the muddy road from Flanders. 'Why didn't he complete his conquest and declare himself King of France? Why is he here on the edge of nowhere?'

'It is one thing to win a battle, Lady Montagu, but quite another to hold the territory you've conquered.' Lady Arundel was surprisingly well informed for a woman. 'You need men to offer up the keys of their towns and cities willing to remain loyal to a new overlord. Would you have His Grace garrison every town and put each man who voiced discontent to the sword? Would you want your husband stuck here trying to hold a town of rebellious Frenchmen? Lord Arundel says even Normandy is too difficult to hold.'

'But why Calais? It's nothing but a mean little fishing town full of pirates. Even the queen agrees.'

Lady Fitzalan nodded to our right. I could smell the salt and hear the sullen roar of the surf and in the louring greyness could just detect a vague outline of sand dunes. But the sea was hidden by a thick veiling of mist.

'Did you know on a clear day the king can see Calais from his castle at Dover?' she remarked. 'Our ships could sail here and back in no time at all and if it was ours, our armies could pass into France with ease. Think what a great advantage that would be. His Grace wouldn't need to bargain with the men of Flanders or the lords of Normandy for a landing ground. If we held Calais we'd have our own harbour on this side of the Narrow Sea.'

'Why not use Brittany?'

'It's too rocky, too dangerous and much too far to the west,' replied Lady Arundel as if she had spent her entire life sailing the seas and knew the whereabouts of every open beach from here to Gascony.

What countryside we could see around us was relentlessly dismal, a flat bleak marshland with not a town in sight. We passed dozens of empty wagons rattling along the causeway, making the return journey to Flanders and occasionally saw a fast-riding group of king's men out looking for signs of trouble, but nothing else. Everywhere there was a palpable feeling of danger and I was glad of our armed escort.

At that moment we both heard the herald's trumpet and raising our eyes, saw figures emerging from the low swirling mist. Riding down the road in great splendour with rain-sodden banners and accompanied by a host of colourful noisy musicians, was the welcome sight of my cousin and his men come to welcome us to Calais.

'This is it,' announced William.

I looked round the snug little hall and was so relieved our home was not a tented pavilion I gave him a beaming smile.

'It's perfect. I couldn't want for anything better and once we arrange for a bigger fire it won't feel so damp.'

In truth, everywhere was damp; damp and cold and gloomy. But at least we had a house. Not one as grand as the Arundel's but ours boasted two tiny chambers as well as the little hall so I was well pleased.

William had grown much older in the six months we'd been apart. He was now almost as tall as my cousin, with the shoulders of a warrior, and one glance at the strength and breadth of his chest made me catch my breath. The soft down on his upper lip which I had often admired had changed to a fuzz of light-brown bristles and his chin showed the beginnings of a fine beard. But his eyes hadn't changed and they weren't particularly friendly.

'Did you miss me, husband?' I said lightly as we sat by the fire that first evening trying to get warm.

'I thought of you sometimes,' he replied evasively.

'Only sometimes?' I teased. 'Was I not worth more? I thought of you every day and remembered you each night in my prayers.'

'As was your duty,' he said shortly.

I wondered what he had done in the nights when he was alone. Had he gone chastely to his bed or had there been other women? I thought there probably had. Six months was a very long time.

'Was the fighting very bloody?'

'Yes. Better than Brittany. The greatest sport you could ever imagine.'

He stared into the flames.

'The king did you a great honour in knighting you,' I said, wanting him to know how thrilled the household at Bisham had been.

'He knighted dozens. I was just one of many. It was nothing special. He could hardly have ignored me when he was knighting men like that oaf, de Ros.'

'But you are now Sir William.'

He turned his eyes to me. 'And you are Lady Joan once more. That must give you a great deal of pleasure.'

It was clear I had displeased him in some way. I knew I had been a disappointment as a wife. I had taken the king as a lover and yet signally failed to gain any benefit for my husband. If I had been cleverer or more desirable I could have held my cousin's attention but as it was I had behaved like a love-struck milkmaid. It was no wonder he had dropped me hastily and never looked my way again. William had got nothing from that encounter other than the shame of an unfaithful wife.

And the prince? It would have been easy to lure Edward between my sheets and talk him into honouring William in some way but I had balked at the betrayal of our friendship. I didn't want him in my bed, I wanted him for what he had always been to me, a loyal and steadfast friend.

'Lady Arundel says there will be a re-telling of the glories of the campaign at the welcome feast,' I said. 'I shall listen carefully and cheer when I hear your name.'

'Nobody will mention my name. You can be sure of that.'

'I'm certain you fought valiantly, William,' I said quietly, nervous of making him angrier. 'Everybody knows what a fine fighter you are.'

I'd not seen him as gloomy as this for a long time and yet I had no idea what was wrong.

'Shall I tell you something?' he said. 'In between charges, when Thomas Daniel slipped in the mud, the prince helped him to his feet with a laugh and a friendly word but when I was knocked to the ground I had to crawl on my hands and knees and get some baseborn squire to haul me up. The prince didn't even notice.'

He kicked a log into the hearth and slumped back in his chair.

'I did miss you, husband,' I said softly, wondering what I should do to improve his mood. 'Would you like it if we went to bed?'

I touched the sleeve of his shirt with the tips of my fingers just sufficiently to let him know what I had in mind but I might as well have been an insect for all the notice he took.

'You go. I shan't disturb you tonight.'

'But William…'

He raised his eyes to mine and I noticed how cold they were, almost as cold as the ditchwater in the trenches outside.

'Go to bed, Joan. I have no need of you.'

For all my good intentions this was not an auspicious beginning. As my maid undressed me and put me to bed, I wondered what I had done wrong.

The next day we broke our fast with a paltry meal of bread and some indifferent cheese. While we ate, I kept up a continuous flow of news and gossip from home, hoping after a night's sleep William was in a better mood but he was as surly as ever.

'You can arrange the house to your liking,' he said into the silence when I finally ran out of things to say. 'I'll send someone to escort you around the town and show you where you can get what you need. Don't go out alone with just your maid. It's not safe. It's not only the enemy out there, there are thousands of men living in those disgusting hovels along the causeways and most of them haven't had a woman in months.'

I dressed in my warmest clothes and stood in the hall waiting for William's man. I surveyed the walls and planned which of the hangings I had brought from home I would use to make the room brighter. It certainly needed improvement. The men of our household bustled to and fro bringing in more logs and stacking the trestle tables against the wall while one of the boys started sweeping out the old rushes. It was a very domestic scene, reminiscent of Bisham.

'My lady? God give you good day.'

The voice was low and came from just behind my shoulder. He could have put out his hand and touched me if he had so wished but of course he didn't. He must have come in very quietly. I hadn't heard the noise of his arrival or even the sound of his footsteps on the stair. I turned round slowly, most unwilling to look at him.

It had been a year since I had seen Thomas Holand and I had no wish to see him now.

'Oh!'

My hands flew to my mouth and I gasped in horror. He was the same man as before but where his left eye had been there was now a black leather patch tied in place by a length of narrow ribbon.

'What happened?'

He smiled grimly. 'I was too slow.'

I felt unaccountably faint.

'But… when?'

'Last summer when we were coming up the Seine.'

He had told me how dangerous this campaign would be but I hadn't understood the reality, not until now.

'Was it a sword?' I asked, remembering William's lectures on how best to kill your enemy.

'Yes.' He gave a short laugh. 'But it could have been worse. At least I am alive; the other man is dead.'

He was very close to me, really much too close.

'Is it… does it…?'

I put my fingers up towards his face but hesitated. I wanted to touch him but I didn't dare. Not here in my husband's house where anybody might see.

'The pain is mostly gone but it aches at night when I try to sleep.'

My lips were trembling and I couldn't drag my eyes away from his patch. It possessed a strange attraction, the way a honey pot does for a wasp.

His smile widened. 'I could have lost my eye but I didn't and now there's only a rather unsightly scar. I don't need this.' He touched the patch, his hand brushing mine, sending shivers up my arm. 'But the women like it. They say it improves my looks.'

He studied me carefully, watching the blush rise in my cheeks. 'What do you think, my lady? Do you find me a more attractive man than I used to be?'

I turned my face away, trying to conquer the trembling sensations in my belly. 'I wouldn't know Sir Thomas,' I whispered. 'I am not in the habit of staring at men like you.'

He laughed.

'Would you like to see it?'

He fingered the ribbon.

I took a step back. 'No, no, not at all.'

He regarded me with amusement.

'When I was a little boy running around my father's hall, I had a nurse, an old woman who'd served our family for years. If I fell over she would scoop me onto her lap and kiss me better. What about you, my lady? Did you have someone to kiss you when you tumbled?'

'No,' I said shortly. 'I was slapped for dirtying my gown.'

'So you have no experience in such matters?'

I put my lips together and said nothing. He was blocking my way to the door and unless I pushed past him I had to stay where I was.

'Kissing is said to be an excellent remedy for all kinds of hurt but I expect you know that already. People say a man can even forget the betrayals of a faithless wife when lying in the arms of a bought woman. Oh those sweet red lips which whisper such tantalising lies! Would it were true that forgetfulness comes so easily.'

He put his hand up to the patch.

'You see, it is at night when I am awake and alone that the pain is at its worst. It is then I wish my wife was beside me putting her soft lips against my skin and kissing the hurt away. Perhaps you, my lady, would care to…?'

That was enough to bring me to my senses.

'Sir Thomas,' I said, gathering my cloak tightly around me as if for protection, 'I think you should remember who I am.'

I said it in as sharp a tone as I could muster but somehow the words trailed away at the end.

He gave a small laugh. 'Oh I never forget who you are, my lady. Never.'

He looked as if he had no intention of moving and was prepared to stand there all morning.

'Why are you here, Sir Thomas?' I said. 'You don't hold a position in my husband's household and I wasn't aware he had invited you to call on us.'

He smiled as if about to divulge a carefully kept secret. 'But that is where you are wrong, my lady. Didn't he tell you? I am his new steward.'

I felt my face redden.

'That's not possible.'

'Possible or not, it is a fact. After Crécy he asked if I would be willing.'

'You should have refused.'

He laughed. 'Why? It is a good position. It suits me and I like the company.'

He caught hold of my wrist and lowered his voice so the others couldn't hear. 'Don't you think we shall get along well, the three of us? I shall enjoy watching you play at being the lady of the house and if there is ever anything I can do for you, any small service: unlace your gown, remove your stockings…'

'Stop it,' I hissed. 'Don't you dare come near my chamber.'

'Why not? You already know what an excellent lady's maid I can be.'

Holy Virgin! What was I going to do? If he was William's steward I would see him every day. He would sit in our hall at the top of the side table, practically at William's right hand, and I didn't know if I could bear to be in the same room as both of them.

At last he grew tired of teasing me and stood aside to let me leave.

In the yard my groom held the bridle of a newly combed and polished Blanchefleur. Her coat gleamed and she looked quite recovered from our journey.

Thomas gave her an appraising look. 'What a beauty,' he remarked. 'You must have pleased Sir William greatly for him to have bought you such a fine animal.'

'It was a gift from the prince.'

He raised his eyebrow.

'Ah, I see.'

'You see nothing. Nothing at all.'

'I still have one eye and it sees everything, believe me.'

And with that rudeness he put his hands round my waist and lifted me smartly up into the saddle. I wished he hadn't because his touch made the skin beneath my linen tingle as I remembered things I would rather forget. My maid straightened the folds of my gown and wrapped my cloak over my knees while Thomas Holand watched with an annoying smirk on his face.

'Leave it,' I said irritably, gathering the reins in my hand and turning Blanchefleur's head towards the gate.

The girl backed away in alarm from the animal's shifting hindquarters, just in time to be hoisted up behind one of Thomas Holand's men.

We rode in silence through the streets of Villeneuve le Hardi, the settlement my cousin and his men had built in just four months. People said it was nothing short of a miracle and showed what the English king could do when God was on his side as He clearly was at the moment.

We made our slow way past the grand houses where the king and queen and people like us lived and on to the lesser houses occupied by the knights of the shires. I had seen with my own eyes the brushwood hovels and little wooden cabins for the common soldiers, where mud oozed round the walls and rainwater collected in puddles in the doorways and was extremely thankful nobody had suggested I should live in one of those.

To my amazement, Villeneuve was like a real town with every convenience a woman could possibly want. If you ignored the stench from the marshes you could almost believe it was Great Marlow or Reading, only bigger.

'It's as big as York,' said Thomas Holand when he saw me looking around in wonder at the sights.

'I've only once been to York,' I said wistfully. 'I've forgotten what it's like.'

'Big. It's the greatest city in the north and only London is bigger.'

As we pushed our way through the crowds of people in the market square, hardly able to hear ourselves speak above the noise, I could see hundreds of traders with their stalls laid out as if for a feast day.

At the far side of the square was a huge building almost as grand as a palace.

'The cloth market,' shouted Thomas Holand. 'What do you think?'

'It's… big.'

He smiled but said nothing.

To my horror, Thomas Holand turned up again the following morning intent on escorting me to wherever I might want to go. The message was brought by our smallest page who was still learning his duties.

'He's in the yard, my lady,' he piped, his scrubbed face beaming with pleasure at the importance of his task. 'He has ordered your horse to be saddled. He said I was to be sure to tell you the day is deceptive and you should bring your warmest cloak. And your stoutest riding boots. He says the mud is something dreadful and it will rain before the end of the day. He says…'

'Thank you,' I said gently. 'You may tell Sir Thomas, I am well aware of the state of the streets and I don't need his advice as to what I should wear.'

The boy gave a quick bow and scampered out of the hall to deliver my reply.

There was nothing to be done. Thomas Holand was William's steward, not mine, and if my husband chose to send him to me as some sort of companion then so be it. All I could do was make the best of an unfortunate and truly embarrassing situation but that didn't mean I had to take pleasure from it.

From my position at the top of the steps he appeared to be in no particular hurry. He was leaning against a stable door with his thumbs hooked into his belt talking to one of the grooms while Blanchefleur was led into the yard. Somewhat reluctantly I came down the steps.

In Ghent I had barely known him. We had used snatched meetings to forge a kind of friendship but until now the longest time I had spent in his company was that night in the house next to the apothecary's shop where I stupidly thought I was taking my future into my own hands.

The little attic room beneath the thatch had been dark and we hadn't talked much. There had been no need and the deflowering of an ignorant young girl didn't lend itself easily to conversation. I had only seen him a few times since then. That evening by the postern gate when I was seduced by promises of a return laden with riches from his Holy War; in the chapel at Bisham, nine months after the horror of my marriage, when all we had done was hurl abuse at each other and deepen our misunderstandings.

Once I had thought I loved him but when my mother explained how he had tricked me and used me, I grew to hate him. It was only later, in the years after he had abandoned me to my life with William, that I came to realise I had hardly known him at all. Our chance meeting last Christmas had prompted sad memories of a stranger who had once been kind but who in the end had proved not to be my perfect chevalier, simply another charlatan. It was a poignant reminder of all I had lost.

After that first day he didn't lay a finger on me, leaving it to the grooms to help me into the saddle and hand me the reins. As the days passed I found myself unreasonably annoyed by his obvious neglect and perversely longed for the feel of his hands around my waist. I recalled the way his hair had brushed against my fingers as he bent to adjust my stirrups and how his shoulder had pressed firmly against my leg.

I told myself he was more competent than my grooms, more able, and that Blanchefleur, who was notoriously fussy with her favours, preferred him. When he continued to keep his distance, I became irritated at this reluctance to do what was only what any knight should do for a lady. If he was my husband's steward he should serve me too. Whatever was my pleasure should be his duty.

'Sir Thomas can do it,' I said to my groom next day in the yard when he prepared to help me into the saddle.

The man backed away and looked anxiously over to where Thomas was readying his own horse. I saw two of the stable lads exchange a grin, noting the challenge in my voice. There was a moment of indecision where no-one moved and nobody spoke and I thought for one dreadful moment he was going to leave me standing on the ground looking foolish.

'As you wish,' Thomas said, throwing his reins to his own groom and strolling over to where I was waiting.

He moved my cloak to one side and put his fingers round the cloth of my thick outer gown. I swayed slightly, aware of his face inches from mine. He kept his hands where they were for what seemed an eternity. I could feel the blush rise in my cheeks.

'Are you ready?' he enquired politely, looking straight into my eyes.

'Yes.' My mouth was dry and the word came out like a croak.

'Sure?'

I nodded, refusing to look away but staring back, unblinking as if none of this was of any consequence.

He tightened his grip still further until I could feel the pressure of his fingers on the flesh beneath my skin and wanted nothing so much as to lean forward against his chest.

Just as I thought I would gasp with something which I told myself was most definitely not desire but more likely discomfort, he swung me up and placed me firmly in the saddle.

'There, my lady. Is that what you wanted?'

'Yes,' I whispered. 'Thank you.'

He smiled. 'Good. I'm glad we understand each other.'

If the hours I spent alone with Thomas on our outings were difficult, they were nothing compared to the horrors which lay within the house. I grew to dread the times I sat at our table in the hall. I schooled myself never to look at Thomas and to my relief he rarely looked at me, directing all his conversation to William. Amidst the noise and bustle of the household eating and talking, William paid no attention to my silence or my unwillingness to be drawn into his discussions with Thomas.

I ate little. There seemed to be an obstacle stuck in my throat which prevented me from swallowing and I began to wonder was I stricken with some terrible malady. I sipped my wine and looked at my shaking hands. Perhaps I had a palsy.

Although I gave him no encouragement, Thomas Holand insisted on conversing with me as we rode together through the streets of Villeneuve. I wasn't interested in what he had to say but it was impossible not to listen and it would have been impolite to turn my head away.

He talked of his family and the life he had led as a child. It was a sad story of fortune's wheel and I realised how much I had misjudged him. He was not some common adventurer dragged up to the ranks of a knight. On the contrary, his father had been a great magnate, a baron, riding at the side of the mighty Earl of Lancaster. His childhood had been one of wealth and privilege which had made his father's sudden downfall all the more shocking. The family had been thrust into obscurity, his father branded a traitor and hunted to his death. With the family practically penniless it had taken his mother and elder brother years to claw back their manors and restore the family's fortunes.

'What of your sister?'

'Which one? I have a clutch of them.'

'The one who wanted to run off with a rich admirer.'

He laughed.

'I didn't think you remembered our conversations.'

'It means nothing,' I said flustered by my stupidity in asking the question.

'Of course it doesn't,' he replied evenly. 'Why would it?'

After a few moments of silence, he said casually, 'As you are now a woman of some experience and know about these matters, which would you have chosen? The dull boy from a neighbouring family offering marriage or the doting greybeard who would keep you in a life of sinful luxury, despised by your friends and reviled by the bishops?'

I thought about it as we walked our horses into the open square on our way home.

'It would be wrong of course but if the old man offered her a manor of her own with a houseful of servants including a seamstress, and an income to spend as she wished, then it could be a good life,' I said. 'But if all she got was a room in the gatehouse with an idiot girl, forbidden to go anywhere, then marriage with the young man would be better. Which did she choose?'

'The rich admirer and she is very content. He keeps her in some comfort and despite his age and infirmity she has given him children; both girls unfortunately.'

'You haven't told me who he is, this rich man who seduced your sister.'

Thomas Holand slid from the saddle and lifted me down carefully placing me on the ground and allowing me a moment to find my feet before removing his hands.

'John de Warenne, Earl of Surrey.'

'Holy Mother of God!' I gasped. 'I know his wife.'

'Ah yes, the intransigent Countess Jeanne. The earl would marry my sister tomorrow if he could so you can imagine what my sister thinks of the countess.'

'I know what the countess thinks of your sister,' I replied sharply. 'The description was of "an avaricious little weasel with the morals of a whore" but she was very fired up when she said it.'

Thomas smiled grimly. 'I think the countess's quarrel is with her husband and not with my sister. But I hear the earl is sick unto death. He is not expected to last the year and my sister is ill with worry. She doesn't know what will happen to her when he dies or how she will live. All she hears is how, despite the earl's best efforts, his nephew is snapping at her heels and she can expect to inherit little beyond some chattels.'

'There are many people who will say she has got what she deserves.'

'But not you?'

'No,' I replied. 'They have both been shabbily treated by the earl. He should have been true to his marriage vows and never taken up with your sister.'

As we walked to the bottom of the steps where he would leave me, he said, 'I quite agree, my lady. If you promise yourself to someone in marriage you should always remain true no matter how great the temptation.'

I could think of no quick retort and realised he had tricked me yet again. He had turned my words around so they had a different meaning.

Alice was horrified when she visited with William's uncle and discovered Thomas sitting in our hall and eating at our table.

'What is he doing here?' she whispered, clutching my arm, her eyes wide with fright.

'He is William's steward.'

'But you can't have him living in your house?'

I pulled a face. 'It seems I have no choice.'

Alice looked totally disbelieving.

'Has he said anything?'

'No, not really.'

I could see her weighing up exactly what I meant by "not really" and wondering if I was already compromised.

'Will he tell William?'

'No.'

I felt sick with fear at the very thought of such a possibility and told myself it couldn't happen.

'Are you certain? He may want to make trouble for you. He looks like a man who might bear grudges. You said he was always sure of himself and men like that don't enjoy having their plans thwarted.'

'I don't think he bears a grudge,' I said carefully. 'It's not like that at all.'

'What is it like?' Alice said, peering once more through the crack in the door.

'I'm not sure. I think he wants me back.'

Alice snorted in disbelief.

'Are you sure it's not you who wants *him* back?'

'Oh no,' I said. 'I have no wish to starve in some hovel with Thomas Holand. In two more years I shall be Countess of Salisbury and sit alongside the queen. I shall have as many gowns as I please and a stable full of the finest horses. What possible use would I have for a man like him.'

'None, unless you have tender feelings.'

With unerring accuracy, Alice had wormed her way into the heart of my private thoughts which I kept well-hidden, even from myself. But she was wrong; I was quite safe where Thomas Holand was concerned. He might desire me but I most certainly did not desire him. I wasn't sure I even liked him any more. He was my husband's steward and I felt nothing for him however much I was beginning to enjoy his company.

'He'd be a dead man if he said anything,' said Alice. 'You know that, don't you? There'd be no trial. My husband would string him up without a second thought. And you don't need me to tell you what they'd do to him first: a man who had defiled the wife of one of the Montagu men. It wouldn't be pretty and I can barely bring myself to think of it.'

I closed my eyes against the horror of Thomas Holand's mutilated body.

'And they'd come for you after they'd dealt with him. I wouldn't be able to shelter you, nobody would, not even your mother.'

'He knows that. He won't say anything.'

'I hope you're right. I can't help feeling that nothing good will come of this. Perhaps you should return home to England. It might be safer.'

'Oh no,' I said quickly. 'I couldn't do that.'

Worst of all were the nights when the candles were doused and the sleepy household settled down in whatever corner they had decided was their own. It was then that William took me to bed. He ordered the curtains drawn and with no preamble turned his attentions to me. Like any husband he expected his wife to welcome his presence in her bed and my newfound reluctance beneath the sheets enraged him.

'In case you've forgotten, I will remind you again that I am your husband and this is your duty,' he hissed into my ear. 'What's the matter with you?'

'Nothing, William,' I whispered, wishing he wouldn't speak so loudly. 'It's just that I'm tired.'

If we had been at Bisham where the walls were built of stone or well-plastered laths hung with thick woollen tapestries, this humiliation would have been bad enough. But here in our makeshift house, where nothing separated us from the hall bar a few strips of wood covered with cheap English cloth, Thomas would hear every word we spoke, every shift of the mattress and creak of the bed and I didn't think I could bear it.

Once the Christmas festivities were over, winter returned across the marsh, baring its teeth and showing its claws. A cold wind blew up from the east, squeezing its way through the gaps in the walls into every corner of our house. No matter how many hangings I ordered placed over the openings, draughts were everywhere. In the evenings the household sat huddled around the hearth but it was impossible to get warm. I thought longingly of the cheerful fires in the rooms at Bisham. Here the logs were damp and our fire smouldered and spat and gave out very little heat.

Despite the cold and my disinclination to spend time with Thomas Holand, I was determined to continue with our outings. I persuaded myself that, as William had ordered it, what I was doing was not for my benefit but for his.

'Where today?' asked Thomas casually as we made ready to leave.

'Would it be possible to visit the walls of Calais?'

He looked amused at my request.

'You wish to make an attempt on the town?'

'No, but I'd like to go closer and see what the king's army is doing.'

'The king's army is sitting around in the mud on its collective backside, waiting.'

'Waiting for what?'

'For the spring, for our ships to return, for the French to come back.'

'Why don't they try breaching the walls?'

He laughed. 'Oh my lady, if only it were that easy. The stone throwers are useless because the ground is too soft; the cannon make a lot of noise but no impression at all, and when we tried scaling the walls with ladders and ropes we were unsuccessful. So now we will starve them out. The king says he'll stay twenty years outside the walls of Calais if that's what it takes, but we reckon another six months should do it.'

We rode past the meat market and the church of St Peter and north out of Villeneuve across the marshes towards the fortress of Calais. Beyond the deep trenches and brushwood hovels I could see endless stretches of muddy, bog-ridden ground, dozens of little streams and banks of sand, and towering over everything, the formidable grey walls of the town.

'Make sure you keep your horse on the path,' said Thomas, watching me carefully. 'Don't let her stray off to the side. The ground is treacherous in places.'

The closer we got to the walls the higher and more sinister they became. There were no signs of life: no women working down at the water's edge, no children playing, no wagons piled high with provisions lumbering through the great gate and no sight anywhere of the defenders. The castle at the top of the town appeared deserted with no evidence of habitation except for the remnants of a tattered flag on the topmost tower.

'Where are the people?'

'Conserving their strength,' said Thomas.

'Are they starving?'

'Not yet. A few supply vessels got into the harbour last month so doubtless their storerooms are not completely empty of grain but the king has plans to stop any further ships.'

'What happens when they have no more food?'

'They eat the horses, the dogs, the cats; rats fetch a shilling and sixpence will get you a fat mouse. Men eye up their companions and wonder what they would taste like.'

'But that's…'

'… what happens when you see death sharpening his knife.'

I thought he must be exaggerating. I couldn't imagine any man ever descending to such depths of barbarity.

'What about the women and the children? Surely they'll be fed?'

'When the garrison commander sees no hope of relief he will open the gate and send the women and children out into the town ditch.'

'Why would he do that?'

'They are useless mouths. They can't fight.'

'What will happen to them?'

'If our king is feeling vengeful he will leave them to starve in full sight of their husbands and fathers; if he is merciful he will let them through our lines to wander off to wherever they can find shelter.'

This all seemed far more horrible than I had imagined. I remembered William saying how my cousin had stood by and seen the women of Caen raped and killed in the streets and I knew that here at Calais he would not be merciful.

'I doubt there'll be any mercy for the men left inside,' said Thomas. 'It's been a foul winter and the king doesn't appreciate being kept waiting in the cold and the rain by a rabble who must realise by now that help is not going to come.'

'Surely the French king will do something?'

'It's said he has no money and some of his great men are already offering assistance to us but I expect those left will force him into action. They'll bless another of their holy flags and come marching across the Somme.'

'At the thought of more fighting I felt scared and pulled on my reins.

'What's wrong?'

'Are we safe?' I asked, looking nervously at the empty walls and thinking of the Valois and his men creeping through the marshes with their swords and daggers at the ready.

Thomas leaned over and touched my sleeve. 'Don't be frightened. I wouldn't have let you come this far if there was the slightest danger. Come on, I'll show you the harbour if you like.'

He turned his horse's head and we set off to our left picking our way carefully past groups of men engaged in digging yet more ditches. I could see the outer moat, a wide grey expanse protecting the walls beyond, and coming up fast towards us, a group of horsemen.

'We have company.' Thomas raised his hand in greeting.

It was Edward and some of his companions. They were dressed in light armour and carrying swords and reminded me of the boys they had once been, playing at fighting across the gardens at Woodstock.

'What are you doing out here, Holand?' said Edward pulling his horse up. 'And why have you Lady Montagu with you? Have you abducted her?'

There was a ripple of laughter from Edward's friends who were busy gauging the significance of my presence out here by the walls of Calais and looking me up and down in the way that men did.

Thomas was not in the least ruffled. He was quite at ease with Edward which was odd because it should have been my husband who could parry a joke and talk in a friendly way with his prince. Yet here was Thomas behaving as if it was he who had spent his boyhood with Edward learning his letters and the art of war, not William. Despite my indifference to his attempts at a renewed friendship, I was surprised and rather pleased.

'Sir William charged me with showing his lady the sights but after a few visits in the town I thought it best to bring my lady here before she bought up the entire cloth market and bankrupted the English treasury.'

Edward laughed. 'It's just as well you rescued her. But you can leave now. I'll take charge of her. I'm sure you have better things to do than act as a lady's maid.'

'Indeed I have, my lord,' Thomas bowed his head to Edward, recognising a dismissal when he heard one. To me he said, 'My lady, doubtless I shall see you tomorrow.'

With a slight frown furrowing his forehead, Edward watched Thomas ride away.

'Do you know Holand well?'

I tried hard not to blush. 'He is my husband's steward. He dines in our hall.'

'Odd choice. Holand is a clever man and had plenty of offers. He could have picked any one of them and yet he chose Montagu.'

'He'd been of service to William's father; perhaps he felt some loyalty to the family.'

Edward looked disbelieving.

'I'm well aware he was the earl's steward but to serve the son is very peculiar. Montagu hasn't received his title yet so he's next to nothing. If Holand wants to advance, and it's obvious he's an ambitious man, then he'd have done better to choose someone else. Why Montagu? What's the attraction?'

'Perhaps he wanted a position which wasn't too demanding,' I said lamely. 'It must be difficult with his eye. It seems to have been a vicious wound.'

Edward threw back his head and laughed. 'Has he been spinning you that old tale? You know he can see perfectly well, don't you? There's nothing wrong with him but a slight scratch. He told me people let down their guard when they think he's a wounded hero of the campaign. He said I'd be surprised what he's learned. It's the same trick men used in the Scottish wars. I remember my father telling me.'

'Well he hasn't fooled me,' I said stiffly.

It was cold within sight of the sea and despite my warm cloak, I shivered, half-wishing Thomas hadn't gone without me. Now I would have to wait on Edward's pleasure and that might be a very long wait indeed. The other men nudged their mounts alongside and tried to engage me in conversation but, with the practised ease of one well-used to serving his prince, John Chandos drew them away leaving me alone with Edward.

'I'm glad you came, Jeanette.' Edward's voice was warm. 'I hoped you would.'

'Your father commanded the wives of his men to accompany your lady mother,' I said, lowering my lashes. 'It was my duty.'

He made an impatient sound and shook his head as if his father's command and my dutiful obedience didn't interest him, only his desire for my presence. I noted his beautifully shaped lips, the long straight nose and the arrogant eyes of a born prince and thought once again how handsome he was.

'I see you brought Blanchefleur,' he said.

'Of course I did,' I said, stroking her warm neck. 'I would never be parted from her. She is the loveliest of animals.'

For a moment he just gazed at me, saying nothing. His eyes flickered but his voice, when he spoke, was guileless.

'You heard of our success?'

'How could I not have heard?' I said calmly. 'They were shouting your praises at every market cross we passed. The victor of Crécy they called you.'

'You should have been there to see it, Jeanette. By God it was wonderful. Two days of fighting and we had the battlefield strewn with bodies. We killed nine princes of the blood and Christ knows how many others. I stood on a mound of French dead and thought I had gone to Heaven. It was glorious.'

We walked our horses slowly along the path.

'Did you hear how the King of Bohemia fell?' he asked.

'William told me.'

'He was shouting his war cry as he went down. What a chevalier! Think of it: a blind man riding into the thick of battle. What courage that must have taken.'

He was flushed by his success as if it was his first kill. I remembered the tremulous excitement of a six-year-old Edward on that winter hunt all those years ago and was surprised the blood of the King of Bohemia wasn't smeared across his face. He might have been fast growing into manhood and learning a taste for war but in many ways he was still a boy.

'And what now? More battles? A great marriage?'

'Ah Jeanette, Jeanette. You know I won't marry if I can't have you.'

'Edward, I am married to William,' I said primly, wondering if, despite our idle flirtation, I would really have wanted to marry Edward.

'He doesn't deserve you,' he said stoutly. 'My father should never have agreed to the marriage. I told him so. The earl was a great man but the son is dross.'

'Edward! You mustn't speak to me of my husband in that way.'

'I can speak of him in any way I like. You're not a fool, Jeanette. You know the sort of man they married you to. He's grudging; he makes mistakes and then whines it is someone else's fault. The men have no regard for him. They want their captains to have blood in their veins, not piss.'

I recognised his description of William and knew he was right but William was my husband and deserved my respect.

'Your father will want you wed,' I said.

'My father may carry on trying to find me a bride but His Holiness will frustrate him at every turn if he can. I don't care. I'm not interested in having a wife, I've got better things to do.'

After the feast of Candlemas, the days grew warmer but with the warmth came rain. The myriad of streams which ran through the marshes swelled and overflowed and the islands where the hovels stood became swamped by rising water. I longed for an English spring, not this miserable existence on the outskirts of Calais. Several women I knew had already left, disliking the incessant damp and complaining that six months of campaigning had turned their husbands into brutes. But I was determined to stay. Despite William's occasional disagreeable moods and the constant awkwardness of being in close contact with Thomas Holand, I enjoyed Villeneuve. The last thing I wanted was to be sent back to Bisham.

On the final day of the Shrove feasting I was invited to the Arundel's house and it was there, in Lady Arundel's spacious and elegant chamber, I first heard the news about Isabella. She was to marry sixteen-year-old Louis de Male, the new Count of Flanders. The betrothal ceremony would take place shortly at Berghes, a little cloth town across the border into Flanders.

'This marriage is going to anger the Duke of Brabant very much,' Eleanor Arundel sighed, gazing round the circle of ladies as if we personally should be able to pacify the irascible duke.

'Surely he doesn't want the Lady Isabella for himself?' I said, remembering the sour-faced duke who had once been our friend but now, it seemed, was our enemy.

Everybody laughed as if I had said something very amusing.

'No, no,' said Lady Arundel smothering a smile. 'The duke doesn't want the Lady Isabella. He's after Count Louis; he wants him for his daughter.'

'I thought our prince was to marry the Duke of Brabant's daughter,' said Alice who was seated rather uncomfortably beside Elizabeth, on the padded settle.

'No,' sighed Lady Arundel. 'That betrothal unravelled and now the duke has his eyes on Count Louis.'

'So the count is very desirable,' said Alice, blinking in her efforts to understand this tangled web of potential marriages.

'Yes,' smiled Lady Arundel. 'He is the hereditary ruler of Flanders and however much the great men of the towns pretend they hold power, without the count they have no legitimacy. Of course he is desirable.'

'I wasn't aware he had expressed a wish to marry the Lady Isabella.' The Countess of Warwick roused herself from her study of the Arundel's musician strumming his lute in the corner, and rather belatedly joined our discussion.

'He hasn't. It is rather the opposite,' said Lady Arundel. 'He was raised at the French court and says he won't marry the daughter of the man who killed his father.'

'I thought as much,' said the Countess of Warwick, picking a fig from the bowl. 'So why is he marrying our Lady Isabella?'

'It isn't his choice,' replied Lady Arundel, clicking her fingers for more wine to be brought. 'Lord Arundel tells me the great men of Flanders make all the decisions and they want the English marriage. They have the count close-guarded and the council packed with their own men so if the count values his neck, he'll do as he's told.' She leaned closer and said in a voice not much louder than a whisper. 'It's said he is watched day and night and can't even piss without a dozen guards in attendance.'

There was a horrified shriek at this ultimate indignity and a snorting giggle from one of the younger maids who should have known better than to be listening.

'Poor man,' I laughed. 'Has he no friends?'

'Only the Valois king and he's in no position to help.'

'So the count is ours for the taking?'

'He is, and the king is determined to have him.'

'I don't imagine he'll make a very happy husband,' said the Countess of Warwick, shifting herself and making her chair creak. 'Let's hope the Lady Isabella will be able to manage him.'

'Of course he'll be happy,' snapped Elizabeth who didn't like the Countess of Warwick any more than she liked me. 'Why wouldn't he be?'

I had never seen Isabella look as beautiful as she did on the day she was betrothed to sixteen-year-old Count Louis. Her robe of heavy green silk, embroidered all over with the finest of silver threads and studded with jewels, suited her dark colouring and the delicate golden tissue of her veil accentuated the high cheekbones and delicately reddened lips of a girl who was now on the brink of womanhood.

As I waited in the unbearably overcrowded hall in Berghes where the gift-giving ceremony was taking place, I felt the lightest of touches on my waist.

A familiar voice whispered in my ear. 'I'll lay you a wager he bolts. Given half a chance he'll be down the privy chute.'

Thomas Holand!

I suppressed a giggle at his vulgarity and glanced to make sure William hadn't heard.

Certainly Louis, the young Count of Flanders, didn't look like a man embracing marriage joyfully. He had a thin, intelligent face and his body, beneath the glittering finery, was lean and made for sport, but his eyes were hollowed pits. They told you nothing of the inner man and I thought the Countess of Warwick's warning was timely.

'The king should have had them wedded and bedded today,' continued the voice.

I turned my head slightly and whispered back. 'It's the season of Lent. The king's daughter cannot marry in Lent.'

'People do, as you should well know, my lady.'

I felt the blush rise in my cheeks as I remembered the Lenten dish of dried fish he had once offered me.

I bit my lip and tried to keep my voice steady. 'The count will honour his word, Sir Thomas. No man would leave his betrothed waiting at the church door.'

'I hope you're right,' he said, 'because there'll be a high price to pay if you're wrong.'

And wrong, I was.

News of the count's disappearance came two weeks later just as the last seed pearls were being stitched onto Isabella's magnificent wedding gown.

'Down the privy chute?' I gasped in horror.

'Out hawking,' said Thomas grimly. 'The messenger said his masters were sitting idly by, congratulating themselves on having ensnared the English king, while the young man put his falcon up after a heron, shouted "Hoie" and was off across the fields. They fear he has escaped into France.'

In the royal lodgings in Villeneuve the jilted bride screamed with rage and collapsed sobbing onto the floor, while in Flanders Count Louis's bastard half-brother was accused of plotting rebellion with French money.

'They say the Flemings wanted him tortured to death in the public square,' declared our youngest page, his eyes alight with joy at such things.

I gulped and the clerk of the wardrobe gave the boy a swift cuff on the ears. 'It's alright, my lady,' he reassured me. 'The Margrave of Juliers put a stop to that. Said some respect was surely due to the man's birth.'

'What happened?'

'They took an axe to him. Cut off his head.'

Almost immediately, hostilities broke out as the English and the Flemings attacked French towns on the Flemish border and for three whole months the town of Villeneuve became a stew of rumour and counter-rumour. Reinforcements from England poured across the beaches in their thousands and by the time a pale summer sun began warming the marshes, we faced the possibility of an attack. The Valois had taken possession of his holy flag and was said to be camped with his army a mere ten days' march to the south.

I wasn't afraid. I knew we were invincible. Gascony was now ours and only yesterday we heard our men in Brittany had captured the nephew of the Valois king. God's blessing was with us and nothing could possibly go wrong.

But somewhere in the darkness, Dame Fortune had stretched out her bony fingers and, as if to teach me a lesson that nothing should be taken for granted in this life, had given her wheel the slightest of turns.

Today was the first day of sunshine for many weeks. The sky was a rain-washed blue with a few puffy white clouds floating gently overhead. But I wasn't deceived and knew it wouldn't last.

There were two armed men in front of me and two behind as I rode through the town gate with that ever-present reminder of things I would rather forget, Thomas Holand, at my side

My maid clung to the belt of one of Sir Thomas's lads, yelping foolishly every time the youth's horse increased the length of its stride. We must have resembled a pretty little cavalcade as we trotted gently along the causeway to the east of the town, waving happily to the men with the vegetable wagons lumbering slowly towards Villeneuve.

Where the road was rutted it was full of puddles and there was still a feeling of damp in the air. Despite the sun, the breeze off the sea was sharp and carried with it the usual smell of salt and various disgusting bits of flotsam. Perhaps there had been a time when these beaches had been smooth and pleasant, washed clean by the swirling waters of the Narrow Sea but the arrival of our army and the constant presence of thousands of men had changed all that.

I had been sitting with my clerk of the wardrobe toiling dutifully over my accounts when Thomas had arrived. He apologised for disturbing our labours but informed me my horse was saddled and the escort waiting so if I would please hurry and call my maid to bring my cloak. I had no idea why he was there as, with the French advancing north, our daily expeditions had long since ceased. I presumed it was at William's command.

We hadn't gone far when we turned off the road down a sandy track towards the sea. Blanchefleur slowed as her hooves encountered soft ground. I looked about me but could see no reason why we were heading along this narrow path banked on either side by great dunes of sand and tussocks of grass with only the sound of the gulls and the sea to keep us company.

When we emerged onto the open beach, Thomas commanded the others to remain at the head of the path while he and I walked our horses slowly across the firm sand.

'Where is Sir William?' I said, my words blowing away on the wind.

'Round at the harbour with the Earl of Warwick.'

'But I thought...'

'Did you?' He smiled, but not, I noticed, with his eyes.

'Are we not going to see Sir William?'

'No. We are going to take a walk on the beach.'

The look on his face was serious and I wondered what he wanted. I didn't trust him when we were alone with no other company.

'Why the beach? Surely we could walk in the town.'

'I need to talk to you and what I have to say is better said here where we cannot be overheard or interrupted.'

'What could you possibly have to say to me which requires a windy beach with sand blowing in my eyes?'

He laughed and slid from his saddle. 'Come down here and we'll go and sit among the dunes. It'll be warmer there and out of the wind.'

I looked doubtful and didn't move.

'I promise you'll be perfectly safe.'

'Oh very well,' I said most ungraciously.

He lifted me down, holding me a moment until I was steady on my feet and then offered me his arm.

I certainly wasn't going to touch him, not here with the inviting privacy of the dunes just ahead and our escort out of earshot.

'I prefer to walk on my own, thank you.'

'As you wish.'

He led the horses a short way into the dunes where we couldn't be seen by anyone. In a little hollow, he took off his cloak and spread it on the ground, indicating that I should sit. I was very suspicious of his intentions and felt a slight frisson of something which I thought might be the cold, but it wasn't and I knew it wasn't.

I sat at the outer edge of the cloak about as far away from him as I could. He smiled at my deliberate decision, measured a distance with his foot and sat down at the other side.

'Comfortable?'

'Yes, thank you.'

'Warm enough?'

'Yes, thank you.'

In truth I felt rather uncomfortable, sitting here alone with a man who wasn't my husband. If William knew he would justifiably be very angry indeed.

'I know you have much to occupy your thoughts, my lady,' said Thomas Holand, ignoring my lack of interest, 'but have you ever wondered where my brother, Otho, is?'

His brother? Why was he talking about his brother?

'No, I haven't, Sir Thomas. Why would I? I don't concern myself with the various members of your family.'

'Would you like me to tell you?'

He really was the most annoying of men sometimes.

'I suppose you intend to tell me whether I ask you or not, so very well – where is your brother?'

He smiled broadly. 'Otho is in England at this moment, guarding a particularly valuable property of mine.'

'I presume you also wish me to ask you which valuable property.'

'I think you might be interested.'

'Sir Thomas, I am not interested in anything you or your brother do. It is no business of mine.'

I *was* curious but I certainly wasn't going to let him know that.

'My brother is working valiantly on my behalf, looking after a friend of mine, Raoul de Brienne, the Count of Eu.'

I must have looked completely mystified because he sighed. 'The Count of Eu is the Constable of France and at present he is my prisoner.'

'Oh!' I said. 'Caen! You captured him at Caen.'

'Yes. The count and I fought together in the Holy Crusade against the heathens. We were friends and when the prince's men stormed the bridge at Caen and he was trapped, he surrendered his sword to me.'

There was a silence in which he idly picked up some sand and let it trickle through his fingers. I stared at the gap in the dunes through which I could just make out the sea, a line of dark blue crested with white. I was beginning to feel sleepy with the warmth and would have quite liked to lie down and close my eyes but I certainly wasn't going to with Thomas Holand sitting beside me.

'The king has offered to purchase the Count of Eu from me for the sum of eighty thousand florins.'

That jolted me out of my drowsiness. Eighty thousand florins!

'But that's a fortune.'

'Yes, it is.'

I remembered the orchard in Ghent where he had once told me how war makes men's fortunes and how the greatest prize of all was a prisoner to ransom.

'So now you are rich.'

'I am. Not as rich as Sir William will be one day. I'll never be that rich. But rich enough.'

Rich enough for what, I wondered. To purchase a manor or two or three, to clothe himself in silks and furs, to have a stable full of the very best horses, to buy himself a wife. Of course, this was why he'd brought me here, to break the news that after Calais he would be going away. He would leave William's service and I'd never see him again except perhaps at some great feast given by the king where

Sir Thomas and Lady Holand would take their places at the lower tables and talk of their happy life together.

A large tear rolled down my cheek.

'Why are you crying?'

'I'm not,' I snapped, wiping my face with my hand. 'Why would you think I was crying? It's nothing but the wind.'

'Aren't you interested in what I'm going to do with my fortune now that I've got it?'

'I suppose like all men you'll use it to enrich yourself further by buying the things men do to impress others.'

He regarded me seriously. 'Not at all. I've decided to use my fortune to settle a long-running dispute over a piece of my property. I wish to see justice done in this matter.'

William was constantly going to law over the boundaries of his manors and the trespasses of others into his parks and it was disappointing to see that Thomas Holand was no different.

'That will hardly use up the whole of your fortune, Sir Thomas. My cousin's justice is not that costly.'

'Oh I don't think I will receive justice at your cousin's hands, my lady. I think I shall have to aim higher.'

'There is no higher justice in the land than the king's justice.'

'Except where the Church rules.'

'The bishops' courts?'

'Not even the bishops. In the matter of retrieving what has been stolen from me I have been told my only hope is to petition His Holiness and that is a very costly business indeed.'

'The Holy Father? In Avignon?'

I couldn't believe what I was hearing. What property could possibly be valuable enough?

His words, when he spoke, came from a very long way away.

'I shall ask His Holiness to order the return of my wife.'

For a moment there was nothing to be heard but the gentle surge of the sea beyond the dunes. The gulls were silent; no voices, no chinking bridles, no passing footsteps, no distant clanging of bells; not even the low rumble of a farmer's wagon travelling along the causeway. I sat perfectly still in this newfound silence as melting ice came slithering through my veins and the little hollow where we sat began to spiral around me.

'You can't do that.'

He gave a half smile. 'I think you'll find I can. You're my wife and I want you back.'

Amongst the sparse tufts of grass, little pink flowers tucked themselves close against the ground as if afraid to push their heads any higher into the air. A small insect leapt onto my hand before hopping off into the sand where it buried itself in an instant leaving behind just a few tiny trickling grains which quickly disappeared.

'I'm not your wife,' I said in a voice which trembled far too much. 'I can't be. I'm married to William. I've been his wife for six years. I sit by his side in the hall. Everyone knows I'm his wife.'

He leaned forward and spoke slowly. I could feel the warmth of his breath on my face and there was nowhere to hide from his words.

'You are not his wife, you're mine. I am the one who will decide where you live and when I tell the Holy Father what happened between us in Ghent, he will agree. It may cost me half my fortune and some months of the king's displeasure, but I want you back.'

'I don't want to live with you in a hovel,' I said in rising panic, imagining the mud and the rush-lights and the hard brown bread. There would be beaten-earth floors and wooden bowls and a pallet bed with dirty sheets. I'd seen how lesser people lived and I wasn't going to give up what I had to starve in a wayside shack with Thomas Holand. I wasn't going to leave the glories of Bisham for some cold northern bogland where the women wore homespun and nobody ate meat except on a feast day.

He gave a short laugh.

'Don't be foolish. You won't have to live in a hovel. I have a good solid manor house where we'll live together. And if you find it too small, I'll build a solar.'

I said nothing, appalled at the thought of losing everything.

'I'll plant you a pleasure garden if that's what you want,' he said softly. 'And there'll be a dovecote.'

'But I'm to be Countess of Salisbury,' I cried, despairing of making him understand how impossible this was. 'I can't sit with you at the lower tables. I have to sit on a velvet cushion alongside the queen and be served from her dishes. I don't want to sup pottage with you.'

He sighed as if explaining matters to a small child. 'My lady, I can't make you a countess. I'll never have as many manors as Sir William and I'll never be an earl no matter how high I climb but I promise I will look after you well. You won't want for anything.'

'What about my household? I can't manage without them. I won't know what to do. I can't brew ale or bake bread or any of those things.'

He had the rudeness to laugh at my panic-stricken expression.

'Don't worry. I won't expect you to bake bread. I have servants. My wife's place will not be in the kitchens.'

'So where will my place be in this house which is not a hovel and which doesn't yet have a solar?' I demanded.

'Where would you like it to be?'

I knew what he was thinking. It was written all over his face. I felt the heat rush into my cheeks as he continued eyeing me like some delectable morsel he could hardly wait to get his hands on. He'd tricked me into his bed once but I refused to be duped a second time.

'Why don't you get yourself some other wife,' I said sullenly. 'It should be easy for someone like you. Why not go back to your manor and find a plump little country nobody with a wealthy father who won't mind the mud or the lack of a solar? Why not put her in your bed?'

He leaned across the gap between us and took my hand in his. I tried to pull away but he had it held much too tightly.

'Because I happen to want you in my bed. You're my wife. It's where you belong.'

'I do not belong in your bed.'

He raised an eyebrow and regarded me with some amusement.

'I thought you enjoyed being in my bed. Was I mistaken?'

He had removed his hat and the sun was gilding the unruly hairs on the top of his head. The sensation which had been steadily growing in my belly sent shivers through the whole of my body as my resolve faltered and I felt faint.

'William will never let me go,' I said in a small voice. 'He won't allow you to take me.'

'I don't expect him to hand you over willingly. It would be a foolish man indeed who'd do that and, whatever else he is, Montagu is no fool.'

'And how will you persuade him? With a band of armed retainers? Swords and cudgels at the ready? You won't get further than the outer gate of Bisham. He'll have you cut down before you set foot in the inner courtyard.'

'He'll put up a fight but if the Holy Father commands your return, he'll have no choice but to obey. I shall bring an order from the papal court and that is something a man ignores at his peril. Montagu won't risk excommunication and the damnation of his soul.'

This was all going too fast. He was going to take me away from Bisham whatever happened. I could be screaming with fear and clinging to the bed curtains but he'd take no notice. He'd drag me outside and throw me up onto his saddle.

'If you force me to leave I shall be penniless,' I said, flatly. 'There'll be no money. Everything I have belongs to Sir William. I shall bring you nothing. The Montagu marriage was a cause of great joy to my mother, and my family would see me dead rather than dishonoured like this. They won't bargain with you or help you in any way. There will be no dowry. Nothing. So why would you want me when all I shall bring you is trouble?'

'Don't you know?'

I shook my head.

'Can't you guess?'

'No.'

'Oh my lady, I thought you would know by now. Wandering round the streets of Villeneuve with you these past months, I realised a truth; one which I have denied for too long. I happen to love you. Not desire you, but love you. Desire is a simple matter and easily cured but love is something else entirely.'

'You've never loved me,' I cried. 'All those pretty words you said in Ghent; you never meant any of them. I thought you loved me but you didn't.'

He moved so that he was next to me and took both my hands in his.

'You know I am a sinner, I've made no secret of it, but even a sinner can be redeemed in this life. You were barely more than a child when I first met you, a pretty young girl I wanted in the way I would have wanted any pretty young girl. Naturally I didn't love you. When I married you it wasn't for love. Only a fool marries for love.'

'I loved *you*,' I muttered.

'No you didn't,' he said. 'It wasn't love, it was a girl's fancy, a green sickness, nothing more.'

'How do you know what I felt?'

He laughed. 'You forget. I have sisters. I know about young girls. In and out of love as often as the seasons change. Think of the men you've sighed over in the years since that night in Ghent, men you have dreamed of, wept tears for. One? Two? Three perhaps?'

When I blushed, he laughed. 'You see.'

'I see nothing but a man who is bent on destroying my life.'

'If I destroy the life you have today, I shall give you a new one. You will be Lady Holand and I shall make you happy.'

Happy? There were few times I could say I'd been truly happy since I married William. Here in Villeneuve perhaps, these past months? But it was Thomas who had leaned against the pillar in the cloth hall while I'd chosen the silks for my gowns: "Not the yellow," he'd said, watching me through half-closed eyes. "The blue. It suits you better."

And when I'd wanted a small gift for Margaret's name day, he'd patiently taken me from shop to shop while I'd hesitated over dozens of little fairings until he'd finally told me which one to buy, the perfect one which had delighted my very particular cousin who had so wanted to be with us but who had been ordered to remain in England by her husband.

It was Thomas who had whispered snippets of gossip in my ear and made me laugh; who'd taken me to taverns and pie shops which William would never have done. He'd shown me the vast warehouses stuffed full of corn and had suggested, outrageously, that we might climb the ladder to the hayloft. "It's dark," he had said in a low voice. "No-one goes there at this time of day. We'd be quite alone". "No, thank you," I'd replied. He'd smiled and said, "Very well, not yet." "Not ever," I'd said smartly and walked out into the daylight.

We'd played this game daily until the Valois king and his army put a stop to it and it wasn't until our time was ended that I realised where it had been leading.

'What if His Holiness denies your petition?' I said. 'What if he decides I am truly married to William? Which of course I am.'

'Then I shall have made both your life and mine that bit more hazardous. Once Montagu knows there will be no unknowing.'

'Is what you're going to do so very dangerous?'

'Yes. Challenging one of the king's friends is always dangerous and the papal court is like a snake pit. Would you rather I left it alone and did nothing?'

I put my head down and looked at my feet. Did I wish him to leave it alone? Did I really wish him to disappear out of my life? I raised my eyes and caught his gaze. There was something in the way he was looking at me that I hadn't seen before, a tenderness which I steadfastly refused to believe was love.

'Perhaps it would be safer to let things lie,' I said slowly, hating myself for being a coward. 'I wouldn't want to see you hurt. We could carry on the way we are, seeing each other like this.'

'So I leave my wife in another man's hall and content myself with the knowledge that it is he who takes her to bed each night, not me. Do you really imagine I can agree to that?'

'I could meet you in secret,' I said, doubtfully. 'I could come to your lodgings if you took a room… I could…' I didn't know how to say the words. 'I could be your concubine.'

He roared with laughter and fell back, his head in the sand, the sun in his face. He grasped my sleeve and pulled me down beside him. There was a sudden shock at the intimacy and then a warm sensation of familiarity. He encircled me with his arms and I found to my surprise I had no desire to struggle free.

'If I wanted a concubine, my lady, I'd choose you above anyone, but I happen to want a wife.' He rolled over and kissed me gently on the mouth. 'And I have a fancy to have a son.'

My lips trembled. I felt blood drain from my face and tears well up in my eyes.

'But what if I can't? What if…?'

He kissed me again, his lips brushing mine in the gentlest of kisses.

'We will make babies together, you and I; of that I'm certain. A clutch of little Holands to grace our fireside in the years ahead. God will bless our marriage because it is a true marriage. It was hurried and the surroundings may not have been as grand as you would have liked but it was no less a true marriage for all that.'

'Was it?' I whispered. 'Was it truly a marriage made before God? I thought perhaps it was a nothing, just a deception.'

'God sees everything we do. He doesn't need a priest or a bishop to open the shutters onto our lives. Even in that tiny attic room He saw and heard what we did. We promised ourselves, one to the other, as husband and wife and when we were alone, we joined ourselves the way men and woman have always done since the time of Adam and Eve. What was that if it wasn't a marriage?'

His eyes were dark and warm with love, and the words he spoke dripped like honey into my ears. But I was not yet convinced by what my heart was telling me.

'Did I really please you?' I said uncertainly,

He tightened his grip and pulled my head onto his shoulder.

'I have had many women in my life and a great deal of pleasure in the having of them, but I have never enjoyed myself as much as I did that night with you. You were a revelation and I could hardly believe my luck in what I had in my arms. It was like lifting a stone at the edge of a stream to find a sparkling jewel hidden beneath and realising it was yours for the taking. Do you understand now why I was so angry with you when you married Montagu? I'd not only lost my path to great favours from the king but also the most alluring young woman I'd ever had in my bed.'

I giggled and settled myself more comfortably in his arms.

'Am I really alluring?'

He kissed he tip of my nose. 'Very.'

He stroked away the lock of hair which had come loose across my face and kissed my forehead, my ears and the lids of my eyes. With my fingers I traced the contours of his face.

'Will you show me your eye?' I asked, curious at last to see what lay beneath his evil-looking patch.

He smiled and guided my fingers up to the narrow ribbon.

'Go on,' he said. 'You do it.'

Gently I undid the knot and peeled back the soft leather. He blinked, his eye half-closed, unused to the brightness. A small puckered scar crossed the eyelid and ran partway down his cheek but the eye itself was whole and perfect. He was not some hideous monster, he was Thomas, the same Thomas who had walked with me in the orchard of the béguinage seven long years ago.

'Can you see me?' I whispered. 'With both eyes?'

'Yes,' he breathed into my cheek. 'I can see you for what you are: the most desirable, most beautiful young woman in the world. And my wife.'

We lay like this for a long time, barely speaking, him stroking my face and my hair.

'I can't do more than this,' he whispered into my hair. 'I want to, Christ knows how much I want to, but if I did I wouldn't be able to stop and I mustn't put you in any more danger than you're in already.'

'I wouldn't mind,' I said, snuggling up closer and feeling the long, lean length of him next to my body. The rough cloth of his padded jacket pressed hard into the soft folds of my gown as I pushed my leg beneath his.

'I know.' His breath caught as I ran my hands over his chest and down his body. 'But you have no sense, wife, so I must be sensible for both of us. There is a long and perilous path ahead and I mustn't behave like a boy beneath a hedge on Mayday.'

'I wish you could.'

'So do I, but I can't. Now, sit up and tidy yourself before I forget my duties completely.'

He removed his arms and gave me a little push.

'What will happen now?' I asked, trying to pin my hair back up. 'Do I go back to William?'

'Yes. Return to Montagu. Do what you usually do and put this out of your mind. Say nothing, but prepare yourself for when he finds out what I've done. Be ready with your story and say to him whatever you need to keep yourself safe because I shan't be there to protect you.'

'What about you?'

'We should be finished here in a week or so. The garrison are close to surrender and if the Valois comes with his army, he won't fight. Not again. We are too many for him. There'll be a treaty and then I'll ask permission to return to England. I now have the name of a man who can help me. He has spoken in the courts at Avignon many times and will know how to do this.'

What had seemed a dream was creeping frighteningly closer.

'Will I see you again?'

He took my face between his hands and kissed my mouth.

'No. It's better we don't risk it.'

'Nothing happened today that need frighten my confessor,' I murmured. 'My conscience is clear.'

'You, my lady, have an extremely adaptable conscience.'

'I know,' I laughed. 'It's a great benefit.'

I didn't see him again. A week later the French army appeared on the heights of Sangatte and one look at the size of our army and the massive defences our men had erected along the beaches and over the marshes brought the Valois king to the negotiating table. For four days he bargained in vain whilst we held our breath and the defenders of Calais moved closer to starvation and collapse. On the fifth night, while I slept fitfully in my bed dreaming of Thomas, the French burned their tents and by next morning they were gone. Calais was ours!

It had taken my cousin exactly eleven months to force the garrison into surrender and he was none too pleased. Together with everyone else, I watched the grand ceremony as six of the richest men of Calais stumbled barefoot with ropes round their necks through the massed ranks of our men and offered themselves up to the English king's mercy in order to save their fellow townsmen. But my cousin chose not to be merciful and ordered their beheading. It was a moment of great drama as the queen cast herself at her husband's feet and begged for the lives of those poor starved creatures and my cousin raised her up and gave her what she asked for. If it had been carefully planned as an entertainment for the watching thousands, it could not have been more thrilling.

'Thank you, Blessed Virgin,' I whispered under my breath. 'Thank you for delivering mercy so speedily and allowing us to go home. It isn't that I don't appreciate all aspects of Our Lord's creation but I really am heartily sick of the damp.'

10

INQUISITION 1347

The drumbeats ceased and with peculiar gracefulness the newly painted Montagu barge glided slowly towards the river bank. I was weary beyond measure but the sight of the Bisham villagers out in force to greet us was like a burst of sunshine on a dull December day. It had taken us the better part of a long and uncomfortable week to make the journey from Calais but at last we were home.

We disembarked at the foot of the jetty to a salute of trumpets and a guard drawn up for our inspection. As we walked together up the familiar path towards the gatehouse we found ourselves surrounded on all sides by a laughing, cheering crowd. Men tossed their caps in the air, women shouted blessings and little children threw bedraggled posies of late-summer flowers at our feet. There was no sun and the grass was sodden but at least the people were pleased to see us.

'What shall we do now?' I asked as we stepped across the threshold into a surprisingly warm and dry house.

'Entertain,' said William, gazing at the soaring glory of the hall as if he had never seen it before.

And entertain we did: invitations quickly sent out; long days of hunting through the woods and open spaces of our deer park; energetic hawking expeditions up the valley of the Thames; and for the older and less able or for the women unwilling to ride far, sedate picnics in the Bisham orchard complete with minstrels and games for the children.

In the late afternoons when the feasting was done and before the younger men drank themselves senseless, we danced and made merry, but as night fell and the torches were lit our neighbours gathered quietly around the fire to listen to William's stories of his part in the king's victorious campaign.

This was a new William. He wanted to be a great man like his father and grandfather before him and, with a knighthood under his belt and the prospect of his earldom less than two years away, he knew it was possible but he needed these magnificent displays of his generosity to persuade everyone else.

'A different woman every night this week,' muttered the eldest of my maids the morning after another rowdy feast which had lasted well into the evening hours.

'It's a disgrace,' she grumbled. 'It would never have happened in the earl's day and the Holy Mother of God knows he had cause enough.'

'Hold your tongue,' I snapped. 'It is not your place to comment on what a man does. He is your lord and you insult him with your gossiping.'

She shut her mouth in a thin disapproving line and reverted to jabbing the remaining pins into my hair. She was a middle-aged woman who had served the Montagu ladies since she was a girl but sometimes she forgot her position and behaved more like my mother.

It was true William had neglected me disgracefully since our return but I didn't care. I preferred to be left alone in my bed. Each morning I would wake, drowsy from sleep, forgetting I was William's wife, in William's house, eating William's food, drinking William's wine. I could feel the warmth of the summer sand soft beneath my head and the blazing heat of the Calais sun dancing on my face; hear the plaintive cry of a lonesome gull and the distant boom of the rolling surf, and in my mind I touched the soft strands of hair which fell across his face and put up my mouth for his kiss. I arched my body with desire and felt myself melt into him until all I wanted was to fall asleep again and dream the day away.

'I shall be gone at least four days,' William announced one morning. 'I have a particularly difficult tenant who is causing problems. You will, of course, look after matters here.'

The following day I took my place on the dais as lady of Bisham, to preside over dinner the way I had a hundred times before. I had no awareness that this day would be any different, there had been no warnings. While everyone ate and drank I amused myself by looking down the length of the hall at the passing travellers who had asked for hospitality and the curious townspeople from Great Marlow who had merely come to gawp.

When the meal was finished and everyone replete, I rose to take my leave. The men of the household scrambled up in haste, pushing benches aside and disturbing the rushes as the rumble of conversation ceased. At the far end of the hall there was some sort of altercation. One of William's new grooms, a big burly man who was not to my liking, was tussling with a small dark stranger barely half his size. An outbreak of fighting in my hall was not something I could ignore so I nodded to my page to go and find out what the problem was while I hesitated at the door.

'The little man wants to see you, my lady,' he said, puffing slightly with the exertion of having run all the way up the hall. 'Says he has a gift for you but yon bully won't let him near. Says he's not fit to wipe his boots on the master's floors and is threatening to throw him out on his arse.'

I sighed, suppressing a smile. I was well used to gifts from passing men with bold stares and beguiling smiles who liked to show their appreciation. I doubted this would be any different.

'Have him brought to my husband's room,' I said. 'I'll see him there.'

I crossed the floor and walked into William's room which had a completely different smell to mine: a low spicy scent of cinnamon and sandalwood and underlying that, a tang of musky male sweat; not unpleasant, merely different. The fire hadn't been lit and the room was chilly but I sat in William's chair and waited.

The man had a ferrety face with small dark eyes which darted to and fro as if seeking trouble, but he looked harmless enough and, thanks be to the Blessed Virgin, he smelled clean. In front of him he held a pedlar's pack, his bent fingers gripping tight to the battered leather, clearly frightened someone would snatch it away.

'You wished to see me,' I said, thinking how unnecessarily rough William's groom had been.

'A small gift, my lady,' he said, dropping to one knee. 'I have eaten well at your table and wish to show my gratitude.'

He placed his pack on the floor and began rummaging around in the depths. The men of the household stepped back and I noticed one or two of them yawning in boredom. Grovelling passers-by were six-a-penny and gifts like this one would be of no consequence. No groom was going to enrich himself with the pickings from this sort of churl.

The man shot me a glance from under his lashes and drew out a short length of ribbon. Black.

'For you, my lady,' he said in a low voice.

I took it in my hand and found my fingers trembling. It was narrow enough to wind around a bunch of violets picked damp from under the hedgerow or to thread through the top of a lady's embroidered sewing bag. Or if you were so minded and had the need, you might prefer to use it to tie in place a man's soft leather eyepatch.

I leaned forward to murmur thanks, my mouth close to his ear. 'Is there more?'

'A message. It is done.'

My eyes widened. 'Is that all?'

'Yes, my lady.'

I wanted more. I wanted to ask how Thomas did. Was he well? Was he safe? Was he bound for Avignon? Did he speak of me? This message was such a small thing to feed upon; so little, so insufficient, so tantalisingly close to what I desired and yet so far away.

One of the grooms coughed and I came to my senses. I could say nothing. Thomas, indeed, had told me to say nothing.

I felt in my purse for a coin but the small man shook his head and murmured, 'No need, my lady. The gentleman paid.'

It is done. So that was it at last. It is done.

I barely noticed the man's departure, the muttered apologies of my husband's men for my being disturbed by such a vagabond, and my stumbling walk back to the solar with the length of ribbon in my hand.

'Is that all?' said my lady companion, echoing my earlier words. 'And why black? Such a dreary colour. Didn't he have a pretty red?'

'For a mourning gown, perhaps,' I said with a little smile. 'Here, have it put in my chest.'

It is done.

But whatever had been done by Thomas, there was nothing I could do but wait.

I gazed across the outer walls of Bisham, gleaming gold in the early autumn sun. So neat and tidy, so sturdy and well-kept; the new buildings, constructed to my father-in-law's design, so beautiful with their painted archways and windows of little panes of Flemish glass. As a boatman had said to me once many years ago, Bisham was a jewel.

In the distance, the fields were shaved and yellow, yielders of a poor damp harvest. Even now wheat was rotting in the barns. Everyone knew the price of bread in the towns would rise and in the winter there would be much hunger. On the dark waters beyond the walls, a myriad of tiny boats like busy ants were ferrying people downstream to Great Marlow or Maidenhythe, perhaps all the way to London. This was the view I had seen most mornings since I first entered the Montagu household as a young girl, what greeted me on rising. But by next summer I would be gone and would never see it again.

'They're saying in the buttery the man as arrived this morning's a bishop,' announced one of my maids as she helped me into a fresh gown.

It was early November, unseasonably warm but with a wind sweeping in from the west, tearing the last leaves from the trees in Quarry Wood and shaking the shutters of the solar.

I felt cold fingers tiptoe down my spine. 'What man?'

'The man as is in with the lord. Blue with three gold mitres on his banner, the kitchen boy said. He's got a fair lot of servants with him. Seems far too many for a bishop. Cook's already complaining.'

I hadn't registered the arrival and didn't recognise the arms. Bishop Simon had been dead these two years and it wasn't Bishop Grandison. But who else could it possibly be? Yesterday I had ordered a man to Great Marlow for needles and English cloth but he would hardly return with a bishop. Perhaps the girl was wrong. And yet – a banner emblazoned with three gold mitres?

I spent the rest of the day trying desperately to concentrate on my embroidery as my needle flew in and out and the pale silk stitches coloured the stem of the Lenten lily winding its way up the sleeve of the gown on my lap. A boy arrived with an armful of logs and the page from the ewery came to ask if I wished for refreshments but otherwise our peace was undisturbed. I had one of my ladies read from the latest romance but found I could barely understand a single word.

It was late in the afternoon when William's groom knocked on the door with a message: my husband would not be joining the household at supper as he was otherwise occupied. There wasn't anything particularly unusual in this but my heart began to flutter and I felt slightly nauseous. My lady companions took no notice as missing husbands were a fact of life and of no concern. There was no reason to be alarmed.

Next morning William was nowhere to be seen and I was informed by a different groom that I was not required to dine in the hall. A selection of dishes would be sent to my chamber, I had no need to disturb myself. My belly churned in the way it used to when I had to meet my mother, and when the boys arrived with the food, I picked at it. I had no appetite and could barely manage to swallow. The day was warm but beneath my linen my body prickled with fear. I felt chilled and the hands which broke my bread were cold and clammy.

In early afternoon the noise of clattering hooves drifted up from the courtyard and one of the maids informed me the bishop, if bishop he was, was leaving. But still no word came from my husband. More dishes were brought upstairs at supper and by now my women had taken to gathering in corners, their hands half-covering their mouths, as they whispered to each other. We all knew something was not as it should be but they didn't know what.

I was about to give the order to retire for the night when the message came, a command to visit my husband in the room where he conducted his private business. No explanation was given and despite the lateness of the hour I knew I couldn't refuse or delay. So I smoothed my gown, summoned up my courage and followed the man down the stairs.

William was seated behind the great oak table with a parchment in his hand and another on the table. He didn't get up. His eyes sought mine but in the looking, changed from their usual indifference to a flinty hardness, the ditch-water darkening to the colour of a storm cloud.

I kept my face composed, a small upturning of the lips to show him I was pleased to be summoned to his presence and gave a little bob. It was what he expected. In his eyes it showed a proper respect from a dutiful wife and I had no wish to anger him at the start of what I feared was going to be a difficult encounter.

He held out the parchment.

It was very fine, very smooth, the words written in Latin. I raised my eyes.

'What is it?' I enquired lightly.

'Can't you read it?' His voice was curiously flat.

'No. We girls were not taught Latin. Your lady mother considered it unnecessary.'

'It is a summons from the court of the Holy Father in the name of Cardinal Adhémar Robert requiring me to appear before his tribunal at Avignon. Now do you know what it is?'

Deny everything, I thought. I shook my head. 'No. Why do they want you to go to Avignon?'

William's eyes narrowed.

'It seems Cardinal Robert is investigating a petition lodged by one Thomas Holand requesting the Holy Father to order the return of his wife.'

There was no sound in the chamber other than the gentle hiss of the fire as I stared back at William as innocently as I could.

'But what has this to do with you?'

'You know Thomas Holand?'

'Sir Thomas? Your steward? Of course I know him. He was with us in Calais. He sat with you in our hall.'

'According to Sir Thomas Holand you know him very well.'

Deny! Don't admit more than you have to.

'William, I've known Sir Thomas Holand for years.'

'How many years?'

'I don't know exactly. I don't keep a tally of your men. I think I recall him being your father's steward and until recently he was yours.'

His hands trembled as he took the parchment out of my fingers and put it down on the table. He kept glancing at it.

'It's not true, is it? Tell me it's not true. It can't be.'

I tried to look puzzled as if I had no idea what he was talking about.

All of a sudden his fist crashed onto the table with such force that the cup at his elbow rocked and wine slopped over the rim.

'Tell me!' he shouted. 'It's not true, is it?'

I jumped and took a step backwards almost falling over the hound stretched out on the floor.

'William, what is this? What's not true? Why are you shouting at me?'

He pushed himself out of the chair and came round the table. He was very much taller than me and for the second time in our marriage I was truly frightened of what he might do.

He put his hands on my shoulders, pressing so hard I feared my bones might crack.

'Thomas Holand claims you are his wife.'

'Me?' I tried to sound horrified. I was so scared of William that my voice dried in my throat and I began to shake.

'He says he married you before I did. He says he lay with you. He says he had you before I did.' He says…' His whole body was trembling in fury as his fingers gripped tighter and tighter until I wanted to scream with the pain. 'Tell me it's not true.'

In the forefront of my mind were my mother's words: it was not a marriage, there was no priest and it was not a marriage. Whatever else it was, it was not a marriage.

'William, this is impossible,' I pleaded. 'There was no marriage with Thomas Holand. I am married to you. We've been married seven years and we've shared a bed for more than five. You are my husband. How could anyone say I was another man's wife?'

'You swear it?'

His face was so close to mine I could feel the heat of his breath.

'We took our vows here, at Bisham,' I stammered. 'In front of our mothers, in front of the king and the queen; hundreds of people watched us marry. Of course I'm your wife.'

'You swear you didn't lie with him.'

'William, please. How could I? I came to you as a girl untouched. I was a virgin. You know I was.'

He paused for a moment and looked straight into my eyes. 'You were ripe and ready for a man. You oozed juice like a bruised plum. I remember that.'

Oh Holy Mother of God! And I thought I'd fooled him.

'I was nervous.'

'You were soft and you yielded yourself willingly.'

Think quickly. What to say?

'You were my husband, William. You had the right to take me. Naturally I was willing.'

He hesitated, still unsure.

'Was I the first? When I took you, was I the first or had you already permitted some other man to burrow his way into your secret parts?'

'William!'

'Do you swear there was no other before me?'

I tried a little smile though to be truthful, I was much too scared to think about smiling. 'Oh William. How could there have been? I was under your lady mother's protection from the time I was a child. I lived here at Bisham. Your mother kept all the girls in her keeping, well-guarded as you can imagine. We never went out without an escort and at night we slept in a chamber with our governess. And when we went to Antwerp in the queen's train, it was like living in a nunnery. Ask your sister?'

'You swear there was no marriage. You weren't his before you were mine, were you?'

I placed my hands on the front of his tunic and tipped my face upwards.

'I was pure when I came to you that night, as pure as Our Blessed Lady. Ask any of the women. They will remember your mother's pleasure when she saw our sheets next morning. The signs were unmistakeable. She knew you had done your duty as a husband and I was now your wife. She knew you were the first.'

He cast his eyes back at the parchment. 'But what does it mean? Why would Holand do this?'

'I don't know but it is a disgusting calumny.'

'He has no cause to harm me. What have I ever done to him?'

William's brow furrowed as he tried to think of a reason. His mind worked slowly as I had learned over the years, but nonetheless I had to act quickly. I was sure the worst of the danger was past but I had to be certain.

'It is the work of someone who wishes to harm you by slandering the Montagu name,' I said with certainty. 'Some enemy of yours who has used Thomas Holand as his cat's paw.'

His face lit up.

'That's it. A slander. Yes. Someone who wishes to harm me.' He chewed his lip. 'But who?'

'You are rising high, William. One day you will be a powerful man like your father and everybody knows a man on the rise makes enemies whether he likes it or not. There will be men who covet what you have and think you should be thrown down.'

'That's true. the king has favoured me on one or two occasions recently. It's obvious he appreciates me as he did my father.'

'And Edward speaks warmly of you.'

'He does?'

I smiled as sweetly as I could manage and placed a hand on his sleeve. 'The last time I met Edward in Calais he sent John Chandos away with the others in order to speak to me of you. He had spent many hours considering you and I think you will soon be the one who rides at his side and receives his favours, not John Chandos.'

'So it could be Chandos who has done this.'

'It could. He is only the son of a gentleman, so a low slander like this would not concern him. He would not consider damaging a man's honour anything other than a subject for mirth.'

William scowled.

'And what about your new brother-in-law, Philly's husband?'

'Young Roger Mortimer?'

'Yes.'

'But he's a friend.'

'William, there are no friends when it comes to matters like this. Men cheat and lie their way to the top and a man desperate to succeed tramples on anyone who gets in his way. It's how men are. You are just too good a friend to see it.'

He started pacing to and fro, his head down, his face sullen.

'But how could he do this to me? When I have welcomed him into our family. And why Holand? Why this particular slander?'

'The Bible tells us the sins of a father are visited upon a son unto the seventh generation and Mortimer's grandfather was an evil man. You remember how they say he attacked the king's father by using the queen as his instrument. Mortimer would think nothing of a deceit like this. He could be rubbing his hands in glee this very moment, thinking of your discomfort.'

William took my hands and gripped them tightly. 'I knew it couldn't be true. I knew all along you were truly mine.' He stopped. 'I shall fight this. I shan't let whoever did this get away with it.'

He folded me into his arms and held me close but it wasn't from love, it was an act of possession. I was his and I knew he would never let me go.

I thought William's suspicions were put to rest but in the days which followed I realised I was wrong. Each morning as I kneeled on the cushioned velvet of my prie-dieu or walked in the dampness of Lady Catherine's garden, I felt the hairs on the back of my neck rise and knew I was being watched. One of my maids fell unexpectedly sick and her replacement, a doe-eyed, mealy-mouthed fawner was seen sidling furtively into William's rooms late one evening. My companions were scandalised, foolishly imagining the girl aimed to replace me in my husband's bed, but I knew exactly what this Judas was doing and it wasn't a matter of lust. I was certain William paid her for information.

When, after a week, William disappeared without telling me where he was going, I knew I was in danger.

'London, my lady,' said the groom, who was supervising the tidying and cleaning of William's rooms. 'To bring back the dowager countess. My, but it'll be a treat to see the good lady again, God bless her. Must be more than three years.'

My mother-in-law! At the news, my heart sank. This was a woman who had said I was dead to her. She hated me and whether she thought me guilty or innocent of deceiving the Montagu family she would use this opportunity to take her revenge and I knew she would be merciless.

As I watched the pale grey dawn lighten the sky each morning I counted the days since William's departure and like a man awaiting the footsteps of his executioner I found myself ever-vigilant to the slightest sound. A week passed, ten days, two weeks, and with each passing hour I became more and more afraid.

One day I woke to a thick late-autumn mist hanging sullenly over the river, obscuring everything beyond the outer walls, giving the world a ghostly appearance and thought this must be a harbinger, but still nobody came.

Then, on a dark morning, well past the Feast of All Souls, when all the world seemed dead, I heard the first sound of an arrival. They came one by one: the soft clip-clop of snowy-white mules drawing an old lady's litter followed by the noisy exuberance of a young man's spirited hunter; the heavy rumble of a widow's magnificent travelling coach, its wheels and axles caked in mud and grime; the steady tramp of an escort which masked the slower pace of a lady's palfrey, and the clattering hooves as a great man and his retinue swept into the yard.

I hadn't been expecting the elegant sounds of Bishop Grandison's private train but when I heard them I was not surprised. And lastly, my husband, the chief witness and prosecutor, announced by an ecstatic yelping from the Bisham hounds as they streamed down the steps into the inner yard to greet their master.

Orders had been sent ahead for me to be kept in my room. I was not to act as the lady of the house in welcoming these guests because they were not my guests and to me they were not welcome. They were my interrogators, my peers, the judge and jury who would determine my guilt or my innocence according to their own set of rules and I had no expectation of mercy or understanding from any of them.

I wore my most sober gown, one of dull grey woollen cloth with a plain white coif, knowing full well that any frivolousness on my part would instantly be seen as proof of guilt. I removed my rings and made sure my shoes were soft-soled in case they remarked on the hesitancy of my coming even though I had no wish to appear anything other than my husband's devoted wife.

As I walked into William's private room with my head held high, the first thing that struck me was the emptiness of the chamber. I had expected a group of local knights from William's council of advisors or perhaps his chief clerk, but no, this was to be solely a family affair.

They were seated at the table but there was no chair set for me. I was expected to stand. William sat in his father's carved chair, flanked by his two uncles, Bishop Grandison and Alice's husband, and by his younger brother, John, whilst on either side sat Lady Catherine, Elizabeth, and William's grandmother, the elderly Dowager Lady Montagu.

I was faced with seven pairs of hostile eyes and not a single smile or greeting.

'Lady,' began Alice's husband. 'You know why you are here and I can tell you this, if you don't give us the truth you will regret it.'

'Uncle, please.' William hunched his shoulders like a stork sheltering from the rain, looking for all the world like a man facing his imminent end.

'I want no lies,' continued Alice's husband as if William hadn't spoken. 'There will be no twisting of the truth. You will answer the questions I put to you and you will answer them truthfully. Is that clear?'

I looked at William but he had his head bowed and wouldn't meet my eyes. I turned to his uncle.

'I have nothing to hide, sir. I am a virtuous woman who has done nothing wrong and anyone who says otherwise is lying.'

He glared at me. 'I have heard of your so-called virtue and let me tell you this, it does not impress me. You know this man, this Thomas Holand?'

'I do. He was my husband's steward.'

'And do you deny this marriage which he says took place between the two of you?'

I chose my words carefully, as I had no wish to imperil my soul further by lying. It was a matter of selecting as much of the truth as could be told.

'There was no marriage between me and Sir Thomas Holand. How could there be? I am married to my husband who sits beside you. There were a hundred or more witnesses to our wedding. It was blessed by your own brother, the Bishop of Ely, may God have mercy on his soul.'

But William's uncle was not so easily fooled. He could smell evasion.

'That is not the question. It seems you insinuated yourself into this family by deceit. A girl in her finery with lies on her tongue is not a bride if she has a husband living. Such an occasion may be witnessed by a thousand men and yet be false. The question is: were you a true bride? Did you come to my nephew untouched by any other man?'

'Your brother himself blessed our bedding.'

'And you were a virgin?'

'Sir!' I wanted to sound as appalled as any woman would whose virtue at such a time was being questioned. I lowered my head as if overcome by shame at discussing an intimate matter. 'Ask my husband,' I said in a low voice. 'He will tell you I was.'

There was a moment of whispers between William and his mother and his uncle. The others looked on in stony silence.

'I saw the sheets myself,' admitted Lady Catherine. 'They were stained but we all know there are ways. She is deceitful. She would have known what to do. My son was raised to be a fine boy and would not have expected trickery. She fooled him.'

'Well, nephew? Did she make a fool of you? Had some churl been making free in the undergrowth before you?'

William shot me a glance of pure hatred. 'I thought she was a virgin. She pretended she was. She squealed like a stuck pig but was very willing. Far too willing for a maiden. And she wriggled like a whore.'

Lady Catherine sat back in her chair. 'Just as I said; a slut and a whore.'

She had already decided on my guilt but her brother, the bishop, being a man of learning, was determined to have proof.

'If this so-called marriage happened before they were wed here at Bisham, where could it have occurred? Where was she?' Bishop Grandison had a silky voice but I wasn't deceived. He was dangerous. 'Was it possible? She was in your household was she not, sister?'

'She was and she was well-guarded. I had several women watch the girls in my house but for a deceitful, determined girl there are always ways.'

She turned to her daughter. 'Elizabeth! She slept with you in the girl's chamber. You must have known her character well. What do you recall?'

Elizabeth smiled thinly as she prepared the revenge she had been waiting to inflict on me for years.

'As you said, lady mother, a whore, and one who knew words which would make you blush. I saw her follow men as they carried provisions to the store rooms, giggling at their jokes, and she made free with my father's squires. Men constantly snapped at her heels and she encouraged them.'

'How so?' said William's brother with a hot look in his eye. 'What did she do?'

'What whores always do. You're a man, John; you surely know how it's done. When we were hidden by crowds at the tourney, men would sidle up and place their hands on her person. It was disgusting.'

'And did she welcome their attentions?'

'She did.'

'She could hardly have married this man and lain with him on the grass at the tourney,' said William's brother. 'That would have been impossible.'

'I didn't say she married him then and there, John, I meant she was the sort of girl who would have done so if the opportunity had arisen.'

'Was there opportunity?'

'How long does it take to wed and bed?' said Alice's husband.

There was a silence while doubtless the women considered the stitching of gowns and the setting of veils and the men pondered the speed with which they might, if the possibility arose, take a willing bride.

'It can be done in a trice,' remarked William's grandmother drily. 'He would hardly have wanted a display of magnificence. He wasn't planning to invite the nobility and give an extravagant feast. All he wanted was the girl.'

'But where was it done? Lady, do you have an answer for us?' said William's uncle, leaning forward and glaring at me.

'Nothing was done, sir. As I told you before, there was no marriage.'

'Perhaps the girl is telling the truth,' said the elderly dowager picking her words with the care of a practised interrogator. 'Perhaps it was not a marriage at all. Perhaps it was a sham. She's no fool. I recall the eve before the bedding.' She fixed her eagle eyes on me the way she had that evening. 'I asked if she was indeed *virgo intacto* and she reddened like an autumn sunset. She was no maid then, I'd swear to it. I thought it was my grandson's doing but it seems not. Thus the question you should be asking is, not when did she marry this man but when did she lie with him and why? Was she tricked or was she a slut as my daughter-in-law proposes?'

'And have there been others?' said Elizabeth. 'We need to know that.'

Alice's husband seized the bone he had been thrown. 'You were defiled before you came to my nephew? You opened your legs for some other man? Is that true? Perhaps this is not so much a matter of marriage we are discussing but one of fornication.'

I stood as straight as I could and looked him right in the eye. 'Sir, I will answer no more of your questions. You have impugned my virtue and it is not what I would have expected from my husband's kinsman.'

'Virtue!' hissed Lady Catherine. 'What virtue do you possess, you disgusting slut? I know exactly what you are and the depths to which you'll sink.' She turned to her brother-in-law. 'She's a whore. She's been a whore since before she married my son and she'll be a whore till the end of her days. She'll rot in the corruption of her own flesh.'

'Lady mother,' protested William's brother, 'You can't say such things without proof.'

'I have proof,' said Lady Catherine. 'I have seen her with my own eyes, crawling into the lap of a man who was not her husband, half-naked, her gowns in disarray and her hair loose on her shoulders.'

'I knew it,' said Elizabeth.

'You know nothing,' said William's brother angrily. 'Where was this, lady mother? Were there witnesses?'

'Her steward was there,' said Lady Catherine. 'A good, loyal man. He saw it all. Her maid had been locked away so she couldn't bear witness to her mistress's sin, but the servants knew; they heard. And she would ensnare you too, my son, if she turned her wiles on you. She has no shame. There is no end to her depravity.'

'And the man?' said Bishop Grandison. 'Who was it?'

'That is of no importance,' said Lady Catherine. 'It is her sins we are examining.'

William's grandmother narrowed her eyes. 'Who would she tell?'

'What do you mean?' said William's uncle.

'Girls always tell someone, my son. If she had a secret she would have whispered it to somebody. The question is to whom?'

They all turned to Elizabeth.

'Not me,' she said. 'We were not friends. I despised her.'

'Who else was there? A sister? 'An old nurse?' said the elderly Lady Montagu.

'She has cousins,' said Elizabeth.

William's uncle laced his fingers together. 'My wife would not be so unwise. She knows well the punishment for disobedience and a sin like this would mean chastisement. She would not dare. If she had knowledge of her cousin's wickedness and kept it hidden from me or if she had so much as lifted a finger to help, she knows I would see she lived to regret it.'

'What about the other cousin?'

'She rarely sees Lady Segrave,' said Lady Catherine. 'We have no connection with the family.

'The mother?' said William's grandmother. 'Would she have confided in her? A girl in distress? What could be more natural than to turn to her mother.'

Lady Catherine hissed through her teeth and turned pale. 'The dowager countess? Never. She would not deceive me. Impossible. We agreed this marriage together. She would not have lied. Not to me.'

'Not then, sister,' said Bishop Grandison, patting Lady Catherine's arm. 'But later. What if knowledge of this liaison occurred after the matter was settled and the contracts drawn up. What if she was caught between a disobedient daughter and the collapse of her plans. Which would be more important to her: to protect her family or to protect her soul?'

The eyes swivelled back to me.

'Did you tell Your lady mother about this man?' said the bishop.

'My mother and I did not see each other until just before my marriage,' I replied. 'She came here to Bisham to prepare me for my wedding.'

'And did you tell her of this man, this Thomas Holand? What did you speak of?'

'Reverend Father, my mother and I spoke of many things. We were a loving mother and daughter who had not seen each other for three long years. She had arranged this wonderful marriage for me but she was concerned because I was so young. You forget, I was only fourteen years old, barely more than a child.'

William's uncle snorted. 'Child? You were a practiced whore. I've seen your sort on the streets of London, plying their trade in the taverns and alleyways, lifting their skirts as they lead a man to the stable-yard.'

The bishop drew his mantle across his chest as if to distance himself from the noxious stews of London and their manifest horrors.

'If there had been a marriage of sorts there would have been witnesses,' said the elderly lady dowager who I thought had been dozing but who had apparently been thinking. 'Every marriage has its witnesses, especially one where a man is trying to trick a woman. Can we find out who they were?'

I shivered, hoping no trace of our witnesses could ever be found.

'A man would take his squire,' said William's uncle. 'Or his brother. Does Holand have a brother?'

'Yes,' said William, in a low voice. 'He does. He sent him home with his prisoner after we took Caen.'

'And a girl?' said William's uncle turning to the women. 'Who would she take? Who would she trust to keep her mouth shut?'

Elizabeth spoke. 'Her maid. But she didn't have one of her own; she shared mine.'

'And where is this maid of yours?'

'Here at Bisham, uncle. She came with me to Hanley on my marriage to Lord Despenser. She is my chief maid. But I'm sure…'

'Get her,' said her uncle.

Ignoring his rudeness, but as always, obedient to his wishes, Elizabeth rose and went to the door where she had a whispered conversation with whoever was outside and a few moments later a frightened-looking young woman whom I recognised from our days in Ghent, was escorted into the room by one of William's grooms. She looked at me with horror and dropped her eyes to the floor.

'You, girl!' barked William's Uncle Montagu. 'You know who this is?' He indicated me.

She nodded. 'Yessir. The Lady Joan, sir.'

'I require you to think carefully before you answer and be sure to tell me the truth. I will know if you lie and I'm sure you have been told what happens to young women who lie, haven't you?'

She looked as if she might faint with fear. She nodded but was unable to produce more than a squeak.

'You know what a marriage is? You understand how a man and a woman promise themselves to each other? You will have seen a priest give a blessing to a couple and pronounce them man and wife.'

She nodded again but I thought she would have nodded if he had asked was I a unicorn or had wings sprouting from my shoulders.

'Did you at any time attend a marriage between this woman, this Lady Joan, and a man, a man other than my nephew, Sir William Montagu? It is very important you give us the right answer.'

She turned her head to me.

'Don't look at her!'

The poor woman jumped and began to tremble.

'Well?'

'No, sir,' she whispered.

'You're quite certain?'

'Yes, sir.'

'You never obliged her by witnessing an arrangement she had with another man?'

'No, sir. Never, sir. I swear, sir.'

'She never asked you to accompany her to some house where a man was waiting to receive her?'

'No, sir.' I could barely hear her reply.

'She never bought your silence?'

This time there was nothing more than a squeak of fright.

William's uncle spat onto the rushes with a sound of disgust. 'Get rid of this fool. She's of no use to us.'

The woman was escorted out still trembling and looking at her mistress to see if she had given the right answers. She would have sworn black was white if Elizabeth's uncle had asked her, she was so frightened. But for me, her denial was an opportunity.

'You see,' I said quietly once the door was closed. 'I have told you the truth. There was no marriage. No witnesses, no marriage.'

'I do not believe you,' snarled William's uncle. 'You are lying.'

But William could face no more.

He was ashen-faced, cringing under his uncle's words like a whipped hound. 'Leave her alone,' he said in a low voice. 'I have had enough.'

'What do you intend to do with her, brother,' said Elizabeth. 'She has sullied your name. Do you propose to allow her liberty to carry on with her shameless ways, letting her and this man spread these slanders abroad?'

'Lock her in her chamber,' said Lady Catherine.

'That's it,' said William's grandmother. 'Lock the bitch in a kennel.'

The men nodded, all certain of my guilt but each one knowing that a plan of campaign was urgently needed regardless of what could be proved or disproved.

Reluctantly William rose and gave his orders. I was to be escorted back to my rooms and was to remain in seclusion until my husband decreed otherwise. A guard was to be placed on the door.

As I walked back up the stairway I sensed a dozen men of the household standing in the shadows, watching in bewilderment at my spectacular fall from grace, and heard them mutter in disbelief: what could the lord's wife have possibly done?

I shivered and wondered how long it would be before Thomas came to rescue me.

It was the Eve of the Nativity of the Christ Child and the comforting sounds of the Bisham household preparing to celebrate twelve days of feasting were filling the air. A tantalising smell of roasted meats and aromatic spices rose up from the kitchens, and from somewhere outside my window men called merry greetings to each other as they dragged great boughs of holly across the courtyard.

The house was full of joyful singing and happy laughter but here in my chamber there was nothing but silence. I sat with almost no company, just two maids who knew better than to utter a word. My hounds no longer lay curled in front of the hearth and the perch where my sleepy falcon had nestled deep in her feathers, was empty. My astonished ladies had been sent home to their husbands without a word of apology and I had been told they would not be returning. William was determined I should have no contact beyond the walls of Bisham. There were to be no letters, no messages and no meetings with anyone not approved by him. I was, as every man in the household must have realised by now, a virtual prisoner of my husband.

'The dowager countess, my lady,' said William's groom apologetically, holding open the door and ushering in a woman enveloped in black.

I looked up, expecting to see Lady Catherine but instead saw the even more unwelcome figure of my mother. She swept in, bringing with her an icy draught which chilled the whole room. She cast her eyes round the poverty of my arrangements and sat herself down in the chair which I had just vacated, leaving me to stand like a needy petitioner.

'I have been told,' she said, without the kindness of a greeting or a kiss on the cheek. 'I knew I should have dealt with that scoundrel at the beginning. I should not have listened to my conscience.'

'Greetings, lady mother,' I said, giving her a daughter's curtsey.

'Well? What have you told him?' she demanded.

'Who?' I asked politely although I knew perfectly well who she meant.

'Your husband. What does he know?'

What indeed? For seven years I had shared William's life, yet he knew nothing of me. He had never asked my opinion on any matter so I had never felt inclined to confide in him and apart from those early months of our marriage when a tentative friendship sprang up as we journeyed into the West Country to visit our marriage portion, we had never been close.

'I'm not sure.'

'You're not sure?' She pulled off her gloves and waved them at her maid who scuttled across the floor to relieve her of her burden. 'You must know what you've said to him. I trust you haven't been so foolish as to tell him the truth because truth will be the end you and let me make this quite clear: when you fall, I do not intend to fall with you.'

'I am quite certain your position is safe,' I said coldly. 'Nobody will blame you. I shall tell them you knew nothing.'

But she was like a dog with a rat, worrying, snarling and snapping, determined to see it destroyed.

'You are a fool,' she said. 'You have no idea what could happen, do you? You think it will be a small matter but let me tell you, it will be utter disgrace: imprisonment, months in the dark, not enough to eat and everything lost. The rings on your fingers, those pretty clothes you wear, the sheets on your bed, they'll all be gone.'

She reached out and grasped my wrist, pulling me close so that I half-knelt on the floor in front of her. 'Once, it happened to me, daughter,' she said, so low I could barely hear her words, 'and I do not intend to let it to happen again. Now, tell me: what did you say to your husband?'

'I denied everything,' I said struggling to my feet. 'You said there was no marriage between myself and Thomas Holand so that is what I told him. I said there could not have been a marriage as I was married to him.'

'Bah!' said my mother. 'Do you imagine that will satisfy him for long? Wait till Lady Catherine and that scheming uncle of his get their claws into him. Once they toss your words around they'll see just how hollow they are and then what do you plan to do, eh?'

I sat down on the stool as my mother was obviously not going to ask me to sit and this was my chamber.

'I shall continue to deny it.'

'And when they produce the Host and ask you to swear on your immortal soul? What then? Will you risk damnation?'

'They cannot say it was a marriage if it was not, can they?'

My mother's eyes narrowed with cunning. 'That won't matter. They will find witnesses: the woman who let you into the house; she will swear you were there with him. She will tell how you went up those stairs before dark and didn't come down until morning. What will you say then?'

'They'll never find her. They don't even know where it happened. They don't know anything about her.'

My mother banged her fist. 'Fool! He has to tell the tribunal everything. He will give them every tiny little detail down to the colour of your stockings and the words he whispered into your ear. They'll want to know if you struggled in fear while he took your maidenhead or if you twisted and sighed with a young girl's pleasure. These are dry dusty men of the cloth and they take their enjoyment that way, through the imagined doings of others. They have never felt the smooth skin of a girl's body and they will want to know what it was like. They will ask how often you cried out his name and whether it was done in fear or in passion. His attorney will make much of his evidence and once he does that, your husband will know everything there is to know.'

Thomas had warned me but, Holy Virgin, I hadn't thought it would be as bad as this.

'Perhaps he won't believe it,' I said lamely.

'Oh he'll believe it, my daughter, and when he does your life won't be worth so much as an empty husk and that piece of scum will be a dead man.'

'Will they kill him?' I whispered.

'Not yet. He's quite safe while his petition is in the hands of the Holy Father. But afterwards, when the case goes against him, what do you think your husband and the men of his family will do? Your Thomas Holand will spend his days looking over his shoulder, avoiding the shadow of an assassin. But he won't escape, there are too many hours of darkness and a man with a price on his head is a tempting target.'

'What if the Holy Father says it was a true marriage? What if he says Sir Thomas and I are truly husband and wife?'

My mother gave a hollow laugh. 'That will never happen. Lady Catherine is on her way to Avignon this very moment with a heavy purse of gold and as Lord Arundel discovered, gold unlocks many a door in the papal palace. Lady Catherine will have the decision on your marriage returned to the bishop's court in England. And the bishops will, naturally, rule in your husband's favour.'

'But what if they…?'

'If they show any reluctance, the king will apply a little pressure.'

I sat perfectly still, considering my mother's words and the hopelessness of Thomas's case. Yet his attorney was a man accustomed to speaking at the papal court and wouldn't be a fool.

'Suppose, just suppose, the Holy Father finds in favour of Sir Thomas. I would be returned to him, wouldn't I? William would have to let me go.'

My mother sat back in her chair and regarded me steadily.

'William Montagu will never let you go. He is not going to relinquish a wife who is the king's cousin, a rich, well-connected young woman. Why would he? He and his uncles will make quite certain you and your wealth remain in the Montagu family until the day you die.'

'But if I am Sir Thomas's wife and he comes for me…'

'Don't be foolish. Thomas Holand won't get within a mile of the gates of Bisham, Montagu will see to that, and if by some mischance he did abduct you, how far do you think the pair of you would get? This is not Camelot. He is no brave young knight in a dark wood rescuing an innocent damsel. This is here, inside the walls of your husband's house and you are not innocent. Within a day Thomas Holand would be dead with his throat slit and you would be dragged back to Bisham.'

The thought of Thomas lying dead filled my dreams. The maid who shared my bed said demons must have taken hold of my soul. There could be no other explanation for a mistress who had defied her husband and was denied the pleasures of the Christmas season, a mistress who wept in her sleep and woke screaming in the dark.

I was permitted to attend the Angels' Mass at midnight in the Bisham chapel but at no time did William let go of my wrist. I stood by his side like a dutiful wife and nobody knew how much it cost me not to rage and scream and pull myself away. My mother, I was told, stayed to the end of the feasting but I didn't see her again. And ahead of me I could see nothing but a long dreary winter and the prospect of a cold and bitter spring.

The queen's *relevailles* took place in her grand apartments at the royal palace at Windsor on a miserably wet midsummer's day. As if in defiance of the rain, every single person present looked magnificent. The ladies of the queen's chamber who circled the great state bed fluttered in their new silk gowns, swaying gently like a field of bright summer flowers, while the men of the household, from the chancellor down to the most menial page, had brand new clothes. Nothing was refurbished or altered to fit, there were no added trimmings to make an old tunic look fresh, everything had been newly stitched from the very latest and richest Flemish cloth.

The queen was dwarfed by the magnificence of her glittering red and purple robes and by the extravagant silks and velvets of the sumptuous royal bed, but her smile was radiant. The baby was another healthy boy and perhaps for the first time in my life I envied her. She wasn't beautiful and her figure after yet another confinement looked more like an overcooked apple dumpling than ever, but everybody said how much my cousin loved her.

I was certain he never gave a thought to women like me, the ones he had selected for their beauty and charm, the ones who had surrendered willingly to his advances, who had given up their virtue, their good names and the respect of their husbands to share a king's bed. The only thing of importance to him were the four beautiful daughters and five strong sons given to him by his wife.

I was there at the queen's request. The invitation, requiring Sir William Montagu to bring the Lady Joan, the king's kinswoman, to Windsor, may have been meant as a kindness but I was the one who had to suffer an angry and reluctant husband escorting me up the hill to the palace walls. He had wanted to leave me behind at Bisham in the seclusion of my chamber where I'd spent the past six months, seeing no-one and with no idea what was happening in Avignon or anywhere else, but he was caught by a royal command.

'If Holand is there you are not to go near him. You will not look at him, you will not talk to him, you will have nothing to do with him. Do I make myself clear?'

'Yes, William,' I said wearily, wondering if the pleasure of seeing other people was worth this incessant hectoring in my ear.

'I have appointed these women to be with you at all times.' He indicated two great harpies whose bulging arms must surely be evidence of a lengthy apprenticeship pounding clothes in the Bisham laundry. 'They will keep you company and ensure your good behaviour. Don't think you can outwit them because I have instructed them carefully. They have been warned of your deceitful nature and know exactly what to do if you misbehave.'

I didn't enjoy the day's entertainments. I was unable to have any proper conversations and quickly became weary of other women giggling and whispering behind their hands as they gazed at my gaolers who were constantly at my back or blocking my way, sometimes linking their arms with mine and even accompanying me to the latrines. Eventually, tired of unwelcome stares and spiteful comments, I retired back to our room, preferring my own company or the even more disagreeable prospect of seeing William.

The pale grey light was fading and the candles had been lit early when one of the queen's pages arrived at the door asking politely if I would please accompany him. He gave no reason and I didn't ask, simply glad for the opportunity to shake off my warders.

He led me to the royal apartments, through one gorgeous room into the next, until we finally arrived at the door to the queen's private rooms. At this point he turned to my two determined companions.

'You cannot come in,' he said firmly. 'Only Lady Montagu.'

They exchanged a frightened look and stepped back, totally in awe of their surroundings, knowing they mustn't incur the queen's displeasure.

I crossed the threshold into rooms which at one time in my youth would have been familiar. Two maids were seated at one end of the room industriously mending, catching the remaining light from the narrow west window while another was attending to the queen's hands, removing her heavy rings and placing them carefully in a silver coffer.

When the queen saw me she waved the woman away and told me to sit. I curtsied carefully and lowered myself onto the little velvet-covered stool at her feet. By the light of the candles she no longer looked radiant, merely tired and pale. She was very plain, her skin spotted with freckles with lines around her mouth, and once again I wondered why my cousin, who could surely have picked any woman, had chosen her. It wasn't as if Hainault was a powerful country with great wealth, it was like Flanders, just another cloth-weaver's county. She would have brought him nothing.

'Lady Montagu. What a trouble you are.'

My eyes filled with unexpected tears. 'Oh Your Grace, I'm sorry.'

'No you're not,' she said briskly. 'You're not in the least bit sorry unless you mistake feeling sorry for yourself with the remorse you ought to be experiencing. You are nothing but a silly vain young woman who thinks only of her own pleasure.'

This was dreadful. I'd known for years she didn't really like me, ever since she'd sent me away from Woodstock, but I had no idea what I'd done to deserve this attack. I bent my head and tried to look meek.

'I've known you since you were a child and I used to have pity for you. It's a curse to be as beautiful as you are, Lady Montagu. I watched you grow and saw how men gazed on your beauty and lusted after you the way they would lust after a rare and precious jewel. In your presence they could think of nothing other than their desire to possess you. It was like a sickness and it affected all of them. Even the king.'

My eyes widened in horror. She knew!

A slow cat-like smile spread across her flat features and I realised she was amusing herself at my discomfort.

'He tells me everything, Lady Montagu,' she said calmly. 'Everything. A loving wife always knows when her husband has strayed and she forgives him when he confesses. For years I watched him struggle against his feelings for you. It was obvious to me how much he desired you. I sent you away hoping he would no longer be tempted but in the end he was not strong enough and you were just a silly little girl who mistook a man's lust for something else.'

I swallowed the shame and the horror of her knowing, wondering how much he had told her but quickly realised it didn't matter how much; it was the betrayal of telling her at all. It cheapened what I thought we had had together and for the first time in my life I truly felt like a whore. I thought he had loved me and yet the moment he had left my bed he had gone running to her and told her what he had done.

'I didn't mean to hurt you,' I wept.

'You didn't,' she said coldly. 'Don't flatter yourself, Lady Montagu. You meant less than nothing to him. Once he'd taken you, it was finished. You were like some insignificant town he'd besieged. Once the gates were forced and the houses stripped of their wealth, he lost interest. I imagine you thought you were the only one, but you weren't; there were others. For a man like him, a great king, there will always be others, women who think themselves irresistible. And I imagine you thought you were somehow special, a true and passionate love, but you weren't that either. You should know by now how men whisper lies in the pursuit of a woman. You mattered not one jot to him. No woman matters to him but me. I am the only one who can hold him because I am the only one he respects, the only one he truly loves. You are not important and you never were.'

I sat in tears, wishing I was back at Bisham and thinking I could never face my cousin again. How could he have told her what we'd done together?

After a while, when I stopped sobbing and started dabbing my eyes, the queen continued as if I were nothing but the stupid little girl she said I was.

'Stop weeping, Lady Montagu. You must learn not to cry over men. It is very irritating and not at all helpful and I didn't bring you here to discuss your girlish infatuation with my husband. Now, this affair concerning Sir Thomas Holand.'

'Oh!' I put my hand across my mouth. 'I didn't know you knew.'

'You foolish woman! Of course I know. Did you imagine a scandal like this can remain a secret? I should imagine half the court knows and is laughing at you behind their hands. Not only have you shamed your husband and caused him great distress, you have near bankrupted him. He has had to ask the king for help. It costs a great deal to involve oneself with the papal court and Sir William does not have the funds. He is still a relatively young man without recourse to his inheritance and you have done him a great disservice with your silliness.'

She stopped and regarded me severely.

'I have been approached by the Bishop of Norwich, Bishop Bateman, who is in a quandary. It seems the papal tribunal will not accept the attorney duly appointed by your husband on your behalf. They say the attorney must be answerable only to you. I gather Sir William has declined to allow anyone access to your person, keeping you in seclusion, a matter for which, I may say, you have only yourself to blame. I do not propose to ask if there is any truth in this ludicrous story, that is not what concerns me. However, I would not see a woman deprived of justice and since we all desire a speedy resolution of this regrettable affair, I have asked Bishop Bateman to find a suitable attorney to advise you.'

She beckoned to one of her maids. 'Take Lady Montagu to the green chamber.'

I tried to tell her of my gratitude but she waved me aside.

'Go away, Lady Montagu. I'm tired of you. You have been nothing but a disappointment to me and I don't want to see you again.'

It was humbling to be spoken to like this by a woman who had once been almost a mother to me but all I could do was creep away with my head bent, wishing I had never come to Windsor.

I followed the queen's maid through a door into a little ante-room and then into another room where the walls were hung with a rich green cloth. A group of men looked up as I came in and from their faces I could tell this was not a place for idle conversations, this was a room for serious business.

I had never met Bishop Bateman before but William's father once told me he spent much of his time in Avignon on the English king's business and was held in the highest esteem by both my cousin and the Holy Father. He was tall and austere and looked much too clever to bother with a young woman too stupid to realise that her royal lover would be bound to tell his wife of his affairs, a young woman who was in so much trouble that even the Queen of England didn't want to see her face.

'Reverend Father,' I murmured miserably as I knelt to kiss his ring.

'Lady Montagu.' He bowed his head and indicated that I should sit.

He regarded me out of a pair of heavy-lidded eyes and his voice when he spoke was deep and sonorous.

'The Holy Father was graciously pleased to receive the petition from Sir Thomas Holand although somewhat surprised, as was I. We do not expect to see cases like this at the Curia.'

He gave a slight cough and looked down his long nose as if both his and the Holy Father's surprise was entirely my fault.

'It has long been understood, Lady Montagu, that the question of the abduction of a wife or the validity of a marriage should be dealt with in the ecclesiastical courts, here in England. That is how it has always been. However, understanding Sir Thomas's difficulties, His Holiness has graciously agreed to appoint Cardinal Adhémar Robert to preside over a tribunal which will investigate this most unfortunate of matters.'

He drew forward another man, a black-robed middle-aged man with a round face and sharp brown eyes who had an ill-clad youth holding a bag of parchment and quills hovering at his shoulder.

'This is Master Nicholas Heath. He will act as your attorney. He is well-versed in canon law and known to me so you can be assured as to his probity. He has great experience in the law and I am certain he will deal with your somewhat unusual situation speedily and to the tribunal's satisfaction.'

The bishop gave a weak smile as if the whole unfortunate matter was extremely distasteful to him. More used to important diplomatic missions, he must regard my marital troubles as grubby and of little importance and he looked extremely relieved to be washing his hands of his responsibility for me. With a brief nod and a curt aside to Master Heath, he disappeared swiftly through a side door accompanied by a swish of his expensive robes and a waft of chill air. His two servants followed hastily after him, leaving me alone with Master Heath and the boy.

I smiled at my attorney who gave a little bow, creasing the immaculate folds of his gown which flowed around his plump middle. He took the stool on the other side of the table and indicated the pimply youth who was busy laying out parchment and inks.

'My clerk. He will take notes if you have no objection, my lady. My memory is good but the written word never lies.'

I gave the boy a brief smile and he blushed like a girl right up to the roots of his straw-coloured hair.

'Before we proceed to the matter in hand,' said Master Heath. 'Let me first make it clear that I am here to represent you and only you. I do not represent Sir William Montagu nor do I represent Sir Thomas Holand and I do not in any way represent the views of His Grace the king nor of any other person. I am totally your man.'

What a pretty little speech. I was impressed.

He steepled his fingers, resting them comfortably against the front of his gown, almost sighing with contentment.

'Let me start at the beginning, Lady Montagu. A tribunal under the auspices of Cardinal Adhémar Robert has been charged by the Holy Father to enquire into the circumstances of your marriage.' He smiled a thin-lipped smile. 'Your first marriage.'

'Oh!'

'Sir Thomas Holand asserts that you are his wife and he wishes you to be returned to him.'

'But I am married to Sir William Montagu. Everybody knows that.'

'My lady, it is not a question of what everybody knows, but of what the tribunal knows.'

'How will they know?'

He smiled at my ignorance.

'They will ask questions. They will listen carefully to the arguments we attorneys put forward and they will consider the testimony of the principals in the case and the testimony of any witnesses. When the tribunal has heard all the evidence set before it, there will be deliberation. The auditor and the notaries will review the evidence and consult their books on canon law and the cardinal and the auditor will discuss the more difficult points. Doubtless they will pray for guidance and then the court will deliver its considered judgement to the Holy Father.'

I thought it very peculiar to think of all these men deliberating and praying about my marriage to Thomas.

'And now, if you are ready, shall I begin?'

I nodded my head in acquiescence. This could not be difficult. Surely it was very simple.

'As you know the case before the tribunal concerns your alleged marriage with Sir Thomas Holand.'

He had a persuasive manner of speaking which spread like ripples on a millpond until all I was aware of was the rise and fall and the rhythm of his voice.

'Before we discuss the facts of your marriages, my lady, you need to understand how much the Church frowns upon private marriages, those without the blessing of a priest. In the eyes of the Church such a marriage – a marriage which is not *in facie ecclesiae* – is illicit and the parties involved may be excommunicated.'

I gave a little gasp and put my hand to my mouth.

'I didn't know that, Master Heath.'

He smiled gently, the way one would when instructing a small child in his catechism.

'There are two elements to any marriage: the consensual agreement between a man and a woman that they are man and wife, *per verba praesenti*, at this present moment, and the physical consummation of that agreement. If the second element is absent we have a cause for annulment of the marriage. If the parties do not have the comfort of their physical union, there can be no marriage in the eyes of God.'

He reminded me of Bishop Simon the way he droned on about the comforts of physical union as if marriage was nothing but the joys of a goose-feather bed.

'However, if the parties agree that they will become man and wife at some time in the future we have a spousal *per verba de futuro*, akin to a betrothal, and there would be no physical consummation at that time, but the parties would be bound to each other and could not marry elsewhere. When physical consummation takes place, the spousal is transformed into a *de praesenti* agreement.'

It was very muddling.

'What if there were no words or the words were wrong? What if there was no consen... consensual agreement?'

He smiled sadly. 'Then it is fornication, my lady. A sin in the eyes of the Church.'

What had Thomas and I done? I was in dread I would be branded a fornicator and be excommunicated and yet we had made an agreement and we had most definitely consummated the agreement. So why would anyone, like my mother, think we weren't married?

He was very thorough. He first asked me about my family and if I knew the day and year of my birth and he asked about my time in the royal nursery with the queen's children and at Bisham with Lady Catherine. He led me through my meetings with Thomas and the words we had said to each other. He pressed me on several points. Was I frightened of Sir Thomas? Had he used violence against me at any time? Did I understand fully what marriage was?

'Who raised the question of marriage between you?'

Even now after everything that had happened I could still remember the day at the béguinage, the softness of the air and the warmth of his words in the orchard: *"You could marry me"*.

'He did.'

'Did he threaten you in any way?'

'No, never.'

'Were you frightened of him?'

'No, he was very kind.'

The young man at his side scribbled away, presumably committing my answers to his long sheet of parchment.

'And you agreed to marry him?'

'Yes.'

'Did you understand what he meant by marriage?'

I laughed. 'Oh Master Heath, all girls know what is meant by marriage. We are brought up to think of little else. It is the most important moment in any girl's life. Of course I knew what he meant.'

He coughed slightly as if this might be a point of disagreement between us.

'My brother has a daughter who is just twelve years of age, a pretty girl and the apple of her mother's eye. She is betrothed to a neighbour's son but I do not think she fully understands what marriage entails; she is barely out of the nursery. How old were you, Lady Montagu?'

'I was thirteen.'

He said nothing but I noticed a slight lifting of his eyebrows as if to have contracted a marriage like this I had been nothing but a wanton.

I was taken through my meeting with Otho and our hurried walk through the streets of Ghent, the house in the narrow street, the woman with her grubby linen cap, the dark stairway and the little attic room.

'This marriage took place when?'

I tried to remember the exact day. 'It was just after Her Grace gave birth to the king's son, John. The king was in England so the princes of the alliance came to see the queen but she was still in her bed. And it was the season of Lent, I remember that.'

He tutted and asked who else was present. I told him about the woman of the house and how she had been brought upstairs. Master Heath wanted to know exactly what words Thomas and I had used when we promised ourselves to each other and he kept asking what Sir Otho Holand was doing and if I was frightened.

No man can understand how a girl feels at her wedding. Of course I was frightened but not in the way he meant.

'And when Sir Otho and the woman left?'

'Sir Thomas locked the door.'

'To stop you from leaving?'

'No, to prevent anyone from coming in. The streets were full of men. We could hear drunken shouting, and there was fighting. It was a sensible precaution to bar the door.'

'What happened then?'

I blushed. I couldn't tell this man I had only just met about that night with Thomas so I said nothing.

'I'm sorry to have to ask you these questions, my lady, but the tribunal needs to know exactly what passed between you and Sir Thomas Holand that night. He took you to bed?'

'Yes.'

'And he had carnal knowledge of you? You understand what that means?'

I turned my head away and whispered, 'Yes, he did.'

'I have to be certain there is no doubt in this matter, so I must ask you again: did he penetrate your woman's parts? Did you bleed?'

Holy Mother of God! Did these men wish to crawl beneath the sheets of a woman's marriage bed? Was every thrust, every sigh, every gasp of pleasure to be picked over and discussed in detail by a group of elderly men who knew nothing of a woman?

'Yes, Master Heath. The answer to your question is yes and yes. He took me into his bed as a maid and when he had finished with me I was no longer a maid. You cannot doubt that Thomas Holand is my husband.'

'I may not doubt it, my lady, but I can assure you, the tribunal will. In a case like yours, all the advantages accrue to Sir Thomas. He was poor, you would one day likely be rich. He was an obscure knight of no particular importance; you were the king's cousin. He was a man no longer in the first flush of manhood: you, if you will forgive the observation, were and still are extremely beautiful. Of course he wanted to marry you.

'The question the tribunal will be asking is how he persuaded you to marry him. If Sir William cannot prove the marriage never took place then his attorney will look

357

for trickery or force and in that way seek to have the marriage set aside. That is why I have to know everything so that if necessary I can counter his arguments. If you tell me you married Sir Thomas Holand willingly and in full knowledge of what marriage entails then I believe you but it doesn't necessarily follow that the tribunal will.'

He sat back and conversed with his clerk who was struggling manfully. He had several rolls of written notes and fingers stained from base to tip with ink. He never looked at me but from time to time I noticed his ears grow red at the very nature of Master Heath's questions and the plainness of my answers.

'After your marriage, later that autumn, Sir Thomas left to go on Crusade. Is that correct?'

'Yes, he wished to demonstrate his devotion to the Church.'

'He told you he would return and yet three months afterwards you went through a form of marriage with Sir William Montagu.'

'My mother persuaded me that my marriage to Sir Thomas was not a true marriage. She said, with no priest, it couldn't be. She told me I was a fool and had been tricked and said I must marry William Montagu. She said I owed a duty to my family and they would be greatly displeased if I did not marry where I was bid.'

'She used force?'

I thought of the blows and the slaps and how she had stamped on my fingers.

'She chastised me, Master Heath, in the way a mother does to a disobedient daughter; that is all. If you wish to be certain you may ask her yourself.'

He shook his head. 'Sadly, the dowager countess is not to be called as a witness.'

'Why not?'

He shrugged. 'Perhaps she knows things Sir William would rather not have brought to the tribunal's attention. It would not help him if Sir Thomas could level an accusation that you were coerced into marriage with Sir William by your family. You see, my lady, undue force by your mother could result in your marriage to Sir William being set aside.'

'I doubt if any man would consider what my mother did to me as undue force. It was painful, yes, but at the time I considered my pain a deserving punishment for what I had done.'

'And so you married Sir William Montagu and later you lay with him and he had carnal knowledge of you?'

I gave him a wistful smile. 'It was a very grand marriage, Master Heath. If you care to look in the priory's *Great Book of Bisham* you will find me. They write everything down. There can be no doubt about that marriage, surely? The king and queen were there, hundreds of people saw us married. No-one can question the validity of my marriage to Sir William.'

He smiled as if I was a boy who has made a simple but crucial error in his schoolwork. 'But what if you were already married to Sir Thomas Holand?'

'Then I would have two husbands.'

'No, Lady Montagu. That is not possible. Neither God nor the Church allows a woman to have two husbands. Not at the same time. It would be an abomination.'

'Is that what I am? An abomination?'

'No, my lady. But only one of your marriages can be valid.'

'So how do I know which one is valid? How do I know which one to choose?'

This time he smothered a laugh at my words.

'You don't, my lady. It is very simple. If you are married to Sir Thomas Holand you cannot be married to Sir William Montagu, Conversely, if you are married to Sir William Montagu you cannot be married to Sir Thomas Holand.'

I looked at him, incomprehension written all over my face. 'But I may not choose?'

'No. The tribunal will, in due course, inform you which of your two husbands is your husband in the eyes of the Church.'

It seemed to me as if we were no further on than we were at the beginning but Master Heath seemed satisfied.

'How long do I have to wait?' I asked.

'It won't be quick, my lady. Even in ordinary times the tribunals of the papal courts are known to be slow but with the dreadful happenings in Avignon and travel being so difficult I don't even know when the next hearing will be.'

'Has something happened in Avignon?'

His face paled and his voice dropped to not much more than a whisper. It was as if he didn't want to say what had to be said.

'Sickness, my lady. We hear rumours of a terrible pestilence which spreads and multiplies. It creeps like an evil spirit from house to house and has no mercy. Four hundred dead in a single day, as if one infected man can infect the world.'

I could barely believe what he was telling me. Surely it was impossible.

'Imagine, my lady. Whole villages with no-one left alive. The sick dying too fast for the living to bury them and bodies flung into the river as the burial pits are full. Bishop Bateman tells me the Holy Father has withdrawn into his inner rooms to pray and is kept safe with huge fires burning day and night.'

'Are we in danger here?'

'No, my lady.' He gave a small smile at the ridiculousness of my question. 'We are in no danger. This is a punishment for the Valois king. It is *his* lands which are being ravaged and *his* people who are dying in their thousands. It is a sign of God's disfavour to Philip of Valois. We are perfectly safe here.'

11

THE PESTILENCE 1348-9

He was wrong. We were not safe. Nobody, no matter how exulted their position, no matter how loved or cared for, no matter how rich and powerful they believed themselves to be; nobody was safe.

William attended a royal tournament at Canterbury and returned with sad news; the queen's baby had died. But there was no time to grieve because within weeks a message from Lady Catherine told us Joanna was dead. Joanna, the fair-haired cherub who was her mother's favourite, the little girl I had comforted in Antwerp the night of the fire, the sweetest and dearest of all the queen's daughters. She had set out for Castile in the spring but had never reached her destination. She had died in a village near Bordeaux in the heat of the summer and been hurriedly buried. The messenger from Gascony said it was "*la morte bleue*", the pestilence, and my cousin had lost two of his children within the space of a single heartbeat.

Death was creeping close but the horrors had barely begun. When I looked into William's eyes I could see mirrored, my own fear: God's anger had reached out and touched one of our own and an enemy even more terrible than the Valois king and his armies could be heard howling at our gates.

'You may dine in the hall tomorrow,' said William in a clipped voice. 'You will no longer be guarded and you will be treated in every way as my wife and mistress of the house. Your ladies may return. I have no desire to distress either of us any further and we will not discuss this matter again.'

I fell to my knees and took his hand.

'Oh William. Thank you.'

He raised me up and kissed me. 'We will talk no more about it. It is over.'

He didn't mention the tribunal in Avignon, or his own attorney, or the one he had appointed for me whom I had never seen. He never once mentioned Thomas Holand or the marriage which was supposed to have taken place between us. He didn't refer to the inquisition I had endured at the hands of his family or the journey made by Lady Catherine to the papal court. He behaved as if none of it had ever happened.

Perhaps it was finished. Perhaps Master Heath's submissions had been in vain and Thomas had lost. Perhaps I was truly William's wife and would have to remain here forever. Perhaps, God forbid, William had given orders to have Thomas killed and I would never know.

The following month William began receiving alarming reports from his tenants in the south west: stories of a strange sickness, of a man dying so quickly there was no time to summon a priest, of whole families stricken in the space of a few days. One man said the stench of the afflicted was as foul as the pit and his master had warned the villagers to use charms to protect themselves from the vileness of the Evil One.

Tales followed of people with black swellings in their armpits which oozed bloody pus, a seething fever, a racking cough and searing pain. Men spat blood and vomit and their excrement and piss were blood-stained and blackened. It was, the horrified messengers said, as if they were putrefying from within.

Fear spread like a winter chill across the land. A letter from William's uncle, Bishop Grandison, confirmed what we dreaded most. This was, he conjectured, the great mortality which had overtaken Avignon. Like his brother in Christ, the Bishop of Bath and Wells, he had ordered processions every Friday to pray for protection from this disease. He said there was much terror amongst the citizens of Exeter and the towns had ceased to welcome travellers. He exhorted us to pray.

That same night William came back to my bed and wordlessly took me in his arms, placing his lips against my hair.

'I am afraid,' he whispered.

'I too,' I said, laying my hands on his chest and wishing we had been better friends. If I was to die I couldn't bear for it to be here, alone and in the dark, unloved and unforgiven.

'I have ordered the gates barred but my uncle says the very air is corrupted and how can I deny entry to the air we breathe?'

I moved closer and kissed the skin of his cheek, feeling the roughness of his beard against my face. 'Do you think we should leave Bisham? Go north?'

'No. I think we will do better here.'

'My maid tells me the king has gone to Calais. One of the men heard it proclaimed in Great Marlow.'

William gave a short laugh. 'Royal business. The king won't flee. He has already decided on his next great tournament and ordered me to attend. He wishes his knights to be seen as not afraid. But I am. I am afraid.'

I lay in silence not knowing what to say for I too was afraid. I thought of the pestilence stealing its way up from the river, slinking along the narrow lanes and spreading its evil breath through cracks in the shuttered windows of every house.

'Can London be safe?'

'My mother writes that one of the lay sisters has died in agony. She says the city is full of panic. Foreigners are being sought out for killing and their bodies thrown in the river.'

I grasped the fur coverlet and pulled it up until we were half-buried beneath its heavy warmth, as if by doing so I could keep us safe from harm. I slipped my arms around him and caressed the coarse hair at the nape of his neck. I could feel his mouth on my skin and hear the uneven threads of his breathing as he began to shiver. Slowly I stroked his naked back beneath his nightgown.

'I would wish to die as a good wife, William,' I said quietly. 'If it would bring you comfort we could forget the past and live as if there is nothing but this one moment which God has given us.'

I slid my leg between his and pulled his head down to mine. I sought his lips and kissed him as if he was truly a beloved husband and I, a loving wife, and from somewhere amidst our terror of what was to come we found a joy in our coupling that night we had never found before.

'I love you,' he murmured, half-asleep, perhaps not even sure who it was he held in his arms.

'And I, you,' I said tenderly, closing my eyes and praying that tomorrow morning would come as I truly could not bear the thought of dying in the dark.

Throughout that winter we learned a new way of living, one which acknowledged the precariousness of what we had, where death might strike at any time and the only breath we could be certain of was the one we took that moment. Each night we said our prayers and carefully composed ourselves for sleep knowing we might never wake, fearing the pestilence would claim us in the hours of darkness.

A maid left my chamber to nurse her sick mother and when she didn't come back I learned the whole family had perished. More terrible were the two village boys seen talking to a passing pedlar, found next morning beneath the trees, their bloated purple-marked bodies lying as they'd died, doubled-up in agony, unwatched, unloved and worst of all, unshriven.

During those short dark days, the elderly village priest came regularly to inform William of the spiritual and physical well-being of his flock. In the priory the canons redoubled their prayers but according to our chaplain some of the younger brothers were already refusing to tend the dying, fearing they too would be struck down. They cited a man's breath as the probable source of his infection which was ridiculous, as stupid as believing a man's look could kill. And yet, who could know?

When I found William on his knees before his father's tomb weeping hot tears of remorse for his failures as a son, I knew just how afraid he really was. He may have been a great soldier on the field of battle and lord of Bisham to our neighbours, but here, in his own house where there was nowhere to hide, he found himself impotent against an invisible foe and that knowledge utterly terrified him.

'I cannot see this enemy,' he cried. 'I do not know how to defeat him. You taught me how to fight, my father, but you never warned me that danger might come creeping like a wet fog across the fields.'

I murmured words of comfort but, in truth, there was no comfort to be had for any of us.

We passed what should have been a merry Christmas at Otford, watching the king's games and exchanging gifts. William, not knowing what else to do, began to follow my cousin's example, holding feasts and increasingly rowdy gatherings for his friends to show he was unafraid. As the weeks went by, the entertainments grew wilder, the music more frantic, with drinking, dancing and displays of debauchery which shocked me so much I refused to attend.

'Each day is precious,' William declared, leaning drunkenly against the door of my chamber with a jug of wine in his hand. 'Join me, pretty wife, because I want you. I have forsworn whoring for Lent.'

He made a grab for the sleeve of my shift but when I pulled away he shrugged and went staggering down the stairway. Next morning, I found him dead drunk in his bed where his grooms had left him.

I called for a bowl of water and sat sponging his forehead and wiping traces of vomit from his mouth until eventually he stirred. He was bleary-eyed from lack of sleep with a sour smell on his breath, but he was still afraid.

'Hold me, Joan,' he whispered. 'Hod me as my mother used to do.'

We called it the season of death and it was in those early days, when green shoots began appearing in the hedgerows, that people started dying. First were the children, then the old people and by the time we journeyed to Windsor at the king's command, the devastation was everywhere. Eastertide was well past yet the land at Westhorpe lay uncultivated and William said the men who worked the strips were either dead or run away and our neighbour sick with grief at the loss of his wife and child.

At the turn of the river by Cock Marsh, beasts with no-one to guard them wandered seemingly at will through the hay meadows and near Cookham we saw a score of bloated sheep lying dead from a murrain. The wharf at Maindenhythe was deserted and beneath the hill on the far bank were empty hovels, plague pits and a clumsily erected cross. The villagers must have thought the sign of Christ's suffering would protect them, but it hadn't; they were all dead.

It was a different world in the king's palace at Windsor in the fresh air high on the hill where we'd come for the St George's Day tournament. Here there was music and graceful living and not the slightest sign of fear. We were gathered to celebrate the creation of my cousin's new order of knights and nobody wanted to think about death or what had been lost forever.

Like Arthur, the ancient warrior King of Britain, friend to Merlin the magician, my cousin was drawing around him a band of men sworn to his service, a brotherhood of knights who would conduct themselves like the brave and chivalrous Arthurian knights of old.

'Twenty-six,' said Margaret in answer to my question, linking her arm with mine as we made our way through the crowded public rooms towards the queen's presence chamber. 'And it's not a matter of rank or money. Nobody can buy a place. Walter Manny says competition for the stalls is tremendous.'

'William was overjoyed to be chosen,' I said as we pushed our way through the throng. 'He considers it the greatest of honours. Apparently the ceremony in the chapel will be very intimate, very spiritual, and most definitely not an entertainment.'

'No,' laughed Margaret. 'That will come afterwards.'

At that moment, a blast of the herald's trumpet silenced the crowd as the doors at the far end of the room opened to reveal the queen. She took her seat amidst a hush of shuffling feet. There must have seventy or more of us tucked into the presence chamber and it was hard to move without treading on somebody's toes.

'I have the list,' said the queen, smiling like an indulgent mother. 'It is only natural that you ladies should wish to take part in today's magnificent entertainment because this event will be as great an honour for each one of you as it is for the men.'

'Hardly,' whispered Margaret. 'All we have to do is learn a few steps and make ourselves pleasant to our partners. How difficult can that be?'

The queen paused for a moment while we held our breath. One or two women were trembling and the girl next to me couldn't stop fiddling with the cloth of her gown she was so nervous.

'I can see you are impatient to know who has been chosen,' continued the queen. 'There are twenty-six noble knights in the king's order of chivalry therefore twenty-six ladies will be selected.'

A groan rippled across the room and the sense of excitement grew. Each woman clearly wanted it to be her rather than her friend, nobody wanted to be passed over. None of us knew exactly what was to happen but if it involved the bravest and handsomest knights in the land, what woman would not want to play a part?

The queen passed the list to the Master of the Revels at her side. As the names were read out, various ladies smiled smugly. Some I knew well, being wives or sisters of my cousin's men and one to my surprise, was the dark-haired young wife of a French hostage.

'And lastly,' said the Master of the Revels, looking round at the sea of expectant upturned faces, 'Joan, Lady Montagu, the king's kinswoman, wife of Sir William Montagu.'

'Lucky you,' said the woman next to me, practically spitting in disappointment.

'Off you go,' said Margaret, kissing me on the cheek. 'Go and learn your lines and your dance steps and don't forget to tie your mask properly. You don't want it falling off half-way through. Nobody will dance with you if they know who you are because by now your reputation is all but destroyed.'

Turning my back on Margaret's rudeness I joined the other women as we trooped into an adjoining chamber to receive our costumes. And what costumes they were! We had ivory gowns embroidered all over with gold and silver thread; chaplets of silver set with pearls and decorated with tiny silken rosebuds, and girdles of twisted gold; we had delicate hose of the finest wool and slippers of shiny white satin. And to ensure we were properly disguised and nobody would know who we were, each of us was given a golden mask with ties of narrow gold ribbon. It was utterly thrilling.

The gowns were exquisitely fashioned from heavy silk with necks cut so daringly low that we showed not only the tops of our breasts but also our shoulders.

'I feel half-naked,' whispered my neighbour. 'I daren't think what my husband will say.'

'I shouldn't worry,' said her friend swirling her skirts and nodding to the two pretty London girls. 'With your mask on, no-one will know who you are. You could be anybody. You can do whatever you like and your husband will never know.'

I could see this was going to be a far more elaborate and surprising entertainment than I'd first thought. We ladies were to be white hinds chased by knightly hunters through the greenwood. I wasn't sure how it was to work but there would be dancing and singing and a lot of running around and by the time it was over each hind was to be paired with the knight who had captured her for a final parade.

There were several dozen small boys playing the hounds. They would be dressed in black and gold and were strictly forbidden from snapping at the hems of our gowns. They had a whipper-in to control them but knowing small boys, I doubted he would be sufficient to ensure good behaviour and made a note to keep my eyes on the back of my skirts.

We spent the rest of the day practising our dances until we were step-perfect while the royal seamstresses pinned and tucked and stitched, making last-minute alterations to our gowns. We even found time amidst the confusion to rehearse our songs and learn the order of events.

'You look lovely, Joan,' sighed Philly, William's younger sister, married to Edward's friend Roger Mortimer, grandson of old Lady Mortimer of Ludlow Castle. 'Are you scared? I hope my husband catches me. I wouldn't want to be captured by Lord Stafford. He looks terribly fierce.' She giggled at the thought of having an older man as her captor and offered to tie my mask.

'Don't worry, Philly,' I said. 'You'll be perfectly safe.'

The silly girl gave a mock shiver and dissolved once more into giggles.

At last it was time. We held hands in pairs and walked slowly in procession down the wide steps, under a soaring archway and out into a vast open space. As I reached the last step I felt a note thrust into my hand. I turned to see who it was but in the flickering light of the torches there was no-one there. Through the eye-slits I could just make out the words,

"Master Nicholas Heath has been arrested on the king's orders and is lodged in the Tower"

My heart lurched and my fingers felt cold as ice. There was no signature and no seal but it could only have come from one person: Thomas. I hadn't seen him but I knew he must be somewhere in the castle.

'Oh look!' Behind her golden mask Philly's eyes glowed with excitement at the scene before us. Lit by the flames of a thousand torches was a glittering display of green and silver and gold. In the centre of the arena was a profusion of trees which had sprung up overnight as if by magic. The trunks were wrapped in silver ribbons and the trees shimmered with gleaming foliage of green and gold. Each branch dipped with the weight of silver coins and delicate jewel-like fruits; and wound over and under the branches were rivers of undulating silk of every conceivable colour.

Around the outside were little pavilions, striped azure and white, flying flags of different colours, each bearing the arms of one of the twenty-six members of the king's new order, and at one side was a small white canvas castle painted with roses.

It was late and the sun had disappeared but the torches had been lit making our world almost as bright as midday. At one end of the arena the royal musicians with their gleaming instruments were grouped high on a dais and all the way round were benches and stands for the onlookers. I could just make out the queen and the royal ladies sitting in canopied splendour beneath a roof of silver and red, but of the knightly hunters there was no sign.

As we ladies entered, the music changed. We danced lightly and elegantly and nobody forgot their steps. When we were finished we collapsed amidst much cheering onto a mound of little white stools looking for all the world like a herd of deer at rest.

The drums began and one after the other the twenty-six knights emerged from the darkness of a hidden tunnel and to an increasing crescendo rode slowly around the arena, pausing only to make their salutes to the queen. We couldn't tell who was who because they were dressed in identical black robes with glittering golden masks hiding their faces. I felt a stir of excitement wondering who would be my partner for the evening: Edward? William? Perhaps John Chandos. None of the women knew the names of all the knights.

The knights halted and dismounted. The music stopped. The drums stopped. There was absolute silence.

Then at a sign from the Master of Revels, trumpets sounded and at once the first of the hinds broke free and fled into the wood pursued by a dozen giggling small boys who had appeared out of nowhere.

It was all a game and the most tremendous fun. We had received our instructions and knew exactly what to do. We were to enter the wood where there was a maze of winding pathways and if we chose the correct path we would arrive in safety at the pretty little castle. Trying to stop us would be two knights. If either of them succeeded in capturing a hind she would be tied with a silver chain and led out of the wood, around the arena and into the pavilion of the successful knight where she would be given refreshments. Those who reached safety had to repeat their race through the wood for a second time and if they had any sense at all would ensure they dallied long enough to be caught.

Lord Henry was cheered to the skies when he emerged out of the trees with one of the city wives who was giggling uncontrollably and moments later Edward's friend, John Chandos, captured the little French girl. One of the women, much to her surprise and dismay, reached the castle in safety and the Earl of Warwick and Sir Hugh de Courtenay returned empty-handed to try again later.

I was next.

In the depths of the wood I could see nothing but flashes of gold and deep pools of darkness. I hesitated at a fork in the path and that cost me dear. I felt a gloved hand placed across my mouth and another on my arm. I had no idea who it was but knew better than to struggle. My captor kept hold of my arm and with his other hand carefully lifted up my mask.

'Lady Montagu! What a surprise.'

The voice was muffled within the confines of his golden eagle's head but I hadn't spent a night in his arms with him whispering love words in my ear not to recognise my cousin's voice.

'Your Grace.'

I dropped a low curtsey.

'I have you caught.' He spoke with some satisfaction.

'So it would appear.'

'I thought merely to win some small creature of the wild wood but it seems I have captured the queen of the herd.'

'You flatter me, Your Grace.'

'I don't think so. I think you are well aware of your worth, my dear Lady Montagu. You don't have two of my best knights fighting over the right to take you to their bed without calculating down to the last penny what you would fetch in the market place.'

He produced a length of silver chain which he proceeded to fix round my wrist, holding the other end firmly in his hand.

'Just a little tether to ensure you don't run away,' he said, giving the chain a sharp tug. 'The whole purpose of this game is to see the knights of my order triumph. If we defeat the French and capture the hinds, this great mortality cannot harm us. People need to understand that their king and his chosen friends will always prevail.'

'But we hinds must surrender to our fate?' I said with some bitterness. 'We are not permitted to fight for our own destiny?'

He gave a short laugh. 'Lady Montagu, the world may be half destroyed but men will always be masters of women. Not even the great mortality can change that.'

I didn't smile. I wasn't going to be amused when I knew what he had done. No woman of any sense laughs at her enemy's jokes.

He put his hand underneath my chin and tipped it up. 'You look delightful when you are angry, my dear, and you really do make an exciting opponent for a king denied a battlefield. If I had all night we could stay here, skirmishing with words, but it's time to give the people what they expect. Come.'

He tugged on the chain and I dutifully followed him along the pathway with ribbons of silk brushing against my face. As we emerged into the torch-lit arena I saw Philly and her husband disappear into a striped pavilion. My cousin raised his hand in acknowledgement while I smiled obligingly and the crowd roared its approval at my capture. One of the grooms carefully removed my cousin's golden eagle's head and the roars increased as the crowd saw it was the king.

He mounted his great black warhorse while a groom knelt, giving me a cupped hand to help me onto a small white palfrey. I reached for the bridle but the groom handed it to the king.

'You are mine,' said my cousin, looking down with some satisfaction from his great height. 'Where I lead, you will follow. You are my captive and I may do with you whatever I wish. You have seen my triumphs against the French and you must know by now that a victorious king is allowed to enjoy the spoils of war in whatever way he chooses.'

With the trumpets sounding a royal fanfare I was forced to ride step by step with him round the arena, paraded like a prisoner in chains. We paused in front of the pavilion where the royal ladies were seated and my cousin acknowledged his wife and gestured to me. I bowed my head politely to the queen and when I looked up she was smiling.

This pretence was all part of the game of courtly love. A knight should woo his lady with words and deeds to show his undying admiration and she would accept his addresses but not relent. He would be ardent but she would be cool; he would cast himself at her feet but she would turn her heel giving only the tiniest hint of a smile. This charade was played by everyone at the king's entertainments and we all knew the rules. It was a foolish woman who allowed herself to be blinded by pretty words, and it would be a brave young man who overstepped the mark and followed a woman to her chamber. My cousin would do nothing to dishonour either his wife or me in front of his people but I could tell from the way the queen inclined her head that she had given him licence to pursue his desires tonight in any way he wanted.

His enjoyment of other women didn't touch her because, as she had said, she was his beloved wife, the mother of his children and everyone knew it. I had been won like a purse at the tourney and could be frittered away in a night's enjoyment and as Margaret had said, my reputation as a virtuous wife was already all but ruined.

The rest of the entertainment passed in a blur of sound: the cheering crowds, the beating drums, the singing, the music, the dancing, the triumphant hunters and their laughing captives. We feasted and made merry long into the night and by the time I retired to our room I was too weary for words. William was nowhere to be seen and I had no doubt he was amusing himself with whichever girl he had caught in the greenwood. He would crawl into her bed seeking comfort and try to forget the horrors of a coming tomorrow.

As my maid combed out my hair ready for the night I heard the sound of a knock and the voice of the king's page asking for Lady Montagu. This was not what I wanted in any way but I could not refuse. I shrugged on my cloak, covered my loose hair with my hood and followed the man through the darkened palace to the king's apartments.

'Lady Montagu,' he said with a smile of satisfaction as the door closed softly behind me.

He wasn't at the king's business; tonight he sat sprawled in his chair wearing a loose chamber robe and drinking wine.

I curtsied low, feeling the coldness of his gaze raise hairs on the back of my neck.

'Your Grace,' I murmured.

He beckoned, watching through half-closed lids as I walked unsteadily across the floor towards him. The sight of his flushed cheeks and over-bright eyes caused my belly to constrict with fear because my experiences with William had taught me exactly how dangerous a man could be when he was half-drunk, especially a man with a score to settle.

'Take it off,' he said nodding at my cloak. 'Or shall I take a knife to the laces?'

I shivered at the thought of him slicing my clothes with his dagger so I undid the ties and slowly slid the cloak from my shoulders. It dropped heavily to the floor where it lay in folds at my feet.

His eyes glittered at the sight of the silk nightgown with my golden hair spread loosely over my shoulders. I felt the intensity of his desire as palpably as if he had it on display. He was holding the silver chain he had tied round my wrist earlier that day, twisting the narrow links in his fingers and pulling them tight.

'I could bind you, Lady Montagu,' he said quietly. 'Or you could sit of your own free will. Which is it to be?' He indicated the dark velvet of his robe where it spread in folds across his legs.

'You wish me to sit on your knee?'

I couldn't believe he would humiliate me in this way but he smiled thinly and stretched out his hand to grasp hold of my waist.

'For old time's sake. Let us pretend you are still that coy little virgin you professed to be when I saw you at Wark.

Let me see if I can make your girlish heart flutter as it must have fluttered that night when I came to your chamber.'

He was furiously angry. Of course he was. That night at Wark I had claimed to be a maid when I wasn't and now the tribunal in Avignon had exposed my lie. He knew I had tricked him and he was not a man who liked to be taken for a fool. I could only guess what he wanted of me but as my attorney was already at his mercy I must show myself willing. If I was to save both Master Heath and Thomas, I had to do everything I could to please my cousin.

'Very well, Your Grace,' I murmured, sliding onto his knee.

The warm cloth felt deceptively comfortable, with its poignant memories of Woodstock and the long years of my childhood, the reassuring solidity of my cousin's broad chest and the heady scent of his skin. I felt myself melt reluctantly into him as he tightened his hold and put his lips to my throat.

'Tell me, my little cousin,' he murmured. 'Do you have men who write verses to your beauty? Do they praise the smooth whiteness of your neck and the roundness of your breasts? Do you have lovers breathing of those pleasures as they move closer in the dance, whispering soft words while they pull you into the shadows?'

'I have a husband,' I said lightly.

'Ha!' he laughed. 'You have two, Lady Montagu. Two husbands. And I ask myself, are your appetites so great that one is not sufficient?'

I flushed at the coarseness of the insult and closed my mouth angrily.

He sat back with his hand still encircling my waist and regarded me steadily.

'Thomas Holand won't win, my dear, so don't imagine it. I won't have my Earl of Salisbury deprived of his wife. Think of the scandal. Think what it would do to my reputation if a marriage brokered by the King of England was found to be invalid and the king's cousin seen busy cuckolding one husband with another. I'd be the laughing stock of Christendom. A king who cannot control his family or his nobles, a king happy to flout the laws of the Church by encouraging a sham marriage.'

'And when the tribunal rules in Sir Thomas's favour?'

'It won't.'

This was a simple recognition of how things would be. If the King of England said the papal tribunal would rule in favour of Sir William Montagu, then that was what the papal tribunal would do. There could be no other decision.

'Your husband wanted Holand killed but I said such a thing was not possible. I did consider a feat of arms, a fight to the death. That would have given us a great deal of enjoyment and satisfied those watching that justice had been done, but in the end I found myself unwilling to sacrifice one of my knights on the altar of a beautiful woman's lust.'

He put his hand to my throat and slowly stroked the skin with his thumb as if testing the smoothness of a piece of rich vellum.

Ah, Jeanette,' he said, sadly. 'You have caused me so much trouble. What possessed you to marry Holand? I could understand if you had slipped into his bed one dark night. He's an attractive rogue and not without charm. But to marry him? You must have known you couldn't have a man like that. I would never have given my permission. You are my cousin. You couldn't just marry where you pleased. Women have been imprisoned for less. Christ's nails! I'd have had you in a nunnery if I'd known.'

The memory of that moment in the attic room before we became man and wife, when Thomas's hand touched mine, when I knew how it would always be between us and understood what a bond between a man and a woman could mean, that was what had quelled my last doubt about marrying him.

My cousin's hand tightened uncomfortably on my throat as if he wanted to squeeze the life out of me for my disobedience and for a moment I was truly frightened.

'It was your fault,' I said breathlessly, pulling my head away. 'I would never have agreed to marry him if it hadn't been for you.'

He seized my chin in a painful grip and turned my face back. 'Be careful what you say, my lady. I am not some cunt-struck boy you can abuse at will. I am your king.'

In an instant he had changed from a cozening lover to the mighty King of England, drawing himself into his royalty. This was a king who could order a man's hanging at the snap of his fingers. 'I think you forget to whom you are speaking, Lady Montagu. It is not for you to lay blame at your king's feet where no blame can possibly exist.'

'Antwerp. The old man. You were going to marry me to him until you changed your mind and sold me to your friend, the Earl of Salisbury, bartering me for favours received.'

He eyed me suspiciously. 'I have no idea what you are talking about.'

'I think you do remember, Your Grace. It was Twelfth Night and there was snow on the ground. The old man was in your private chamber at the abbey. The servants said he came up from Koblenz with you. They said he was a friend of yours. He touched my face and stroked my hair and you asked him what he thought of me. You offered me to him.'

He looked puzzled and then began to laugh.

'Oh my dear little cousin,' he said. 'That was no friend and I certainly wasn't planning to give you to him in marriage.' He shook his head, still chuckling. 'You could never have married him. It would have been impossible.'

'He wouldn't pay your price?'

'Price was never an issue. I would never have sold you, not to any man, not even to the Emperor himself. You were far too precious to me.'

'He didn't consider me worthy?'

'No, no, it was not that. You couldn't have married him. He had a wife still living as I well knew.'

For a moment he hesitated as if pondering the wisdom of what he was about to say. Then he reached for my hand and brought it up to his lips. Gently. one by one, he kissed my fingers.

'He was my father.'

I felt the cold slap of truth on my face.

'But that's impossible.'

He smiled sadly. 'Nothing, it seems, is impossible in this world.'

'But your father was dead. You told me he was dead.'

'I told you the truth as I believed it when it happened.'

'I don't understand.'

He touched his lips to my hair.

'I told you once there was a secret, a secret I couldn't divulge because it was not mine to tell.'

I nodded, remembering the night in the Tower when he had made me promise to give myself to him and in exchange he had told me about my father.

'Everything is changed now and the secrets and lies of yesterday have been laid to rest. God has given us the gift of this brief moment poised between life and death and perhaps it is time you, of all people, should know the truth. Give me your hand.'

Reluctantly, I held out my hand and his fingers closed over mine. His grasp was as firm as it had been all those years ago.

'Lord Mortimer didn't have my father killed. He had him taken secretly from his prison at Berkeley and a letter sent to my mother and me at Lincoln telling us he was dead.'

'But why? Why would he do such a thing?'

'It doesn't matter why he acted as he did, suffice to say it was a deception done to fool others.'

'But the funeral?'

I remembered him telling me of the funeral and how he had walked with his mother behind the body of his father and seen him lowered into the earth.

'I don't know whose body he put in the coffin but it wasn't my father's. It was the most diabolical deceit to bury an ordinary man and pretend he was an anointed king. It was an abomination.'

'And this was what my father discovered?'

'Yes. So Mortimer had to silence him. There was no other way. Whatever I said or did, Mortimer was going

384

to have him killed. He couldn't let him live. He knew too much.'

'And my mother?'

'He would have kept her imprisoned and you, my little cousin, would have wasted away in the dark. Perhaps in time he would have had you all murdered, when everyone had forgotten.'

'But you rescued us.'

He pulled me against him so that I lay half-cradled in his arms, the way I used to as a child.

'I rescued you.'

I was rigid with shock, my face in his hair, breathing in the scent of him, trying to reconcile these truths: my father's death, the identity of the old man, the deceptions, the untruths, the bare-faced lies. There had been no plot to send me away, no cruel foreign husband and my efforts to thwart my cousin's will had been pointless. I had been a fool.

Eventually I raised my head. His eyes were glittering in the candlelight and I knew immediately what he was going to say.

'Sweetheart, I am going to take you to bed.'

He could command my obedience and to lie in his arms would not have been unpleasant but it was not something I desired. I was not the green girl I had been all those years ago and he no longer had my heart. He had done things to harm me and I had ceased to trust him.

'I should prefer to return to my room if Your Grace permits.'

For a moment he said nothing but I knew he was not pleased.

'This is not a game, Lady Montagu, and I did not invite you here tonight to be insulted. I have done everything I can to help you and gratitude if nothing else should make you want to share my bed. And never forget how well I know you, my dear. It's not as if we are strangers to each other's desires.'

'I am sorry, Your Grace, but I should like to go.'

He twitched his lips in annoyance and for a dreadful moment I thought I had miscalculated and he was going to take me by force.

'And if I command you to stay?'

I thought of the note Thomas had sent.

'Then I would have to be obedient to your will in the same way that Master Heath has no choice but to remain in the Tower where he has been sent at your command.'

He put me off his knee and stood up, keeping a tight hold of my wrist.

'God's nails, woman! Am I supposed to know who Master Heath is?'

'Master Nicholas Heath, Your Grace. You had him arrested and thrown into prison.'

He narrowed his eyes and frowned. 'The name is not familiar but I don't keep a tally of all the miscreants in the kingdom. What has he done?'

I hesitated but anger made me brave.

'I think you know exactly who he is, Your Grace. He is my attorney.'

'Lady Montagu. I advise you to be careful. You have a husband. You cannot bring a case in my courts. Why would you need an attorney?'

'Master Nicholas Heath was introduced to me on the orders of His Holiness, Your Grace. He represents me at the papal tribunal in Avignon.'

My cousin reached for more wine, raised the cup to his lips and then offered it to me. I turned my face away

'A matter of a disputed royal grant if I remember correctly,' he said at last. 'You see it doesn't do to go against a king's desires, Lady Montagu. Never. If I choose to assign a rectory to my clerk it is not for Master Heath to dispute my right to do so. He should have known better.'

'That wasn't why you had him arrested.'

He sighed, took another sip of wine and smiled very slowly.

'What other reason could there possibly be?'

I opened my mouth to reply but he put his hand out to silence me.

'Go home, Lady Montagu. A wise woman always knows when she is beaten. Go home before I change my mind and do something I shall really regret. Go back to Bisham and make a dozen babies with young Montagu. Mend your marriage and learn what it is to be a dutiful, loving wife because, Christ knows, I no longer have any appetite for you.'

'And Thomas Holand?'

'Forget him. You can never be his.'

Our homecoming should have been triumphant but at the foot of the steps we were met by a messenger dressed in black. He knelt at William's feet and with tears in his eyes told him that Lady Catherine, the dowager Countess of Salisbury, was dead, a victim of the pestilence.

And she was not the only one we lost. Hundreds were dying and my Uncle Wake was another who followed the path to God before the mid-summer fires burned brightly in the villages. Eight years earlier he had walked me to the door of Bisham chapel to marry William. I remembered his heavy tread on the crimson carpet and the uncomfortable bulk of his body next to mine, but little else. His face was a shadow. I received a curt note from my mother informing me of his death which she said was a result of the great mortality. There were no other words of sorrow or comfort and I had no idea whether she mourned his passing or not.

At the height of the summer William had to return to Windsor to take delivery of his lands and receive his title from the king.

'You will stay here,' he said, wrapping his arms around me and holding me close. 'You will be safer. I won't be more than a week. It's not a grand affair like when my father became Earl of Salisbury, just a brief ceremony. I expect there'll be feasting but half the men call me "Earl William" already. I have no idea how many documents require my seal or how slow the royal officials will be but I'll hurry back as soon as I can.'

'Take care,' I said, glad I was not going with him as I had no wish to face my cousin again so soon.

I gave him a wife's blessing and we walked together down to the Bisham jetty. Just before he stepped into the barge he turned and kissed me softly on the mouth. 'You'll be a countess when I next see you,' he said. '*My* countess.'

I waved farewell, watching the oars dip and the barge move away from the bank out into the current. I kept watching until I could no longer see the lonely figure of my husband sitting beneath the canopy and the Montagu standard fluttering proudly on the prow. I turned and walked slowly back to the house pondering on the difference it might make to my life to be Countess of Salisbury and whether after all it might not be a better life than being Lady Holand.

The days passed idly by with no word from William until one morning there was a commotion in the yard and the sound of men's voices. One of my ladies peeped out of the window.

'Oh!' she squeaked.

'What? Who is it?' I asked.

'A most handsome and richly dressed young man in the courtyard,' she said breathlessly.

The others rushed to the window to take a look but from the expressions on their faces I gathered the handsome young man had disappeared.

A moment later there was a clatter of footsteps outside my chamber, the door swung open and in strode Edward with a companion at his heels followed by my steward calling rather belatedly, 'Edward, Prince of Wales, my lady, and Sir James Audley.'

Clearly this was not a royal visit which required the splendour of heralds and a liveried retinue of a hundred men on horseback, otherwise I would have been summoned to the courtyard as lady of the house. This was a private visit, possibly even a secret one since Edward must know William wasn't here.

I rose from my chair and gave a respectful curtsey desperately trying to recall how low I should go if I was now a countess. I decided humility was preferable to correctness and lowered myself right down to the floor.

'My lord prince,' I murmured. 'You are very welcome to Bisham.'

He nodded his head curtly. 'I thought of sending a note ahead and signing myself Perceval,' he said with a careless laugh, raising me up and casting a glance round the room.

I smiled. How long ago that childhood summer of Perceval and Blanchefleur now seemed and how innocent we had been. It was a time when a boy's kiss meant nothing more than just a kiss. Now, when our lips touched, each one of us wondered if this would be the last time. Would we be spared?

'Have you come from my husband?' I asked, wondering what he wanted.

'No,' he said bluntly. 'Montagu doesn't know I'm here.'

He turned to his companion whom I recognised from the St George's Day tournament.

'Go and entertain those damned women, James,' he said, indicating my ladies who had withdrawn politely to the far end of the chamber with their sewing but now sat with their ears pricked, attentively listening to every word we said. 'I wish to speak with the countess alone.'

Sir James strolled over, leaned down to look at a piece of embroidery and made some comment which caused a ripple of girlish laughter and a couple of flushed cheeks.

'Jeanette.'

Edward grasped my arm and pulled me over to the settle in the window embrasure where we were mostly hidden from view. His hands felt hot and sticky through the light cloth of my gown and his face had an expression of annoyance as if I had displeased him in some way.

'You are such a fool, Jeanette,' he said, the moment he had me seated amongst the cushions with his knee pushed hard up against my leg. It wasn't a very comfortable position and I was rather surprised at his lack of courtesy but I didn't protest. Edward had grown to be a young man who liked his own way in all things and I didn't think he would appreciate any criticism of his behaviour.

'My father told me everything,' he continued. 'Why didn't you come to me? If you were so desperate to be rid of Montagu, why didn't you ask me? I'd have helped. I'd do anything for you, you know that. I could have had you freed from him if that was what you wanted. Nothing is impossible. But why in the name of Christ did you devise this stupid plan involving Holand? If the Holy Father's tribunal frees you from Montagu, you'll be shackled to Holand for the rest of your life. He'll be able to claim you for himself and that's lunacy. What were you thinking of?'

He had both my hands grasped and had pushed himself so close that his angry breath warmed my mouth and I could see myself reflected in his eyes.

'You don't understand, Edward,' I gasped, aware of his lean hard body pressed against mine.

'Of course I understand. I know you, Jeanette. We shared a nursery when you were in short skirts and I remember just how stupid you can be. But all is not lost. I've talked to Bishop Bateman who tells me the Holy Father has appointed a new investigator, Cardinal d'Albi, the Cardinal-Bishop of Porto, and he has demanded you be properly represented with an attorney of your own.'

I tried to wriggle away but he was pressing against me and I could barely move. I imagined he must feel the rise and fall of my breasts against the gorgeous silk of his tunic because I, most certainly, was aware of the thudding beats of his heart.

'I had my own attorney, Edward,' I said, hoping he might let me breathe a bit more easily. 'Master Nicholas Heath was my attorney but your worthy father had him thrown into the Tower. He said there was good reason but I don't believe him. He was lying. Are you not afraid of defying the king's will?'

'No. My father has been less than honest in his dealings with you.'

'He is determined I shall remain with William. He told me so.'

'Whereas I am determined to keep you from falling into Holand's clutches. I shall deal with Montagu later. I shall agree a settlement with him. You will claim you only married him under threat of violence from your family. You will say you were afraid for your life. The Church will annul your marriage. Montagu is a man of honour and I shall persuade him to release you to me. Whatever he thinks, he won't want to cross me. Oh God, Jeanette, I never thought it would come to this.'

He gazed into my eyes as if he would penetrate my soul and before I could say anything else he kissed me hard on the mouth.

'I love you Jeanette. I love you and I want you. I'll wait for you however long this takes and I'll do whatever needs to be done. Nobody is going to stand in my way because I intend to marry you. Now do you understand?'

'Marry me?' I felt the breath knocked out of my body.

'Yes. I shall make you my wife. You will be my beloved princess and one day you will be my queen.'

He wanted to make me a princess? A queen in waiting? The idea was preposterous. It was ridiculous. His father would never agree and neither would his mother. They wanted him to make a great alliance. They wouldn't let him marry me. But oh, the thought of being a queen! All that splendour, all those jewels and the richness of the furs! Of course it was quite, quite ridiculous but it was also curiously seductive. Edward wanted me to be his queen. Was such a thing possible?

'You want to marry me?' I said, struggling to speak. 'You want to make me your wife?'

'Naturally. What else?'

'But what about William?'

'I told you, forget William. Let me deal with him.'

'And Sir Thomas?' I said softly. 'What about him?'

'Damn Sir Thomas,' he said.

He kissed me again, this time with more determination and a great deal more passion and to my eternal shame I found myself responding with a very guilty pleasure.

'Oh God, Jeanette. If only...'

'I couldn't, Edward,' I said hastily, gasping for breath and coming rather belatedly to my senses. 'Not here in my husband's house. It wouldn't be right.'

He sat up, letting his breathing return to normal while I smoothed my skirts and rearranged the neckline of my gown, wondering what on God's earth I was going to do if he decided to carry out his plan to marry me.

We stared at each other, rather surprised at what had just taken place, almost embarrassed at what had been said and done. Then with a grin he reached over and stroked my cheek.

'One day, Jeanette,' he said. 'One day soon. We can wait, can't we?'

I nodded mutely, too afraid to tell him the truth, that being shackled for life to Thomas Holand was the one thing I really desired and that he, a nineteen-year-old prince who had just offered to share his life and his crown with me, could only ever be second-best. That sort of insult he would never understand.

'Very well, Edward,' I said, softly. 'Whatever you say.'

'I have brought your new attorney here. I had him sent to your husband's room. When you see him you will tell him that Holand is lying. You will say there was no marriage and anything you said previously was because you were mistaken. Tell him you were frightened and became muddled.'

'But Edward...'

'Do you understand?'

I opened my mouth but he silenced it with a kiss.

'Do you understand?'

'Yes, Edward. Of course, Edward. I understand completely.'

My new attorney was Master John Vyse, a sub-dean of the diocese of Salisbury, who announced by way of introduction that he was a bachelor both of arts and canon law. He was also a man of stern resolve who, when faced with an obdurate Edward, showing every sign of staying and not the least sign of leaving, told him that he needed to speak to the Lady Joan alone and in private.

'I am her friend,' said Edward, looking down his long nose at the lawyer. 'And in case you were unaware, Master Vyse, I am also a prince of royal blood.'

But Master Vyse was not cowed. 'That is as may be, my lord, but not even the Holy Father himself is permitted to be present when a principal in a case is giving a statement to her attorney. It is as sacred as the confessional so I very much regret that I must insist you leave us.'

He folded his arms and waited quietly. After a few moments when Master Vyse showed no sign of backing down, Edward swung on his heel and left the room, all but slamming the door.

Master Vyse smiled thinly. 'Now, my lady, from you, I need the truth.'

And so I told him. Sitting in William's chamber amongst the trappings of William's life with Edward's kisses still warm on my lips, I told him everything from the very beginning. I made no pretences and no evasions. I told him how I had voluntarily and wittingly become Thomas Holand's wife in the spring of the year that the king's son John was born in Ghent and how a year later I had submitted to a marriage with William Montagu only under great pressure from my family and in fear of the consequences if I refused to obey their wishes. I told him that despite having lived with William Montagu for several years in apparent contentment, I still considered myself Thomas Holand's wife in the eyes of God. And I told him it was my most fervent wish to be reunited with my husband.

Two days later the angry tramp of feet on the stair outside my chamber gave me just enough time to compose myself and greet William with a smile on my lips and a sweeping curtsey.

'My Lord Salisbury,' I murmured, wondering from which direction the attack would come.

'You couldn't wait, could you?' he snarled. 'The moment my back was turned, you have him sniffing around your skirts, paying you pretty compliments. Doubtless you welcomed him with open arms. I should have known better than to trust you.'

'What are you talking about, husband?' I said opening my eyes wide and trying to appear the model of innocence. 'The only visitor when you were gone was Edward and he stayed barely a few hours.'

By now he was practically on top of me, his hand grasping my arm and pushing me back towards the bed.

'Oh yes, your beloved Edward, your little playmate from the nursery who is planning this very moment how to get you for himself. Don't think I don't know what is going on because he told me everything. He threatened me, said he'd make you his if it was the last thing he did and if I didn't stand aside I would regret it.'

I twisted my head away and put my hands on his chest trying to hold him off.

'William, what nonsense is this? I don't know what you're talking about. Are you sure Edward wasn't drunk?'

'And who was the other one?'

'Which other one?'

'With Edward. And don't lie because I know there was somebody else here.'

My heart leapt as I recalled the long afternoon I had spent with Masgister Vyse and the evidence I had given him.

'Sir James,' I said, remembering the name of Edward's friend. 'Sir James Audley. My ladies made a great fuss of him. It was a merry gathering and I said at the time it was a great shame you weren't here.'

'You mean to tell me he brought Audley with him?'

'Yes, they were travelling upstream and called in to tell me you would be returning soon. That was all.'

'Edward said nothing of his plans for you?'

'Oh William. I am certain you are mistaken. He has no plans for me. How could he? You are my husband.'

William let me go and walked to the door. His groom hastily opened it but William paused on the threshold.

'Yes, my lady. I am your husband and don't you forget it. Don't imagine the Holy Father is going to undo the ties which bind us together because that won't happen. There is only one key to unlock a marriage and that is death. You would do well to remember that when you are considering your lovers.'

'I have no lovers,' I said steadily. 'Only you.'

'I wish I could believe you,' he said. 'But I don't.'

He didn't come near me for the rest of the day and he supped alone in his chamber.

By the time what little harvest there was had been brought into the barns and the last of the fruit preserved for the winter, it was time to compute our losses. I counted on my fingers numbering each death in this year of death. Five, ten, twenty… a hundred. There was Lady Catherine and my Uncle Wake, both laid to rest as the trees came into bloom; Elizabeth's husband, Sir Hugh Despenser; the young Courtenay heir to the earldom of Devon; the

397

elderly Archbishop of Canterbury and just last month his nominated successor, the Dean of Lincoln who had been my cousin's confessor at Calais. The Bishop of Worcester was dead as was the Abbott of Westminster; also Sir John Pulteney, four times Lord Mayor of London; and Sir John Montgomery, the Governor of Calais, and his lady wife.

A dozen faithful servants struck down in Montagu manors up and down the country, with each day bringing news of further deaths. And the children; hundreds of them, some scarcely breathing before they were taken. I knew of mothers who had lost every child they had ever birthed and others, like Alice, who wept inconsolably over their firstborn.

In his letter, William's Uncle Montagu rained scorn on his gaggle of useless daughters, fit for nothing but milking cows. His only son was dead and he could not forgive his wife for allowing such a disaster to happen. That a punishment of such magnitude should be visited upon a man like him who was pious and deserving of God's grace, meant that his wife must have committed some unforgivable sin. In the chill of the Bisham chapel I prayed, not only for the soul of the little boy who lay wrapped in white velvet in some Montagu vault but also for Alice who was now in more danger than ever.

It was into this well of misery that I had another visitor, my cousin, Margaret. No-one announced her coming and the sight of her black-clad figure standing at the door filled me, not with joy, but with apprehension.

She walked swiftly across the floor and instead of a greeting, wrapped her arms around me in silence and laid her cold cheek against mine.

'What has happened?' I whispered.

She continued to hold me close.

'Dearest Jeanette. It is bad news.'

Thomas? I felt my heart flutter and my belly fill with ice.

'Tell me,' I said quietly.

'It is your mother. She's dead.'

The sudden pain took me by surprise. I didn't love my mother, I never had and she didn't care for me so why did my heart feel sliced in two? I sat down hurriedly lest my legs gave way because there was no doubt the news of her death was a terrible shock. It was more shocking than the deaths of all those great people, more horrible even than the death of Alice's child because we were used to little children dying. But my mother?

'When did she die?' I said, aware of the unnatural quiver in my voice.

'Three weeks ago. It was not unexpected.'

So strange not to have known. I should have known. She was, after all, my mother. She had given birth to me and must have held me in her arms and called me, her Jeanette. There must once have been a season when she had loved me.

'What did she die of?'

Margaret touched my hand. 'She had been unwell for some time but at the end it was the pestilence. It was very quick. She didn't suffer.'

I knew of the horrors of the pestilence and heard the lie on Margaret's lips. Of course my mother had suffered.

'I shall arrange for a Mass for her soul and I shall light a candle as is only right, but you know she never loved me, not the way a mother should.'

Margaret took my hand in hers and pressed it gently. 'You are mistaken, Jeanette. She did love you. She told me so. I saw her a week before she died. She asked me to come to her. I didn't want to go but felt it was my duty.'

I thought of my mother writing to Margaret when she didn't write to me, of spending her precious time with my cousin when she rarely bothered to visit me. And when she did come all she did was berate me for my foolishness and complain of my behaviour. I knew I had been a disappointment to her because she had told me so.

'Why you?' I asked grudgingly. 'What would she want with you?'

'She wanted to talk of my mother and my father and of the plans for my children's marriages. Like most old ladies she dwelt mainly in the past and talked of people who were already dead and things which happened long ago but at the end she spoke of you.'

Margaret delved into her purse and brought out a tiny package wrapped in dark green cloth.

'She gave me this to give to you. She knew she was dying and she wanted this to be yours. She didn't dare send it by messenger in case your husband took it. She had no illusions about how he treats you so she asked me. She said to tell you it was sent with a mother's blessing and a mother's love.'

The knife twisted a little more and I blinked back the tears.

With trembling fingers, I undid the ribbon and unwrapped the cloth to reveal a dark blue velvet drawstring pouch. Inside was my mother's ring, the gold and ruby ring she always wore. She had sent it to me. At the end when she knew she was dying she had sent it to me with her love and her blessing.

'Your father gave it to her,' said Margaret. 'It was a love token. It belonged to our grandmother, Queen Marguerite. It's beautiful, isn't it?'

It was. I slid it onto my finger. It fitted perfectly.

Margaret smiled. 'I wonder who gave it to our grandmother? I asked but your mother didn't know.'

I smiled through my tears. 'Our grandfather? Or perhaps a lover?' I suggested, smiling through my tears.

'Oh no,' said Margaret. 'My father said she was the most perfect example of womanhood, full of grace and kindness, a pious woman loved by everybody. She would never have taken a lover.'

'Why did my mother never tell me these things, Margaret? Why did she remain silent? She never talked of my father and their life together, not once.'

'Guilt,' said Margaret.

'Why would she feel guilty? What had she done?'

'Oh Jeanette. Surely you know the answer to that by now? She blamed herself for your father's death. She believed it was her fault. And for your imprisonment in Arundel Castle. She blamed herself for that too. She was trying to protect her family. She only wanted the best for you. She vowed she would never allow you to repeat your father's mistake.'

'Mistake? What mistake?'

'Marrying her.' Margaret smiled sadly. 'She was, like my own mother, considered unworthy. She may have been a baron's daughter but she was far beneath him. He was a king's son and should have married a great foreign princess who would have been of advantage to his family, not someone like her who was nothing but a widow with a lost dower living on the king's charity. So when you told her about Thomas Holand…'

I thought of my mother's fury when I had first revealed the story of my secret marriage and at last I understood why she had acted as she had.

'She had to stop me.'

'Yes. She was determined on the Montagu marriage. She saw it as a way to redeem her failures of the past and ensure your future.'

'No wonder she hit me.'

I tried to recall the words she had spoken but could remember nothing but the emptiness of her eyes and the pain of her blows.

We sat in silence for a while, staring into the embers of the fire, while I twisted the ring on my finger, noticing how the huge ruby caught the light. I thought of what my chaplain had told me, that a virtuous woman is far above the price of rubies. Our grandmother had been given this magnificent jewel. Was it a recognition of her virtue? Probably, but we would never know for certain.

'Has there been word from Avignon?' said Margaret breaking into my thoughts.

'No. There are times I think I'll be waiting for a decision until the end of my days and I'll die not knowing who is my true husband in the eyes of God and the Holy Father's tribunal. How can it take so long?'

Margaret laughed. 'Easily. The mills of God grind slowly and Pope Clement is rumoured to be an extremely diligent miller.'

'Master Vyse believes the new cardinal will decide within a year but who knows? He says the pestilence has come back. It is killing hundreds each day and when it disappears nobody knows where it has gone or if it will return. People are walking in fear for their lives.'

'It is everywhere,' whispered Margaret in a low voice. 'Everywhere. I have heard half the people of Bristol are dead and Norwich is stricken. It has reached as far as York. Nobody knows where it will go next but I have made a decision. When winter is past I shall travel to Avignon and seek a divorce from John Segrave. If God grants that I live to see the end of this horror I shall choose a new life.'

I recalled the women at the béguinage all those years ago who took the future into their own hands and chose the lives they wanted and thought how like them my cousin was, not just brave but determined and resourceful.

'And you, Jeanette?' she said. 'What will you choose?'

Since that day in the sand dunes of Calais I had not allowed myself to consider that I had a choice in the matter. I was a married woman, the possession of my husband and could have no desires other than his. If in the depths of the night I dreamed of a different man and another life it was just that, a dream, and dreams should be set aside in the light of day.

Master Heath had told me the choice was not mine to make but that of a group of men in far away Avignon, men of the Church about whom I knew nothing. He had said it was not a question of what I wanted but of what was the truth and that the truth was known only to God. When I had pressed him further he had said that God's truth was conveyed to his servants in ways that a woman like me could never understand.

William or Thomas? Which one was God's truth and was the papal tribunal really listening?

The women with whom I was intimate knew what I was supposed to have done. They had heard how this man, who had once been my husband's steward, was demanding I should be given back to him, but we didn't talk about it. No-one mentioned Thomas's name and not even my maids dared gossip about William's lack of interest in my company. Nobody suggested he might not be my husband because they all remembered the magnificent wedding in the Bisham chapel in front of the king and queen and the costly gifts we had received. If they thought about it at all, they would have said that Thomas Holand was mad.

As the days stretched into weeks and the weeks into months I wondered if I would die not knowing which of my husbands was the true one. Margaret had asked who I would choose but that was a question I never allowed myself to answer. William or Thomas? The splendour and luxury of life as Countess of Salisbury: the precious silks, the jewels, the richness and wealth of my surroundings, tied to a difficult and occasionally violent husband who didn't entirely trust me; or the unknown low-lying pastures of life as Lady Holand, with a man who could offer me little, a man I barely knew but thought I might just possibly love?

William and I sat together in our hall. He extended his hand as he helped me to my seat and accorded me the reverence that the household expected from a lord to his lady, but there was little warmth in his touch. The closeness we had experienced in the months after the coming of the pestilence had dissipated like a handful of chaff in the wind and there was nothing left now but duty. He came to my bed with a dogged regularity but there was no joy. I tried my best to give him pleasure but it was like blowing on the long-dead ashes of a cold fire.

12

INTO THE UNKNOWN 1349

The wind had turned to the north. It was getting colder and one of the grooms brought in a second basket of logs for the fire. My maid gossiped to him as I sat sewing by the meagre light from the window wondering if it would snow and if the soft white flakes might suffocate the pestilence in an icy tomb.

As soon as the man had gone the girl came over and gave me an awkward little bob. 'He says the bishop's here, my lady.'

I'd heard no arrival which was surprising as the courtyard was mostly empty. These days there was not much journeying and William continued to bar the gates to passing travellers.

'Did he say which bishop?'

'He didn't know, my lady. He said the men had blue badges on their sleeves with fancy gold decoration.'

Not Bishop Grandison then. Perhaps it was Bishop Bateman. Perhaps there was news.

I barely had time to consider what this meant when another of William's grooms came through the door at a run.

'The Bishop of Norwich, my lady. Downstairs in the master's chamber. He's asking for you.'

'Is Sir William there?'

'No, my lady. He was but he's gone to the yard.'

There was no time to prepare, and delay would not change what was to come so I murmured a quick prayer to Our Lady and followed the man down the stairs.

Bishop Bateman was standing with his back to the door studying the drawing of William's new coat of arms which lay on the table. He turned as I entered. There was none of the magnificence I'd noticed at Windsor the summer before last, none of the gorgeous splendour of the king's favourite and most valued diplomat. He looked an old and worried man.

'My lady.' His voice was cold.

'Reverend Father.'

I knelt in meek submission and dutifully kissed his proffered ring.

He regarded me with muted sadness, a sinner in need of redemption rather than a countess and cousin of the king. I rose to my feet keeping my head lowered and my eyes on his hands.

''I have in my possession, my lady, a letter from the Holy Father.'

I could see quite clearly the roll of parchment with its heavy seals, a parchment which had travelled all the way from Avignon and surely contained the decision of the papal tribunal. In a wave of utter terror, I half-closed my mind to what was happening.

The bishop watched me gravely as if expecting a response and when none was forthcoming returned his gaze to the smooth vellum and the crabbed black writing.

'The Holy Father's letter is addressed to the Bishop of Comacchio who as papal nuncio has travelled to England to deliver it to myself and to my brother in Christ, the Bishop of London.'

He looked up enquiringly but my face like my mind was a blank.

'I shall not read the whole letter, my lady, as it is long and detailed and difficult for a woman such as yourself, untrained in ecclesiastical matters, to understand but the essence is that His Holiness is pleased to accept the verdict of Cardinal d'Albi's tribunal in the matter concerning Lady Joan, daughter of Edmund, late Earl of Kent, Sir Thomas Holand, and Sir William Montagu, Earl of Salisbury.'

He paused and gave me a look which contained a sliver of distaste as if the whole matter was something disgusting which carried with it an offensive odour.

'Cardinal d'Albi has concluded, after reviewing the evidence presented both to Cardinal Robert and that offered to his own tribunal, and with careful deliberation on his part, and after consultation with other legal experts...'

He paused yet again as if the words had stuck in his craw.

'... that the contract entered into by Sir Thomas Holand and the Lady Joan was and still is a valid marital union.'

I began to tremble. A valid marital union. Thomas. A valid marital union. I was Thomas's wife. Not William's. All this time I had been Thomas's wife.

Bishop Bateman continued reading. 'The Lady Joan is to be restored immediately to Sir Thomas Holand and their union is to be solemnized publicly.'

I could go back to Thomas. Immediately. To Thomas.

There was more. 'The de facto marriage entered into by Earl William and the Lady Joan is null and void.'

He put the parchment down on the table and looked at me with the satisfaction of one who has delivered a damning verdict of a richly deserved and terrible punishment.

'Do you understand the meaning of what I have told you?'

Mutely, I nodded my head.

'You realise this decision means you are no longer Sir William's wife. You have no further claim upon him. He has cast you off and you are required to leave his house so that you do not bring further shame upon him and his good name.'

So my tenure as Countess of Salisbury was finished, but I didn't care. Flooding my mind was an image of Thomas. The Thomas who was my true and most beloved husband.

'The wrong that you have done Sir William is a truly dreadful thing,' thundered Bishop Batemen. 'It is beyond anything that I have ever had to deal with in a dispute between a man and his wife. It was a vile and despicable deceit practised upon a wholly blameless young man and before you can be received back into God's good grace you will be required to make a full and frank confession of your sins and accept whatever penance is given to you. Do you understand?'

'Yes, Reverend Father,' I whispered, unable to think of anything other than Thomas and the enduring warmth of the sand dunes of Calais.

'Very well. If you would make yourself ready, my lady.'

'Ready?'

'To leave.'

'Now?'

'Naturally. Sir William will not countenance your presence under his roof for another night and I must return to my diocese. If this had not been a command from His Holiness I would not be here. Now if you please, my lady, make haste.'

I walked unsteadily out of William's chamber into the familiar sights and sounds of the busy hall. I could see a dozen grooms and pages going about their daily business and heard them talking but was unable to comprehend what was happening. Nothing made any sense. All I could think of was that I was leaving; leaving my friends, my lady companions, my maids, my steward, the clerk of my wardrobe, my little page. In a few hours I would be gone and I would never see any of them again.

And Bisham? What about Bisham? I felt a pang of loss and immediately thought of William, the William who was no longer my husband. Where was he? What was he doing?

As soon as I reached my chamber I gave swift instructions to my maids for the packing of my chests. I held the hands of my ladies and told them gently that I was departing.

'Where?' they asked and when I explained, their eyes filled with tears.

They had admired my position as Countess of Salisbury and when they held me in their arms they cried not just for their own loss but also for mine.

'How will you manage?' said one, sniffing miserably. 'Nobody will want to know you.'

'I shall still be a lady.'

'Yes, but…'

To both of them, my fall from grace was an utter disaster and they could not understand why I was not in despair.

'What are you doing?' A cold voice cut across the room.

Holy Mother of God! It was William!

'Sir William,' I said bravely, trying to remember he was no longer my husband and had no power over me. 'Bishop Bateman has ordered me to make ready.'

'So I repeat. What are you doing?'

'The bishop has commanded me to pack my things.'

William cast a glance at the gowns, folded and layered neatly in the two chests, the books and my sewing bag and my silver mirror placed in a smaller box.

'Those are not your things.'

'They are my robes and my…'

'Those are *my* things,' he said flatly. 'Everything in this room belongs to me. Everything in this house belongs to me. I thought you were mine but it seems in that I was mistaken.'

'William,' I pleaded. 'I didn't mean to deceive you. You must know I didn't.'

He swept on as if I hadn't spoken. 'Since you are not mine you may go. Everything else remains here.'

'But my gowns?'

'Mine.'

His voice was sharp enough to splinter stone and I could detect no softness, no forgiveness, no sign of weakness or sorrow.

411

'What am I to wear, William?'

'That is not my concern. Ask your so-called husband.' He spat out the last word with real venom. 'And don't imagine you're taking that coffer of jewels I see on the table. I gave those to my wife, the wife I married in good faith, and since you are not my wife and never have been, they cannot be yours.'

'But…'

He crashed his fist on the table making the maids cower in fear and both my ladies retreat to the edges of the room.

'They are mine, as are the rings on your fingers.'

I looked at my hands. I only wore two rings today: a small sapphire William had once given me as an Easter gift and my mother's gold and ruby ring. I removed the sapphire and closed my fingers tightly around my mother's ring.

'That one too.'

'No, William. That was my mother's ring. It belongs to me.'

For a moment I thought he would rip the ring from my finger but he still had enough of his temper under control.

'If that lying whore, your mother, was here and not rotting in her tomb, I'd throttle her. I hope she burns for an eternity in purgatory for her part in this. My parents should never have trusted her. Very well, keep your witch's bauble. But get out of my sight. I never want to see or hear from you again.'

My maid held out my winter riding cloak: thick blue Flemish cloth, lined with lambswool. William glanced at it, then at me.

'Leave that.'

'Bring me one of the others,' I said quietly to the girl.

'Oh no,' snarled William. 'You'll leave them all. They're mine. Every single one of them. No whore leaves my house clad in the best that my money can buy, and you won't need them in the shit-hole where you'll be going.'

I touched the fine wool skirt of my gown, feeling beneath its meagre thickness my single linen shift and my elegant hose.

'William, it's winter. I'll freeze without a cloak.'

'I'd send you out in your shift, you bitch, if I didn't think it would offend the bishop. I don't care if you freeze. I don't care if you starve or get eaten by wolves. The ravens can peck out your eyes if they so wish. I hope the pestilence gets you, you and that scum you lay with. I hope you both rot together in hell.'

I turned to my maid. 'Give me your cloak and fetch the old one you were going to patch. You can wear that for the moment. I'll find you another once we're away from here.'

William shot out a hand and pushed the girl out of the way.

'You won't be taking your girl with you. She belongs to me. They all belong to me, every one of them. I house them, I clothe them, I feed them. They are *my* chattels.'

The girl looked at me with mute terror. She'd served me for more than half her life and didn't understand what was happening.

I placed my hands gently on her shoulder. 'Don't worry,' I said quietly. 'Stay here and be a good girl. Say nothing. There'll soon be another mistress for you to serve. Just fetch me your cloak.'

She practically ran to the closet and brought out her cloak of plain English cloth; the lining was budge and there were no trimmings. It was a very mean affair and not the sort of cloak a lady would ever dream of wearing. I put out of my mind the velvet cloaks and wonderful gowns I was leaving behind: my favourite blue silk, the green brocade, the delicately embroidered nightgowns and the sparkling jewels.

I threw the cloak quickly over my shoulders and walked to the door.

'Fare you well, William.'

He said nothing. His face was hard and he didn't even look at me as I slipped out and went down the stairs. My footsteps echoed forlornly and I felt a shaft of pain at the thought of the women huddled upstairs who were no longer part of my life.

Bishop Batemen was in the hall. His eyes took in my peculiarly lowly appearance but he said nothing. Perhaps as a man of God he despised a woman's liking for finery and was glad I was demonstrating a suitable repentance for my previous vanity. He glanced behind me.

'Where is your woman?'

'There is only me, Reverend Father. My…, Sir William will not permit either my maid or my chests to accompany me. I come as I am.'

'But you have a horse?'

He looked alarmed at the thought of having me hoisted behind one of his men in plain view of anyone on the road.

'Yes. I have my own mare. She was a royal gift. I don't think Sir William would dare to keep her.'

I followed him and his servant down the steps to the courtyard where the bishop's men were waiting.

As I set foot on the bottom step, a man detached himself from the shadows. It was my steward. His eyes were full of tears.

'My lady,' he could barely utter the words he was so upset. 'We heard, my lady. It is the most grievous news and even the boys in the kitchen are weeping to see you go. We of your household wish you well. Wherever you may find yourself our prayers go with you.' He thrust a small piece of folded cloth into my hand and I heard the chink of coins. 'The men want you to have this. It is all they can manage but they wouldn't want you to go hungry. You have been a good mistress to us and it distresses them to see you leave like this.'

I grasped his hand. It was firm and warm and I knew I would never feel it again.

'Thank you,' I whispered, almost choking at his kindness. 'Thank you. I shall think of you all and remember you in my prayers. May the Holy Mother of God keep you safe in the years ahead.'

It was noon when we rode under the gatehouse and down the track to the river. I didn't look back although every bone in my body screamed for me to do so. I wanted to linger, to let my eyes wander over walls which gleamed rosy in the pale winter sun, across steep tiled rooftops where in springtime rooks built their twiggy nests, down to the tall glazed windows of my solar where I had spent so many hours staring out across the fields.

I wanted to stay and gaze at this house which had been my favourite home since I was nine years old, which I would never see again, but Bishop Bateman was eager to be on his way. Like all bishops, he had the liveried splendour and magnificence which accompanied him everywhere but as we rode down the river track, I saw dozens of armed men ahead of us, far more than was usual for a bishop's train.

'Dangerous times, my lady,' said Bishop Bateman dourly.

A mile downstream we crossed the bridge and rode quickly through the town of Great Marlow, looking neither to left or right. Doors were closed and the streets filthy with human waste. The road outside the walls, leading up the hill, was not well-used and the few people we met moved hurriedly into the bushes when they saw the bishop's outriders. I had no idea where we were going.

After a while the road dipped to a narrow wooded valley and before long I saw ahead of us the walls and rooftops of a small town.

'Wyccim,' said the bishop.

The town must once have been prosperous but now the market square was empty and the shops deserted, only one man sheltering in a doorway observed our procession. Set back from the other buildings was a sturdy church and standing by the gate in the middle of a small group of men was Thomas Holand.

There was no doubt that my first two marriages had both taken place in a climate of fear: fear of my cousin's plans for me and his anger if I did not conform to his wishes. In Ghent, I took the only escape offered when I chose to run away from a marriage I did not want and at Bisham I was so cowed into a state of obedience by my mother's threats and the violence she had already meted out that I would have married whoever she put in front of me.

This time was different. This time I knew what I wanted. I thought it was love but the moment I saw Thomas standing by the church gate I knew it was more than that. It was desire of a most unseemly sort.

It had been more than two years since the sand dunes in Calais and I had quite forgotten what he looked like. He wasn't dressed in his best clothes, that was obvious, and for a moment I thought he might have changed his mind. How dreadful if after everything he didn't want me. If that happened, I would be utterly shamed and have nowhere to go.

I stayed in the saddle, too embarrassed to move, until Thomas strolled over taking all the time in the world as if he was an idle passer-by come to ask what we were doing.

'My lady,' he said giving a nod of his head and cursory glance at my cloak and my everyday boots. 'God give you a good day. I see you come prepared for our second wedding, beautifully gowned just as I expected.'

He wasn't smiling.

'I come as I am,' I retorted, sounding braver than I felt. 'If you don't like what you see, Sir Thomas, I can always return to Sir William. He has my robes and my furs and my jewels and my women. Perhaps he would like to keep me as well.'

'So there is no wagon with your chattels creaking along behind?' he said, staring down the track as if one might magically appear out of a mist.

'No, there is not. There is nothing. You're lucky I have a gown on my back. If it hadn't been for the bishop's presence, I'd be here in my shift and that would be to shame us both.'

He gave a short laugh and held out his hands to lift me down.

'Come on then, let's get this done.'

He glanced back the way we had come. 'Do you wish to wait for your girl?'

I flushed. 'I thought you understood, Sir Thomas. I have no girl. I have nobody; nobody to dress me or brush my clothes, nobody to comb my hair or help me with my shoes. I am entirely alone. I have been cast out with nothing but the clothes I stand up in.'

'No gems? No trinkets?'

'None. Just my mother's ring.'

The disappointment showed in his face. He must have expected a small fortune in jewels to accompany his bride. Instead he had a penniless woman in a plain cloak with no attendants and no dowry. It was a most unpromising prospect for any man, especially one who had just risked his fortune to retrieve a lost wife.

At that moment Otho Holand emerged from the church bringing with him a nervous-looking priest. At the sight of Bishop Bateman, the priest fell to his knees and kissed the bishop's ring, stuttering a greeting in Latin. I was surprised how gentle the bishop was with the man. He spoke kindly and after a moment, raised him up and went with him to the church door.

Otho nodded to me and then whispered to his brother.

Our first wedding had been quick, simply a matter of clasped hands and whispered vows and to be truthful this one was not much better. The little priest gabbled his way hurriedly through the words and blessed the ring. To my surprise it was the very same one Thomas had produced for our first wedding nearly ten years before. Had he kept it as a keepsake or was he reluctant to buy a better one? Was this all I was worth? Even now?

When the priest was finished, Thomas kissed me briefly on the cheek but without much enthusiasm. At the bishop's insistence we went inside the church where I was to make a stumbling confession of my sins before we celebrated a hasty nuptial Mass. A purse of coins changed hands and the priest mumbled his thanks. He gave a final curious glance at our odd little group before scuttling away through a door at the side of the church.

I thought Bishop Bateman would stay for the celebration feast but he was anxious to return, looking at the sky and murmuring about the lateness of the day.

'I left my diocese, Sir Thomas, because I was charged by the Holy Father to undertake this task. It is no pleasure to remove a man's wife under circumstances such as these no matter what the reason. But all is done as was required and now I have more important matters to concern me. The great mortality is killing thousands and I have clergy dying in their scores. I cannot leave the people without the benefit of a priest in their parish and every day I must bring dozens of young men into the priesthood. It is an unending task.'

'We are grateful for your concern,' said Thomas, looking at me.

Clearly both men expected my gratitude so I knelt uncomfortably on the muddy ground and kissed the bishop's ring.

'Thank you, Reverend Father,' I whispered. 'You have been more than kind and I am truly sorry if I have caused you or those you serve any distress.'

Somewhere behind me, Otho coughed.

Thomas nodded his head to Bishop Bateman and raised me up.

'We must leave also. I have no desire to stay a moment longer than necessary.' He turned to me. 'On your horse please, my lady.'

This wasn't what I had expected. Where was the feast, the entertainment, the singing and the minstrelsy? And where, now that I thought about it, were the silver coins which had been so conspicuously absent at my first wedding?

I was hoisted unceremoniously into the saddle and told to make ready. Apart from that one brief brushing of lips across my cheek, Thomas had shown no sign of affection and no indication that he thought of me as his wife. I was treated like a maidservant, told to get in line, be silent and keep up with the others.

We parted company with the bishop's cavalcade and took a well-trodden road towards the west.

'What lies this way?' I asked Otho as we passed through the town gate.

'Oxford,' he said with no further elaboration.

I indulged myself imagining a small inn somewhere in the narrow streets of the town and a comfortable bed for the night with Thomas and I wrapped in each others arms, but as night crept up and over us, we didn't stop. Nobody bothered to ask if I was tired or hungry or if I wanted to rest, and nobody seemed interested in telling me anything. We just kept going, mile after mile after mile. When the others took a track to the right which appeared utterly deserted and led into even deeper darkness, I began to be frightened.

The sky was a deep velvet black spangled with tiny stars and between the criss-crossed branches of the trees there shone a huge white moon. We had stopped in a clearing but there was no sign of an ale house or anywhere to sleep for the night. Perhaps a priory was nearby, a place where we could shelter and be warm. And eat. I had begun to feel very hungry.

'Where are…?'

'Shh!' hissed Thomas.

He slid off his horse and the others did likewise. Thomas whispered instructions and the four young men disappeared into the darkness of the trees. Otho came to help me down.

'What are we doing here?' I whispered.

'Taking a rest.'

'Here?' I said in disbelief.

Thomas came over with a flagon of ale which he proffered to me.

'You'd better drink something, there's a long way still to go.'

'Where are we going to sleep, husband?'

I saw his teeth gleam in the moonlight. 'We're not; not tonight.'

'But why?'

He removed the flagon from my hands and took a drink himself. He wiped his sleeve across his mouth and passed the flagon to his brother.

'Because by now Montagu will have men on our trail and the faster we get out of here the better our chances of staying alive.'

'I'm sure Sir William wouldn't...'

'Wouldn't what? You think he'll let you ride away and do nothing? If a thief steals a lord's best horse, he gets his throat slit, so why not the man who steals the lord's wife? With the bishop gone, Montagu will have sent men to hunt us down and it won't take them long to discover which way we've gone.'

'How will they know?'

'Anyone who saw the bishop's train will have told his neighbour. The news that the Bishop of Norwich rode by with a pretty young woman at his side is choice gossip. Someone may even have recognised you.'

'But...'

'And you can be sure the priest at Wiccim is entertaining his parishioners in the alehouse this very night with his tale of the bishop's visit and the marriage of some knight to his kitchen wench of a wife.'

'They know which road we took,' said Otho. 'It was no secret but I doubt they'll notice the track, not in the dark. We're as safe here as anywhere.'

'Can't we stay awhile?' I said, wondering how much longer I could ride at this pace.

Thomas regarded me unsympathetically. 'No. This is how men travel, my lady. We ride, we stop, we eat, we drink, we piss and sometimes we sleep. Then we ride again. Now which is it to be first – bread or piss?'

I lifted my chin and stared him straight in the eye.

'Piss, my lord, if you please.'

By the time we stopped again, I was nearly asleep in the saddle. We had ridden for hours, first along a rough track, picking our way around outcrops of rock, following the path of a stream; then through stretches of open woodland studded with dangerous bogs and shallow pools where we had to ride in single file. For the past hour we had been climbing.

We were at the edge of a thick wood. In the distance, dozens of lights flickered in the darkness and, to our right, a pale grey horizon heralded the dawn of another day.

Two of the young men got down from their horses and melted into the shadows.

'Off,' said Thomas briefly.

I slid into his arms and almost collapsed onto the ground. I wanted to lie on the cold leaves, I didn't think I could stay awake a moment longer.

Thomas hauled me upright. 'There's a hut back there amongst the trees,' he said. 'They're making sure it's empty. You can sleep there.'

I didn't care if the hut was inhabited by a tribe of woodland creatures or if the Holy Father himself was in residence. A hut would be dry and surely couldn't be as cold as staying out here in the raw morning air.

The roof thatch reached almost to the ground and the doorway was low, dark and unwelcoming. I stumbled across the threshold and without thinking, lay down on a pile of musty bracken piled in one corner. I had a vague recollection of a heavy cloak laid over my legs and the brush of a finger across my forehead as I tumbled over the edge of wakefulness into the depths of sleep, and then nothing.

Someone was shaking my shoulder but I didn't want to wake, I was far too comfortable. I grunted and pushed whoever it was away. The shaking became more persistent and the warmth on my legs suddenly vanished. Someone had stolen my cover. I opened my eyes in bewilderment.

'Sister,' whispered Otho Holand. 'Wake up. It's time to go.'

I struggled to a sitting position. There was just the two of us.

'Where is my husband?'

'Seeing to your horse.' He smiled and handed me some bread and a chunk of cheese. 'You'd better eat this. We've another long ride ahead.'

'Where are we going?'

'North. Many days' ride, so you'll need all your strength.' He went to the door of the hut and paused. 'Be as quick as you can.'

It hadn't been much of a wedding night, alone in some wood-dweller's hut. A thought struck me. Perhaps I hadn't been alone. Perhaps they had all slept in here beside me, all six men, and that was why the hut had felt so warm. I wondered how many women in their dotage when such things might be said, could tell the story of how they spent their wedding night alone in a hovel with six men!

It was late in the morning when we set out and the sky to the north was dark with the ominous sight of those deep-bellied clouds which herald snow. Whilst I had slept two of the others had ridden to the nearest settlement to make enquiries about strangers and buy feed for the horses.

'Did nobody sleep?'

'We took turns,' said Otho shortly.

We wound our way down from the ridge and for the rest of the day rode along the flat lands, skirting several villages and stopping only once to ask directions. At a crossroads we met a monk with his dog who told us he'd been travelling for six days looking for his bishop. All the brothers in the priory were dead, he'd buried them with his own hands. When God didn't take him too, he gathered up his bowl and his dog and set out to find his bishop to ask what he should do.

'I wrote down the names,' he said plaintively. 'It's all recorded just as it should be. I prayed for guidance but there was no answer and nobody came.'

We left him wandering down the road, complaining of the injustice of it all. By now I was losing track of time in a misery of hunger, cold and tiredness. It felt as if we had been riding north for ever.

Sometime in the late afternoon we turned our horses off the road. As we plodded further and further into the deserted countryside I kept my head down, wondering what malign trick of fate had conjured me here into the middle of nowhere with a husband I barely knew who paid no heed to my comforts.

I thought of William and how angry he had been and of Edward who, when he heard, would be incandescent with rage. He had warned me of the dangers of being shackled to Thomas Holand and I had chosen to ignore him. As darkness fell, I thought of my royal cousin who would never again acknowledge me. He would instruct his clerks to erase my name from every register. There would be no more invitations to Windsor or to his private palaces for the festivities; there would be no royal gifts of costly furs, no jewels, no fond kisses and never again would he pull me onto his knee and call me his little Jeanette. I would be dead to him.

'We'll stop here for the night.' Thomas's voice broke into my indulgence of self-pity.

I sniffed and looked up. Even with the moonlight casting a ghostly whiteness over everything, I could see no house.

Here turned out to be a cave cut deep into the rock, half-hidden by a tangle of overgrown ivy and sheltered by the trees. It was large enough for the horses to be stabled at the entrance and for us to sleep at the back.

After the usual meagre meal, I lay down next to the rocky wall, shivering in my cloak. I curled up as tightly as I could but my teeth were still chattering and I couldn't feel my toes.

'Are you cold?' Thomas whispered into the darkness.

'Yes,' I said, thinking miserably of roaring fires and warm spiced wine and wondering who was making merry in my solar at Bisham now I was no longer there.

Thomas crawled over and moved behind me, covering us both with his cloak. His arm came round my shoulder and in the darkness he gathered me tightly against him. We lay like small children tucked into a cradle with me barely daring to breathe at his unaccustomed closeness. I felt the warm roughness of his face against my hair and the touch of his hands on my waist but he didn't kiss me or whisper any words of love. He behaved like an old man with a five-year-old granddaughter.

Reluctantly I felt myself drift off to sleep in the warmth of his arms and when I awoke he was gone.

It must have been the third evening when we stopped at the deserted ale house. It stood on its own in a clearing by the side of what must once have been a well-used track. It looked as if no-one had passed this way for weeks.

Thomas was careful and made us wait in the trees while he and one of the others went to see if it was safe.

'Are you afraid?' I whispered to Otho.

'Of what?'

'The pestilence. Dying in the night.'

'It would be a foolish man who was not but men are well used to fear. And I have these.'

He delved into his pouch and produced a small packet. Inside were four grey pills.

'Stag's horn,' he said with satisfaction. 'I bought them from an apothecary in Lincoln. Swore it was better than bishop's piss for the plague. Promised me my money back if it didn't work.'

'Has my husband got some?'

Otho laughed. 'Thomas is not a believer in remedies for which you have to pay hard coin any more than he is a man who depends on the parings of a saint's toenails to save his life in battle.'

'What does he depend on?'

'God and his sword.'

Thomas had paid hard coin to retrieve me from William. I wondered if he regretted it.

The door to the house opened and Thomas emerged looking none too happy. 'We'll take the stable,' he said.

'May we not use the house?' I knew an ale house would have a hearth and perhaps a pallet bed for travellers.

'No.'

'But surely…'

'If you wish to share your night's sleep with a woman hanging from a beam, my lady, then you are welcome, but I have no liking for corpses and prefer to sleep in the stable.'

I felt my belly turn over in fear. 'A dead woman?'

'Frozen stiff. Dead about a month, I'd guess.'

Holy Virgin! What sort of place was this where a woman could be strung up from a beam in her own house and no-one would take her down?

'Hanged herself,' whispered Otho. 'The pestilence came. Lost her husband, her children and her wits. What else could she do?'

This was worse. If she'd hanged herself, she was unshriven which meant her soul was wandering out there in the darkness.

'Should we not fetch a priest?'

'For a suicide?' said Thomas. 'He'd not thank you for disturbing his rest and besides, I doubt there's a priest to be found anywhere for miles. The bishop said they're dying by the score.'

There were no animals but the stable was dry and to Otho's satisfaction the racks were full of hay. Thomas made me sleep in the loft but refused to follow me up the ladder, preferring to remain on the ground with the others. I remembered how in the darkened warehouse in Calais he had dared suggest that I might care to climb into the hayloft with him and wondered where the joy had gone. Once he had professed to love me but now it seemed all his tender feelings had gone and I was nothing but a burden, an extravagance he no longer wanted.

Next morning, we left before dawn as everyone was anxious to be gone from the dead woman's house. It was colder than ever with frost on the branches and gilding the bushes.

The only people we met all day were a group of bedraggled men and women who told us they'd lost their village when men fired the thatch.

'It were our lord's men,' said their leader, a squat little man with red hair. 'They came when we were asleep. They had swords and killed our pigs. Said they had a murrain. Pushed them into the flames.'

'Why would your lord burn his own village?' said Thomas, disbelievingly.

'Afeared of the pestilence. Said we were foul sinners and would bring sickness to his door. So he burned our homes and turned us away.'

It was a sad tale but there was nothing we could do. As Thomas said, it was not our quarrel and we would not be thanked for interfering. But afterwards we travelled in silence for the rest of the day.

On the fifth day it began to rain, a wet sleet blowing in from the north and smelling of snow. By midday I was sodden in my saddle and drooping with tiredness.

'We need shelter for the night,' said Otho bluntly. 'And unless you wish to carry your wife home along the corpse road you'd better find her a bed.'

Thomas put his bare hand against my cheek. 'You're cold?'

I nodded. 'Yes.'

He turned back to Otho.

'How far to the crossing?'

'Half a day, if that.'

Thomas chewed his lip. 'Right. We'll find somewhere in the town.'

'There's the priory at Tutbury.'

'I think not. The brothers have loose tongues. I'd rather the ale house.'

I knew the River Trent crossed England cutting the kingdom in two, separating north from south. It was as mighty a river as the Thames and Otho told me its crossings were few and well guarded. Nobody could hope to cross unnoticed.

Shortly before the gates shut for the night we passed over the bridge into the town and the men began scouring the streets for a likely place to sleep.

'We are taking you to your brother at Nottingham if anyone should ask,' instructed Thomas. 'You are recently widowed and we are your late husband's retainers.'

I nodded. I would be the Queen of Sheba if he wanted me to be. Anything to be out of the rain.

The woman at the door eyed my sodden garments suspiciously. 'Widow eh?'

'Yes,' said Otho. 'Left in a sad way.'

'So I see. Hmm. It'll cost yer.'

'We can pay,' said Otho proffering two coins.

'By the nails of Christ young man, where've ye been? Ye'll not get a hen coop for that. Sixpence for the woman. She can have the dog pen. There's been naught in it since the old bitch died last summer.'

'Have you no rooms?'

'No I have not. I've a chamber packed like a fish barrel with folks lying head to toe and men on top of their wives, and a dozen boys bedded down by the hearth in the kitchen. But yer widow can have the dog pen and the young men can take the stable. There's straw in both.'

'Can you…?'

She folded her arms across her massive chest. 'Take it or leave it. There's nowt else and ye'll not find anywhere better, unless the lads wish to wash their wicks in the bath house down Duck Street.' She cackled deep in her belly like a rumble of thunder.

'It'll do,' interrupted Thomas. 'We'll take it.'

The dog pen was a narrow space between two buildings where someone had erected planks for a wall and constructed an adequate thatch. It smelled of something I didn't want to think about, something putrid, but there was a good supply of dry straw. The door could only be bolted from outside. Otho brought me a bowl of pottage and some ale which I demolished with amazing speed.

There was raucous singing coming from within the ale-house and every so often I heard men stumble into the yard to piss in a corner. I was about to lie down when I heard the bolt undone. Thomas stood in the doorway blocking the torchlight with his face in darkness. He stayed completely still, watching me crouched on the straw. He didn't move and he didn't speak. I wasn't sure what he wanted but along with the pottage and ale warming my belly I felt the remembered stirring of desire.

'Husband?' I said softly.

'I wish you a good night, my lady. Get as much sleep as you can,' he said curtly, backing away and closing the door, leaving me once more in the dark.

I woke to a noise and someone collapsing on top of me. A heavy weight crushed my chest and I couldn't breathe. There was a hand across my face and a voice in my ear. 'Open yer mouth and I'll slit yer throat.'

I struggled but the man was much too strong. He pressed me into the straw. His breath smelled foul and full of drink. In the darkness I couldn't see him. He grabbed the folds of my skirts and hauled them up. I felt him fumble at his belt and realised at once what he wanted. I tried to kick but I was pinned to the ground with his knee shoved between my legs. If there had been more room I might have been able to roll away but the walls of the dog pen were too close and the two of us filled the tiny space.

I had lain like this on many occasions, crushed beneath the weight of William's body with him hissing obscenities in my ear, but this was different. This man, whoever he was, was not my wedded lord and master, but a stranger intent on rape. Here, I was not a wife sworn to obedience but an innocent victim.

I bit hard. The shock made him jerk his hand back.

'Thom . . ' I screamed, before he hit me. A stinging blow to the face.

'Whore!' he growled. 'Want it rough do yer?'

He wrenched at the top of my gown and I heard the cloth rip as his hands clutched at my breasts, squeezing them painfully.

He grunted as his groin thrust against mine. In my panic I tried to turn my body to one side but I couldn't move. With one hand he seized my chin and turned my face to his. His fat lips were all over me, his tongue pushing deep into my mouth till I began to choke while all the time he was grinding against me, trying to find his way through my clothing.

'Agh!' The momentary shriek of a man in agony. A strange gurgle. His arms flailed and I could smell blood as he collapsed on top of me.

'Get his legs!' It was Thomas.

With a horrible slither and thud the man was hauled off me.

I heard Otho's voice. 'That's it.'

Thomas crawled in beside me and pulled me up until I was sitting with my back to the wall. I was shivering and felt cold. He pushed the hair out of my eyes and found my cloak to wrap over my ruined clothing. When he put his hands on my shoulders, I could feel they were shaking.

'Did he hurt you?'

'N-no.' I could barely speak I was so shocked.

'He didn't. . . ?

'No, No. He didn't, but he tried to. He... he... I thought he was going to kill me.'

I could feel his smile. 'I don't think he wanted your life, my lady. He was after something else entirely.'

'But he had a knife.'

'Well, he's dead now, knife or no knife.'

'You killed him?'

'Would you rather I'd left him to finish what he'd started?'

'No.'

It was too horrible for words. A man dead. I swallowed hard and tried not to cry.

'I'll give you a bit of advice for next time,' said Thomas, in a voice which carried an undertone of fury.

'What?'

'Pretend to welcome it. Tell him what a big man he is and how you can't wait. A man with a willing girl rarely slits her throat and if it's inevitable you might as well get some enjoyment from it.'

'But I'm your wife.'

'Yes,' he said scrambling to his feet. 'And my duty is to keep you alive.'

'Your duty, Sir Thomas,' I said angrily, 'is to protect my chastity.'

He regarded me with an amused smile. 'What chastity?'

In the end they could think of nowhere to put the man's body other than hidden in the straw at the back of the dog pen.

'I'm not spending the rest of the night with a corpse,' I said firmly.

Thomas smiled at Otho. 'Remember Caen?'

Otho smiled back. 'Yes but he was a man-at arms and deserved our respect. This is just a piece of scum.'

'Ill sit with you,' said Thomas, turning to me.

The dog pen was small and we sat squashed together by the door.

'Thomas,' I began.

'Go to sleep,' he said, closing his eyes.

I rested my head against his shoulder and he didn't move away but neither did he put his arm around me. After a while, when I looked up at his face, I could see his eyes were wide open. He was staring into the darkness.

Surprisingly, I slept.

We left just before dawn. The body of my attacker was dragged from its hiding place and left in a dark corner of the yard.

'Nothing to say it was us,' said Otho, rubbing his hands.

'Will they raise a hue and cry?' I asked nervously.

'We'll be long gone if they do and nobody knows who we are. A poor widow being taken to Nottingham? Could be anyone.'

We roused the sleepy porter to open the town gate and rode fast out along the deserted road to the north.

We rode for two days almost without stopping and then two more. At one point we crossed a wide river over a good stone bridge which according to Otho meant we were now among friends.

It was late in the afternoon when the snow came at last. I was almost asleep in the saddle, swaying forward and laying my head on Blanchefleur's neck. I felt the first flake settle gently on my cheek, melting as it touched my skin, then another and another until the ground beneath the horses' hooves was white and the way ahead a mass of swirling snow, grey against the blackness of the trees.

'Hurry,' urged Thomas. 'It's not far. There's the priory. And the gate lantern.'

By now I was seeing apparitions in the dark: gigantic shapes of grinning demons; William waving a huge sword, shrieking, "You took my cloak! You can freeze to death for all I care." His blade swooped down and severed the ties at my throat. 'Thomas!' I screamed as the cloak flew away in the wind. 'Thomas!'

A hand reached out of the darkness and grabbed my sleeve. I was falling. I tried to hang on to Blanchefleur but my assailant was much too strong.

I slipped, I slid and felt myself let go as I fell into the void.

I awoke to silence. I was lying in a bed in a room I didn't recognize and had no idea how I had got there. My last clear memory was of sliding forward onto Blanchefleur's neck and falling into darkness.

Pale grey light from an unshuttered window filled the room. It was morning. The wall by the bed was plain plastered and decorated in an old-fashioned way with yellow curling tendrils and little brown flowers. There were no hangings except for a dull brown curtain stretched almost the whole way across one end of the room. I moved my eyes. A doorway. A chest.

The sound of a stool scraping against the floor made me turn my head. It was a child, a girl, not much more than seven years old. She had scrambled to her feet and was staring at me with wide, frightened eyes.

I smiled.

She muttered something and fled out of the room. From beyond the curtain I heard the murmur of voices and a moment later there was Thomas.

He nodded at me. 'You're awake.'

'Yes,' I replied, thinking it must be quite obvious to anyone that I was awake.

'Good.'

There was a pause while we eyed each other.

'Where am I?' I asked politely.

'Upholand,' he said shortly. 'My father's manor until he lost it to the king. Now it's ours again.'

I wondered if this was the good solid manor house where he'd promised to build me a solar.

'I don't remember anything.'

He smiled briefly. 'You tumbled off your horse. Luckily for you I was there to catch you. I carried you in.'

'You put me to bed?'

'Yes.'

I was no longer wearing my gown but a strange shift-like garment which had tangled itself around my legs. I touched the ties at my neck.

'This?'

'My shirt.'

'Oh! Where is my gown?'

'It was filthy. I gave it to the women to wash.'

'You took off my clothes?'

'Yes.'

His mouth twitched in amusement at my horror. 'I am your husband, my lady. I have the right, in case you have forgotten. And I've seen many women's bodies over the years, so you can stop blushing.'

'No, I haven't forgotten,' I said, covered in embarrassment at the thought of him peeling off my sodden clothes and seeing the paucity of my torn and soiled undergarments.

'The girl will bring you some water.'

He put out his hand and ruffled the child's hair in an intimate gesture which made my heart beat faster. As he had just told me, he hadn't spent the past ten years without a woman, so what else could I expect? But I hadn't counted on a bastard child to greet me in my own house.

'Is she yours?' I asked, afraid of the answer.

'No,' he laughed. 'She's not. Now get yourself ready. The household will expect to see you at supper.'

It seemed I had slept the day round.

The girl pattered in and out bringing a bowl, jugs of water and a large drying sheet. While she helped me wash, she chattered away but her accent was so strange I could only understand one word in ten. She was entranced by my hair, stroking the wet strands, sighing over the colour and the way it gleamed in the candlelight.

'Pretty,' she breathed.

When I was clean, she wrapped me in the drying sheet.

'My gown?' I enquired.

'Wet,' she said in reply.

This posed a problem. I couldn't appear in the hall in Thomas's shirt.

'You'd better fetch my husband,' I said and when she didn't move, I said more clearly. 'Sir Thomas. The lord. Bring him to me.'

She slipped out and a moment later returned with a husband who had clearly been interrupted in the middle of something more important than his wife's clothing.

'Yes?'

'I have no gown to wear, Sir Thomas. Mine is wet and there is nothing else.'

'So? Wear my shirt. Or the sheet.' He put his head on one side and regarded me critically. 'Yes. Wear the sheet. You look very lovely in a sheet.'

'I absolutely refuse to take supper in a sheet, or in a man's shirt,' I said indignantly.

'Then you'd better stay here, my lady, because there's nothing else.'

He turned his back and left the room as hurriedly as

he had entered. He clearly had no desire for my company whether wrapped in a sheet or not.

'I'll go back to bed,' I called after him but he'd gone.

I lay in bed feeling very cross but when, later, the girl brought me some food and ale, I felt better. He would come soon, when prayers had been said and the household was ready for sleep, of that I was certain. He would be as impatient as I was.

I lay, wriggling my toes in anticipation, wondering what he would say and what he would do. But one by one the candles guttered and died, the noises from beyond the curtain ceased, and the house was still. A final bark from a distant dog elicited a curse. Then nothing. He wasn't coming. He didn't want me. It had been too long. After the years of waiting he hadn't wanted to marry me and had only done so because he had been ordered. He would have left me at Bisham but it was too late. He had made his move and now he was paying for it. A single tear rolled down my cheek and I buried my head in the pillow and cried myself to sleep.

By next morning my gown was dry and the girl helped me dress, stroking the fine wool which was very much the poorer because of our flight from Wiccim. Whoever had washed it had done their best but there were stains which would never disappear and clumsily mended rents across the bodice. In my other life I would have tossed it out to one of my maids but here it was the only gown I possessed.

The hall was small but comfortable with a central hearth and three tables; one for Thomas, Otho and I, one for the men and another for the three women and the girl. I, naturally, was the object of everybody's curious gaze and I was glad I had refused both the shirt and the sheet. Thomas sat by my side but talked to Otho. It was like Calais when William would talk to Thomas instead of me. Perhaps all husbands were like this.

That afternoon to my annoyance I felt the familiar cramping pains and, after counting the days of my courses, realised any further hope of marital intimacy would have to wait. I explained to the girl what I needed and she trotted off to ask the women. When she returned, Thomas was with her.

'You're bleeding,' he said abruptly.

I kept my head bent so that he couldn't see the flush of embarrassment on my face. This was a private matter for women, never discussed with any man, not even a husband. 'Yes,' I whispered.

'The women will look after you,' he said. 'I shall be leaving tomorrow as I have matters to attend to. Otho will remain so you'll be perfectly safe. If I can, I'll bring you some cloth for a gown.'

'Thank you,' I muttered, still refusing to meet his eye and not liking to ask where he was going or who might be there.

I knew he was staring at me.

'Take care of yourself,' he said softly.

I looked up, surprised at the warmth in his voice, but he was gone.

With my husband absent, I found time to explore the manor house and its surroundings but the daylight hours were short and so cold that I achieved little else. I exhausted my conversations with Otho, who proved most unwilling to tell me much about his brother, and there didn't seem to be anything for me to do. I couldn't understand the women, who scuttled away every time I made an appearance, and the men, although friendly, seemed discomforted by my presence. There were no minstrels or books and with no sign of neighbours or passing strangers, nobody had the inclination for telling stories.

It was evening on the sixth day when I heard the sound of his return. The shutters were closed for the night and the candles lit in the little chamber beyond the curtain. I was making myself ready for bed. The curtain which hid the doorway billowed open and my heart leapt most unreasonably at the sight of my husband. His head and shoulders were covered in a fine dusting of snow.

He walked across the floor towards me and in a single movement scooped me up and held me tight against his chest. The folds of his cloak flapped against my legs and a snowflake settled on my face where it melted to nothing. I could feel the metal of his buckle pressing hard into the soft wool of my gown.

'Thomas…' I was silenced by his cold mouth on mine.

He kissed me the way he had always kissed, the way I remembered him kissing me in Antwerp after the fire in Sir Two-Faces' house, the way he had kissed me in Ghent, in the chapel at Bisham, by the banks of the Thames and two years ago in the sand dunes at Calais. He kissed how I had imagined him kissing me in a hundred thousand dreams over the years but no dream could possibly have matched the gloriousness of this moment.

'I thought you didn't want me,' I whispered.

'Oh I want you,' he said.

And with that he proceeded to gather me up and carry me off to bed.

He was still fully dressed and the first time he didn't even take off his boots.

'I can't wait,' he said. 'I really can't.'

Afterwards I whispered into the warmth of his mouth, 'You didn't come near me. All that time. I thought you didn't care.'

'Sweet fool,' he said, nibbling my ear. 'I cared, and you can't imagine how much I wanted you, how many times I had to stop myself from touching you. But I had to be certain.'

'Of what?'

'That your child will be my child. A man must know that his heir is his own and not some other man's bastard. Montagu had been in your bed.'

'Not for months,' I said untruthfully.

He put his head on one side and looked into my eyes. 'The next time you lie to me, Lady Holand, I shall...' He whispered something quite outrageous into my ear which reduced me to helpless giggles

'You wouldn't?'

'I most certainly would.'

'Very well, he hasn't been in my bed for at least a month.'

'That's better.'

He picked up my hand and gently kissed the soft pulse on my wrist, the palm, the tips of each finger.

'You must always tell me the truth. A man has to trust his wife. Whatever you've done, however bad it is, you must always tell me.'

'He was meant to be my husband,' I said sadly, thinking of the many occasions William and I had clung together for comfort, and the bitter parting when he knew I was leaving. 'But at the end I was unnecessary to his pleasure.'

'Well, you are not unnecessary to mine,' said Thomas firmly.

I lost count of the number of times he made love to me that night but there was light in the morning sky when we finally fell asleep, locked in each others arms.

When I awoke, Thomas was watching me from across the pillow. He smiled. I smiled back, thinking how handsome he was despite the scar on his eye and the grey hair touching his temples.

'Greetings, husband.'

'Whose wife are you?' he asked lazily.

'Yours, Thomas.'

'Are you sure?'

'Yes.'

'You don't want me to ask the tribunal to reconsider their verdict?'

I touched his lips with my finger. 'Don't tease. I love you.'

'Ah, you may say you love me today but I happen to know just how fickle your affections are.'

'For ever. I am going to love you for ever.'

'Unto death?'

'Unto death and beyond.'

He made to sit up. 'Good, so that's settled and I can get back to work.'

I didn't want him to go, not yet.

'Work, my lord?' I said, stroking my fingers up his thigh. 'What kind of work?'

He rolled on top of me and pressed me deep into the mattress. 'The making of our first little Holand, my lady. What else?'

Much later we sat, wrapped in the bedcovers, idly discussing the future.

'Must we stay here?' I asked.

'For now. But come spring, if we are still alive, we'll travel south and throw ourselves on the king's mercy. He'll be planning his next move against the French and he knows I am a very fine soldier.'

'What about me?'

'You, Lady Holand, will be sewing baby garments for our first son.'

He was so certain, I could almost believe it myself.

He hauled himself out of bed. Oh, but he was beautiful to look at in the light of day as he walked across the floor. He turned and noticed my gaze with amusement.

'Am I to your liking, my lady? It's been a long time.'

'You have always been to my liking, my lord. From the very first moment I saw you.'

His clothes were strewn where he'd thrown them the night before. He bent down, picked up his belt and retrieved his purse.

'When I was away, I bought you something.'

'Cloth for a gown?'

'This is something else.'

He walked back slowly, stretching his body, easing his muscles, and stood beside the bed. My belly felt weak and my heart turned over at the sight of him.

'As you know, Lady Holand, I am a man who keeps his promises and a long time ago I told you that if you married me I'd cast jewels across our marriage bed. Not as many as I'd hoped and probably not as many as you would like but...'

And with a carelessness which astounded me he threw a handful of seed pearls right across the coverlet. They lay there, shining like little drops of holy ice, nestled against the roughness of the dull brown cloth.

'Oh Thomas,' I whispered. 'Oh Thomas.'

He put his hands on either side of my face and kissed me softly, and the pearls were all but forgotten, lost in a tangle of bedclothes, falling one by one gently onto the rushes on the floor.

EPILOGUE

BROUGHTON 1352

Somewhere in the snowy countryside of England, the lady of the little manor of Broughton stood staring at the letter in her hand. She read it twice and then, in disbelief, read it a third time. The exhausted messenger kneeling at her feet wore a black tabard and when she'd seen him leap from his sweating horse her first thought had been for her husband.

Thomas Holand was doing his duty in Calais. It was his first command and she had wanted to accompany him.

'It's a garrison town,' he had said. 'No dancing, no women.'

'You're certain?' She had tried her hardest not to sound like a jealous wife. 'I won't stand for women.'

He had laughed and kissed her firmly on the lips.

'Give me a daughter to keep our little son company in the nursery and I promise you faithfully there'll be no women.'

'I shall have your brother keep me informed.'

'Otho would never betray me, not even to you.'

'I wouldn't be too sure,' she had said, smiling.

That had been six months ago and Otho had never said a word. Naturally the baby had been a girl. She had called her Maud as they had agreed and her brother had sent the child a silver bowl.

'He can't be dead,' she said at last. 'It's not possible. He's my brother; he's only twenty-two.'

'I'm sorry, my lady,' said the messenger, thinking how beautiful Lady Holand was, even in her present distress. 'I saw his body myself.'

Joan called for food and drink for the man from Woking but at the back of her mind she was already planning. She was in disgrace with the king for having defied him in the matter of her marriage and her royal cousin was not inclined to do her any favours. She and Thomas were still waiting for the rest of the money owed to Thomas for the prisoner he had captured at Caen on the French campaign, and when Thomas had asked for help with the expenses of his new position the king had offered a mere hundred marks a year. Such meanness when they had so little and once she had been her cousin's favoured Jeanette.

But now? She hardly dared think of the possibilities. Her brother had no children and she was his heir. She would be Countess of Kent. All those manors her brother had talked about incessantly, and best of all, Castle Donnington with its flower-strewn meadows and stretches of beautiful woodland. It would mean an end to their poverty, a return to court because her cousin could hardly ignore her, not when she would be so very, very rich.

Thomas could give up soldiering if he wished. He could manage their estates and they would live a life of ease and contentment. There would be more children, more time together. Broughton could be forgotten, leased to someone else while they climbed back into the sunshine. There would golden years ahead with Thomas: twenty? thirty? Who but God knew how long. They would spend their money and enjoy it. After all you couldn't take a rent roll to the grave.

And this time she would have a solar.

What happened next

In the ten years following their second marriage Joan gave Thomas four children, two boys and two girls. Thomas was summoned to parliament in 1354 as Baron Holand and in 1359 took the title Earl of Kent in the right of his wife. His military career culminated with his prestigious appointment as the king's captain and lieutenant in Normandy and France.

Shortly after Joan left him, William Montagu married Elizabeth, daughter of John de Mohun, Lord de Mohun of Dunster. They had one son.

In 1352 Edward Montagu, was arrested, suspected of being responsible for the death of his wife, Alice, following an assault. No charges were ever brought.

After her husband, John Segrave, died in 1353, Joan's cousin, Margaret, married Walter Manny.

Within four months of Thomas Holand's death in Rouen on 28th December 1360, his widow, Joan, secretly married the king's son, Edward, Prince of Wales.

Bibliography

Richard Barber	Life and Campaigns of the Black Prince
B.C. Hardy	Philippa of Hainault and her Times
Lisa Hilton	Queens Consort
Penny Lawne	Joan of Kent
Ian Mortimer	Medieval Intrigue
Ian Mortimer	The Perfect King
Ian Mortimer	The Time Travellers Guide to Medieval England
Compton Reeves	Pleasures and Pastimes in Medieval England
M.M.N. Stansfield	Holland, Thomas: Oxford Dictionary of Biography
Jonathan Sumption	Trial by Battle. The Hundred Years War I
Jonathan Sumption	Trial by Fire. The Hundred Years War II
Barbara Tuchman	A Distant Mirror: The Calamitous14th Century
Jennifer Ward	English Noblewomen in the Later Middle Ages
Alison Weir	Isabella, She-Wolf of France, Queen of England
Karl P Wentersdorf	The Clandestine Marriages of the Fair Maid of Kent
Kathryn Warner	edwardthesecond.blogspot.com

Acknowledgements

Many thanks to Nick for getting me started and to Jackie, Jane and Ken of the writing group for keeping me at it. Without the Danish pastries, the chocolate cake and the endless cups of coffee this book might still be languishing half-finished on my computer. Also thanks to Ken for help with the editing.

Thanks to my husband, Richard and to my daughters, Natasha and Alex, for their help with choosing the cover image and to the team at Matador for all their advice and support.

But most of all I need to acknowledge the debt of gratitude I owe to my father for introducing me to the world of my mother's family tree and to my mother for having the good sense to be born with Joan as her sixteen times great-grandmother.

Contact

If you enjoyed *The Fair Maid of Kent* and would like to know more about Caroline's forthcoming books please visit:

Website: carolinenewarkbooks.co.uk

Facebook: carolinenewarkbooks

Blog: carolinenewarkbooks.co.uk/blog

COMING SOON

The Pearl of France

JOINED BY GOD, FUSED BY PASSION, TAINTED BY JEALOUSY

In the autumn of 1299 as part of a treaty of peace with England, Marguerite, the French king's young sister, marries her brother's enemy, the elderly Edward I.

Marguerite expects nothing from this marriage other than a life of duty and obedience but Edward is a man experienced in the art of pleasing a woman and he awakens unexpected passions in his young wife.

Used by her step-children as a peacemaker and by her husband as a vessel for the sons he craves, Marguerite believes she is content until she comes to desire a man who is not her husband and whose interests run counter to those of the king.

When the quicksands of a Scottish war open beneath her feet and her beloved stepson finally rebels against his father, she is engulfed in a nightmare world of treachery, murder and hideous bloody revenge.